MAXIMUM IMPACT

MAXIMUM IMPACT

JACK HENDERSON

sphere

SPHERE

First published in Great Britain in 2005 by iUniverse.com
This edition published by Sphere in 2007

A CIP catalogue record for this book
is available from the British Library.

Hardback ISBN 978-1-84744-027-3
C format ISBN 978-184744-028-0

Typeset in Sabon by M Rules
Printed and bound in Great Britain by
Clays Ltd, St Ives plc

Sphere
An imprint of
Little, Brown Book Group
Brettenham House
Lancaster Place
London WC2E 7EN

A Member of the Hachette Livre Group of Companies

www.littlebrown.co.uk

for Lori and the girls

Those great and good men foresaw that troublous times would arise when rulers and people would become restive under restraint, and seek by sharp and decisive measures to accomplish ends deemed just and proper, and that the principles of constitutional liberty would be in peril unless established by irrepealable law. The history of the world had taught them that what was done in the past might be attempted in the future.

The Constitution of the United States is a law for rulers and people, equally in war and in peace, and covers with the shield of its protection all classes of men, at all times and under all circumstances. No doctrine involving more pernicious consequences was ever invented by the wit of man than that any of its provisions can be suspended during any of the great exigencies of government.

Such a doctrine leads directly to anarchy or despotism, but the theory of necessity on which it is based is false, for the government, within the Constitution, has all the powers granted to it which are necessary to preserve its existence, as has been happily proved by the result of the great effort to throw off its just authority.

—U.S. *Supreme Court Ex parte Milligan, 71 U.S. 2 (1866)*

As the circle of light increases,
so does the circumference of darkness surrounding it.

—*Albert Einstein*

PART I

0

The sun had been up for over two hours, and as the city outside got itself underway on a bright late summer morning, the world turned into just the position to put the coffee on.

High on a shelf before his kitchen window was a small model of Stonehenge. The sarsen monoliths were shaped of polymer clay, oven-cured, weathered, and airbrushed in obsessive detail. The monument was not fashioned after the vandalized and ragged shadow of itself that survives on the bleak chalk plains of Salisbury today, but as it had stood in its full Pagan glory five thousand years before.

The ancient circle was modeled in precise concentric scale on a miniature landscape of stubbly green grass and scattered rock, rotating infinitesimally to compensate for the tilt and orbit of the Earth around the Sun. The intricate mechanism was built on the guts of a pawn-shop Pioneer turntable, though its original manufacturer wouldn't have had the clues to claim it. It had pleased him to rescue the old-tech of this record-playing machine into a new form and a more timeless purpose. Now as the sun rose over Manhattan, just as it would have in a cool September two millennia before the dawn of the Iron Age, a ray of morning light filtered through a warren of calendar stones to mark the coming of the new day.

The pencil sunbeam struck the face of the coffeemaker, itself a Sunbeam, and illuminated a solar cell that activated the highly modified machine. A measure of espresso beans skittered through a funnel into the electric mill, spun down to a play-sand grind, dropped into a filter in the grip of an advancing articulated arm, and the strong coffee began to brew.

Back when he'd still been ship-shape to do so, his father might have tut-tutted at such elaborate mechanics applied to a simple manual task. The same class of mind, of course, would have looked on in clueless wonder as the ancient Britons dragged their 50-ton quarry stones for twenty miles into the middle of nowhere to build a mystery for the ages.

The apartment was awakening. Here and there a relay or solenoid clicked in response to an infrared or RF signal from a timer, sensor, or from a complementary device in an ensemble. Over two decades he had patiently handmade his space to be as alive as a thing that was not alive can possibly be. Normally in robotics, the goal was to miniaturize and make independent an analogue of some living thing. Those were trinkets, crude science-fair novelties, and John Fagan had gone in the other direction. His idea of a mechanical companion was writ 4,000 square feet large, the walls, ceiling and floor humming with hundreds of trillions of bits of silicon intelligence, and he lived inside of it.

The clear weather outside selected two CDs to spin-up in a rack of players, one of autumn bird songs and the other Rautavaara's *Angel of Light*. Indirect lamps hummed gradually to their gentle dawn settings. He preferred artificial illumination since the Sun signaled a day too short by half for his body clock. Today, his morning actually happened to be morning.

John had slept at his desk as he usually did, reclined in an electronically tricked-out La-Z-Boy worthy of a spot on the bridge of the Starship Enterprise. He would never have made the Trekkie reference himself, of course. Everything after the second season had been horseshit of Shatnerian proportions.

4

And besides, this was the real deal.

Behind him, a rectangular mosaic of hundreds of salvaged LCD screenlets flickered alive in a domino sequence, row upon row, to form a twelve-foot diagonal, 16×9-format high-definition window on the outside world. Every small screen had an intelligent feed from a separate source of news on the Internet, from favorite sites, RSS feeds and newsgroups to hacked satellite and cable video, tapped surveillance gear, Webcams and instant messaging streams.

Each screenlet chose and displayed its content based on a buzz algorithm that parsed for personal relevance, keywords, proximity, source and substance. They could work together or individually, forming larger or smaller subscreens in the array as the significance of the content warranted. It was an ever-changing symphony of visual input that CNN would have paid billions to develop, if such a thing could have crossed a corporate mind.

John was becoming conscious, and it wasn't a welcome sensation. Along with his usual discomforts something warm and wet was slapping the back of his hand as it hung over the arm of the chair.

"Boner, please, for God's sake," he said. The dog sat, and gave a low, timid bark in answer. He looked something like a small Shepherd, though with a healthy mixture of many other fine breeds in patchy evidence.

"Feed the dog, please, and make it a half-hour earlier tomorrow, all right?" he said.

"Understood, and adjusted," a digitized voice answered, in a refined emulation of Kate Jackson, of *Charlie's Angels*.

A spout extended from a cabinet near floor level by the door, and a cup of lamb-and-rice kibble filled a low dish adorned with cartoon pawprints. Thin beams of sentient light danced briefly across a nearby bowl, confirming the level, temperature and clarity of the water within it. Boner trotted over to his breakfast.

John lifted a hand to rub his eyes awake, and a hangover was pounding just behind them. He reached out blind for the remains of a pint of Old Crow on the arm of the chair, and killed the last two swallows. His dad would have called this a little morning pick-me-up. The old prick had been right, though, about the nuances of alcoholism if nothing else. The pain in his head began to dissolve, and he cracked opened his eyes.

Near the upper left-hand corner of the media wall, a new image abruptly replaced the talking head that had occupied the spot a moment before. In the mirror of his darkened desktop computer monitor he only noticed the reflected image as it expanded to take up four, then eight, then sixteen segments of the array behind him. Something was growing newsworthy, at least in the group-mind of the news services and the Net. He reached for his glasses, put them on, and swiveled his chair to face the screen.

The image he saw there in the corner took several moments to begin to register. He had seen its subject a thousand times, but it looked so different now that his mind wouldn't immediately accept it as itself. The image doubled in size again, blotting out border wars, famine and disease, George Clooney and Chandra Levy.

It was bigger now, but still not real. There was so much smoke, far too much for a fire that could ever be contained. The picture took two jumps larger then, pushing aside politics, Palestinians, earthquakes and all manner of human mayhem, as all the world's attention began to take focus on a single spot.

John stood up slowly, and walked a few steps toward the moving image that now rippled outward to fill the entire wall. Then there it was, realization.

A quarter of a mile up in the sky, tower one of the World Trade Center was burning.

Scrolling text at the bottom of the screen said the north tower had been struck by an aircraft, possibly a small private plane, about fifteen minutes ago. He took another step closer to the screen, which was now showing a wide GyroCam shot from

News Chopper 4 of the unreal scene unfolding only blocks from where he stood.

John checked his watch. It was 9:03. He was growing numb, but his mind was still working.

"Any second now," he breathed.

A moment later, United Flight 175 outbound from Boston sliced into the south tower, releasing thirty thousand liters of jet fuel and all souls on board into the conflagration.

1

Jeannie Reese looked out through the tint of the wide conference room window, took a deep breath in, closed her eyes and exhaled on an eight-count. She was calm, and for the moment she was allowing herself to consider that she wasn't reacting rationally to the situation. Two passenger airliners, after all, had been driven into the World Trade Center twenty minutes ago, and clearly this was no accident. All hell was breaking loose throughout the building. But here of all places, didn't business still have to be done?

Her meeting had been interrupted by the news, and if there was one thing she hated more than waiting, it was interruptions. She'd called a ten-minute break, and her audience had scattered like fifth-graders at the bell on the last day of school. We were now at sixteen wasted minutes and counting.

No, not irrational, she thought, *by all evidence you're the only one on the floor with your wits about you. There's work to be done, and this attack only underscores the urgency of that work. People are dying, yes, I understand. People die every day. If I'm the only one who sees the need to keep my head on straight, so be it. I will not be terrorized. We must focus. Extraordinary times demand extraordinary people.*

That word, extraordinary, had been yoked to her for as long as she could remember. By age ten, she had achieved more notoriety

9

as a theoretical heurist than the combined army of Princeton mathematicians they'd deployed to evaluate her. She had been a rare find, a true math prodigy and a computer wunderkind wrapped in a single, recruitable unit.

Before she'd hit puberty she had proven herself capable of thinking deeper and wider than the best in the field, and a precocious Mozart in the emerging art of differential cryptanalysis. And though she had only achieved legal drinking age last year, it was Jeannie's charge to design and marshal the government's eyes and ears in the electronic battle zone, translating what she saw, suspected or forecast into the language and tactics of war.

And she got things done. The day she'd met Don Rumsfeld, a few days after his appointment as Secretary of Defense in the new administration, he'd given her his signature squint and intoned, "And you, young lady, I'm led to understand that you are the grand mistress of the instrumentality."

Damn right, Rummy.

Jeannie checked her watch. There were no friends in New York to call, even if the land-lines and cell carriers weren't log-jammed already. She had no idea where her parents or any of her siblings were, and she was dead certain that the inverse was true. Everything she could do in the face of this crisis she could do here, now, but not before an empty room.

She closed her eyes and tried to clear her mind, but it wouldn't rest. The thought of her family had reliably triggered a spate of memories, and before long she was mentally fast-forwarding through the details of the events that had both launched her career and robbed her of her childhood.

By 1990 Jeannie Reese had turned eleven and the telephone system had grown so complex and so dependent on lightning speed that moment-to-moment control of it had been turned over completely to computers. Human hands simply couldn't move fast enough, and human minds couldn't meet the demand for the required instantaneous reactions. The network nearly ran itself, with the help of software programs designed to execute literally billions of routing and management instructions every second.

Phone traffic is extremely variable, and the thousands of inter-linked networks had been painstakingly designed to share their power to keep the calls going through at all costs, regardless of the ever-changing load. The system was built with a great deal of flexibility, so when occasional problems did occur at a station the load could be switched out to that station's designated back-up, and the extra traffic would be seamlessly handled until the afflicted section of the network had cleansed itself of the error. This scheme of programmed backups was the fundamental safety valve that allowed the phone system to weather virtually any traffic storm, automatically.

But there had been a weakness built into the programming, a narrow doorway through which a brilliant opportunist would send a silver bullet to the heart of the Bell System. The Achilles' heel in the code was actually documented in the AT&T technical manual for the new 4ESS Digital Switching System, on page 114, and again in Appendix G. The subroutine wasn't listed there as a weakness, of course, just as a beta-level feature of the upgrade that facilitated a quicker response to potential system crashes.

In the event of a problem in any individual 4ESS switch, that switch would take itself offline by shutting down and restarting, wiping out its glitch by committing digital suicide and then coming back to life a minute later, born again, all clear. Just before it did so, the switch would send a "Get Ready!" message to the next 4ESS down the line, which would slow itself down temporarily to handle the incoming extra traffic from the failing switch. When the troubled 4ESS was ready to come back online, then it would send an "I'm Back!" message to its helper switch, and the traffic would be re-diverted back to its original pathway.

The flaw was this: in the few seconds that the traffic was being diverted, if during the transition just two phone calls happened to arrive within the same hundredth of a second, the helper switch itself would momentarily overload, causing it to fail as well. The traffic of both switches would then be sent to the next station down the line. Under innocent circumstances, this was still a perfectly reasonable, nearly fail-safe little routine. To a malicious hacker, however, it was to become the lynchpin of the mother of all domino effects.

The virus that brought down the entire phone system of New York City had four simple functions: 1) wait for a legitimate triggering of the fail-safe system in a 4ESS switch, 2) follow the "Get Ready!" distress call that the failing switch sent down the line to its helper, 3) route two simultaneous phone calls to the helper switch, and 4) go to #1.

This self-replicating code was released into NYNEX on that Monday morning in 1991, and within an hour, one 4ESS in downtown Manhattan experienced a routine, minor overload. That switch followed its programmed orders, and dutifully prepared to send its "Get Ready!" warning to the next station in line as it shut itself down. The virus infected that first distress call, and the now-diseased alert message shot down the phone lines to its helper switch. The second failure triggered, the infected switch called for help, and the snowball had begun its roll.

The resulting cascade of unrecoverable system crashes didn't end until the Basking Ridge technicians literally pulled the plug late in the day, counted to ten, and then plugged the whole thing back in again. This effectively destroyed the virus, of course, along with every other byte of running software in the telephone system. They had cured the disease by killing the patient.

The only thing that had prevented a widespread, region-hopping phone-out on that day was an accidental firebreak, a single outdated station, still sporting electromechanical switches, on the outskirts of the NYC service area. This hub was at the narrowest part of an electronic funnel that connected New York City to the rest of the interstate phone network. The old switches were immune to the virus, being just smart enough to either shut down completely or explode with a bright, purple bang when hit by the tsunami of diverted phone traffic that smashed down on them that morning.

Though still two years a pre-teen, little Jeannie Reese had earned a top spot on the FBI's short list of potential perpetrators of the NYNEX hack. Between cello lessons and karate class, she'd been finding time to write some of the nastiest computer viruses on record. The tiny agents of chaos she'd unleashed from her upstairs bedroom were of a new breed entirely, hiding themselves perfectly amongst the background code of the fledgling Internet, spreading like an e-pandemic. Her work was inspired, revolutionary, the agents had said, if only for its wickedly elegant inventiveness.

Her parents had seemed suitably surprised and affronted when the Feds had come calling, but though she'd never gotten a full confession Jeannie was certain that her mother was the one who'd dropped dime on her.

It turned out they'd been watching her for a while, and in the profilers' opinions her psychological dossier had *prime suspect* written all over it: *A loner, IQ off the scale, not socially integrated, child prodigy, prominent family/broken home*, that sort of thing. In any case, within a week of the attack they came to either arrest her or hire her. To this day she sometimes wondered which one they'd actually done.

Since the evidence had been destroyed in the brute-force disinfection of NYNEX, they'd needed to reconstruct the virus so measures could be taken to prevent a repeat performance. While the technicians sat with her, Jeannie spent an hour with the 4ESS tech manual and had written her version of the malignant code before her Saturday afternoon soccer game. She had crossed paths with her first computer criminal, and to her government's delight, she had risen to the challenge and was eager for more.

After the folks and the family lawyer had signed her over, she passed a polygraph and the agents relaxed a bit and gave her the scoop. The man who was probably behind this, they told her, was the uber-hacker, long thought only an urban myth, a shadowy rumor of the Usenet counterculture. They had no name and only a sparse description, but his work, when it emerged, was as unmistakable as a fingerprint. On the newsgroups this man was called Phr33k, with a "Ph" instead of an "F" and two 3s for the "ea" sound, because it was hacker jargon.

At that tidbit she'd given them a naïve little *oh-my* worthy of a vintage Shirley Temple flick. She'd been fluent in the lingo of the cyber-underground since she was eight, of course, but there was no reason to let the stiffs know that.

She'd heard of this Phr33k, and now she felt as though she'd met him, the author of the brilliant seven-line masterpiece she'd just reconstructed for these serious men in their dark suits. There was an unfamiliar stirring down in her stomach as she looked over what this anonymous, faceless genius had made, and that she had reverse-engineered *in simpatico* with him. In her young life, this was the first piece of someone else's work she'd yet come across that actually earned her respect.

From that day forward she'd been a government asset, and on the day she got her driver's license, her last zit and her doctorate from MIT, she punched-in full time as a federal asset.

Today's presentation was the culmination of six years of work, her grand unified strategy for security in the age of electronic warfare. The broad concepts of TIA, or Total Information Awareness, had been floating around since she'd proposed them in her first months with the Agency, and this morning she was to make a strong case for final approval and deployment of the whole shebang. In a nutshell, TIA would link all the US intelligence data, foreign and domestic, into a single cyber-supermind. At the same time, it would revoke or relax most of the outdated and overliberal privacy protections granted to the burgeoning millions of Internet users. These rights were a treacherous holdover from the days when most online citizens were themselves government entities, and it was way past time to tighten the screws.

But things moved so slowly. The glacial pace of government galled her on a daily basis, as did the impassable walls that had been erected between factions of the intelligence community. Tens of billions were being spent on duplicate research, offices refused to collaborate for fear of getting their lunch eaten by rivals for budget dollars, and it went on and on. The result was an almost perfect lack of communication. But TIA would fix that too.

This morning's terrorist attack only confirmed that the time had come to circle the wagons and make security our nation's prime directive until further notice. We had long needed to act with authority, to do some perhaps unpleasant and unpopular things in order to avoid some truly unthinkable consequences in the future. And today the unthinkable had finally happened.

Okay, enough.

She shot a signal to Rudy Steinman, her boy Friday, to go into the hall and muster the meeting back to order.

Gradually the group began to filter back into the room, with many still wrapping up their cell conversations. She had a genuinely heavyweight audience today; every intel, counter-intel and DoD department was represented here, along with emissaries from House and Senate subcommittees and senior White House staffers. Rumsfeld himself was downstairs making a similar case to an even higher level of decision-makers.

When they had taken their seats Rudy lowered the lights, and as the room quieted, she picked up her presentation.

"Thank you in advance for your time and attention, everyone. In light of the disaster at the Trade Center, I trust you've made the calls you need to make and have cleared yourselves for the next hour or so. If you're feeling an impulse to run from this room to go and do something about the attack we suffered this morning, let me assure you that by giving me these few minutes, you will be taking direct and immediate action, right here and now. If you get an urgent call, of course I'll understand."

Jeannie clicked her remote to display the next slide on the screen behind her.

"In January of 1991, a hacker brought down the telephone system in the five boroughs of New York City, with seven lines of code and a stolen tech manual from the phone company." She advanced to a God's-eye-view graphic of the tristate area, with the critical telco stations circled in red.

"SysAdmins at NYNEX had seen the first signs of something serious coming at 8:30 A.M. Service outages started to appear one after the other, and the automatic countermeasures were failing to keep up. The superstructure of software and hardware charged with managing the most performance-critical phone network in the US was cracking, and the human managers were proving equally inadequate. The network was coming unraveled as they watched, and everything they did to try and stop it only made things worse."

On the screen, concentric circles were radiating out around the scattered central office locations, like fallout zones in a nuclear-war training film.

"Something exponential was happening, something working from the inside. By 10:00 A.M. the NYNEX status wall was lit up like a roller disco with warning lights that never came on outside the monthly diagnostics. Then some big, bad things started to happen."

Jeannie quickly scanned the conference table for full attention. She had it, with the exception of a young Navy man who seemed to be intensely daydreaming about the contents of her blouse. Without a pause in her presentation, she shot from the hip with her laser pointer and nailed him in the left eye.

There, now he was listening.

"At 10:20 A.M. the New York Stock Exchange lost all contact with the outside world. Ten minutes later, 911 emergency services went down all over the city. At 10:45, the air traffic control systems at La Guardia, Kennedy, and Newark airports began to fall apart, and within minutes they all went blind, deaf and dumb, having lost all their vital data and voice uplinks. Then, at noon Eastern Standard Time every phone in the New York City metropolitan area rang once and went stone dead.

"The crisis lasted seven hours, and the phones were back by sundown. By then, though, the damage had been done. The stock market had taken an eight per cent correction, triggered by the disruption of tens of thousands of automated computer transactions and the resulting waves of investor panic. The airlines recorded five near-misses over the metropolitan area, four of which they managed to keep out of the papers. Business ground to a halt, and traffic completely clogged the bridges and tunnels. Those of you who were in the city at the time will remember, the police were overwhelmed, emergency services were in disarray, and Manhattan was effectively shut down for the day.

"This was not an equipment failure, an innocent glitch or a legitimate software bug. For the first time, we had hard evidence of computer sabotage, electronic terrorism. We were hit by a logic bomb, and like any other bomb, its only possible purpose was to cause destruction.

"This was a big one, and it really opened our eyes," Jeannie said, "but there've been other attacks before and since, to the power grid, 911 emergency, military installations, government databases and satellite communications. Most of these crimes were perpetrated through the Internet, and we believe that many of them can be attributed to the work of one man."

She advanced to the next slide. It showed a composite line drawing of a man's face, Caucasian, perhaps thirty years old. It lacked human detail, like most such drawings; it could have been nearly anyone.

"This is all we have of a physical description, and we have very little else. The anonymity of the Internet continues to tie our hands as we endeavor to bring this man and the thousands who aspire to his capabilities to justice. We are ready to address that challenge, and we need your cooperation and support in some critical areas. That's what we're here to discuss today."

As she clicked to the next slide, she noticed that the young man to her right, the breast man, was now looking out the conference room windows. She cleared her throat and waited. He didn't seem to get the message, but his eyes narrowed a bit.

The ensuing silence in the room put everyone's attention on him, but he didn't seem to notice at all. He rolled his chair back a few inches, and as he stood slowly, others followed his eyes outside, and Jeannie followed with them.

The Pentagon was not a tall building, but in this wing they had an unobstructed view for several miles. Way out over the western suburbs of DC, a jet was making a wide turn. Dulles and Reagan National were nearby so the sight should have been nothing at all unusual. But she fixed on it, like the others were beginning to.

It was too far away to pinpoint the class, but it was an airliner, not military, and it looked to be in a landing pattern. She followed its descending flight path as it came around ninety degrees onto final, with two thin lines of black exhaust now tracing straight back toward the horizon, and she saw what was wrong. It was going too fast, true, much too fast, but even at this distance and at that speed, looking head-on at what was now clearly a 757, she was able to spot the really obvious flaw in the image of a landing jumbo jet.

No wheels.

It seemed for the next few moments to be suspended in the air, only growing gradually larger and settling gently lower to the ground as it came. It hung over the landscape, the aileron corrections of its pilot causing it to rock left, then smoothly right to wings-level again. And then suddenly, the illusion broke and the plane accelerated to half a thousand miles per hour, struck streetlights cartwheeling in its wake turbulence, the ascending whine of its engines almost but not quite outrun.

The room was quiet. There was only one last moment to accept, and surrender.

2

Edward Latrell awoke with a flinch and a start, snapped back to his bedroom from the still depths at the center of his mind, and now suddenly, intensely aware.

The first light of sunrise had awakened him, and then the words. The staticky snippets of sentences and muttered anticipations that had quietly mingled with his own inner voices as he slept had now become shouts of joy and triumph from the all-band transceiver on his roll-top desk. The banks of indicator lights chased and paused as the receiver scanned the frequencies for witness from his people, searched the invisible waves countrywide for the news that would be coming on the air.

A doubt suddenly chilled him.

He turned his eyes to the windows of his room, sought an affirmation there. The day as always had begun early, life had been underway for over an hour outside his home, and the sight of his people never failed to bear him up.

The camp had grown over decades, enfolded by a rough ring of minor mountains in the Sangre de Cristo range not far from San Luis. It was ragged and inaccessible country, cruel and kind at its whim, but always the land had provided. Game was plentiful for much of the year, and the streams ran rich with trout in the spring run-off and through the summer months. And the land protected

19

its own. Even standing on the ground within the camp's borders, but certainly from the vigilant sky above, there was little to suggest that many hundreds of families, soldiers and guardians of liberty made their home in this place, beneath the sheltering umbrella of an ancient pine forest. Here all was peaceful, self-sufficient, self-governing, self-defending, untainted, incorruptible. And waiting.

The scene outside was a realized vision he'd nurtured for years, but it was not his sole creation. In the very founding days of the United States, Thomas Jefferson had dreamed of the life in this small nascent corner of the nation he had made. The gentlemen farmers bearing their crop to the local markets and canneries, the herdsmen tending, the wives and daughters making homes, the town militia honing their cold discipline. And fathers teaching sons to become men, free men in whose hands now lay the future of a once-great republic.

The girl had been resting with him, cradled at his shoulder after the long final night's preparations, and his movement had roused her. She was warm from sleep, slower than he to come to consciousness, and unlike him still blissfully inclined to the deep slumber of youth, faith and clarity.

He met her eyes as she opened them, watched them brighten at the recognition of him, saw them widen as she heard the excited words amid the windy rush of the shortwave, as she remembered the order of the day.

He nodded to her, laid his head on the cool cotton down, and pulled her close. His eyes found an engraved river stone on his side-table, a gift from her the evening before. He read the inscribed words, and in them he found the strength their author had meant to commend to generations.

We have it in our power to begin the world over again.
—*Thomas Paine*

"Stay with me," Latrell whispered. "It begins."

3

File: NSA/FBI joint op code: Rugbeater
Source: Internet Relay Chat (IRC)
Channel: #26, el33tzCafe
—Transcript follows—
Start of #26 buffer: 21:48:39

Wednesday, March 10, 1993

*** Now talking in #26 [in progress]
*** Topic of #26: .:[{1066}].:[high.crime.critique]:?

*** Set by ChanServ 75 minutes ago
*** Users on #26: +TheHelix +reZ|sham +cavebear +spazWarz
+shazam +KhZ2600 +L0pht_01 +saint_Ted +theprisoner +phr33k
+blitzCraig +roobiTuesday +jiffypoop +dragonlord +STaSHoLa

*** End of /NAMES list.
*** User mode for channel #26 is "+tnl":|stealth
*** Channel #26 was created at 21:42:46
*** Join to #26 completed in 1 second(s).

-reZ|sham- I'm not playing right now.
-TheHelix- What's the matter, can't keep up?

-LOpht_01- Nah, he's prolly got some homework.

-reZ|sham- My mom walked in, and she's got that 'quality time' look.

-TheHelix- ROTFLMAO

-roobiTuesday- :)

-saint_Ted- Maybe after she tucks you in, you can sign back on.

reZ|sham** has left the conversation

-dragonlord- thumbsucker

-theprisoner- Okay, time for tonight's main event: the perfect murder.

-STaSHola- ive got one

-theprisoner- Bring it on.

-STaSHola- alright you put a pencil mark on your passenger side dash in your car and you slide the seat way up forward then you take the guy for a ride and you say dude could you get that pencil mark off there for me and you hand him a sharp #2 pencil and when he starts to erase it with the eraser BAM you rear-end the car in front of you pop the airbag and the guy stabs himself in the heart

-roobiTuesday- Thats actually not bad...

-TheHelix- The pencil would break on his breastbone

-STaSHola- huh uh

-TheHelix- uh huh

-STaSHola- huh uh

-TheHelix- uh huh

-theprisoner- Let's try to keep the discussion above playground level, please.

-TheHelix- sorry

-STaSHola- huh uh NO TAGBACKS

-shazam- Even if the pencil didn't break, which it might, you might just wing the guy, and if you didn't kill him, he would know what you did and you're busted.

-KhZ2600- Okay Im next. You get a big meat stick, like a giant slim jim, put it in the freezer for a couple days, break into the guys house and beat him to death with the meat stick, and then microwave it and eat it. NO MURDER WEAPON NO FINGERPRINTS BWAAA haa ha ha

-theprisoner- Slim jims aren't kosher, could I use a kielbasa?

-shazam- Your fingerprints would be on the Triscuit box. :)

-KhZ2600- I dont need no stinkin crackers

-STaSHola- plus the cops could suppena your dooty

-TheHelix- LOL

-phr33k- You know, no offense, guys, but this group used to be a lot cooler.

-roobiTuesday- Well, the lurker speaks.

-shazam- Whose that?

-phr33k- I'm just saying, I started this group six years ago, and it used to be we had some serious thinkers here. Maybe it's time to move on.

-shazam- That nick is retired, you know. Nobody uses 'phr33k' around here, dude

-phr33k- Nobody but me.

-shazam- What's that supposed to mean? You saying you're him, bullshitter?

-KhZ2600- ooo, a celebrity

-phr33k- I'm not saying anything. BTW, is that 'shazam' like from Gomer Pyle? Shuh-zay-um!

-STaSHola- who is it???

-shazam- Nobody, just some homo lurker with no respect for his betters.

-KhZ2600- Dude, how do you know its not him

-STaSHola- ?

-jiffypoop- you guys are off topic

-KhZ2600- Off topic my schvanz

-shazam- So you're the man? Mr. Nynex? You wrote the Valentine virus? Phr33k, of the '77 east coast blackout? Riiiiiiiight.

-STaSHola- i was born in 1977

-KhZ2600- Just shut up, stash

-STaSHola- i was

-shazam- All you've gotta do is prove it. Prove you're the guy.

-STaSHola- yea

-jiffypoop- put up or shut up man

-shazam- Show your cards, you hump. Hold em or fold em, chicken shit. You know I can get your IP? You don't know who you're messing with. Your gonna get flamed off IRC, dude, and I'll hit you with an email bomb youll never forget. Whatd you do, disappear? I don't see anything, did you poo your pants, big shot? come on, phr33k, lets a;k#

-KhZ2600- Shazam?

shazam** has left the conversation

-STaSHola- ?

-jiffypoop- What happened to that guy?

-phr33k- I think he might be having a little trouble with the boot partition on his hard drive.

-STaSHola- whoa

-theprisoner- Its him guys. HIM

-STaSHola- 8^)

-phr33k- Now, where were we?

-theprisoner- Man, I'm your biggest fan

-jiffypoop- He trashed the guys hard drive over IRC? Can you even DO that?

-theprisoner- Kid, this guy probably *wrote* IRC

-phr33k- No, that was Jarkko Oikarinen. But I did consult.

-STaSHola- whoa

-KhZ2600- Id like to here your perfect murder, ph

-STaSHola- me 2

-phr33k- You guys are thinking too small.

-dragonlord- Okay, something major . . .

-phr33k- Pick a victim, but think big. Not the President, that's been done to death.

-KhZ2600- A couple of weeks ago, you know what happened at the World Trade Center?

-saint_Ted- Truck bomb in the parking level, some towelheads tried to blow up the building

-phr33k- Okay, good example.

So here's what they thought they were going to do. They thought they were going to blow out the foundation and tip over one tower onto the other, and both of them would fall on the surrounding buildings and kill 100,000 people. AND, they loaded the truck up with cyanide, hoping to gas anybody who survived the blast.

-theprisoner- dumbasses

-phr33k- So what did they do wrong?

-STaSHola- needed a BIGER BOMM (sp?)

-phr33k- Bigger bomb wouldn't have done any good. Those buildings are supported by huge steel columns sunk 60 feet into the bedrock under Manhattan. To take those out, you'd need giant linear shaped charges on at least half of them, and some serious timing electronics to set them off in sequence. You'd never get the opportunity to place the LSCs, even if you could get ahold of the right materials and technology, which requires a serious license, which you can't get. The cyanide, of course, was stupid, since it burned up in the explosion. They had no chance whatsoever.

-theprisoner- So how would you do it?

-phr33k- Do what? :)

-theprisoner- Come on, how would you have taken out the World Trade Center

-phr33k- Well . . .

To start with, that wasn't what they wanted to do. They wanted to commit the ultimate terrorist act, to fuck up the US economy and scare the living shit out of the population. That's very ambitious for a loose band of amateurs.

-KhZ2600- So............?

-phr33k- Alright. Guided missiles.

-STaSHola- awsome

-saint_Ted- wait a minute, thats lame. where are they gonna get missiles that are big enough to take out a giant building, and how are they going to get them into the country????

-phr33k- We launch 40,000 of them here every day...

-KhZ2600- WTF?

-dragonlord- . . . Airliners . . . !

-phr33k- Airliners. Now you only have one shot to do this, because it will never work after the first time.

US borders leak like a sieve, so you get your people in the country on student visas, work visas, any kind of visa you like. Enroll your moles in private pilot school, just a bunch of friendly foreign guys with cash who want a private pilot's ticket. Remember, you just need to learn how to FLY a jet, not to takeoff or LAND a jet, that's the hard part. Basic instruments, stick and rudder. You're going to be taking over the controls in the air. If you want to, take some of your oil money and buy yourself a full-size simulator. Remember, this is America, and everything's for sale.

Once your pilots are trained, then, lots of test runs. Buy first-class tickets, one-way, early morning non-stop cross-country flights, so your jets are full of fuel for a long trip. Test and see what weapons you can get through the joke of a security screen, but stick with small knives, like case cutters, the kind of harmless utility piece you might forget to take out of your pocket after work. Perfectly innocent, and they're all you're going to need.

.You want flights that consistently have a small number of passengers, and the ticket agent on the 800 number will give you that.

-KhZ2600- why is that, with the passengers?

-phr33k- Crowd control. You don't want a big mob to worry about.

-KhZ2600- o

-phr33k- Watch the procedures, watch the cockpit. See that little, flimsy door that your grandmother could kick open? See any air marshals? Didn't think so. How many flight attendants? You want four, five, maybe six of your guys per plane. A timekeeper, two guys who can kill hand-to-hand, one or two pilots, and a comm guy to coordinate with the other flights.

Only the pilots know the whole plan, so you don't get any chickenshit defections from your fellow radicals. Like everybody else, they think we're just joyriding to a friendly tropical neighbor with our hostages.

Like I said, this is a one-time-only deal, so you get all your teams on flights across the country, 100, 150 of them, whatever you can swing, taking off within minutes of each other.

They're all in communication right up to take-off. Targets are set: World Trade Center, Empire State Building, Stock Exchange, White

House, Capitol Building where hopefully Congress is in session, CIA headquarters, Sears Tower, the Hancock, O'Hare and the Board of Trade in Chicago, the Library Tower and the Department of Water and Power in Los Angeles, the Golden Gate Bridge and the Transamerican in San Francisco, Hoover Dam, the Gateway Arch, nuclear power plants, pipelines, refineries, ports, electric stations, reservoirs, communication hubs, sports arenas, you pick them for maximum impact, 30 or 40 landmarks, power and transportation arteries and centers of commerce across the country. Everybody's got their coordinates, aerial photos and flight plans committed to memory. Okay, the planes take off, around start of business in the morning. In a few minutes, during the climb-out, your team stands up and immediately makes an example of a nearby passenger or flight attendant.

You cut their throat, a quick ugly murder to show that you're off-the-deep-end, wacko serious, to keep people in their seats. You tell the flight attendants that it's a hijacking, and you want into the cockpit. If the pilots don't come out, you keep killing bystanders until they do. Remember, the rule for hijackings is to lie down and comply. After all, they figure all you want to do is fly and land somewhere, and the law will deal with the situation when the plane gets back on the ground.

Now you're in the cockpit, and your muscle either kills or trusses up the flight crew so they can't interfere. Turn off the transponder, and stay off the radio. When and if the ATCs realize there's a hijacking, they'll probably get around to scrambling some fighters, but the procedures will be rusty and it'll take a half hour to get the jets armed and into the air. That's more time than you'll need, even IF they'd shoot, which would take a direct order from the President. Change course and head for your target. This is happening fast, and it's happening everywhere, so the authorities can't possibly keep up, and they've got no clue what you've really got in mind. The passengers are calming down, and on the ground they'll be lucky if they've figured out that anything is wrong by the time you're on vector to your final destination.

Let's take the WTC example, cause it'll be the most spectacular. You want to hit your building about 3/4 of the way up, and dead center if you can. There's 40,000 liters of jet fuel in your rig, and you need to get all of that inside the shell of the building. So, kiss your ass goodbye and drive that sucker straight into the 80th floor.

-theprisoner- Those buildings can take a direct hit from a 767, I've read about it.

-phr33k- You're right, they can. They're super resilient, and they're built to absorb lateral loads, like high winds or jumbo jets, much more than a gravity load, which is supposedly known and constant. They could probably take five times the impact of the plane, and still be standing. But it's the gravity load that we're going to fuck around with.

Now, stay with me. It's hard enough to fight a conventional fire in a high-rise, but this is a fuel-fed inferno from hell 800 feet off the ground. The WTC is about 95% empty air, so the fire's not going to get snuffed from lack of oxygen. It burns for 45 minutes or an hour, and the steel columns that support the weight of the individual floors start to soften.

-KhZ2600- The fire wouldn't be hot enough. You can't melt that steel with an acetylene torch.

-phr33k- Now you guys are thinking. This is good.

You're right, KhZ, this is what is called a diffuse fire, like the one in your fireplace, extremely inefficient compared to a pre-mixed flame in a stoichiometric ratio, like a welding torch. But I said soften, not melt. Each floor of the WTC is designed to handle over a thousand tons more than its own weight. It is a strong and sturdy motherfucker. But remember, we just drove a jet into the side of it, so at least some of the supporting members are now out of commission. And the fire's getting hot enough now to compromise the remaining members a bit, and they're getting weaker. The killer, though, is temperature differential.

The inside of the support steel is super hot, and the outside away from the fire is relatively cold. Thermal expansion caused by the internal heat disparity in the steel columns produces stress, then

28

irregular distortions, then loss of structural integrity, then buckling failures. There's a lot of building above where you hit, and as the members start to give way the weight falls on the intact floors below. The angle clips that support those floors fail, the weight and momentum builds, and the whole thing comes straight down in 10 seconds like a stack of flapjacks.

-STaSHola- . . .

-theprisoner- Straight down? Why doesn't the top just fall off, above where you hit?

-phr33k- Newton figured that out. Each of those towers weighs half a million tons, and that's a lot of inertia. Nothing's going to push that much mass sideways, so it's got no choice but straight down, at 125 miles an hour.

-KhZ2600- You ...... are ...... GOOD.

-phr33k- Now, with the Trade Center, you've got a media bonus, because there are two targets. Remember, you want massive psychological impact, and that means you need good pictures.

Of all your targets, you do this one first, because it's got some terrorist history and a lot of shock value. And you want everyone to get a good look at your handiwork.

Now you might get some accidental camcorder footage of the first collision, just because there are thousands of fucking tourists running around every day. But who has an idea on how to get extreme close-ups and lots of angles without tipping anyone off that you know what's going to happen?

-theprisoner- ......?

-KhZ2600- Hit them with the first plane, then wait half an hour and hit them with the second one...

-phr33k- That's right. Half an hour's too long, though. Think about dramatic pacing. You're in Manhattan, during the morning shows, and they'll have helicopters in the air within minutes and crews down there right after that. Do the second tower in fifteen minutes or so, and the reporters will be right at the scene, talking about this terrible accident. They'll be holding all commercial breaks. All eyes everywhere are on the spot. Then BAM, second plane hits the second tower. And that sinking feeling sets in that America is not just unlucky today; we're under attack.

Then terror, as they say, ensues.

-KhZ2600- Alright, you WIN. :^0

-phr33k- Think about it. A storm of jumbo jets raining down all over the country, in one day. Tens of thousands of casualties. The WTC is toast, Washington is devastated, landmarks are destroyed, power, phone and utilities are in disarray, Wall Street is shut down, nuke plants are leaking doom and destruction, and panic reigns. You want to be a terrorist, that's the way to do it. And you could pull it off for about half a million bucks.

-STaSHola- dude, u rool

-phr33k- Not bad, I think, for straight off the cuff. Take care, boys. Keep the group going.

phr33k** has left the conversation

End of #26 buffer: Wed Mar 10 22:19:51 1993

Xref: DoD subcontract 202(h)8015893(IRC)

First viewed: – –/– –/– – – –

Last viewed: – –/– –/– – – –

Date archived: 3.10.1993

4

The newspeople, always reliably untouched and animatronic, were nevertheless feeling it. This was their island after all, and the skies above it were darkening with a cloud of brown-black smoke from enemy fire. They were stumbling over the words, and long silences broke their thoroughbred delivery as the humans inside those talking heads really saw what was happening.

John realized his leg was aching, and he lowered his eyes from the burning towers to check the time in the corner of the wall-sized video screen. It was 9:30. He'd been standing transfixed for almost half an hour. He backed to his chair, felt for it, and sat down, watching.

This is not your fault, he thought, and he said it out loud.

He was not in any way responsible, of course. He'd been part of a discussion, eight years ago; he'd shared ideas as free-thinking people are allowed to do. Novelists and screenwriters make their living spinning tales about all manner of crimes, and if some idiot takes those ideas and murders their boss, or robs Fort Knox, or blows up a few buildings it isn't the ideas that are to blame. This is America, and freedom of expression is a goddamn built-in, unalienable principle.

You did not cause this, you did not drive those jets, nor are you driving the hundred or so others that must now be on their

31

way to rain hell all across the country. It's out of your hands. And not only that, by the way, and let me reemphasize this, it was never in your hands to begin with. You're clean on this one. It's going to play out now, but you have no involvement what-soever.

The FAA had closed the airspace around New York only a few minutes ago, but most of the morning's scheduled flights were still in the air. *Too slow,* he thought, but he heard the words and the dog cocked his head, so he must have spoken them again.

They weren't thinking fast enough, not by half.

There was the President on TV now; he was somewhere in Florida and looking understandably flummoxed, but he was keeping his grip. We had suffered an apparent terrorist attack, he'd just said, and the scrolling caption on the lower third of the screen repeated his assessment.

Well, no shit, Sherlock, just like the Titanic hit an apparent iceberg. And I've got a news flash for you, chief. It'll be getting a lot more apparent straight away.

The dog was staring at him, had been for a while now.

"What, Boner?" John said. "You're not going out, so you can either hold it or go in the corner." He didn't look like he wanted to go out at all, though. He looked like he looked before a trip to the vet, and he was scared shitless of needles.

John was on his feet without thinking about it, and he found his cane. His leg was acting up a bit, but the cane would keep it steady. He walked to the tower of his computer and pulled the small memory stick from a USB port on the front panel, slipped its dogtag chain around his neck, and tucked it under his shirt. He was still in the clothes he'd slept in, but he didn't think anyone was going to notice that.

He felt in his pocket for the key, and stopped to look for a long moment at the video wall. People were jumping from the buildings now, and the networks had gradually mustered the good judgment to turn our eyes away from that horror, at least.

32

The mayor was down on the scene, and firemen and police were rushing to their duty.

He checked his watch. "I'm not going to be gone for very long," John said, quietly and mostly to himself. He hated going out like Boner hated distemper shots, but he wouldn't be gone for very long.

The door to his apartment opened not to a hallway but to an ancient Otis elevator car. It was original equipment for this building, a perk for the old executive office level, ornate with brass fittings and varnished wood panels. There were no buttons, only an operator's lever that swung through an arc to take you either up or down. John had added floor-level controls so the dog could come and go unaccompanied, with permission. Boner was no Stephen Hawking, but he picked things up quickly when food was involved. To go out, push the checkered pedal, get a treat. To come back up, push the one with stripes, get a treat. The first day he'd gotten it the elevator had run up and down nonstop until the entire reservoir of Snausages had disappeared.

There was no traditional exit or entrance to his place. In a city as dense as New York, a hermit needed a man-cave that drew no attention and invited no visitors. The elevator ran directly to the basement, a labyrinth of stuffy cubicles and decaying storehouse inventory. A chain of floor-level guidelights marked the circuitous path toward his door to the outside. A short concrete stairway led up to padlocked double steel doors that opened outward onto the sidewalk above.

His home was all but invisible to the self-absorbed public that flowed past it every day. Sandwiched between similar buildings on either side, from the street it looked stately but gray and archaic, just the fading former home of another dead American industry. John's great-grandfather had built his fortune through the invention and manufacture of an innovative hook-race mechanism used in foot-pedal sewing machines. His granddad had navigated the business through the Depression, but by his father's day it had become a daily losing battle against changing times and overseas knock-offs.

The factory doors had closed for the last time in the mid-seventies, but they'd held onto the real estate. The years of stress had pretty much killed his Mom and certainly started ol' Pop on the downward spiral to his last address at Highland Eldercare up in Nyack. Alzheimer's had arrived a little later, just to put the sprinkles on the cupcake. The disease had come on slowly. Until the yearly unanswered birthday letters had stopped arriving John could read the annual, gradual drawing away of the man. It was as if his mind were leaking memories bit by bit, last-in, first-out. He would never know for sure, but he'd always felt that his father must have welcomed the departure of all but a very few of his recollections.

A sole heir, a trust fund and the building were all that remained of the Fagan legacy today. And since the day he'd signed-by-proxy the final admission papers for dear old Dad, the building was his, all to himself.

Like his home John was invisible, or as nearly so as he could manage. He rarely ventured outside. All his needs were delivered in packages, left by various delivery boys in an automated receiving box in exchange for cash in labeled envelopes. When he did step out he was hidden by the cloaking effect that obscured all New Yorkers from one another. On the outside, John was simply an overweight, pasty, plain and unassuming nonpresence, aged thirty-five to forty-four.

Sunlight was as always an irritating shock to his system. He'd climbed three of the six steep concrete stairs that led up to street level from the basement, and the glare broke in as he pushed upward on one of the double-metal doors set into the sidewalk above. He opened it just slightly to make sure no one was walking or standing on it. He took another step up then, and the hinges creaked as he pushed both doors up and out. They fell with a double-clang onto the sidewalk, and the sharp sound stung him. He stepped up, bent and lifted the heavy doors, and lowered them closed. Already breaking a sweat.

You're going to be okay, he thought, and he walked out into the morning air.

There were people on the street, but they weren't concerned with him. Everyone who was out was either headed down toward the Trade Center, or directly in the opposite direction, both with comparable urgency.

John made his way down the block, looking up as he walked. There was a great deal of black smoke, but it was up high and the wind was carrying it east. The effect at street level was just an eerie darkening, like the early phase of an unforeseen eclipse.

He was getting winded by the time he saw the rough police perimeter. Looking up now the twin buildings were surreally tall, his insect's perspective rendering them massive at the ground, narrowing as they rose into the sky. People from the lower floors were still coming out, some at a dead run, most stopping when they were clear and turning to look back up at where they'd just been, what they'd just escaped.

Fire crew chiefs were yelling to their teams over the din, trying to formulate and mount a response to the fires. Some of the men had already been up there and back down again, their faces smudged and red from the soot and the hellish climb.

Team by team, he watched as they came to their agreements, and started back for the towers.

What were these people thinking? Everyone above the fires was toast already. Anyone could see that, couldn't they? And everyone below the fires was walking out on their own. You can't pump water that high, you don't have an 80-story extension ladder, so what's the point of going in there? Do you think those people would be jumping if there was any other way down? Or up?

Bodies were hitting the ground every twenty seconds or so, and he let his eyes travel up the side of the south tower, the one nearest him. He saw something descending, reflected in the bright glass sides of the building. It looked like debris at first, falling smoothly from way up high.

Not *it*. She.

She was not flailing her arms or kicking her legs, there was no screaming that he could hear. Her fear was behind her. She was simply coming down.

John pressed his way forward against the slow current of a river of humanity, faces blank, troubled, relieved, crying, heaving for breath. He reached a cop who was holding the line, and the young man took a grip on his shoulder.

"Go back, pal, let these people out. Go home."

"Look, I'm a doctor," John said. "I need to talk to someone in charge."

"Where's your bag, doc?" the cop said, dismissing him. "Go on, get back so we can work here, bud."

John caught a glimpse of the guy's badge, and he looked him in the eye. "Officer Perrone," he said. "I can help. Let me help."

Something in the tone did the trick.

"Go help, then, doc. Go talk to that man over there." The officer stepped aside and ticked his head toward a tall ruddy man in a navy blazer, standing on the open tailgate of a fire department vehicle, bullhorn in hand.

It was an imaginary line, but as he stepped across it he could feel he was now on the inside of the disaster. There were civilians passing through, and some newspeople, but the power on this side was all police and FDNY. These were not John's people, not by a long shot, but he was sure he could communicate with them.

It was a mess out there, chaos. There were men and women on stretchers and gurneys, but even more of the injured and some of the dead were still on the pavement. In the midst of a field of broken glass and blowing paper, he saw a line of black medical bags in the open bay of an empty EMS wagon. He walked over and picked one up, hefted it. Felt like a full kit.

As he worked his way through the crowd toward the field

commander, his foot caught on something in the street, and he was down on one knee before he regained his balance. There in front of him was what had been a man in a suit, lying motionless on his side and curled in a fetal position. He was nearly all the same color, burnt to a dark brown, suit and skin alike. The fabric of his clothing looked fused and brittle, as though it would puff into ashes if he moved. One of his arms, from the elbow down, was perfectly normal, pink and alive, but was stripped of both the shirt and the jacket sleeve that had covered it when he had dressed himself this morning.

Hurricanes drive soda straws through oak trees, tornadoes pick up cows and lower them gently onto the roofs of houses, and explosions sometimes burn you lifeless except for one sleeveless arm.

Miracles.

The eyes moved in the bronze statue's face, and they met his own.

He didn't think about what to say. The very-soon-to-be-dead required peace and consolation only.

"It's gonna be all right," John said.

The man's head was suspended a few inches above the asphalt, as if it were resting on a pillow. The lips didn't move, but John heard a version of a word come through them.

"All right."

People were rushing past them on all sides, but no one was paying them any mind. Thirty yards away, an EMT was putting a field splint on a child's leg, and he caught John's eye. He shook his head, indicated the burnt man and flicked an index finger across his neck. He wasn't being cruel, only realistic, and efficient. *That one had already been triaged,* said the gesture, *and your time would be better spent with someone who might actually live until lunchtime.*

Well, nevertheless.

John opened the bag beside him. He felt through the gel dressings, antiseptics, aspirin *(aspirin, for God's sake)*, instruments and test strips, and he found what he was looking for. He held the small vial up to the light, shook it and peeled off the anti-tamper seal.

"This is going to make you feel better, and then we'll get you all fixed up before you know it."

"Thank you," the man said. It sounded more like "tank oo," but the sentiment came clear.

Providence had left a strong blue vein ready in the ruined man's untouched arm. The Lord moves in mysterious fucking ways, John thought, as he slipped a plastic hypodermic from its holder and punched the needle through the stopper of the vial.

Morphine in the burn unit, he thought, and he closed his eyes.

Photographic memory, like genius, was a power claimed by many but gifted to only a handful, most of them institutionalized savants. It wasn't wisdom, his early teachers had been fond of pointing out, but more like a filing cabinet, a personal reference book. They had expected the skill to fade with adolescence, but he had held onto it and strengthened it with the years. Now at forty-one, his memory had grown as deep and wide as the Library of Congress and the Smithsonian combined, and everything stored there was only milliseconds away. Billions of cross-referenced blocks of knowledge were etched in his brain, filed alphabetically, chronologically, categorically and permanently, everything he'd ever seen, ever read, and ever heard.

His mind's eye flew over the landscape of memory until it slowed and arrived at what he was seeking. Between Christmas and New Year's eleven years ago, he'd read Goodman & Gilman's *The Pharmacological Basis of Therapeutics*, and he hadn't really thought of it again until this moment. The answer was there, on page 537, lines 9–17. For good measure he mentally scanned several other related clinical papers and treatment protocols for guidelines and contraindications.

John pulled the plunger out with his thumb, and watched the clear liquid rise against the hatch marks. Ten milligrams were recommended to swap a dressing. This was no bandage change, though, this guy was one solid third-degree burn. *Maximum recommended IV dosage, 30 mg slow push, in field trauma sit-uations.* He stopped the rising column just past 35, and squirted a bit into the air to clear the needle. In the hospital, an allergy to opiates might be a concern, but this was no hospital, and John, of course, was no doctor.

"You're going to feel a little pinch, now," he said, and he would have sworn the man's eyes narrowed a bit, the most of a smile he would ever manage again. John thumped the vein three times, and rubbed it with an alcohol swab. The thin-gauge needle slid in, and he pushed the plunger gradually to its stop, withdrew it, and swabbed the skin again.

He checked his watch, took a marker from the bag, and wrote in clear red letters on the man's unburnt forearm.

end-stage injuries, admin 35 mg IV morphine, 9:55 A.M., *9/11/01*

"Now try to rest," John said. "You're going to wake up and this is all going to be fine."

The man's eyes stayed with him as he disposed of the hypo in the kit's sharps container and snapped the bag closed. John looked at him, gave him a nod, and walked to the makeshift command point at the tail-end of a fire department SUV.

"Chief, I need to talk to you."

The man looked down at him. "It's assholes and elbows right now, doc, let me do my job."

"Listen to me," John said, glancing at the man's security badge. "Mr O'Connor, you've got to get your men out of the buildings, now."

"No, I've got to get my men into the buildings, and then I've got to get 'em out, and you're not helping me do that." He turned his attention back to the chaos in front of him.

"Listen!" John shouted, slamming his cane against the side of the vehicle. "The fire is weakening the support beams, and when they're weak enough they're going to buckle, and when that happens the upper floors are going to fall down onto the lower structure and then it's all going to come right down here where

39

we're standing. Everyone in those towers is going to be dead in a few minutes if you don't clear them out right now."

He got no response, but the other man lowered his bullhorn slowly.

"Are you listening to me? Am I getting through to you?" John shouted.

The man dropped down from the tailgate and faced him. He was drenched in sweat and smoke, and there were tears in his clear blue eyes. "Are you getting through to me?" he said. "What are you trying to get through?"

"Everyone in those buildings," John said, "all your men are going to die if you don't get them out—"

"Do you think I don't know that?" He waited for an answer. "Do you think they don't know that? I know my job, and they know theirs; my brother and my son are in there, and so are people they signed on to serve and protect. You took an oath too, didn't you? Now get about your business before I send you to the hospital in the back of an ambulance." He turned away, put his walkie-talkie to his ear, and walked toward the building in front of them.

John looked after him, followed his progress until he disappeared into the entrance of the south tower. Other men were heading there, too, firemen and cops, some with helmets and oxygen, others in their shirtsleeves and only barely in uniform, as if they'd come down on their day off, to pitch in against the insurmountable.

He looked up, backing away slowly, heard glass crunching under his heels. This hadn't been the best idea, he thought, if duty was going to outweigh reason. He'd tried to tell them. He'd tried to help them, but they wouldn't listen.

"Get back," he shouted, continuing to retreat, watching the top of the enormous building in front of him. "Everybody get back," he repeated, his voice rising and disappearing with the other shouts, sirens, and screams into the furor of the scene. "Everybody get back!"

High up in the sky, the sides of the near tower seemed to shimmer for a moment.

The mass of the uppermost twenty-five stories pressed down on the ruining steel, by only fractions of inches at first. The columns began to bow, outward and inward, and at last the burden could no longer be resisted, and they sighed and let go. The reinforced concrete and structural members that had held the 85th floor in its place were pulverized to dust and broken steel by pressures unimagined by their architects. Gravity seized the now-detached upper floors, inertia released its grip and momentum took its hold and drove the top of the tower earthward like the falling head of a sledgehammer.

Running would be of little use now. He would live or he would not. John watched as the building came down and down before him, heard and felt the freight-train roar of its dying breath, and was swallowed whole by the rolling gray-white avalanche of ash and dust that would settle as a shroud for thousands dead.

5

Before she was awake, she became aware that something was wrong, not dangerous, just different, unfamiliar.

The smells were wrong. There were flowers somewhere nearby, and she hated cut flowers. This was not her apartment, and these were not the sheets of a hotel room against her skin. The light that came through her eyelids was too bright, and the air was too dry.

She kept her eyes closed, and decided in her half-consciousness to make it a game.

Where was I when I went to sleep? she thought.

I don't remember, she replied, and isn't that a little odd? I don't remember going to bed, but I'm definitely in a bed, and it isn't mine. There are flowers, and those aren't air-freshener flowers, those are roses and, what is that other subtle stench, lilies? There's something else, now. The scorched odor of a high-volume laundry was in the bedclothes, and there were other traces, of synthetic pine, ammonia, peroxide and alcohol. Institutional smells.

Well, against all common sense and my better judgment, she thought, I have an answer. I'm in the hospital.

She opened her eyes, saw the IV tree up above her and to the side, the clear liquid dripping into a curling tube. There was the dull beige blandness of sickroom walls, the pitted white tiles of a suspended ceiling, the curved metal track of the privacy curtain.

She felt a hand holding hers. There was a twinge in her neck as she let her head roll sideways, and a sharp pounding started in her temple.

Her eyes met those of a young man. Hazel eyes, tan and fit, short dark hair and maybe eight years her senior, he was sitting there with the cool confidence of a guy who knew he could take out a half-dozen armed men without unsnapping his holster. Even before she registered the uniform she'd pegged him as military, probably Special Forces.

His face was kind. He smiled a little smile at her, and then she remembered.

The wall of windows in the conference room had turned bright orange, and then the wall was gone and everything around her was flying. The sound of the explosion wasn't what she would have expected at all. She'd heard a *whump*, a pillow-fight noise, followed by only a ringing in her ears. A wave of heat and light had washed over her, and then it was dark. And now she was here.

Jeannie looked at the man who was next to her, and realized she was gripping his hand so tightly that his fingers were nearly blue. If it hurt, he wasn't showing it. She let go and pulled her hand away, and focused on the ceiling.

"What happened?" she asked him.

"We were—the Pentagon was hit by an aircraft, and you were injured in the—"

"I'm well aware of that. What I'm asking you is, what happened, what happened that a jumbo jet crashed into the side of the Pentagon?"

"I'm sorry, I didn't know if you—"

"Yes, yes, I'm lucid and in full possession of my faculties. My name is Jeannie Reese. This is September and the year is 2001. I'm in a hospital room with a strange man who's about to get busted a rank and replaced by someone who can tell me what the hell I need to know to deal with this situation. Now help me sit up and tell me what happened."

He stood and spoke as he propped two pillows behind her, and lifted her slight form gently to lean her back against them. "Multiple hijackings, the planes were apparently taken over and piloted by terrorists on discrete suicide missions," he said.

"How many attacks?"

"Just the Trade Center and the Pentagon. One jet went down in Pennsylvania, definitely hijacked and bound for DC. We might have shot that one down, or the passengers might have tried to retake the plane, we don't know right now. There might have been other teams that were in place but failed to see it through, good chance of that, but it's early—"

"Anyone taken responsibility?"

"No, not yet. All the money's on radical Islamists, Hamas, al Jihad, bin Laden, Jemaah Islamiah, maybe a state sponsor. This was a precision, coordinated attack, that much we know."

"What time is it?"

He checked his watch. "It's 4:15 in the afternoon, still on the eleventh. You've been out for a few hours."

"Where's the President?"

"They've kept him moving, we picked up some chatter that Air Force One was targeted, but he's on his way back to town now. The VP's locked down at Raven Rock, and they're both in communication with the Cabinet."

"Get me a pad and a pen, and sit down," Jeannie said.

He found some writing materials in the bedside drawer, and passed them to her. She began to make notes, and he watched her complete two dense pages and begin a third.

"The other people in your meeting," he said. "It hasn't all been sorted out yet, but some of them are down the hall here. Your assistant, his name is Rudy I think, he's okay, just some cuts and a burn on his leg, but he's okay."

Jeannie laid her pen down. "Who are you?"

"Lieutenant Robert Vance, Rob, you can just call me Rob. I'm a Navy SEAL attached to the Defense Intelligence Agency, I was in your meeting. You shot me in the eye, with your laser pointer, remember?"

She looked up at him.

"They've assigned me to stay with you," he continued. "They don't want anything to happen to you, so I'm here to act as a, whatever, I'm here to stay with you and protect you." He waited for her to respond. "So anyway, that's who I am."

"Lieutenant," Jeannie said, "I can tell you're a talker, and I'd love to sit here and listen to you go on and on, but I have work to do, so I'm going to ask you to step outside and let me work. I'll be perfectly safe in my bed, so if you don't mind." She picked up her pen and went back to her writing. "I'll need my cell phone, a laptop with a secure broadband uplink, a conference room and a meeting in ninety minutes with my team. Wake Rudy up, and he'll tell you who to call."

Rob leaned back for a moment, and then stood to leave.

"I'll be outside," he said.

"Yes, I'm looking forward to that."

Jeannie heard the door hiss shut a few seconds later. She put down her pad and capped her pen, covered her face with her hands, and wept until no more tears would come.

6

The room was lit yellow-orange by the sun as it began to settle behind the mountains, and it was quiet. The men around the long table were still, stock-still like a doe frozen by a boot-crunch behind her in an open field. There was no cover here, and though he did not look at them, they felt his fury passing among them, from man to man.

Spaced along the walls of the room were scores of display screens, showing remote faces of others in the coalition, watching and being watched via Webcams and satellite videophones. They too were silent, as if in full knowledge that the man before them could reach through the wires and put an end to them with a gesture.

Edward Latrell stood at the head of the table, his eyes on the floor in front of him. His rage was strong, he nearly glowed with it. His fists at his sides were working, relaxed then tightening, as if he were trying to pump the anger down to the point of control, so he might speak without the wrath in his words turning this room full of worthless humanity to dead stone.

Ten minutes passed, then fifteen. One of the young men, one of the foreigners, let out his breath with the slightest hiss, a sound of impatience meant for his companions but heard by all.

Latrell's eyes darted to him, then to a figure in the shadows at the far end of the room, then back to the spot at his feet. An instant later, the young man was jerked backward out of his chair and onto the floor. The guard who'd unseated him pulled him bodily up onto his knees, stepped in front of him, and pressed the barrel of his revolver to the man's forehead.

The tall man at the far end of the table started to rise. Joe Lange, head of security and seated next to Latrell, caught the man's eye and lifted the flat of his hand an inch above the table. Joe raised his eyebrows, then lowered his hand slowly back to rest. The man followed the silent order, and sat quietly back down.

"He," Latrell began, pointing to the kneeling man, "has just died. Feel for him, gentlemen, look at his position, because that is the position – precisely the position – that we are, all of us, in at this moment.

"He made a gesture, he sent me a signal, did you all hear it? He didn't realize what room he was sitting in, what the stakes of the game at this table really are. So he made a noise, with the air in his mouth. He wanted me to know that he was ready for me to get on with it. Shit or get off the pot, he told me, fish or cut bait, mister, because I'm tired of sitting here waiting for something to happen."

He addressed the kneeling man. "What was your name, boy, when you were alive?"

The man didn't speak immediately, until he felt the barrel of the gun tap twice on his forehead, *knock knock.*

"Khalid," he said.

"Kyle?" Latrell said. "Do you know, I've never known a Kyle that was worth his candle?"

"Khalid," the young man repeated, louder, but before the word had fully left his lips the cold flat of the pistol barrel struck the side of his head to silence him.

"Well, Kyle, you made a sound, and now I'll make one. And I want you to listen to it very carefully."

Everyone, eyes forward, heard the hammer of the pistol cock

with a sharp metallic *click-clack,* overloud in the stillness of the room.

"You, Kyle, made a gesture, in good faith and for the benefit of all. But it was weak, do you see that now? You wanted to get things started, and now they're started, but are things going as you'd hoped? I got your message, but are you getting mine?

"Kyle's impatient little sigh, and three airplanes, *three,* three little airplanes hitting three little targets. Do you see the correlation, gentlemen? Kyle there is fully aware of my point, but are the rest of you? Do you feel the gun at your head? Do you feel the government that you hate galvanizing, not destroyed, but hardening, angry and vengeful and mobilizing and a hundred times more powerful than it was yesterday? And their only thoughts are of you, of us here. We hissed our limp, impotent impatience into the face of a superpower, nothing more. We shucked open the eyes of millions of soldiers, agents, lawmen and citizens, Democrats, Republicans and Independents in search of an ideal, and we have in one master stroke awakened their naïve patriotism and shone a spotlight on the perfect enemy to rally against. Last week they were lost, adrift, preoccupied, disparate and shallow. Tonight they are an army a third of a billion strong."

He looked around the table, to each of them there.

"It was to be not three planes, but over one hundred and fifty, or am I mistaken? The President was to be dead, the seats of power, energy and commerce were to be in ruin, dams were to be broken, great cities in flames, tunnels flooded, bridges fallen into the waterways, both houses of Congress were to be eviscerated, the populace huddling terrified and leaderless. Was I misinformed? You," he said, pointing to the tall man, "Was I misinformed?"

The man spoke carefully, and in English. "There were teams in place for every flight we had chosen. But there were . . . logistical problems . . . beyond our control when the operation had begun."

48

"Your men were cowards," Latrell said. "When their time came they would not give their lives, not for your cause, their God or the virgins you promise in paradise."

"With all respect, it was a failure of strategy, not of my men." The tall man glanced to the side of the room. "Not of my son. It was the . . . insistence on the timing, the delay between the first and second strikes on New York, it was an . . . error, that allowed them the time to—"

"My only error," Latrell snapped, "was putting my trust in you. And now it falls to me to pull us back from the grave you have dug for us. We will arrange for you to contact your leadership, and I have a message for them."

One of the seated men put pen to paper, ready to transcribe.

"As you are by now aware, this day was a failure, but the battle is now joined. We have planned for this contingency. As we make our preparations, we must have a distraction. You will be implicated in today's attack; they will come for you with all they have, with the world united against you, and that is the way it must be. Leak the identities of the teams who succeeded, issue statements and lead them to evidence that confirms their suspicions. Give them clarity, al Qaeda will be the focus of the war they will wage, and you must keep their eyes on Afghanistan. Many will be martyred to glory in the coming weeks, but our aims will be achieved on these shores, and all will be avenged. Contact me directly within a week's time. Your men who are stationed here will be gathered to my headquarters and will be in my care until they are needed for what will follow.

"That's all, send it." He turned from the room, and motioned Joe Lange to stand near him.

"Joe, there is a man we need to find," Latrell said quietly. "I need for you to find him, and bring him here to me, alive and well. This is for Mr. Krieger. Come to my quarters this evening, and I'll tell you what I know. But we have no option, we need his mind. If we have him, we can still win. It's as simple as that."

"We'll find him, Ed. Count on it."

49

"That's good. Good man." Latrell turned back to the table, where all were still seated.

"Our next moves were to be political, but we have no choice now; we must proceed otherwise, and with speed, and force. We have forever lost the element of surprise, and make no mistake, that is the single element that allowed you to succeed in even the trivial way you did this morning. Human weakness and dull minds led us to failure. But I will not fail."

His voice had grown low and calm. "Just one more thing," Latrell said. His eyes moved to his right, his head gave the slightest nod, and the room rang with the sound of a pistol shot to the head of the kneeling man.

7

It was a motley crew, she thought, sitting there around her table. With a few fifes and a snare drum, she'd have a July Fourth marching band.

They fumbled to open their laptops with bandaged hands, searched their bags for pens and pads with slung arms and eye patches, punched keys with splinted fingers, and helped each other to become settled through fresh pains and disabilities.

For her part, she had removed the ridiculous cliché of a head-injury bandage they'd trussed her in. Whatever good it had been doing could not outweigh the indignity of it. There was a shiny red scrape on her cheekbone and a cut on her forehead, and they would heal just fine in the open air.

"Let's get to business," Jeannie said.

As she looked up from her notes, Rudy caught her attention from the back of the room. He let his eyes circuit the people around the table, and he looked back at her, expectant.

"I, um," she began, "I'm happy to see you all here. And, I know that it is taking a great deal of . . . commitment . . . for you to interrupt your convalescence to attend this meeting. Thank you."

She looked to Rudy. He blinked a few times and smiled, like a father at his backward child's Bat Mitzvah. Clumsy, his eyes said, but considering the source, it was a warm and heartfelt overture.

Jeannie took a quick tally of the attendees. "We're missing . . . who, Nicholas. Is he able to come?"

Some in the room exchanged glances, others looked at their hands, the floor, or the table in front of them.

"Boss," Rudy said, "I'm sorry, I didn't think to tell you. Nicky was in the hallway this morning, down the hall from us on his way to the conference room, and we lost him. He was killed in the fire."

The room was still, the hospital sounds outside having quieted in the late hour. As seconds passed the silence seemed to amplify, a seashell pressing to each ear. She took them in, a tenuous circle of confused and wounded individuals, herself among them. They wanted to grieve, to sleep, to hold their pillows over their eyes and forget, and she could not fault them. They were hurt, their friend was gone, their world was in a flat spin, and she would gladly join them as they let go of the controls and fell apart in the face of it.

But she was the one standing at the head of the table.

"I'm going to be perfectly honest with you about something," Jeannie said. "I don't know anything about some things, anything at all. I don't have a boyfriend, never have, and I'm fairly sure my ongoing virginity is a reliable source of mirth around the water cooler. I don't believe in God, I don't know how to pray. I learned the words like everybody else, but they just don't make sense to me. I'm not sure what a religious person would feel right now, but I know I'm not good enough to forgive the people who did this, and I will not forgive them.

"But I want you to pray if it helps you, pray for Nicholas, and the thousands of others who died this morning. I just want us to take a moment and think about them."

She waited and watched them. Some lowered their eyes, others bowed their heads and knit the fingers of their hands together, their lips moving silently. Nearly a minute had passed before they finished, and they looked to her again.

"Amen," Jeannie said.

"There are tens of millions of people, maybe billions of people around the world praying those very same prayers tonight. Even countries who hate us don't necessarily want us to fold up, and some of them are praying for us, too. But I'll tell you what I think. I think those people are praying *to* us, as much as for us. To us, here in this room. They don't know who we are, but they know we're out there, and they are all looking to us now to keep them safe. They're realizing tonight that this country might not be invulnerable. They're in the process of figuring out what all of us have known since our first days on this job. That what has been built in this country may not be under God's protection after all.

"This American way of life, in fact, you and I know it, it's just a tissue of ideas, it's a soap bubble. It's built to operate right on the edge of viability, pushing and pulling itself in every direction, and testing its limits. It's an experiment, and it's only held together and maintained day by day, hands on, by people like you and me. We are a paper-thin line, and chaos is on the other side. And people, we let chaos get in this morning.

"So, in addition to asking for divine guidance, I think all of those hundreds of millions of people are praying to us, to you and me, to stand up, dust ourselves off, get our heads on straight, twist the balls off the people who did this, and remove their ability to ever do it again.

"And that's what we're going to do," Jeannie said.

"I do not make promises easily, because I don't break my promises, but I'm going to promise you something now. I promise you that I know what to do. As frightened as you may be, as uncertain as you may be – and I understand that completely – what you need to know right now is that I know *exactly* how to proceed. All that you have to do is come with me, and I promise you we will get these cocksuckers."

She looked toward the back of the room. "No offense, Rudy," she added.

53

The legendary status of Jeannie's chastity was matched only by the renown of Rudy's fat catalog of sexual exploits. He was a proud icon in the tight gay underculture of the defense intelligence community, an otherwise tense and hyper-paranoid secret society.

"None taken, sweetheart," Rudy said. "Besides, I'm a pitcher, not a catcher."

They all looked around at each other, scared and bandaged and in no mood for levity. But they had a laugh, and when it had nearly passed it restarted around the table once again, and they began to feel a little like who they had been before. Early this morning they had been directors, leaders, heads of initiatives, strategists and tacticians, the brightest thinkers their government could muster, and they would be those things again. They were shaken, yes, but not beaten, because if this room was beaten then so were we all.

"I had a call with the President and his Cabinet this afternoon, and I received a green light, and that's good news for us," Jeannie said.

"A green light for what?" someone asked.

Though her young and beautiful face looked like it had weathered a bar fight, her smile was pure Mona Lisa.

"For everything," she said.

8

Outside of Jeannie Reese, no one alive really knew what to expect from IRIN, the cybernetic backbone of the Total Information Awareness program. It was like contemplating the fetal sonogram of some dread, wondrous new lifeform, straining at the womb with the combined genetic jackpot of Plato, Fischer, Newton, Nostradamus, and Attila the Hun. Until she threw the switch and it was born, it had been no more real than the scattered Internet rumors of its declassified component parts. But at 2:21 in the morning on September 12, 2001, it opened its great eye, and saw.

Jeannie had once said that all IRIN was really capable of doing was putting two and two together. Of course, its inference engines performed this simple math nine hundred billion times per second, and it added not numbers, but knowledge.

Despite Americans' cherished rights to privacy, a great deal of highly sensitive data about each and every one of them hummed openly over the wires on a daily basis. This fact had been tacitly accepted on some level for many years, as a cost of convenience, and in part because there was a vague feeling that these electronic whispers revealed so little, taken individually.

IRIN, however, took things collectively.

In its first warm-up nanoseconds of operation, the system

decisively nailed Arnold "Bud" Blaustein of Cicero, IL. Bud's iPass had earlier greased his reverse-commute passage along the tollway, his debit card paid for a dinner for two at Houston's downtown, the security cameras at Walgreen's recorded his cash purchase of a tin of Altoids and a package of Trojans, and his keycard time-stamped his return to the office after hours. This sequence of events, overlaid with the congruent movements and chronology of his administrative assistant, Universal ID # 003-760018-7152, equated to *extramarital affair* with 82% confidence. Of no immediate interest to law enforcement, perhaps, but a damn nice piece of subsecond gumshoeing to be sure. Noted and filed.

As of 2001, US citizens were often on camera for well over three-quarters of every day, on the street, in waiting rooms, stores, restrooms, lobbies, and workplaces. The Internet connected over eighty per cent of them to news, shopping, entertainment and associated spyware. Credit cards kept a continual feed of behavioral and positional data streaming into deep data mines. And most of these tidbits, packaged as lightspeed 1s and 0s, had stopped for the briefest moment in Langley, Virginia, to be etched on spinning tapes and silver platters for a day (may it never come) when they might be called up to serve their country.

In the phone system IRIN passively listened to every single conversation, as its precursors had since late 1989. Context algorithms allowed it to distinguish homophones, flag conversations based on voice-stress levels, and discern the difference between a *joke* about a bomb and a *plan* about a bomb. No law had been passed or circumvented to achieve this surveillance; it was a business arrangement, and a de facto opt-in agreement with every customer. After deregulation there was even a surcharge on phone bills to cover the system's overhead.

Computer-based data gathering was much easier. IRIN had become a part of every commercial computer operating system, virus scanner and firewall software and firmware, with the creators' passive contractual blessings. It couldn't be detected because it was on the inside all along, reading, recording, and deliberating.

Pick an individual, and IRIN knew their movements, activities and attitudes to the minute, for any day in its memory. Pick an organization, and IRIN knew the probability that some among them were plotting something unsavory. Pick a crime, and IRIN could reconstruct its storyboard and predict and describe the criminal, without the entanglements of a judge or jury.

Until today what it knew could neither be seen nor spoken of, its accumulating open-and-shut cases lay encrypted and unaccessed. The truths in its files had to be ignored and adjudicated in analog time, as often as not to be lost under the blinding rhetoric of defense attorneys and due process. A sufficient threat had never yet existed to outweigh the fear of what total information awareness might bring. Never until today.

Success came quickly. Within fifteen minutes of light-up, the names, photos and last known addresses of all 9/11 hijackers were released to an astonished but receptive press corps. Three minutes later, the text of an obscure IRC thread from March 10, 1993 was printed, stamped *Eyes Only: Above Top Secret* and hand-delivered to the hospital room of Jeannie Reese.

9

"**K**ate," he said in the dark and quiet of his living room, "what day is it?"

"Unrecognized," the soothing digital voice replied, "Please repeat and verify."

He cleared his throat, and it felt as dry as burnt white toast. He hadn't spoken in what might have been weeks, and bourbon was the only food he could remember taking in. "Fagan, John," he said. "The quick brown fox jumps over the lazy dog."

"Verified. Good afternoon, John. It is 6:22 P.M., and today is September 19, 2001."

He knew better than anyone that no password was secure, and biometrics were far harder to break. Still, a 128-point voice-print challenge was probably excessively paranoid, considering that he was the only human who'd set foot inside this room in the past eighteen years.

"Would you like to see what is going on in the world, John?"

"No, I would not, thank you." He noticed a small video picture of himself in the upper corner of the media wall. "And stop fucking watching me, I've told you before." The picture winked out. "Just mind your own business, no cameras on me, forever, got me?"

"I understand."

"Oh, do you really."

"Shall I choose some music?"

"No, no goddamn music. Where's the dog?"

"Boner is outside in the back courtyard, fourteen meters from his exit door. Should I call him in?"

"Please do. Has he been fed and watered?"

"Last feeding was at 8:15 A.M., and the water dish is at seventy-two per cent capacity, at fifty-five degrees Fahrenheit—"

"Fine, great. Give me the news," John said.

"Local, national or international?"

"Local."

"Business, technology, entertainment—"

"What's the fucking local news, Kate? And summarize."

"Power was restored this morning to thousands of residents of lower Manhattan, after eight days of—"

"Next."

"A prayer service is scheduled at Yankee Stadium on Sunday, September—"

"Next."

"Over three hundred firefighters are missing and feared lost in—"

"Next, next."

"Thirty-two thousand workers are searching in shifts in rescue operations at the site of—"

"Stop." There was only one good slug left in the pint bottle in his hand, and he knocked it back, then laid his drinking arm over his eyes. "Rescue operations," he whispered. "After eight days."

The dog nosed open his swinging pet-door. When he saw John was awake, he scampered and slid across the hardwood floor and jumped into the chair beside his master.

"You're wet, buddy," John said. "Is it raining? Did you get wet?"

Boner shook himself, spraying droplets of dog water in all directions. John wiped his face with the back of his wrist, and his eyes stung. He looked at his sleeve, his hands, the arms of his chair, and then slowly around at his desk, the floor and the shelves of books that lined his walls. Everything around him was whitened by the thinnest veil of dust.

He heard the rain then, pecking on the windows. John held his dog and his empty bottle, and sat still among the ashes.

Sleep had come again at some point, full of dreams he was glad to watch recede as he gradually awoke. *Enough*, he thought. There were things that needed to be done.

For instance, this dust needed to go. There was nothing worse for computer hardware than fine dust. John set about wiping everything down with damp paper towels. He needed a drink and a cigarette, but if he stayed at it, this would go quickly.

Boner was big on exploring in trash bags, but he was staying clear of this job. A billion pounds of matter had been pulverized to 30-micron wisps of concrete, fiberglass and asbestos, desks and picture frames, gym bags and Day-Timers. And people, of course, first to mind but last mentioned. Three thousand or so was the last estimate he'd heard. It was the people that were bothering the dog, most likely. But it was nothing to be afraid of, not at all. He had touched the dead before.

His grandmother on his father's side had expired in the family home when he was eight. While they waited for the hearse to arrive, Dad had brought him into her room.

Feel her hand, John, his father had said.

No fucking way, thought young John, but Dad had taken him by the wrist and put his hand on hers.

What do you feel, John? the old man had asked.

It's cold.

What else?

And it's empty. Daddy, her ghost is gonna get mad.

There are no ghosts, Johnny.

Is Gramma in heaven?

No, son. She's just gone. They'll put what's left into a box, and bury it in the ground, and she'll just gradually disappear, and that'll be it.

Will she know she's in the box?

I don't think so, John.

But what if she does?

Well, that would be pretty bad, wouldn't it?

Dad, if I die—

When you die, John.

When I die, don't put me in a box, don't let them put me in a box, please Dad—

Shhh, listen. Listen. The horror is not in the box, Johnny. Only peace. All of the horror is here.

Another Norman Rockwell moment. Why that scene had never graced the cover of the *Saturday Evening Post*, well, it was a goddamned mystery.

As each paper towel became gray and saturated, he folded it carefully and placed it in the open black plastic bag. Whatever horrors they'd faced in the end, they were gone now, and at least they wouldn't have to be buried in a box. They were gone, and there were no ghosts.

There were no ghosts.

10

The sparse offices of *MHz* Magazine went dark an hour after sunset, and the last of the employees walked out three minutes later. Still, he waited and watched from high vantage, two-hundred yards west in the shelter of the woods.

Nathan Krieger had hitchhiked from San Luis to New Paltz, New York in just over thirty-six hours. One of the truckers had wanted a conversation, so he'd opted to hop out and risk a delay rather than make an issue out of it. He was to leave no trace or trail, no memory of his passage, whatever steps that required.

After a quarter-hour more, he'd seen no movement from the building and heard nothing but night sounds in his headset. He'd aimed the handheld parabolic ear at each window in sequence, listening for footsteps, papers shuffling, machines whirring, the asymmetric sounds of human activity.

All quiet. The building was clear.

A keypad secured the front door, but the fire escape led to an unlocked outside exit on the second floor. Smokers, no doubt, had left it open after their last break of the day. He let his eyes adjust to the ambient light for several minutes, and then with a dentist's mirror he checked for security cameras at each corner as he padded through the hallways to the editorial offices.

MHz was a semi-underground hacker rag, printed on second-rate stock and barely a magazine at all, but in the early nineties it had been nothing more than a hand-copied, stapled-in-the-corner newsletter sent out to booksellers that catered to computer geeks and other assorted feebs. The filing cabinets were unlocked and out on the open floor, typical of a grassroots, shoestring operation. He pulled on thin cotton darkroom gloves and found a drawer labeled "Archives '90–'92."

The target had submitted a number of articles here, but he was looking for one sent before e-mail had become mainstream. His finger moved over the tabs in the hanging files. There, August 1991, marked for publication on pages 11 through 15.

Phree Long Distance: Redboxing is Not Dead, by phr33k.

Krieger pulled the first folder and then found the others on his checklist, eleven in all. He laid the sheets in careful order, side-by-side on a long worktable in the layout room, with the folder for each file under the last page. Every step he took needed to be reversible, made invisible when he was done, and organization made that easier.

He clipped a miniature LED worklight to the band of his wristwatch, clicked it on, and bent low to his work to keep the glare contained. With a loupe in one eye, he puffed a thin warm vapor from his small rechargeable atomizer over each sheet of the articles, front and back, and when it had been included, the stamped envelope each submission had arrived in. This was old paper, almost certainly far too old to react with the shit he was spraying. Ninhydrin was what he needed, but you do what you can, with what you brought. After fifty-five minutes, he'd worked just over thirty of the pages with only dim and useless results, but there were at least that many more to go.

There now, what was this?

A printed word was smudged near the margin, the inkjet ink hadn't quite set before the author had pulled it from the tray. The blur was broken here and there by the loops and whorls of a thumbprint. He sprayed it lightly, then again, and then watched as scant hidden details of the full print began to emerge on the yellowed paper.

With the flash shielded, he took three quick photographs of the smudge with his tiny black Minox. He applied clear tape from his kit, gave it a few minutes to set, and then peeled it carefully back and held it up to the dim blue-white glow of his wristlight. The print wasn't perfect by any stretch, but it was better than it might have been. He pressed the adhesive tape to a backing card and slid the card into a compartment in his vest.

More like this would be a comfort. The fact that the partial print was set in the original ink meant it belonged to the author himself, with at least enough certainty for his needs. Mr. Latrell's moles had access to the FBI's vast fingerprint database, but they would need the best image he could find so they could finish quickly, and in secret. And there were a hundred ways to find a guy once you knew his name.

He decided to take another pass through the pages he'd misted already, to have a second look for similar ink smudges and any latent development. He walked the length of the work table to the first page in the line, leaned close to it, and froze.

"Idiot," he whispered, but it was Latrell's voice he heard in his head.

In the upper left corner, on page one of the first manuscript, clear as son-of-a-bitchin' day, staring at him, there it was. *The guy's return address.* He could have been out of the woods and on his way home an hour ago.

He smacked himself hard in the forehead with the heel of his hand and paced for a few steps, muttering. He had been punished since childhood for this, and all through his years of training, endlessly he'd heard it: you have overlooked the obvious. *It will kill you someday*, Latrell had said, *the obvious will kill you someday, or one of us, or all of us, and you will learn to see it.*

He took a deep breath. *Shake it off, let it go. Nobody saw. You did fine, got what you came for, so cut yourself a break, God knows nobody else ever has.* And sooner or later he would learn, learn to read the moment, learn to look first for what was right before his eyes.

Now, focus.

Krieger committed the Manhattan P.O. Box on the manuscript to memory, returned each of the files to their original location in the cabinet, and was finishing his wipe-down when headlights swung past the line of windows facing the parking lot.

He was being careful not to leave things any cleaner than he'd found them, to erase only his own signs. Outside a car door opened, then closed, and a single set of footfalls crunched in the gravel toward the building. The gait was uneven, Krieger noted; the man outside (and it *was* a man) was either disabled or carrying an uneven load, or both. He closed the last filing cabinet drawer, and then pulled it back out a fraction of an inch, just as it had been when he arrived.

Keys rattled downstairs, and the front door opened and closed noisily, with a clatter of buckets and long wooden handles. Krieger made a last deliberate check of the scene, flicked off and stowed his small light, noted the time, and then found his spot. This should only take another minute.

The man was singing softly as he made his way up the long hallway, limping and pushing his rolling mop bucket. Krieger knew the words, but he'd never heard them sung in Spanish before. He decided to allow himself a little twist of a smile, no more, but it did sound funny.

"*Gonna jump down, turn around, pick a bale a cotton,*" he mouthed the English words along with the janitor. "*Gonna jump down, turn around, pick a bale a day.*" Second verse, same as the first. Oh, he was definitely going to laugh if this went on much longer.

The knob turned, and the door to the room swung open. The

cleaning man's hand was almost to the lightswitch when a dark form dropped silent from the ceiling beams like a black widow, and he was dead before his song had finished echoing down the corridor.

11

IRIN was earning its funding this week. The leads were coming in fast and furious, and the main challenge was to sort and route them before they backed up and bogged things down.

In her main conference room a vast flat-panel screen showed a map of the US, populated in real-time with potential threats color-coded by source, severity and immediacy. The eastern seaboard from Maine to Florida was awash with red, orange and yellow pixels, and the West Coast glowed with deep concentric pockets of high alert. Major cities across the country radiated warnings, real and projected, and scattered locations in the heartland pulsed with danger signs.

Those were the easy ones. Thousands of people had already been picked up, questioned and detained in the past few days, most from no-brainer warrants autogenerated and passed directly to the Justice Department. These were known Islamic radicals, qualifying associates of said radicals, watch-listees, contributors and members of suspected front organizations and assorted dissident-sympathizers. The dusty INS records had been little help in tracking these down, but with IRIN homing in on their pagers, cell phones, Net-surfing patterns and e-mail traffic, it was like shooting pigs in a stockyard.

There was a second and much larger stratum of suspects that

were less concrete and more problematic. These were open expressers of anti-American views, antiestablishment activists and ultra left- or right-wing agendists, all abusing First Amendment rights to spout their poison and recruit to their causes. They ranged from columnists in the popular press to bloggers and Webmasters of amateurish, nut-job Web sites, all testing the border between dissent and treason. The system flagged them for deeper analysis, sorted them carefully and turned over a daily list for surveillance, and in the odd case, detention and questioning. It was open season on subversives, but even in the current climate it was a delicate game.

IRIN was sending up other red flags, though, in a category that Jeannie had christened *critical anomalies*. These went directly to her desk, and her team of specialists was charged with interpreting and hand-routing them. They were pieces to a troubling puzzle, the size and shape of which was yet to emerge. And they went on and on.

A massively inflated number of speculative investments preceding the attacks, shorting airline, tourism and insurance stocks.

High-volume pre-9/11 retreats to five-year US Treasury notes, including a single, incredible $5,000,000,000 trade on September 10th.

Scattered urgent e-mails and heavy IM traffic in the days before, all still being traced, warning recipients to stay away from listed landmarks across the country that morning.

The strange downfall of WTC 7.

An unusual cash-out of US dollars across the former Soviet Union, encouraged by foreshadowings in the press of a coming "financial" attack here.

Unexplained seismic spikes at Ground Zero, preceding the collapse of each of the twin towers.

A sixth-grader in Dallas, and his art-class picture of the Manhattan skyline, the World Trade Center circled in red crayon. He'd told his teacher that World War III would begin tomorrow morning. On the 11th.

"What have you got there?" Rudy asked. He'd brought her a cappuccino, but she hadn't heard him come in.

Jeannie held up a twenty dollar bill, folded symmetrically like the nose of a paper airplane. "Take a look at this," she said.

He put down their coffee cups and took the bill. The simple folds had formed a new picture from the art on the back of the note. Without any undue imagination, it depicted a long low building, the Pentagon, burning from the center of one of its faces.

"That is so weird," Rudy said.

"Yeah? Turn it over."

On the other side, clear as day, rose two tall buildings, side by side, with their upper floors obscured by fire and rolling black smoke.

"You're freaking me out, punkin."

"Rudy, it doesn't mean anything. It's a completely improbable fluke; these bills were redesigned and printed in 1998. Do you see what I'm saying?"

He was still looking at the bill, first one side, then the other.

"I'm looking at reams of ironclad evidence here," she said. "It's doubling every day, and I need to separate what could be real from the perfectly credible bullshit. It's not easy."

"Well," Rudy said, "I guess that's why they pay you the big bucks."

"Oh, I thought that was why I'm a 22-year-old workaholic type-A battleaxe with no social life."

Rudy stood up to leave. "That reminds me, I was supposed to bring you a big glass of whine."

"Fuck off, Rudy."

"I love you, too," he said. He held up the twenty. "Oh, do you want me to—"

"The engraver and the printer are already downstairs. Let's sweat them a little longer, and then give them to George and Eileen."

"Good cop, bad cop, that's nice. See you later, hon."

"And send in the lieutenant, I'm going to need some lunch."

Alone in her office, Jeannie closed her eyes and took in a deep breath, then let it out slowly. She clicked open a window on her computer's desktop and entered the twelve digit password, changed this morning and every morning. The window was labeled *Phr33k*, and it contained only a graphical progress bar, advancing very slowly on a scale from 0 to 100.

As she worked through the day and far into the night, IRIN was spidering farther and deeper across the vast fields of data. By the time she checked again, the bar had ticked from 48 to 66 per cent, out of the yellow and into the green.

12

Joe Lange listened patiently. His face was a kind one, grand-fatherly, with bushy eyebrows and a generous beard and moustache. Every Christmas, he was the people's choice to play Kris Kringle for the children of the camp. But what he was hearing now was more than troubling; it was treason, and the wisdom of his years offered no reaction, none at least that he could voice at the moment.

"Joe, I hope you're hearin' me in the spirit I brung in here tonight. This ain't no revolt. I cain't imagine it's just me, neither, but I'll just out with it, I am not on board with this, it's not why I come here, it's not why I pulled up stakes and brung my wife and my children here. And I guess it took seein' those buildings comin' down, Jesus Christ, pardon my French, but you know? I'd take a bullet for Mr. Latrell, and for you, Joe, but all those people. Do you see what I'm saying?"

"Lower your voice, Ben," Joe said.

"We just want to go, we'll keep our mouths shut and just disappear, like we was never here. You'll have nothin' to worry about from us, we just, we just want to go."

Joe only sat looking across at the man, a friend and, he'd always thought, a compatriot. Ben Morrison was not so much a warrior as he was a supplyman, he was the camp's chief baker and brewer.

But in war all of them were soldiers, and across his dining room table sat a soldier talking desertion. Asking *permission* for it.

"Joe, can we do that? Can we go?"

"Ben," Joe said, "I want you to get up now, and leave my home, and I swear to you that I'll forget this conversation, but you will never mention this again."

"Hell, Joe, I'd stay on myself, but for Edie and the kids, I don't want this for them, and they couldn't make it out there by themselves. I got to take care of them, Joe, that's a vow I took, too, and I'm bound to keep it. Now, we didn't want to just steal off in the night, we wanted to talk this out with you, and if we could, get your blessing. But I can't see a choice."

The big man didn't answer. He stood up slowly from his chair, and turned to face the window. The moon was a waxing crescent and nearly setting over the mountains, and the sky was full of stars.

"I said what I was going to say, Ben. You said you hoped I was hearing you, and I did. And now I hope you heard me."

After a moment, his friend pushed his chair back with a rasp on the oak floor, and he rose and went to the door.

"Goodnight, Joe," he said. "And all the best to you."

The door closed. Joe Lange watched the moon until the point of its opal sliver touched the high horizon out in front of him.

"Reilly," he called to his bodyguard, always on station now, always within earshot.

"What do you need, Joe?"

"Send a runner to see if Mr. Latrell is awake."

"What's the deal? I don't wanna get my head bit off, it's awful late."

Lange didn't answer, but he sat and swiveled his chair around to look again out his window, at the mountains under the setting moon and the bright stars in the clear air.

"Joe?"

"Forget it," Joe said. "Changed my mind. It's nothing to trouble him with."

13

The Internet was different tonight.

He'd been in no shape to go about his normal online routines since . . . well, for several days. But now in the wee hours there were things going on out in the digital landscape that were clearly out of kilter, no two ways about it.

John was a long-standing Microsoft resister, but he'd found the latest version of Windows interesting enough to back-engineer it to run under Unix. He called it Johndows 98, and it was still being debugged after three years. Just like the original.

In the millions of lines of spaghetti-bowl source-code he'd disassembled, there had been a number of subroutines whose purpose he couldn't decipher. Now his homebrew firewall was getting hit hundreds of times a day, by something that was looking for the same ports, pointers and handles that the extraneous code had referenced. It was bizarre.

It could be Micro$oft creeping out to look for unauthorized copies of its operating system, but that was unlikely. They talked a good game about hunting software pirates, but they also knew full well that a huge chunk of the illegal copies belonged to otherwise legitimate citizens who'd borrowed a CD from the office, so they could work or play at home. In other words, the very customers who'd made M$ the richest corporation in the industry. Start kicking in those doors, and you look a little ungrateful.

No, this was darker, and there were only two other real possibilities. It was either a sophisticated, coordinated assault from an organized group of vandals, or it was the government. And that distinction was a fine line indeed.

"Kate," he said, "is there anything on the wires about a new virus, or a worm or Trojan horse, anything about a hacker attack?"

"Give me a moment," the computer said.

"Take five minutes. Drill deep, international, all languages. And Kate?"

It took her an extra second to respond, since her search had already started in earnest.

"Yes, John."

"The next time the firewall gets hit by a port query, do your best to finger the source."

"Acknowledged. Search in progress. I've put some coffee on for you."

John had devoted years to making his interface to the computer as anthropomorphic as possible. By the standards of the day she was a world-class, fifth-generation natural language interpreter, hashing spoken input and forming realistic and thoughtful responses with a surprising level of personality. It was a convincing illusion. In fact, though, Kate was a glorified chatbot, and grasped only the essential parts of what she heard. "*Next . . . firewall hit . . . port query . . . finger . . . source*" was closer to her native tongue, and she would have understood that string of words just as well. But he had given her the power to learn, too, she had been with him for almost 20 years, and sometimes he wasn't so sure she hadn't evolved right out of his hands.

He walked to the kitchen and watched the coffee drip into the pot. Supplies were getting low, he knew. Most of the neighborhood had shut down for several days after the 11th, but the shops should be reopening by now. Time to order in, as soon as the sun was up. He picked a tall mug from the shelf and poured it full.

"Search completed," Kate said.

"What did you find?"

"No reports of widespread computer attacks, no out-of-norm reports of new virus strains."

"Nothing?"

"Nothing out-of-norm."

"Kate, search on keywords, National Security Agency, Department of Defense, DARPA, CIA, DIA, FBI, NIMA, NRO, domestic surveillance. Tell me what you find."

"Depth?"

"Everything you can dig up, as far as you can go. Sort for relevance, start with queries under the Freedom of Information Act."

"Searching. This may take a short while."

"Take your time."

Cigarettes were always the first vital commodity to run out, and after he'd finished his first cup of coffee it had taken a few minutes to track down an acceptable butt. It was bent almost ninety degrees, looked weeks old and tasted like charred baling twine, but the first drag was very, very good.

Boner had found his tennis ball and brought it over, for a game.

"Not right now, boy," John said. "How're you doing, Kate?"

"In progress."

"Give me the interim results."

"FOIA document 858-38118-19, request for funding, integrated electronic surveillance and reporting system, January 16, 1998."

"Put it on the screen please, and keep searching."

The media wall came to life, displaying an image of a paper document, titled as she'd read it. Toward the bottom of the page, it was stamped "Classified," and there were typewritten additions by the FOIA reader.

```
Pages reviewed: 1,146
Pages released: 0
```

"Next page," John said.

The image of the sheet was there all right, but every line was covered by the thick stroke of a black marker.

"Find all related, and show them as you find them."

"Searching."

One after another documents flashed on the screen, all with disturbing titles and the same redacted content.

"Extract keywords and cross-reference on the Web, ftp, telnet, Usenet, everything, and be stealthy," John said.

The FOIA files were not going to yield anything useful. Now he was looking for something under the veneer, something on an errant server or in unsecured personal files, anywhere on the Net. He was stubbing out his half-cigarette and picking through the ashtray for the next candidate when a new document filled the big screen.

By the header it was sidebar copy from a freelance reporter for the *Washington Post*. The dateline was August 4, 2001, but the story had been spiked in editorial, it never ran. The guy had saved a copy on his hard drive though, and he hadn't been too careful with his network security.

The title was, *What is IRIN?*

John scanned the text quickly. This was exactly what he was looking for. And in all likelihood this was exactly what was looking for him.

"More like this, and print what you find," he said.

Before the computer could acknowledge his request, the warning tone from his firewall went off like a jostled car alarm.

"Port query, level severe," Kate said.

"Follow that, backtrace, put it on the screen," John ordered.

The wall filled with a graphical map of the earth, in a standard 2-D projection. Glowing lines showed the topography of the Internet, with key nodes along the backbone and the streams of digital tributaries that connected most of the world. A red pulsing bull's-eye appeared near Dallas, Texas, denoting the origin of the attack. Then there was another, in Toronto, then another in Kansas City, then in Portland, Tokyo, Tampa, and Seoul. Source hits were appearing all over the map.

It was coming from everywhere.

"Clear that, push harder, Kate, we're getting yanked around," John said.

He watched as she pressed on through the phantom leads, tracing them back to their roots through onionskin layers of electronic countermeasures. The map zoomed in until it showed only the United States, then down to all states east of the Mississippi.

He lit another butt, one far below his standards, and dragged deep on it. This was no time to be choosy.

Getting closer. East Coast.

"Kate, slow down."

No answer.

South of New York.

The little hairs on the back of his neck began to rise. "Kate, I am dead serious, listen to me, slow it down."

Then there was the curve of the Potomac, the tangle of the Beltway. The moving mural dissolved one last time, to its maximum level of detail. There, between Wilson Boulevard and Quincy Playfield, was 3701 North Fairfax Drive.

HQ, Defense Advanced Research Projects Agency.

"Kate, pull back, blank us out, NOW!"

He heard a noise then, an impossible noise, behind him.

He'd bought a vintage payphone four years ago on eBay, hacked it onto his Wi-Fi network and mounted it on his kitchen wall, with a plan to someday experiment with voice-over-IP. This phone had no number, no dialtone, no connection to the phone system whatsoever.

Nevertheless, it was ringing.

14

"**H**ello?"

Though it was unquestionably the thing to say when picking up a telephone, John noted that he sounded like a complete dumbass saying it now, given the circumstances.

No voice came back, but he was connected to something. Under the quiet on the line he heard the high rasping drone of broadband digital, the audible thought process of a network of computers.

"Kate, did you do this?"

She didn't answer.

"Kate, acknowledge me."

"Acknowledged," she said. Her voice was an octave lower and a tad slower than normal, as if someone was dragging their thumb on a turntable playing it. "Priority function call, embedded opcode exploit, momentary firewall breach activated all TCP/IP-enabled local devices."

"We got backdoored, son of a *bitch*," John said. "Diagnostics."

The wall of pixels lit up with graphs, moving lines and shifting bars, the EEG of the computer's core functions. Nearly all of the system's processors and resources were being diverted to reinforce the firewall against what must be a colossal brute-force probe. Of course, it wasn't enough to simply block the assault; the block itself would be an indication of his presence. She was taking every query on a wild-goose chase out into the cyber-wilderness, creating a hopscotch string of false addresses and fictitious locations for the attackers to follow. It was drawing a lot of power, but this was her strong suit, and she could handle it.

"Background task," John said.

"Ready," the computer responded, her voice now as deep as DeMille's burning bush.

"Patch that hole when you get a chance, like it was never there, Teflon-coat it."

"Acknowledged."

He still had the handset to his ear, and as he moved to hang it up he thought he heard a sound amidst the electronic undertones. It could have been, must have been his imagination, but he would have sworn he'd heard someone inhale. He pressed the receiver close and covered the mouthpiece with his free hand.

There, now a slow exhalation, unmistakable. In through the nose, out through the mouth. In some unlikely marvel of star-crossed technology, he was connected to a yoga-breather.

"Who the fuck is this?" John shouted, and he heard an authentic Three Stooges spit-take on the other end of the line.

"What?" a voice came back, tentative and surprised. A young woman.

"You heard me, spook. Get your supervisor on the phone so I can find out who the fuck has balls big enough to invade my privacy."

"Who is this?" she said evenly.

This broad was either dense or dangerous. "Listen, moistie, I've got a network log here that's got Senate subcommittee written all over it. You wanna know who this is? My name is cease and desist. You're ass-deep in ACLU territory now, baby-cakes."

She didn't answer right away. He heard her keyboard clacking away for a few seconds, probably initiating some sort of trace. Good luck with that.

"To whom am I speaking?"

The question in her voice had an alarming coolness to it, and he felt a chill tingle up his back. It was not the tone of an intern, a student or a script-kiddie, though she couldn't be much more than twenty or so. It was dead calm that he heard, and a self assurance that belied her obvious youth. She asked the question as if she somehow already knew the answer.

"You're speaking to a US citizen, on a secure encrypted non-commercial line that should in no way be accessible to an incoming call. Unless you've got a brand of warrant that I've never heard of, you need to break this connection right now. Or I can just patch you straight through to my attorney, if you like."

"Why do you need an attorney? Did you do something bad that you'd like to tell me about?"

"This is not amusing to me."

"Who are you? I'd really like to know who you are."

"You don't want to tangle with me, let's leave it at that."

"Oooooo." It was half sigh and half moan, as though she was cat-stretching, just releasing a little tightness in her smooth shoulders in the late hour. "I hope you don't mind my saying it, but when you talk like that I'm finding it something of a turn-on."

"Do you know how incredibly unprofessional that is?"

"Oh, I know, but it's late and I'm tired, and I'm just curious about what I've stumbled into here."

"Stumbled? Like how Sturgis and McCord stumbled into the Watergate? This is breaking and entering, jail-bait."

"The system that found you, you could say it has a mind of its own, it freelances a bit. My phone rang, and I picked it up and no one was there, and then you shouted something and I almost choked on my cappuccino. And now here we are."

"Oh yeah? Where are we?"

"I read a very interesting IRC thread the other day, from way back in 1993. In light of recent events, I'd like to talk to you about it. Phreak."

"All right, I'm hanging up now," John said.

"Oh, I don't think you're going to leave me just yet."

"Why is that?" he asked, and he really wanted to know.

"Because I think you're as curious as I am," the soft voice replied.

On the face of it the trace seemed to be making good progress, but looks were deceiving. So far she'd managed to precisely pinpoint his location in rural Iowa, at an internet café in Sarajevo, and at a dumb terminal at the guest relations desk of the White House.

She'd been tired earlier, but now as the horizon out her east-facing window was going pink-orange in the pre-sunrise, she was wide awake, and her heart was thumping triple-espresso.

"You still there?" Jeannie heard him say.

"Of course I am, where did you go?"

"I needed a carton of cigarettes, and a candy bar."

"So you walked to a store and back in two minutes? So that would put you in a major metropolitan area?"

"Okay, you got me. I live in a city somewhere. Should I expect you to bust through the door shortly? Gee, I'd better put something nice on. Like pants."

"Every little bit helps. Who's this woman I hear you talking to? Kate, you called her? Who's that?"

"You wouldn't believe me if I told you." She heard unwrapping sounds, and then he spoke again, his mouth occupied with his snack. "Hey, how's that trace-route going? Did I miss anything exciting while I was out?"

Whatever she was up against here, it was good, better than she had ever run into. There didn't seem to be anything real to fix on, just clouds of digital chaff and false targets. "How are you doing this?" she asked.

"I noticed you breathing kind of heavily earlier. Are you overweight or something?"

"You could bounce a quarter off my ass cheek."

"If I turn myself in, would you let me?"

"Turn yourself in and find out."

Jeannie leaned back in her chair and brushed the blonde hair from her eyes with the back of her wrist. She'd returned to the DARPA complex after the gym, and now she'd been up all night. She was going to need a shower and something to wear other than gray cotton shorts and her junior-high Bon Jovi tank top.

"Look, I've got to run. It's gonna be a blast interrogating you in person, but I've got plenty of other fish to fry, too," she said.

"Tell you what. I'll make a deal with you."

"That sounds mildly interesting."

"Let's play a game of chess. If you beat me, I'll fly out with my lawyer and hand myself over."

"That's such total bullshit."

"No, I will, I promise, or if you'd prefer, I'll shut off my firewall and you can find me yourself, and come over with a SWAT team and a news crew. I won't put up a fight."

"Now why would you do that?"

"Well, I'm not going to do it, because you're not going to beat me."

She checked her watch. There was plenty of time before even the early risers would arrive.

"Okay," she said.

"Do you know how to play?"

"I think I remember." Jeannie had become bored with the competitions when she was 11, but her last formal rating had been around 2340.

"Do you want white or black?"

"I'll go first, since you're obviously so talented."

"No cheating, now, this is all in our heads, right?"

"Just slip into an orange jumpsuit and start limbering up for your perp walk," Jeannie said. "D4."

"Queen's pawn game? Okay, let's see. D5."

"Bishop to F4."

"C5."

"Bishop to B8. You just lost your bishop, big shot," Jeannie said.

"First blood," came the reply. "And the first of many blunders to come."

"Don't beat yourself up."

"I'm talking about your blunders, snotnose. Rook takes bishop."

"Big deal. D4 to C5. Say goodbye to your pawn."

"You're a hungry little minx, aren't you? I'll bet you're a real handful in the sack."

"That is a bet you would certainly lose." She heard him lighting a cigarette, drawing on it. "Nervous?"

"No," he exhaled. "I always smoke after I talk about sex. Um, pawn to E6."

"Have you played this game before?"

"It's been a while."

"I can tell. Queen to D4."

"Now, who told you it was a good idea to bring out your queen on the fifth move? Queen to C7."

"Don't worry about me, this is going to be over before you know it," Jeannie said.

"I agree."

"Pawn to B4."

"Pawn to B6."

"Pawn takes pawn at B6. Do you want to give up now?"

"Not just yet," she heard him say. "Rook takes pawn at B6."

Something about that move troubled her. She closed her eyes, looked down on the imaginary board from above in her mind, rotated it 90, then 180 degrees.

Oh, Jesus H. Christ.

"Pawn to C3," she said.

"That's not gonna help you. Rook takes pawn at B4."

"Pawn takes rook at B4."

"Queen to C1. Check. Grab your ankles, girlfriend."

"Queen to D1."

"Big, throbbing bishop takes frightened but strangely aroused pawn at B4. You're in check again, chickie."

"Knight to D2."

"Bishop takes knight, that's mate," the man's voice said, "and I have a genuine Eagle Scout puptent in my shorts! Boo yah!"

She was speechless.

"You're not saying anything," the man said. "Still basking in the afterglow?"

Her voice was small. "I haven't lost a game of chess since I was five."

"That makes us almost even. I haven't won a game in under twelve moves since church camp."

"How did you—"

"Okay, that's enough fun. Go take your shower now, and try not to think about me as you're getting all sudsy. And honey?"

"Hmm? What?"

"Run that game over and over in your head today, buttercup, because that's why you're never going to find me."

The line went quiet, with a click.

Later, she did try not to think about him as the soap and warm water washed the long night from her body, but she did not succeed for long.

15

Her office was empty, unlocked, and the lights were off at 9:30 in the morning, and that was highly irregular.

Lieutenant Robert Vance, the most decorated warrior in his elite and classified division, was finding this babysitting assignment more stressful than any live-fire exercise in SEAL school. His charge kept unbelievable hours, disappeared and reappeared like Siegfried and Roy and, let's be frank, was treating him like an amusing but dimwitted busboy.

He had her morning bottle of mineral water in his hand, for God's sake, and she was nowhere to be found, and now it was getting warm.

He leaned back slightly to check the hallway once again, up and down, and then walked to her desk. It was the picture of organization, of course. Neat stacks of color-coded files, clean work area with a pen canted at a perfect diagonal in its center, on a new legal pad. No desktoys, no photographs, of loved ones, pets or anything else.

Rob kept his eyes on the door and casually pulled open her right-hand drawer. Office supplies, and some assorted girl-stuff. He sat in her chair and swiveled to the left, to the right, and then once all the way around. Halfway through his second revolution his shoe brushed a half-open file drawer, and as he bent to close it, he caught a flash of color down inside.

He opened the drawer a bit further. It was a book cover he'd seen, several paperbacks in fact, dog-eared and well-read. *Amanda's Passion*, *Miss Lockhart's Mischief*, *The Scoundrel's Embrace*, *Dahlia's Demise*. The covers were all practically the same, a tanned, bare-chested manly man pulling a corseted, reluctant young hottie into one embrace or the other. The only change was in the background art, an ornate drawing room here, a stormy cliff or medieval boudoir there.

And what was this? He reached in and came out with a small shirt, a pink tank top. It had *jovi girl* laid in rhinestones across the chest, and the *j* and the *i* were dotted with little hearts. This would be tight on a ten-year-old, he thought. On her, it must look, well, incredible. He held it closer, and then slowly closer until the cloth was against his face, and he breathed her in. It smelled like fresh air, Ivory soap, clean sweat, and peaches.

"Oh, you nasty, nasty boy."

The voice was right behind him, and only his commando training kept him from screaming like a schoolgirl. He shot to his feet, banging his knee hard on the metal desk, and turned around.

It was Rudy.

"I was just—"

"You were just sniffing my boss's gym clothes, if I'm not mistaken."

"I was—"

"Buh-sted," Rudy said, singing the syllables in doorbell notes.

"Look, man to man, can we just forget about this?"

"Oh, lighten up, sailor." Rudy looked him up and down. "Say now, is that a torpedo in your pocket, or are you just enjoying the show? It's a good thing I came in before you found her shorts, you might have blown a porthole in the front of those nice khakis."

"Look—"

"All hands on dick! Hoist the coxswain! Batten down the snatches! Blow the tubes, boys! Dive, Dive!"

Rob sat down, and only fortunately found the chair waiting under him. Rudy moved a stapler and sat on the desk facing him, his legs tucked Indian-style.

"Okay, okay. Talk to uncle Rudy, Lieutenant, what's on your mind?"

"You're not going to tell her about this, are you?"

"Oh, please. You like her, huh?"

Rob was silent, mortified, completely at a loss.

"I can see it," Rudy said. "Everyone can see it. Hey, we're rooting for you, pal."

"What do you mean?"

"She likes you, too, I think. I don't know, she's a complicated person, but all of us here are kind of hoping, you know, that maybe you two can get something going. She needs somebody to – what am I trying to say – take the edge off. But you like her, right?"

Rob looked at his hands, still holding the shirt. "Of course I like her, I mean look at her, she's a—"

"Goddess?" Rudy said.

"She's a goddess, yeah, and I've, believe me, I've had a lot of girlfriends—"

"Oh, I'll bet you have, with your broad shoulders, and your chiseled features, I'll bet you've got more miles on that penis than my mother's old LeSabre."

"But how am I supposed to do this? I mean technically she's my superior, and it's just, why am I talking about this with you? I must be out of my mind."

"Okay," Rudy said, rubbing his hands briskly together, "I can see that an intervention is necessary here."

"No, don't do that—"

"No no, listen to me, *shhh*, just listen. I'll talk to her. It's going to be okay. Come on, stand up, thaaat's right, big hug, there, he's gonna be just fine. Okay, big fella?"

Rob wasn't hugging so much as simply standing there, but gradually he brought his arms up around Rudy and gave him a squeeze. "Okay," he said.

A familiar voice came from the doorway.

"What are you two doing?"

"Hey, there, wow," Rudy said. "We've got a big morning, and Lieutenant Rob and I were just—"

"Cuddling?" Jeannie said.

Rob managed a lifeless chuckle, and Rudy stepped subtly in front of him just long enough to allow the tank top still in his hand to be secreted away.

"What's he doing behind my desk?"

"I'll talk to you about that later, okay? Hey, how about some breakfast? Rob?"

"Fine, yes," Rob said. "What sounds good to you, an egg sandwich? How about an egg sandwich?"

Jeannie considered him for a moment, quizzically. "That sounds fine."

"Rudy, how about you?"

"You know, Rob, you've got me thinking about sausages. How about something warm and steamy and salty, wrapped around a nice big sausage?"

"Okay! I'll just go and get the breakfast," Rob said. He started for the door, and he almost reached it.

"Hold it."

He stopped at the sound of her voice, and turned back to face the two of them.

"Yes, what?"

She walked to him, her eyes never leaving his, and stopped less than a foot away.

"What have you got there, sailor?"

When he didn't move to answer her, he felt her take the tiny corner of the shirt that was poking out from his pocket, and then she tugged it out into full, incriminating visibility.

After a moment he mustered his most winning, boyish smile,

but it withered gradually to half-mast as he saw she wasn't buying.

"Sorry," he said.

"Sorry?" she asked. "Sorry for what?"

"I'm—"

"For pawing through my belongings? Sorry for what?"

"I—"

She held up her hand, and it silenced him. When she spoke again her words were halting, her voice controlled against a slowly rising anger. "If I find anything disturbed, at all, beyond my personal things which you obviously feel I keep here for your amusement—" She took in a deep breath. "One document, one file, any one of which if violated will put you in shackles in front of a board of inquiry before the sun goes down today, Lieutenant, I will see you court martialed."

He lowered his eyes. "I'm sorry," Rob said.

She didn't answer.

The few moments it then took to turn from her, open the door, walk into the hallway and listen to the door whisper closed and latch behind him felt to be the longest stretch of seconds in his thirty-one years.

16

She'd told him more than she'd intended to, or maybe she was simply underestimating her opponent, just as she had in the chess game.

The backtrace had put her at DARPA. Hint of a Boston accent, the majority probably ironed out in finishing school. She was damn young, and yet in the upper ranks of the technological engine of the Department of Defense. She was in good shape, and competitive, and if her voice translated in any way to physical form, she was real eye-candy, tight and pert and sassy.

That last part was probably not germane to his investigation, but he allowed it into the record.

"Kate, are you feeling yourself again?" he said.

"Good afternoon, John. The firewall is secure, and I am operating within normal parameters."

"You sound much better."

Boner was on his back in the other room, trying to inchworm his nose under a cabinet where his ball had become wedged. That dog would play fetch for hours at a time, and every toss was a new, glorious chase.

"Do a search for me, Kate."

John rattled off a careful string of keywords. "Look in the

Northeast US, but don't restrict yourself too much. And while you're working show me what's going on in the world, please."

"Give me a few minutes," she said. "Here are your headlines."

The news just kept getting more and more ominous. The normal snail's pace of the US legislative branch was quickening to a sweatshop tempo, and every closed-door committee seemed aimed at putting the hammer down on civil liberties.

They'd pulled something out of a hat this morning called the Combating Terrorism Act, suspiciously finished and ready for perfunctory debate and ratification only ten days after the attacks that supposedly spawned it. On the next screen was another salvo, news that broad changes to wiretap and domestic surveillance regs were creeping in through little kneejerk tweaks to the Foreign Intelligence Surveillance Act. Since the terrorists were here among us, why shouldn't FISA be relaxed to include our own citizens?

Sure, why not? Thurgood Marshall must be spinning like a Skilsaw.

The next story hit much closer to home. It described the Anti-Terrorism Act, a 25-page opus introduced just yesterday, that among other atrocities made "hacking" a federal terrorism offense, right up there with political assassinations, and punishable by up to life, *life*, in prison. Qualifying offenses included "advice or assistance," which meant, presumably, just talking about shit.

Or writing about it on IRC, for example.

There had been a five-year statute of limitations on even true computer crimes, but the new ATA was going to blow that away, too. Abolished retroactively, so even offenses decades old could be prosecuted, starting today. And note this on your dance-cards, kids, there's no parole in the federal justice system.

The previous administration had already sold us halfway down the river with sweeping assaults on electronic privacy and due process, from CALEA to ECHELON and beyond. There were hackers in prison, for years, charged with possession of modified telephone hardware they'd bought at Radio Shack. And now the Bushies had something new in the works – they were calling it the Patriot Act – that looked like an overreaction of historic, jack-boot proportions.

The name was the biggest red flag on this one, the Patriot Act. That's like calling for a measured, thoughtful deliberation on the pros-and-cons of the Stop Ass-raping the Altar Boys Amendment. This beast was obviously going to be rubberstamped on the fast track.

The doorbell rang, probably the groceries, and some new delivery kid who didn't know about the drop-box. John told the dog to stay, and made his way through the circuitous route to the street entrance. He pushed the metal doors up and open and walked up the concrete stairs partway.

"Hey," the young man said, "dude, you have got one cool front door."

"Yeah, it keeps out the riff-raff." He pointed to the waist-level, key-padded sliding door of the dumbwaiter. "Just stick the stuff in there next time, all right? Your boss'll give you the code."

"Shit, sorry man. Can you get all this stuff?"

"I think so," John said. "This is the only exercise I get, so I'd better give it a try." He handed the teen three hundred-dollar bills.

"I can't break this, I don't have that much change."

"No, keep it, happy birthday, okay? I appreciate it."

The delivery boy was still looking at one of the bills, holding it up to the sunlight and turning it over in his hands as John closed the doors. So he was a big tipper, so what? The kid needed it more than he did.

He was finishing stocking his cabinets when he heard Kate's voice. "Search completed," she said.

"Show me what you've got."

He walked in to see the wall filled with windowed Web pages

and documents. He touched the screen to select and scan them, discard the flotsam, and narrow the results to the ones he'd been looking for.

Oh, this had to be her.

"Kate, sort on this name, ascending, chronological." He touched the first letter, dragged his finger to highlight the rest, and the screen filled with her history.

Tyro vs Machine: Child Wonder Beats IBM's Deep Blue

There was a picture and an article, on the People page of the *Boston Globe* from 1988. She was a little blonde thing, a grandmaster in a sailor dress, sitting in front of a big-screen chessboard and smiling like Christmas morning.

"Doogie Howser" Accepted at Cornell

She was older now, but not much older. The McGraw clock tower was in the background and she was standing with her parents, holding a football pennant in an oversized Big Red sweatshirt. The smile, he noticed, was almost gone now.

There were others, from her undergrad, master's and doctoral days, but the articles got gradually smaller. Freaks of nature became less amusing and more creepy as they got older, but she'd held up. She was hardening, though, straightening, and in the later photos she was always working, and always alone.

The last item was from August just past, in an unclassified, desktop-published DARPA newsletter. She'd won the All-Agency Triathlon, a loose Olympics-style competition for government employees. There she stood in her ponytail and baseball cap, Jeannie Reese, a garish gold trophy in her hands and a big blue banner across her chest. And that smile was back, if only for the moment.

The doorbell rang again. *Jeez.*

He had been looking forward to the liquor delivery, but not to dragging the cases up from the rear. *Ah, well.* Maybe he'd go out for a little while this time, just to walk. He pulled the memory stick from the front of his CPU, put its bead chain around his neck, and headed out.

He couldn't get her out of his mind as he walked through the dank lower floors, and in truth he wasn't really trying to. He hadn't spoken to a woman like he'd spoken to her, well, ever. She'd looked out at him through those pictures, and he felt her eyes with him even now.

He smiled and shook his head. If he were thirty pounds lighter, twenty years younger and an entirely different person in basically every detail, she was exactly the woman for him.

The light from the sun was fading in the late afternoon, and as he pushed open the double doors his arms told him he'd exceeded his maximum daily lifting allowance. Nothing a few snorts of Black Label couldn't fix right up.

"Hey, let me give you a hand with those," the delivery guy said. He pulled the doors the rest of the way vertical and let them clang outward onto the pavement. "Tried your little booze elevator thingy over there. Guess I got the code wrong, it locked me out."

"That's okay, it's been acting up," John said. "What do I owe you?"

"Two-twenty should do it. Where do you live, in the basement?"

John looked at him, and counted out two hundreds and a fifty. "Doesn't sound like enough," he said.

The man took the money, pocketed it. "Runnin' a sale."

"Are you new?"

"Nah, I just drive a different route. Your usual guy, he had a little accident this morning."

"Looks like you had a little accident yourself there."

"This?" There was a clumsy bandage of tissue and Scotch tape wrapped around his arm, with a spot of brown blood in its center. Running through it and along each side were four parallel scratches, like a ragged trail of fingernails. "Little cat-fight with my twat of a girlfriend." He hefted one of the liquor boxes. "You know how I know the bitch is stronger than I am? She can bleed for a week, and still not fucking die." The man chuckled, and started down the stairs.

94

John put his hand on the case to stop him. "No, that's okay, really, I can get them myself."

"Listen, I insist," Nathan Krieger said evenly, a smile curling at the corner of his mouth. "We gotta look after our valued customers. And I'm gonna take real good care of you."

17

There was a new word buzzing through the agency memoranda today, though thankfully not yet on the newswires.

Anthrax.

Great.

Commercial jets were flying again, and amazingly, the ban on unscreened mail and cargo had already been lifted under pressure from industry. We're capitalists, and the capital needed to flow, but she'd been dead-set against any artificial return to normalcy when it came to aircraft. General aviation was still grounded around major cities, and over most of the US the skies were unnaturally vacant, save for the occasional contrails of an Air Force scramble.

Yes, they felt it was necessary to engender the public feeling that everything was becoming A-OK again for air travel. But no, they'd still ordered her not to fly. Not just yet, they'd said. So here she was, in the back of a limousine from the White House pool, on the last leg of a five-hour drive to upstate New York.

Nearly a week had passed since her conversation with Phr33k, and it had been all dead ends ever since. IRIN had been unable to reestablish the fluke phone connection, and every other lead just lily-padded off into empty space. Which was precisely what he intended, no doubt.

It had been a quiet ride. She looked across at Lieutenant Rob, almost ten feet away in the limo's ornate rear compartment. He had been avoiding her, too, to the extent that a soldier could avoid the person he'd been ordered to accompany at all times. He was wearing headphones and his dress blues, looking out the row of tinted windows at the scenery, and probably farther.

Well, she could not be a nursemaid to bruised male egos, or God knows she would have time for little else.

US human intelligence assets were splitting into two camps these days, and that was fine with her. A good number of departments were being redirected to focus solely on the military response, which would first and foremost involve blowing the living shit out of Afghanistan and rounding up as much of al Qaeda as possible, dead or alive, and ousting the Taliban in the bargain. This was happening fast, and it wasn't her kind of process; there was only time for pure, regimented logistics. We were going in strong, because we were pretty sure, and because we had to, that was all. Still, it would take at least two more nonstop weeks of intensive preparations just to make it happen.

Though no one had asked, Jeannie was one-hundred per cent behind the military counterattack, for any number of reasons. It was the region's most fertile ground for a terror magnet like Usama bin Laden to build a foundation, and he was there now, by all accounts. In any case, the average American just didn't realize what a savage, hopeless, desolate hellhole Afghanistan was, and an especially horrible place to be a woman or a child. The people would certainly be better off once the United States had come and gone.

Bin Laden was involved, no question. He'd declared this war on the West years ago, and we'd been inexcusably unhurried in dealing with him and his like. But there were always greater depths to be plumbed, and the tracks she was following kept leading her much, much closer to home.

So her department was to stay focused domestically, and if DARPA's top-secret budgets and programs had been black before, they were to be absolutely invisible from here on. The outcome in Afghanistan was known even now, weeks before the first bomb would be dropped. But what she might uncover no one yet knew, and the possibilities that were beginning to emerge struck a fear for the very fabric of the nation.

Rob Vance had been called back to his combat unit, but she'd put a stop to that before he even got the notice. He would have gladly gone, she knew, and it had taken five telegrams and a personal call to a fleet admiral to release him. She had spent too much time breaking him in, and she wanted him here, that was her story. She needed him here, and she would have him.

Jeannie had asked the driver to take them a little out of the way, up the coast of the Hudson and along the cliffs of the Palisades. They'd rounded a long corner and the limo slowed, and now across the stretch of windows before them rose the skyline of Manhattan. Her parents had always taken her this way on weekend visits to New York, and it was the most wonderful view of the city from the ground. She kept her eyes to the north, but gradually they moved across the landmark architecture, to the Chrysler Building, the Empire State, and on downtown toward the Battery.

She'd known what to expect, but knowing and seeing were two different things. Where the shining silver majesty of the Trade Center had been, there were now only columns of dead gray smoke rising into the empty sky.

She looked at Rob. His expression hadn't changed, but his jaw was tight in profile, and his eyes were wet, but hard with the ice of a Navy pilot.

"Rob?" she said.

He didn't answer.

"Robert?"

He turned to her, pulled his headphones from his ears, wiped his eyes with the back of his hand.

"Would you be able to come over here for a minute?"

"Sure, okay," he said. He crouched his way across the compartment, and sat down next to her. He began to ask her what she needed, but she shook her head, lowered her eyes, put her hand softly on his knee.

Slowly, tentatively, he brought his palm to her cheek and caressed the tear there away with his thumb. She leaned to him, curled to his chest, and he held her. She pressed herself to him, her small hands gripping his jacket, pulling him closer and closer until she knew that nothing bad could reach her behind the shelter of his strong arms.

Her breathing gradually changed, and soon only a very occasional little catch and gasp broke its regularity.

He had been watching the scenery as they rode on upstate, as she cried herself out, as he stroked her hair and spoke soft words to her. He had held her as the tears of loss and bottomless despair gradually became those of unrequited fury and yearning for a pending vengeance she would deal with her own two hands. Through it all, she hadn't hidden her face from him. And then finally sleep had come.

She stirred now in the grip of a dream, and he looked down at her. Her lips moved as she spoke to her dream-partner, she shook her head lightly, *no,* a frown clouded the angel's face, and she balled a limp fist and drove a weak right-cross into his stomach. But it was weak only in this imperfect world. Wherever she was standing now, before her enemy's dying eyes she held his still-beating heart in her hand.

Shhhh, Rob said gently.

Her eyes moved beneath the lids as she took in a changing dreamscape. Her features softened little by little, a smile touched her mouth.

And where are you now? he wondered. A vestal maiden robed in pure shimmering white, maybe, descended to the green fields of Elysium, a garland of pale flowers in her hair, sent by the gods as a forbidden reward to a fallen hero of Troy. Her fantasies would not be small.

She breathed in sharply, exhaled slowly, pulled herself closer, an *mmmmmm* from her soft lips sent a tingle through him as her fingernails dragged a wicked, urgent inch down his chest.

He brushed a wisp of blonde from her brow, leaned into an even more uncomfortable position, and with a sensuous stretch she drew herself into him, closer still. He watched her as she slept, held her as the long highway passed behind.

There were a thousand reasons why he was no match for her, but as he watched her there in his arms he let himself forget them all, and he dreamed with her as the minutes and the miles to the next stop in the destiny they now shared wore steadily on. And somewhere a little farther down the road, the man came to terms with what the soldier had always known, from the moment he'd first been ordered to her side. He was hers, and whatever she needed he would be.

"Jeannie?"

She stirred against him, shifted her head. "Hmm?"

"I think we're almost there."

She opened her eyes and looked up at him.

"I think we're almost there," he repeated.

"Oh," she said, straightening up. "I'm sorry, I didn't mean to fall asleep."

"It's all right."

"Are you okay? Have you been sitting like that all this way?" She was looking around her seat, gathering her things.

"I'm fine."

"What's that on your lapel?"

He looked down. "I think you might have drooled on me a little bit."

"Oh, let me get that," she said, and she began to look for a tissue in her bag.

"No, it's okay, I'll wear it like this, it's fine."

She took a deep breath, and looked up at him.

"You know, Rob. It's not good, for people who work together to become—"

"Hey," he said, "you just took a little nap on me, it's not a big deal."

"Really?"

"Really."

"Because people have gotten the wrong idea with me before, guys, and I wouldn't want that to happen with you, okay? Because it's never ended up very well, and despite the bumps along the way, I like you, I like working with you."

"Fine. I'm good."

"Good," she said. "Oh good. Then so am I."

"Good."

The convoy was pulling into a gravel parking lot, in front of a plain two-story building. A wooden sign over the entrance said *MHz Magazine*.

As soon as they'd come to a halt, the doors of the long black sedans in front and behind swung open. Agents in dark suits exited the vehicles, one after another, their black shades glinting in the sun, the eyes behind them quickly scanning the perimeter. It was like clown cars at the circus, the way they just kept folding out; they must have been packed in like Pringles.

Jeannie had resisted the heavy escort from the Bureau, but her fallback position was an insistence that she and Rob have a car to themselves. This had obviously put an unpleasant crimp in their normal seating arrangements, but *c'est la vie*.

"All set?" Jeannie asked quietly. She was checking herself up close in a mirrored interior side panel, and she might have been talking to Rob, or she might not have been.

"Let's go," he said.

The two of them walked to the door, with a cortege of four FBI men behind. The rest had fanned out and were busily securing the surrounding area. The location was rural and remote, but there were many cars in the lot to be checked and acres of land with sporadic cover to be cleared.

This looked to be an old residence, converted to ivy-covered

101

office space by the low-renters who ran this fringe-interest magazine. Jeannie had been a clandestine subscriber since her pre-teens, and had seen *MHz* grow from mimeographed obscurity to the near-legitimate quarterly it was today. The content, often brilliantly written and sometimes on the edge of criminality, was an excellent window into the guarded realms of the hacker elite, and a guilty pleasure for her. She'd even sent in a few articles and letters-to-the-editor under a *nom de plume*, but her submissions had never yet seen publication.

As they walked into what used to be the foyer of the grand old house, a loud alarm sounded and two young security men in faux police uniforms stepped up to them.

"Would you empty your bag for me please, ma'am, on the table there?" one of them said.

Jeannie let her eyes narrow a bit. "Not for a plastic badge," she said, and she started between them for the stairs.

The bigger kid raised a hand to stop her, and what happened next happened fast.

Before Rob could move, she'd caught the guy's little finger and bent it back toward him hard. He went to his knees with a squeal. The other one grabbed her shoulder and her arm whirled up and around it, bending his elbow in the direction elbows don't normally bend. She pivoted a half-turn and swept his legs, and his off-balance mass sent him flat onto his back. She dropped to a knee to maintain her holds, with the hands that had touched her now twisted back almost to their fore-arms.

She looked back and forth between the two of them, and applied enough additional pressure to make them wince as she met their eyes.

"Keep your hands to yourself," Jeannie said. "Okay?"

They nodded their heads, and after a moment she released them and stood up.

"Nice," Rob said.

"That?" she replied. "That's just blind-date kung fu. We should spar sometime, and I'll show you what I've really got. Wear a cup, though." She thumped his crotch with the back of her hand, and winked him a sly smile. "Where were you, by the way, while I was getting manhandled?"

"I was right behind you."

A lanky man in John Lennon wire-rims had come down the staircase to their right. He surveyed the assembly: his two security guards on their backs, a preppy blonde with a Navy officer, and four men-in-black bringing up the rear.

"Now what on earth," he said.

"Mr. Smith, we've got a situation here," one of the guards said, from the floor.

It was hard to place the man's age, he could have been anything from a road-worn, time-weary fifty-five to a spry and well preserved seventy-two. His hair was long and gray and somewhat unkempt, and he wore jeans and a pastel cardigan with a moth-hole at the shoulder. There was the feeling of a man who in his mind had not aged a day since his twenties. He carried himself like a long-limbed kid, but the lines at the corners of his eyes led back decades, through activist college years, Woodstock and Hoffman, Vietnam and Kent State, Timothy Leary, and the summer of love.

"You called about a break-in," Jeannie said.

"I called the local cops in New Paltz, not the fucking thought police. Who set off the metal detector?"

Jeannie met his gaze, coolly. "I don't know, it might have been this." She reached down with her right hand and drew up the hem of her skirt, just far enough to show him the nickel-plated Walther holstered at mid-thigh.

"This might have done it, too," Rob said, patting his sidearm. "Or it could have been those." He jutted a thumb over his shoulder, and the four G-men pulled opened their coats to show the hoglegs in their shoulder holsters.

The spectacled man shook his head, and smiled. "Get off my land," he said.

"All right, men, we're not getting anywhere whipping our dicks around," Jeannie said. She pulled her ID from her bag, walked over and flipped it open. "My name is Jeannie Reese. You're right, you called the local police, and then they called me. It's the nature of the break-in here that we're interested in, and we have reason to believe it could be a matter of national security. That's why we're here, and we'd appreciate your cooperation."

The man looked at her identification and blanched a bit, in spite of his staid composure. He took in a breath, and let it out with a sigh.

"No guns," he said.

"Fine." There was another quick flash of black garter as she retrieved her pistol. She popped the clip and checked the chamber, then tossed it to one of the rent-a-cops who had now regained his feet. "Keep that warm for me, killer."

Rob unbuckled his holster and handed it to the suit behind him.

"Okay, let's go up," Jeannie said. "The rest of you bad boys stay down here, and keep an eye on each other."

"Winston Smith, is that actually your name, like from Orwell, *1984*?" Rob was handing their host back his driver's license.

"I had it legally changed, and it's been that way for a lot of years. But you've checked that out, I'm sure."

"I was just curious. It's kind of neat."

"Don't patronize me."

Jeannie was looking over the copy of the police report he'd given her. "This is very detailed. And nothing was stolen, you're positive?"

"Look around you. What's to steal?"

"None of the files are missing?"

"No, like I said. They were only disturbed."

"And where are those files now, the ones that were disturbed?"

"I shredded them actually, when I saw you drive up."

104

Jeannie held up a finger, found her cellphone, and speed-dialed one of the agents outside. "It's me. We're going to need Jay's team. Right. Call him and do what he says. Okay. Get it rolling." She closed the phone and dropped it back into her bag. "Why would you do that?"

"Because they were still my property, and something told me it was the prudent thing to do."

"All right, you panicked, but as of now you know better than to do anything like that again, don't you? There are only about five minutes separating what you did from obstruction of justice, and those guys downstairs, they're a little twitchy these days, if you know what I mean, so just cool it. You don't want to die in federal prison. No more shredding."

Smith pulled a cigarette and a book of matches from his desk, and lit up. "Look," he said, "if we're going to stay on friendly speaking terms, you're going to have to tell me what this is really about. I'm not going to sit here without a lawyer, with the place crawling with pigs."

Jeannie looked at Rob, then back to the man across the desk. "We're looking for someone, one of your contributors. He's a person of interest in the September eleventh attacks, and our filing system caught some details you provided in your police report, and correlated them with our guy. Somebody broke into your office and touched only the files with his name on them. We need to know why that happened."

Smith didn't say anything, he only nodded.

Rob looked around, found the filing cabinets, all closed and looking perfectly unmolested. "Is this how they left everything?"

"Yes, it is," Smith said. "Just like you see it, everything in its place."

Rob blinked. "How did you know what'd been done, or that you'd even had a break-in?"

Smith took a long drag on his Marlboro, and rubbed it out in a Mason-jar lid on his desk. He opened his middle drawer, and took out a wrinkled tube of airplane glue. "Let me show you something," he said. He walked them over to the row of filing cabinets. "Every night before I leave, I do this." He opened the silver tip of the tube and touched the edge of the cabinet, and then the edge of the top drawer.

"So?" Rob said.

"Do you have a laser pointer on you?"

Rob didn't, but Jeannie did, and she fished it out of her bag.

"Point it right there," Smith said.

The bright red spot of light searched around for a moment, and then revealed the microscopic, wispy strand of polymer now connecting the two points. "It's the last thing I do before I leave, and the first thing I check in the morning."

"So if anyone opens a drawer—"

"I know about it, right. They'll never see it, so they won't know to replace it, no matter how careful they are."

"Paranoid?" Rob asked.

"You tell me."

Jeannie's pager chirped, but she side-buttoned it to silence. "How about the individual folders, how did you know what he'd seen?"

"This guy was careful, professional. I always leave the bottom drawer here open just a crack, and he was good enough to leave it that way, too. When we file things, we reverse a sheet or two here and there. Casual snoopers will right the page to read it, and they'll almost always forget to put it back like they found it. He remembered. I went over every page in every drawer he'd cased, and there was one trace he didn't count on anyone picking up." He pulled his middle desk drawer again. "Close your eyes," Smith said.

She did. Rob kept his open.

Winston Smith withdrew a single leaf of manuscript from the drawer. He stood and walked to her, held it under her nose. "Breathe in," he said.

"Smells like paper."

"And what else?"

There was another odor there, faint, from a long time ago. But gradually clearer, and then unmistakable.

Her eyes snapped open. "Iodine."

"Iodine," Smith said. "And with plenty of newer technologies available, why might some people, your colleagues for example, use iodine to try and raise old fingerprints on paper?"

"Because the image comes up long enough to photograph—"

Rob finished her thought. "And then it disappears."

Smith took his paper back to the far side of his desk, sat down and looked at her, expectantly.

"It wasn't one of us," Jeannie said.

"Oh, don't bullshit me further, please. This so-called filing system you're talking about, there's no way a police report of a petty break-in from a one-horse town in upstate New York gets cross-referenced with your most-wanted list a few days after it's filed, no fucking way in hell. I didn't just fall off the turnip truck, I've had a peek behind the curtain, cookie, I know what you goose-steppers are dreaming up out there. So we're left with two possibilities. Number one, you and your plumbers pulled a G. Gordon Liddy here and are now trying to play innocent and backpedal into the shadows again. Or number two, some rene-gade double-0 seven broke into my office and is hunting for someone I care about."

Smith looked back and forth between them for an answer, and didn't get one.

"Look, I'm not kidding myself," he said. "I know I'm on a watch list, you guys have been demonizing hackers for years, all of us, with the same broad brush. You've seen my crack security team, they're all I can afford, and I'm only a little better off in the legal department. I know you don't have to tell me jack shit. Hell, these days you could disappear me into Leavenworth with one call on that phone, just for doing what I've always done with this magazine. But human to human, lady, I'd really like to know what happened here."

107

Jeannie leaned forward in her chair. "It wasn't one of us, that's a promise."

"You said you know what all those files had in common, you know who this guy is looking for?"

She nodded.

"And you're looking for him, too?" Smith said, and he cocked his head toward a splash of years-old Keith Haring graffiti over the door to the coffee room. A circle of Haring's rhythmic, white chalk stick-figures were genuflecting around a string of block letters.

PHR33K R001z, it said.

"That's right."

Her cellphone twittered, sounding its priority tone.

"Now what," Jeannie whispered, and she answered it. "Reese." She listened for a while, and her eyes found Rob's. "All right, stay there, and have them cordon off the area. No, the entire area, nobody in or out. And bring up my kit."

Smith stood up. "What is this, now," he said.

She closed her phone slowly.

"Do you know a man named Emile Arias?"

"Yes, he cleans the place, nights." He looked back and forth between Jeannie and Rob. "Oh, no way, don't you dare try to lay this—"

"Sit down, Winston," Jeannie said.

He did.

"The agents found him, in the woods about a quarter of a mile away. In a shallow grave."

18

He felt fingertips on his forehead, and a thumb on his eyelid pulled it up and open. A blaze of white light seared into his retina, so bright that he saw the blood vessels and pink striations of its surface. He felt his brain send an impulse to his arm to strike the hand away, but the signal went slow and weak, and only his index finger moved. His eye closed but the other was soon peeled roughly open, and the brightness burned in again, and then darkness returned. There were voices, but only the sounds of voices, the meanings of the words were somehow not penetrating.

He opened his eyes. There was warm, blurry light now, amber and flickering, and a smell of woodsmoke and creosote on the air. There were dark figures standing, and one seated near him, leaning close. A hand from that one drew back and moved as though to flick a persistent insect away, and the other muttering specters quickly disappeared. He heard a heavy door close, with a metal latch and the turn of a lock, and it was quiet.

"John?" a voice said, near his ear. "John Fagan?"

A sharp new smell slammed into his brain and jolted him to sudden consciousness. Ammonia, his mind said first, but after a moment it issued a correction. Make that ammonium carbonate solution, $(NH_4)_2CO_3 \cdot H_2O$. *Smelling salts.*

"There you are," the man's voice said.

"Get that shit out of my face," John replied weakly. He started to bring himself to an elbow, but there was pain everywhere in him, from his joints to the surface of his skin.

"Take it easy, just relax."

"Where are my glasses?" John said.

"I'll get them for you."

The man carefully opened the frames and gently slipped the spectacles into place, but everywhere they touched him they burned like the tip of a soldering iron.

"I'm sorry you're hurting, but we're just going to have to wait it out. My man got a little reckless with the fentanyl, we weren't even sure you were going to pull through. They tell me the pain is a side effect of the overdose, it's rare, but—"

"Hyperalgia," John said. At least his mind was beginning to clear.

The man settled back in his chair. "I'm impressed," he said.

"Don't be. My dad wanted me to be a doctor, so I've read a few books."

John swiveled his head against the feather pillow, and he felt the vertebrae in his neck rasp and scrape like barn hinges. He looked into the face next to him, and it registered before he'd even called upon his memory to retrieve it.

"Do you know who I am?" the man asked.

John nodded his head. The eyes were distinctive, and the deep voice was as he remembered it. But in his heyday, the press had made this man most distinguished by his freakish smoothness. From the crown of his head to the floor, he was completely hairless, no eyebrows or lashes, no stubble, nose, ear or body hair.

"Yeah, I know who you are," John said. "You're Ed Latrine."

From the corner of his eye, John noticed the armed man standing guard at the door stiffen visibly.

Latrell's left eye ticked almost imperceptibly, but he smiled, in control. "They did call me that, didn't they?"

"Well, mostly during your presidential campaign in seventy-six," John said. "Hey, look, Ed, I'm a big fan, I've still got a Nigger-Go-Home fanny pack from one of your whistle-stop rallies."

The guard at the door was still motionless, but his eyes were growing wide.

"You're a cynic," Latrell said.

"I suppose you're right. What did Oscar Wilde say? When I smell flowers, I generally start looking around for a coffin."

"Are you wondering at all where you are, and how you got here, and why we're talking now?"

John's eyes were getting heavy, and he felt the cottony opiate sleep descending again.

"I'm still a little stoned here, Ed," he murmured, his lips barely moving, "Can you help me out with any of those?"

"I can help you, yes," Latrell said. "I'll help you, John. And then you'll help me."

19

As it turned out, Winston Smith hadn't just shredded the Phr33k archives. He'd practically annihilated them.

His office was outfitted with an authentic, DoD-class shredding machine. It was the size of a small refrigerator and must have cost more than the car he was driving, but it had done a bang-up job on the files. Each one of the pages he'd fed it had been torn to nearly 6,000 tiny, indistinguishable cross-cut rectangles.

There was no way to know how many sheets he'd put through, or how much irrelevant paper was now mixed in with the target files, but it was conservative to estimate that there were now half a million needles hiding in one motherfucker of a haystack.

The fun was just beginning, however. Before Smith had come down to meet them in the lobby, he'd taken a moment to swing the contents of the shredder's receptacle out a second-story window at the back of the building.

It was a breezy afternoon, and the shards had fluttered everywhere. Jeannie had deployed most of the agents from her escort to the grounds surrounding the building, armed with handheld vacuums, tweezers, magnifiers and grid-coded evidence bags. Standing there in the parking lot, she could make out only the faintest pattern of the wide debris field, with little angular points of white scattered over thousands of square feet of gravel, sidewalks, grass and shrubbery.

This was a tall order, so she'd called for the best in the business. And now forty-five minutes later, Jay Marshall and his team were rolling into the drive.

This man had almost single-handedly created the document reconstruction industry, and he was the leading private-sector consultant on secure information destruction as well. She'd worked with him years ago at MIT, when he was still using Pakistani rug-weavers to physically reassemble shredded strips of paper into their original form. Jeannie had brought a revolution of computers, digital microimaging and fuzzy logic to his process. And for his part, Jay had helped her through some things, as well.

"Little Jeannie Reese," Marshall said when he saw her, and the big man approached, shaking his head lovingly with his arms outstretched.

"Jay, I haven't seen you in, what's it been?" Jeannie said, bracing herself.

He wrapped his grizzly-bear arms around her, squeezed her close, and made a caveman growl as he lifted her off the ground. These hugs, she knew, were like quicksand; it was better not to struggle. At length, she was back on her feet.

"Too long, little girl, too goddamn long. I was so scared for you on the eleventh, I'm just glad to see you in one pretty piece."

He looked around them as a dust-devil zigzagged through the lot, whipping up flecks of paper, with a pair of vacuum-wielding field agents in hot pursuit.

"What have you got here?"

"Snowstorm," Jeannie said. "Some files we've really got to see."

"What did they use to destroy the documents?"

"The antichrist," Jeannie said. "An HSM 390, the same model you installed down the hall from me."

Marshall grunted. "How much of this is target material?" he asked, sweeping his clipboard around the speckled landscape.

"Don't know, maybe half, maybe less. The guy's not hostile, he just flipped out when the line of black government limos drove up. He told us he hadn't emptied the bin in a few days." They both surveyed the depressing landscape. "Jay, we need this," Jeannie said. "Can you do it?"

He snorted. "Girl, listen to me. That shredder meets NSA specs, and I know you know what that means. That means when something goes in, it don't come out, right? It's gone, it's pulp. On top of that, look around you here, at this confetti party. Mix a thousand one-thousand-piece jigsaw puzzles together, paint all the pieces white and crosscut them into perfect little parallelograms, then blow those itty-bitty little bits over an acre of land on a windy day, and you're asking me if I can put that back together?" He shook his head, and sighed.

"You insult me," he said. "Give me forty-eight hours."

She'd stayed with Jay as he supervised the retrieval operation, including all trash from the office bins and nearby dumpsters. The sun was getting low by the time they'd finished and every visible scrap of paper had been gathered. The FBI entourage was packing up, and the two of them were having coffee, sitting on the tailgate of one of his SUVs.

"So," Jay said. "You look good, kitten. You're a woman now, no doubt about that."

She'd been studying her coffee cup, and not saying much.

He leaned to her. "You seeing anyone?"

She smirked, shook her head.

"Why the hell is that funny, why not? You're a knockout, you're brainy, you should have to beat the boys back with a broom handle."

"It just doesn't click, Jay, for some reason. Every so often I'll meet a guy, and we'll have dinner, and I'm physically sick of him before dessert. And I don't get that many offers anymore. You'd think I was intimidating, or something."

"I can't imagine that."

She looked up at him. "You can't?"

"Sorry, I was mocking you. You're intimidating as hell."

She took in a deep breath, and sighed. "I did meet someone, the other night on the phone."

"On the phone?"

"Yeah, it was just one of those fluky things. But we talked all night, and he was always one step ahead of me, you know? He was funny, smart, he beat me in a game of chess, Jay, *me*," she said. "And strong, he wasn't afraid of me at all."

"Are you going to see him?"

"No," she said, "not even in the realm of possibility. It's doomed. It's so doomed you can't imagine. Like J. Edgar Hoover with a crush on Pretty Boy Floyd."

"If I remember correctly," Jay said, "there actually were some sparks between those two."

She swung her legs off the back of the tailgate, and looked to the side where the sun would be setting soon. "It's messed up, I know, but I can't stop thinking about him."

"Well," he said, "it's crystal clear to me that you need a long vacation, and a good lay."

"I'm not familiar with either one of those concepts," she said. "I'm tired, Jay, you know? Between you and me, I'm dog tired."

"You're where you are because there's no one else like you," he said. "Hell, at your age I was still shotgunning beers and hazing freshmen during rush week at NYU. You grew up pretty young."

"But how can I stop?" she asked. "I can't stop. You're absolutely right, there's no one to step up if I give out, no one who wouldn't screw up everything I've built, but where does that end? I've got so much in my head now, Jay. There's a picture materializing, of what happened on the eleventh, what's still happening now, it's still unfolding. It all fits together, I can see that it does, but I can't fit it together yet."

"And this here today, you said, these files, this is a key?" he said. She nodded. "I think it is."

He studied her. "Do you have an idea what's behind the door this key might open?"

115

She didn't speak, but the weight of the answer was in her eyes.

"Jeannie," Marshall said, reaching into his inside breast pocket, "will you have a drink with me?"

He withdrew a thin silver flask from his coat, unscrewed the cap, and poured a few ounces of auburn liquor into his coffee. She shook her head, put her hand over the mouth of her cup.

"You're legal now, right?"

"Yes, I'm legal, I'm twenty-two, but I'm on duty," she said.

"All right," he said. "More for me, then."

He took a healthy sip from the cup, and put it down between them.

"Jeannie, you operate in a sphere that's way over my head, you have since I met you, when you were twelve. But I'm older than you are, and I'm going to give you some advice."

"Okay," she said quietly.

"There are things in the world, some old, old things, that have always been working, they've always been here since men first stacked two rocks on top of one another. Governments come and go, but there's a unity of power up at the top, that's underpinning everything, always."

She looked at him. "Give me that," she said. He passed her his flask, and she twisted off the cap and tipped it up unselfconsciously, wiped her lips with her wrist. "You haven't gone one-worlder on me, have you Jay?"

"Call it what you want, kid. I'm saying that not much happens in the course of human events these days that's not agreed upon, on some level that even you aren't a party to. And this, these attacks, somebody went off the playbook, and I think they were trying to do more than declare war on liberty and freedom. I think they were trying to make a cut that was deep enough to expose the clockworks, things none of us are supposed to see."

"Bullshit," Jeannie said. The bourbon was warming her in the cool evening air, and she took another drink.

"Jeannie, we closed the airspace nationwide after the eleventh, didn't we. That had never been done before, everything was grounded, right?"

She was concentrating on screwing the cap onto the now-empty flask, and running her thumb over the embossed scene that was etched into the pewter. It showed a hunter and his dog in a field of tall grass, a vee of wild geese in the air over their heads.

"But there was a plane in the air on the thirteenth, though, Jeannie, one plane, and you know who was on it?"

"That's unconfirmed," she said.

"I'm sure it is. It was bin Laden's family, and a hundred-forty or so Saudi nationals, wasn't it? While we're rounding up ten thousand suspects on evidence that wouldn't have gotten a second look a month ago, we're escorting a group of Saudis out of the country, unscreened and unquestioned, back to a nation that we know fifteen of the nineteen hijackers came from. Why do you think we did that?"

Jeannie handed him his flask.

"First of all," she said, "bin Laden has fifty-three brothers and sisters, and most of them haven't seen him since they were kids. He's disowned, he's dead to them, and that goes for most of the other relations, too. You may think we're not watching, Jay, but we are."

She paused, let her eyes drift out to the graveled turf in front of them.

"That flight you're talking about, that's a red herring, Internet bullshit," she said. "But there are other things."

"Jeannie, I'm just telling you to be careful. They've got you on the inside because you're a genius, but you're also on the inside because they can't risk having somebody like you on the outside. You may be finding stuff that shouldn't be found, and there are lines they won't let anyone cross, no matter who you are." He put his hand on her shoulder, and squeezed it. "Just be careful, is all I'm saying, and watch your back."

The reassuring smile she gave was unconvincing, to either of them. "I'll be careful, Jay. You just get me those documents as soon as you can." She gathered her bag, and looked around briefly. "Have you seen that fellow who was with me earlier?"

"The hot Navy boy with the cute butt?" Jay asked.

"That's him." She stood up and brushed herself, straightened her skirt. "I cut him loose a couple of hours ago, he's probably taking a nap in the back of one of the cars. He's been trying his best to keep my hours, poor thing."

"You know? I think he's on the roof of the building, up with the FBI lookouts."

"Oh," she said. "He is?"

"Yeah, I think so, I think I saw him up there."

"Well, then, Jay," she said, holding out her hand, "I'm going to be getting back."

Ignoring the handshake offer, he stood up and took her in his arms, hugged her tight. "Take care of yourself, little girl," he said. "Anything you need, ever, I'm there. Remember when I made you that promise?"

"Yeah," Jeannie whispered.

"And try to let yourself go once in a while."

She patted his shoulder, and took a step back. "Call me when you know something on this," she said. "In fact, call me tomorrow even if you don't know anything yet."

"Will do," he said, and he watched her turn from him and walk toward the fire escape that zigzagged up the outside of the building.

She didn't see him immediately as she topped the last staircase. There were snipers at the four corners of the flat roof, and a number of other agents were milling about, collecting their gear and preparing to leave. She walked to a block of tall maintenance vents and peeked around the corner, and there he was, sitting cross-legged on a blanket on the black tar surface. He'd changed into a pair of faded jeans and a tight gray sweatshirt from his travel

118

bag. He was wearing a backwards baseball cap, with *FBI* embroidered on it.

Next to him on the blanket sat a young female agent, wearing khaki slacks, a ski-bunny sweater and a flak jacket.

She watched them for a minute as they talked quietly. The girl was sitting close, listening to his stories and laughing with him. He leaned to her and whispered something, and she pushed him away in feigned offense. She shook her head as if she knew better, then pulled a pen from the clipboard next to her, took his hand and wrote something across its palm.

"Well," Jeannie said, taking a few steps toward the two. "Wrapping up?"

The young agent stood quickly. "Yes, ma'am," she said. She began collecting her things and stuffing them into her duffel.

Rob got to his feet and stretched. "So you're all set?" he said.

Jeannie looked at him, and then at the girl.

"Oh, Jeannie Reese," Rob said, "this is Agent Woodruff. She, uh, attended a close-combat seminar that I facilitated at Quantico last spring, and we were just catching up."

"Well, that's nice. And how was it?" Jeannie asked. "The seminar?"

"It really was awesome," the agent replied. "He's a great teacher." She looked at Rob, smiling. "He really knows how to pound a point home, so you never forget it."

Rob blinked, and smiled back. "I believe that's the nicest thing anyone has said to me all month long," he said. "Do we need to get going?"

Jeannie nodded.

"Okay, then," Rob said. "Let's see, this is yours." He took the cap from his head and handed it to Agent Woodruff.

"Oh, my goodness, I almost forgot," the girl said, and she removed the Kevlar vest she was wearing and returned it to Rob.

"She was chilly," Rob said.

Jeannie nodded.

"So, see you around, and call me sometime," Woodruff said,

and she squeezed his arm as she left them. "And nice to meet you, ma'am, I've heard so much about you."

Jeannie smiled thinly, and watched the girl until she'd disappeared down the fire escape.

"Let's go, Lieutenant," she said.

It was a beautiful clear night, and the moon shone full and blue-white through the tinted glass panels in the roof of the long car. The lights were cocktail-lounge low and warm, and the faint vibration of the road was soothing.

The two of them hadn't spoken a word in sixty miles.

"Rob."

He didn't move. He was reclining on the long bench seat with his eyes closed, and he'd put his headphones on twenty miles back.

"Rob," she said, louder this time. He craned his head back to look at her, and pulled one pad away from an ear.

"Hmm?"

"Would you mind sitting up and talking to me?"

He brought himself up onto an elbow and laid his 'phones on the seat next to him. "What do you want to talk about?"

"Do I need to post an agenda? It's a long ride and I'd just like some company. Jesus."

He sat up the rest of the way, and moved closer to her. "I'm sorry, I sometimes don't know whether I should bother you or not."

"Don't apologize, it's my fault, I'm sure." She brushed her skirt with the back of her hand, and then looked out the window. "That girl on the roof," she said. "What were the two of you talking about? Just talk to me like that. You were having fun, and I need to have fun."

Rob hesitated, shifting in his seat. "We knew each other from that class, I mentioned that, and she and I . . . unwound together a couple of times."

"Unwound?"

120

"Yeah, so we were talking about, you know—"

"Unwinding," she said. "I'm afraid I don't know very much about that."

"Let's talk about something else, then," Rob said.

"What were you listening to over there?"

"You'll think I'm an idiot."

"No, no I won't, what is it?"

He leaned back. "Okay," he said, and he slid over and transferred the CD from his player into a nearby console, and pushed play.

The haunting opening notes were familiar, but she couldn't place the song. "What is that? I think I like that."

"It's vintage Fleetwood Mac, 'Gold Dust Woman.' I'm a seventies nut." he said. "My mom told me once I was conceived to this song." The lost, waifish voice of a young Stevie Nicks came over the speakers.

"So, you were conceived to this? Doesn't it make you think about your mom and dad having sex?" she asked.

"Never actually teased it out to a full-blown visual," he said. He winced and covered his eyes. "Oh, man, this little dirty movie is completely stuck in my head now, thanks."

She smiled, her first real one of the day.

"Rob, do you want to have a beer, or something? I think they've got everything in this car."

"You know," he said, "that sounds pretty nice. How 'bout you?"

"A beer or something stiffer would be perfect."

"Stiff, now let me see." He thought for a moment. "Ever do a Cruise Missile?"

"I think I'd remember that, and I don't believe so."

He opened the minibar, and returned with four airline bottles of Jack Daniels, along with two icy Stolichnaya minis from the freezer.

"I'm not a very experienced drinker," she said. "What do I do?"

121

"You said you wanted fun, right?"

She smiled, and nodded.

"And you're feeling adventurous?"

"Truth? I feel like bungee-jumping naked off the 59th Street Bridge."

"Okay, then. I'll show you how to drink like a seadog," he said, and he rubbed his hands together briskly. "Now, you've got to hit all three of these, the whiskey and then the vodka, and you've got to kill them all, no hands, no spitting up, or you lose."

"What happens to me if I lose?"

"Well, you have to go again until you get it right," he said. "We hold the bottles for each other, just like this. Here's what you do."

He twisted the tops off all three, then held one of the little whiskey bottles upright between his knees and put the next one at mid-thigh, followed by the vodka bottle about an inch from his zipper. "See that? It looks a little racy, I know, but it's fun." He removed the bottles he'd placed, and held them out to her. "Now you set me up, take these, I'm gonna go first, to demonstrate."

"I'm wearing a skirt."

"I don't give a damn, sailor. You've seen one, you've seen 'em all. Hike it up and let's go. Unless you're chicken."

After a last moment's deliberation she took the bottles, leaned back against the leather seat, edged her skirt up tentatively, placed the first two little bottles as he'd shown her, and braced herself.

"Oh, good God that's cold," Jeannie said, as she got the frosty Stoli bottle situated.

"All right, are you ready?" he asked.

"Just go, yes, I'm ready, I'm ready."

He knelt in front of her, held up a finger for silence, then lowered his lips to the mouth of the bottle between her knees. He took it up, tilted back until he'd swallowed it all, and then tossed the bottle back over his head with a flip.

"See how I did that? Right back over your head, no hands," he said. "Oh, my, that's tasty."

"Come on, come on, I'm getting a frostbite over here."

"Here I go, I'm going in, so stop squirming." He shrugged off his bomber jacket, cracked his knuckles, took a deep breath, and then bent and grasped the top of the second bottle in his teeth. After a moment, he looked up at her.

"You're clenching, Jeannie, you've got to help me out a little."

"I'm sorry," she said. "This is my first Cruise Missile."

He nodded his head, and put his hand gently on her thigh. Her skin was hot, but she was trembling. She sighed, and closed her eyes.

"Just relax, yeoman," Rob said. "That's the most important thing, just relax."

He went down for the bottle again, and this time it slipped free. He drained the whiskey, and spit-tossed the empty back over his head onto the floor behind him.

"Home stretch," he said.

"You're telling me this is what sailors do with each other when they go drinking?"

He put a hand on the seat on each side of her, and his eyes were close to hers. "I can't lie to you. I totally made this up just now."

"Oh, you are such a rotten bastard."

"Never said I wasn't." He handed her one of the unopened bottles. "Drink that down, and I'll be right back."

She felt the liquor warm her throat as he moved slowly past the curve of her neck, and as his lips brushed down the front of her sweater she caught her breath and arched to him. His head was against her stomach as she felt him slowly tug the cold little bottle free, near a delicious ache that was knotting there.

He raised himself back up, close in front of her.

"Woof," he said, around the top of the bottle in his teeth.

She smiled with him, took the cold vodka bottle from him and drank from it, closed her eyes, and he kissed her gently. Her hands pressed against his chest, as if ready to push him away and make her escape if need be. But she pulled him closer as his lips touched her cheek, the lobe of her ear, and her nails dug in

123

as the things he whispered sent a shiver from the nape of her neck to her toes. She felt his fingers deftly slipping the first button of her blouse, and the second, and the third.

Deftly.

She opened her eyes, caught his thumb back-hand and twisted it down so his palm was flat to the warm sidelight of the interior.

It was the hand Agent Woodruff had autographed on the roof in New Paltz. *Shari*, it said there in round flowery script, and a phone number curly cued below. She looked up at him, and narrowed her eyes.

"Don't move, just one second," he said. He emptied the last of the vodka into the hollow of his palm, rubbed his hands together and then opened them to her. The writing that had been there was gone.

At length she lowered her eyes, and pulled his hand back to where it had been.

"She called me *ma'am*," Jeannie said quietly.

He bent his head to her bosom, and she felt him undo the next straining button there with his mouth, and the next, and the next.

"Let me try to make you forget about it," Rob said.

She lay back against the cool, creamy leather, closed her eyes and stretched her hands over her head, and he held them gently there. His touch was tantalizing, light and maddening at first and then firm and sure and knowing, knowing the places her imaginary lovers had always known, as they lured her late at night to a breathless but unfinished ecstasy. She turned her face aside in surrender, moving under his hands, pulling away and then pressing back again, a fiery coil of wanting tightened down inside, edging her toward a coming release with every tease of his mouth, his fingertips, his warm breath. And as his lips finally found hers again, as her fingers tangled in his hair and raked the tensing muscles beneath his clothing, as she felt his heart pounding with her own in every inch of him as she gave herself over to it at last, there was one small part of her that held back, recoiled, and stayed behind.

Because a different face had faded in behind her eyes. It was not that of the young Navy lieutenant who had sworn his life to her safety, no, that small part of her noted, with a distant sting of judgment she blithely chose to disregard. This face was of another, his features vague and indistinct as the composite sketch of a most-wanted man, a mask of secrets, but his mind, his mind the one that could finally complete her, and own her, body and soul.

"You have to show me what to do," Jeannie whispered.

"I will, baby," the man said, against her skin.

Another song was playing now, music from before she was born. In the light of day, playing from a car radio or in an elevator, it might have passed unnoticed with the other maudlin noises of the world. But now under the moon, with the great bright city sliding by them outside the long windows, it surrounded them, revealed them, and entwined with them.

20

Breakfast here, John thought, was nothing if not voluminous.

He had been eating only lightly, but that hadn't deterred his hosts from rolling out the county-fair chuck wagon at every single meal. This morning it was buckwheat pancakes, eggs over easy, bacon, biscuits, gravy and jo-jo potatoes, all right off the greasy skillet and arranged on a white china plate the size of a turkey platter.

Still, he didn't feel much like chowing down. This might have been due to the fading remnants of the anesthetic he'd been shot full of days ago. It could also have been that he hadn't experienced home-cooked food in almost twenty-five years, and this fare was clearly from a real pan-frying, lard-slinging country kitchen. It wasn't bad, but it was heavy.

Most likely, though, it was the nagging certainty that every meal they brought him was very possibly to be his last.

He looked over at the burly, lumberjackish fellow by the door, and tapped the cup beside his plate with the edge of his fork.

"Yo, Boxcar Willie, you think you could rustle up another cuppa java for a brother?" he said.

The man's jaw tensed. He turned slowly until they were face to face, letting the business end of the 12-gauge shotgun in his hands swing level past John's chest.

Their eyes met, and held for a while.

"Should I draw you a picture, Jethro?" John said. He picked up the cup and slid it across to the edge of the wooden tabletop. "I'd spell it out for you, but in your case I don't think that would help."

The man's face reddened, but after a moment he walked to the table, took the cup and turned to leave.

"That's a good man," John said. "Coffee and a cigarette for Uncle Johnny. And don't stop to fuck your sister."

The door clicked shut, and he heard the deadbolt slide home on the outside. His heart had begun to pound, and a thin icy sweat broke on his forehead. He wiped the moisture away with a cloth napkin. *Nicotine withdrawal,* he assured himself, or, perchance, his edginess was somehow related to his very first look down the throat of a fucking Remington 11-87 semi-auto. His hand on the table was trembling, and he made a fist, tensed it until the subtle shaking passed. *If they wanted you dead, you'd be dead. Fear is a weakness to this kind. You show an animal no fear.*

There was no way to be sure exactly how long he'd been here. He remembered the liquor delivery man on the back stairs of his home, a brief scuffle and a choke hold, and there were swatch recollections of a hot, dark ride, cramped and drifting in semi-consciousness. Latrell's bedside chat had been two nights ago now, and since then he'd only seen his sentry, the odoriferous old gentleman who was passing for a doctor, and the wispy young woman in gingham who came in to clean and bring him his meals.

Boner would be fine, he thought to himself. The apartment would take care of him, and if and when these yahoos decided to quit screwing around and put a bullet in his head, well, the dog could find his way out of the courtyard and fend for himself when the food bin ran out. New York was a big city, with table scraps from 20,000 restaurants and plenty of good souls. He'd been a street mutt once, and he'd be one again. The dog would be fine.

Each of these mornings he'd awakened to find fresh clothes laid out on a sideboard in the corner of the room near the lavatory, and today was no different. There was no modern plumbing, but the basins of hot and cold water had been rinsed and refilled for him, and he washed and dressed himself. The dyed wool and cotton fabric of the clothing was rough against his skin, and the seams were meticulously hand-sewn.

Whatever universe this was that he'd landed in, there were almost certainly worse places to die.

There was a polite triple-knock, and he heard the locks outside being thrown. The heavy door opened, and four men in dark fatigues came into the room and took post by the entryway. A few seconds passed, and Edward Latrell walked in.

"Good morning, John," Latrell said. "My, but you look fit as a fiddle."

"You look just great too, Ed."

Latrell smiled, and motioned him to the table. "Would you have a seat with me? I have something I want to talk to you about."

John pulled a chair back, and sat down.

"You can leave us," Latrell said to his entourage. "We need some time alone here. And John, did you need a coffee and a smoke, is that right?"

"That would be just awesome," John said.

"Wilson, ask Gretchen to clear these dishes and bring us some coffee, and some tobacco for John."

One of the exiting men nodded sharply, and the door closed behind him.

The two of them sat regarding each other, and John mirrored the small, expectant smile Latrell wore.

"Quite a place you've got here."

"You have no idea," Latrell said.

The girl he'd caught glimpses of since he'd been conscious stepped quietly into the room and put a tin of tobacco and a few rolling papers on the table between them, then quickly gathered

128

the dishes and silverware from the table and left the way she'd come.

"So Ed," John said. "What the fuck?"

"By that you mean, what are you doing here?"

"I meant what I said."

Gretchen returned with their coffee, and she carefully placed a steaming cup in front of each of them.

"That's a good girl," Latrell said. He patted her on the behind, and his hand lingered there. She froze in place, and kept her eyes on the floor. At length, he smiled and gave her a sharp swat, and she left them again.

"By the way, John," Latrell said, cocking his head toward the door. "Do you want her?"

"What is she, Ed, sixteen?" John said. "Now what would I do with a tenth grader?"

Latrell had been rolling a cigarette, one-handed, from one of the papers and a large pinch of the dry leaf tobacco. He ran the finished product across his tongue to seal it, and passed it across the table with a wooden match.

"Why, anything you want," he said.

John only looked at him, bemused, as he struck a match against the grain of the table and lit the makeshift cigarette. The raw smoke was pungent and strong, but the stinging in his lungs was welcome.

"You want a drag?" John asked, offering the cigarette. "Maybe it'll put some hair on your chest."

Latrell's smile hardened a bit around the edges, and he shook his head, no.

Edward Latrell's textbook case of *alopecia universalis* had struck in his first weeks as an inmate at Marion, back in the late seventies. The newspapers had detailed his trial and conviction back then, painting him with lurid tabloid prose as a crazed, racist zealot. The last story of note had told of the aftermath of a ferocious three-day rave he'd thrown in solitary, after the news had come that his wife had mysteriously passed away in custody.

129

The bulls had elected to strap him down for his own protection, but the rabid screaming went on and on. When it finally became quiet in the tiny cell, they'd flipped on the light to check, and they'd found him sleeping peacefully. Every hair on his body had fallen out, never to return.

And clearly, he was still a little touchy about that.

"Look, Ed," John said, "I'm as patient as the next guy, and I realize that there's probably some personal risk for me in pissing you off, but I'm really going to have to ask you to get to the point."

Latrell nodded his head thoughtfully, and then his face brightened. "Let's go for a walk," he said.

The air here smelled different, or maybe this was just the way air actually smelled. It was cool and sunny as they walked, and the breeze brought scents of spruce and clean turned earth. These aromas were nigh alien to the nose of a New Yorker, but not entirely unpleasant.

The two of them were walking together, about ten yards ahead of an armed cadre of guards. His eyes moved across the encampment around them and to the mountainous horizon beyond. There were no landmarks that he recognized, but that was to be expected. An operation like this would have to be remote to stay hidden, as far from the realm of the recognizable as possible.

There were vehicles here and there, but the people by and large were moving on foot or on horseback. There was a stark separation, too, between soldier and citizen. Here a blacksmith was hammering out a wrought-iron pot rack at a coal-fired forge, and there to the side was his waiting client, in polished boots and camouflage, an Uzi hanging by his hand. It was Colonial Williamsburg with submachine guns.

A simple but effective woodland cover had been applied to the structures and to the grounds. It took a second look at times to discern the outline of a residence, bunker or storage building amongst the surrounding landscape. For the most part, though, it was clear that the ingenious mix of natural and manmade cloaking was designed to obscure the camp from the air.

"John, you recognized the details of the September eleventh actions, didn't you?" Latrell said.

John didn't answer.

"And you've deduced, I'm sure, that the . . . terrorists took advantage of your thinking, that their leadership had been auditing your IRC forum there on the Internet, and that they formed their plan for that day based on your ideas?"

"Yeah, I deduced that. And Nobel invented dynamite to make the world a better place. Ideas get loose," John said.

"That's certainly one way to look at it."

They were approaching a series of long open-ended Quonset huts, and Latrell steered them into the wide mouth of the first one as they walked on. There were four Piper Cubs there in various models and states of repair, with men and women in overalls hovering around them. At the end of the hangar, he saw three old Cessna Agwagons, with their wing tanks being changed out and steam-cleaned.

Cropdusters.

"You also know that the scope of the attacks was very small compared to the grand day of terror that you'd outlined in your writing."

"Well, thank God for human frailty, right?" John said. "I guess you can convince a few assholes to die for an asshole cause, but cowardice or good judgment sometimes prevails for the rest."

They were passing into the second hangar, and to the right and left were a number of oblong wooden crates, stacked like cordwood, with *Medical Supplies* spray-stenciled in black on their facing sides. One of the crates lay open, and it contained straw packing and a heavy dark tube, about six inches in girth by seven feet, with a grip and trigger along its length.

The concave metal wall to his left was papered with a gallery

131

of four-by-six-foot architect's blueprints, originals by their texture and condition. The World Trade Center was first, with sheet after sheet detailing its structure down to the foundation. And there were others down the line. The Sears Tower, the Empire State Building, the Hancock, others. One toward the end took an extra once-over to register properly, its layout being such a departure from its companions.

Hoover Dam.

"You're exactly right," Latrell said. "That's exactly why I've brought you here."

There were larger crates on wide pallets as they continued on, and a long white cylinder with stubby wings and silver exhaust nozzles was suspended in a chain lift beside them, its maintenance panels open.

"Jeez oh pete," John whispered.

He'd seen pictures of the Tomahawk, of course, but in person it was bigger than he'd imagined. The missile was as long as a Cadillac, and the deployed winglets spanned almost twelve feet. His mind took a quick snapshot of the scene, and he mentally counted the surrounding crates as the tour continued.

Forty-one.

"We picked that one up in Baluchistan. The others were duds recovered after the strikes on the aspirin factory in Sudan, and in Afghanistan and Iraq in the nineties. They were repaired in China and shipped over, in exchange for two working models to reverse-engineer.

"Oh, by the way," Latrell added, "no smoking up ahead."

The next building was bristling with guns of all shapes and sizes, racks and racks of them. Many of the tall stacks of boxes here were labeled by type of ammunition, and others were stenciled in dark red letters, *C4, Semtex, RDX, HMX, PETN.* John took another quick set of mental images. There was enough high explosive and detonating hardware here to blow the side off a mountain.

One more thing. Along one wall stood a line of twelve stain-

132

less steel refrigerators, chained and padlocked. A sweaty man with a slung M-16 and a respirator hanging from his neck was tending the gas generator that ran power to them. Whatever the guy was guarding in those coolers, it probably wasn't Jolt Cola.

The group passed through, and headed into the final hangar.

"Now this I'm proud of," Latrell said.

John stopped in the doorway, and had to let the scene before him sink in for a moment. He searched his memory for some possible explanation, and in a few seconds he'd found what he was looking for. He let the recalled headlines scroll past his mind's eye.

Air Force Baffled by Pilots' Disappearance

Debris on Mountainside May Be Missing Planes

Investigation: "99.9% Sure" Mystery Planes Crashed

In April of 1997, two Air Force jets had been flying a routine training mission near Gila Bend, Arizona, carrying a full load of armament. At around 10:00 P.M. their radios and transponders had gone silent. Their fellow pilots reported that the planes broke formation, changed course, lit their afterburners and headed north-northeast at terrain-hugging altitude. Search teams were deployed, but after weeks the investigation ended with no convincing explanation of the event. The planes and the pilots had disappeared and were presumed lost.

Lost somewhere in the mountains of Colorado.

In front of him was an A-10 Warthog, a flying Gatling gun capable of raining 4,200 Coke-bottle-sized incendiary rounds from the sky per minute. On rolling cradles under the craft's empty hardpoints were four 500-pound bombs, JDAMs by the look of them.

Farther down the large hangar, though, was the *pièce de résistance*. There in majestic and deadly profile stood an F/A-18 Hornet, with a full complement of Sidewinders and a long-range AMRAAM slung under its sleek gray wings.

A goat had wandered in through the open corrugated doors,

and was now nibbling grass from between the wheels of the most formidable tactical fighter aircraft that had ever flown.

Unreal.

"John?"

"Hm?"

"Come on, let's have some lunch," Latrell said. "And then you and I have some planning to do."

21

Jeannie sat alone in the semi-darkened room, clicking through her electronic slides. Her eyes flitted over the words and pictures projected on the wide screen, anchoring key points and making an occasional edit for clarity or emphasis.

The upcoming meeting had been a drag to prepare for, but it was an important and necessary step. IRIN had been delivering a steady flow of suspects at the foot-soldier level, but this was to be a status update on the big picture, requested from on high. All agencies were to be represented by direct decision makers, and they all were to leave with actionable paths forward.

She paused on one of the slides, and sat back to consider its unnerving contents. It was a tree diagram, the type law enforcement sometimes used to depict the structure of organized crime. This one was an extreme simplification of the data that lay behind it, but its form met its function well.

Big picture indeed.

Rudy had stepped into the room with her mid-morning latte, and he sat down across the conference table.

"Where have you been? I was worried about you," Jeannie said. "Did you sleep in this morning?"

"Doctor," he replied. "Just poking my prostate, nothing to worry about. Come to think of it, though, I went in for a throat culture."

She smiled. "I'm a little sleepy today."

"Let me get a look at you," he said, sizing her up. "My, your cheeks are rosy. And there's a peculiar twinkle in your eye."

She looked at him, put her palm to her chest, and sighed.

"Oh, no you did not," Rudy said.

She covered her face with her hands, nodded, and giggled.

"Why you little skank," he said. "You took Lieutenant Rob to the secret garden, didn't you? Didn't you?"

"Oh my God, Rudy. I'm still . . . fluttery down there."

He checked his watch. "Okay, we've got a few minutes, tell me everything, come on, spill."

"I'm not gonna tell you anything, it's private," she said, blushing.

"Well, it's not going to be private for long, I can tell you that much." He was flipping through the pad on his clipboard.

"What are you looking for?"

"I'm seeing who had the box for last night."

Her mouth slowly dropped open.

"You have Got to be kidding me," she said.

Rudy found the sheet he was looking for and ran his finger down a column, then across a row on the hand-drawn, photocopied calendar grid. "God, damnit," he said, thumping his finger on the paper. "That little bow-tie-wearing, lactose-intolerant pretentious Harvard prick, Tyler. Like he needs the money, he still lives at home, for crissakes."

"You little wankers were running a pool on when I'd lose my virginity?"

Rudy looked at her, and blinked innocently.

"What?" he said.

She looked across the table at the sheet in front of him. "I've seen that up in the Xerox room, on the bulletin board. I thought it was fantasy football."

"Sports betting is against the rules," he said.

She shook her head, disbelieving. "How much did he win?"

"Well, it's a progressive, so let me see." He pulled over his TI-

83+ and punched buttons, hit memory-plus. "Shit," he said, sliding the calculator across the table to her. "There goes my Lexus downpayment."

She read the digits on the display. $9,624.80.

"How long has this been going on?" she asked.

"A little over two years, quarter limit," he replied. "Hey, don't you look at me like that, you're the one who's always telling us, no secrets, we don't have any secrets, secrets are weapons, yadda yadda. We love you, baby-doll, we believe you, and we do what you say. You sauce-box, you."

Rob breezed into the room, and put a bottle of water on the table in front of her. "Good morning," he said. "Rudy, do you want an Evian, or anything?"

"Good morning, Rob," Jeannie said quietly.

"No, I'm good on fluids, Rob," Rudy replied. "Just a little short on cash." He watched the other man find his seat for the meeting, three places down from Jeannie. "You couldn't have waited until next Thursday, could you?"

Her presentation had gone well, with much discussion, and she had just finished taking them through the tree diagram that would impel the remainder of the meeting.

At the root of the structure were representations of hundreds of *Feeders*, her term for minor entities or individuals that had in some way contributed momentum or aid to the September 11th attacks, through overt commission or informed omission. The list was long, and comprised constituents ranging from front-charities and radical church leaders to professed US allies in the Gulf states and Near East. Those who were citizens or tracked illegals were in the process of being rounded up and brought in, both here and in their homelands.

The next level, the *Actors*, included the hands-on perpetrators, smugglers, conspirators and button men. Beyond the dead hijackers themselves, there were a surprising number of their associates who were known and still at large. It was estimated that many thousands of young males had passed through terror training camps in Afghanistan, Iraq and elsewhere. These trainees were now thought to be waiting in clusters at hundreds of launching points, within the US and abroad.

Next were the *Drivers*, leaders of terrorist cells with access to laundered money and logistical support. This level had strategic autonomy to plan and carry out acts of terror, large or small, on their discretion. Mohammed Atta had been the Driver on the 11th, and he had uncharacteristically given his life in the operation. Perhaps he'd wanted to ensure that at least part of that attack actually went according to plan.

A very small part, they were learning now.

The Drivers had direct responsibility for individual atrocities, and their past actions were presented in bold type and attached to the relevant boxes by thin lines:

Khobar Towers
USS Cole
US Embassy, Tanzania
US Embassy, Kenya
World Trade Center bombing, 1993

The list of attacks went back through recent history, but three incidents, though separated widely by time and geography, seemed to rise up off the screen together.

Murrah Federal Building, Oklahoma City, 1995
TWA Flight 800, 1996
Anthrax mailings, 2001

Finally, there were the *Leaders*. Usama bin Laden and Ayman Al-Zawahiri were featured in boxes at this level, of course. But there were many other blank squares on each side of them. These had no names or pictures yet, but IRIN had hypothesized their logical profiles in brief descriptions.

The projected deep-cover locations of these Leaders were wide ranging. Some would have been apparent even to a middle-school World Issues student: *Afghanistan, Chechnya, Syria, Iraq, Iran, North Korea, and the Philippines.*

Others were less apparent, but still not surprising: *Indonesia, Columbia, Greece, Spain, Turkey, Peru, the Congo, Pakistan, India, and Liberia.*

Still others would raise the hackles of the most seasoned intelligence operatives in the room, for differing but obvious reasons: *China, Russia, Mexico, Canada, France, Germany, and Great Britain.*

The neural network had generated text that described each of these unknown Leaders in varying depth and detail. IRIN was still working and watching, and as the days passed there would be more clues and clearer sketches of the individuals at this highest level.

The last box on the right was the same size as the others, but it stood out nonetheless. It stood out on its content, but also on the alarming number of black lines that connected it to other cells, other acts, other agendas. Other allies.

US neo-revolutionary faction

Radical anarcho-libertarian/racist/separatist/Constitutionalist influences

Focal point of a nationwide network of armed and active local cells

Headquarters (confidence: 44%): Western US

Deportment: PARAMILITARY

Jeannie had called a break, and her guests were now returning from their phone calls and Blackberry exchanges to take their seats. The NSA man, Walt Kamuck, was the last to reenter the room. He remained standing.

"Before we get started," he said, "who are these two again?"

With the thumb and little finger of his right hand, he was pointing at Rob and Rudy.

"They're on my team," Jeannie said.

Kamuck shook his head, and walked to the head of the table. "I don't think it's appropriate for them to sit through this next section. Or to have been here at all, for that matter."

Rudy raised his eyebrows, and looked to Jeannie.

"They both have standing Top Secret clearance, with an SCI rider and special access waivers from DSS for this program," she said. "They went through the same screening you did to get in this room."

"I don't want to get into a pissing match," Kamuck said. "Are we really going to have to take this upstairs?"

She looked at the thin, bookish man evenly.

"You *are* upstairs, Walter."

A voice with a familiar accent spoke up from the dim seating area at the back of the room.

"Jeannie. I have to agree with Walt on this."

It was Ari Darukyan, an old mentor from her early days at DoD. She hadn't seen him in years, and he'd apparently come in during the break.

There was a sinking hollow in the pit of her stomach, the first physical symptom of a power shift in the room. Someone somewhere must have determined that it would be most effective if the rug were jerked out from under her by a father figure.

She leaned back in her chair, looked at Rob, then at Rudy, and then down at the table in front of her. Without a word, they gathered their things and left the room.

"What's going on here?" Jeannie said.

Kamuck smiled. "DARPA is about research, Jean, and you do a fine job with the data," he said. "But we're at war now, and there's precious little time for conspiracy theories. You've given us a blizzard of detail here, and plenty of trails we could all follow right out the window, but it's not what we need right now." He waited for her to acknowledge him, but got no response. "Understand?"

Ari had walked to the head of the table. "Sit down, Walt, while you still can," he said softly.

Walter Kamuck found a seat.

"Jeannie," Ari began, "what we've been discussing, and what we're about to discuss cannot leave this room, under any circumstances. That's why we asked your associates out. The risk of a leak is just too great, and I hope you'll understand."

"A leak? My office doesn't leak. My people don't leak. It's the FBI that's topping the *New York Times* bestseller list this morning, not us. Never us." She was referring to the blistering biography of double-agent Robert Hanssen that had hit the shelves in the past week. There were three more similar exposés coming out on its heels, one after another, and the Bureau was stinging over the embarrassing, inexcusable ineptness Hanssen's fifteen years of undetected subterfuge was highlighting.

Darukyan put up a hand to quell a threatening eruption from the right side of the table.

"Jeannie, listen to me," he said. "We have nothing but confidence in you, and appreciation for your work in getting toward the bottom of this rat's nest. There is a feeling, however, that the knowledge you are uncovering must be managed by a broader team."

She didn't respond, and he came nearer, and lowered his voice.

"Look at me, Jeannie."

She did.

"On the one hand, *bien aimé*, we have the truth. And on the other, there's what really happened. You know this as well as I do. We are all here in this room, all only concerned with the truth, until further notice. And the truth is, al Qaeda attacked us on September the eleventh, and everything, everything depends on the focus and the might we must now bring to bear in response."

"You don't understand," she said.

"This country has to run, Jeannie, and it runs on confidence, it is fueled by confidence. We need to give confidence back to the people of this country, show confidence to our allies, and our enemies, and our corporations, and most certainly to Wall Street. And the path to confidence is straight and narrow. It can't look like this," he said, pointing to the elaborate network diagram IRIN had created.

141

"You're talking about public relations," Jeannie said quietly. "This is real, Ari."

Walt Kamuck puffed his cheeks and exhaled, shaking his head.

"We know that it is, Jeannie," Ari said. "But the minute what you've presented here leaves this room we're at a whole new level of terror, by orders of magnitude. It could sink us, our economy, our government, beyond our ability to recover, do you see that? It would be exactly as the terrorists intend. The population will accept a faraway, credible enemy and a band of radicals that blindsided us on a single day. They have accepted that. And we can hit back at that, we can win against that, and we must win."

He tapped the illuminated screen. "But this?" he said. "This is panic. Hell, even the *Los Angeles Times* would be clamoring for martial law."

"So what then?" Jeannie said. "You're going to bury my work, and me along with it?"

"Don't worry your pretty head, Jean," Kamuck said. "IRIN is too valuable to bury. It's now a shared NSA, CIA and FBI asset, by order of the Directors, and you and your people can go back to doing whatever it is you all do. We'll need some of them, of course, for tech support and training, but those have already been requisitioned and moved over."

Jeannie ignored him, but she felt the color rising in her face.

"Ari," she said, "don't do this. If you take our eyes off what's here, if we don't move on this, you're leaving this country open to something unimaginable. Keep a lid on it, by all means, but we have to act. It's in the works, it's coming, they're not finished, and you're going to let it happen if you do this."

"It's already done, Jeannie," he replied. "Your work won't be forgotten, it's just got to go on the back burner for a while."

She stood up, snapped her laptop computer shut and tucked it under her arm. "This isn't over," she said, and she headed for the door.

"Oh, it's over, honey," Kamuck said. The door closed behind her, and he looked around at the other men. "What a piece of ass, huh?"

"Walt," Ari said, "I'm not going to warn you, because I've warned you before. Just know this about Jeannie Reese. She keeps score. And she never forgets."

Rudy and Rob were outside the conference room when she emerged.

"Did that go as well as I think it did?" Rob asked.

"Walk with me," Jeannie said.

There were a lot of strange faces here, and she waited until they were in the elevator to speak again.

"They're taking IRIN, refocusing it," she said.

"Refocusing where?" Rudy asked.

"FBI, CIA, NSA," she said. "On leads they should have been following all along. You read the papers, they're getting pilloried for failing to anticipate the eleventh. They need to dig themselves out of the hole they're in, and IRIN will give them enough intel to fill in the blanks and deflect the fingerpointing. They're going to use it to look back, and stop us from looking forward."

"They can't do that, can they?" Rob asked. "You've got autonomy on this, from the Oval Office, right?"

"This is war now, Rob," Rudy said. "And in this town that means politics and PR. You're in the Navy, you should know all about the wisdom of a bureaucracy."

"The President is just taking counsel from his advisors," Jeannie said. "It's these agency wonks that are screwing us over. They're guarding their turf, in the guise of protecting the country. Sons of bitches just squeezed me out of my own meeting."

The elevator doors hissed open at their floor.

"If you liked that, you're gonna love this," Rudy said.

Across her huge office level, Jeannie saw that her people were in their cubicles, but they were all standing behind their chairs. In their seats were white-coats from Information Systems, pecking away at the keyboards.

Her keyboards.

"What's happening, Rudy?" she said.

"They're shutting us out, changing passwords, creating a new administrative layer," he replied. "Starting tomorrow, we have to go to NSA for access."

"My office," she said.

The three of them walked briskly to the corner suite. She put her hand on the doorknob and tried it.

Locked.

She slid her keycard through the reader.

Red light.

"You or me, Rob," she said.

"Oh, let me," he replied. He gave the door a flat-footed kick at latch-level, and it banged open hard.

Inside, a soldier with an assault rifle wheeled and leveled his sight at Rob's head.

Jeannie stepped in front of him. "Secure that weapon, mister," she said, "or I swear to God you'd better kill me before I get across this room."

The barrel of the gun didn't waver. At a quiet word from the man seated with his back to the door, the guard snapped his rifle to his side in three taut motions.

Jeannie's office chair swiveled around, and she recognized the middle-aged, intense man in uniform who occupied it.

Deputy Director of the Defense Intelligence Agency, Benjamin Fuller, and Rob's commanding officer.

The man stood, and returned Rob's salute.

"Ms. Reese," Fuller said. "It's a pleasure to see you again, and I apologize for the circumstances. We'll be finished here in a few hours, and I suggest you find a conference room and cool off. And Lieutenant Vance, I wanted to be here to thank you personally, for all your help in this."

Jeannie looked at Rob, and it took her long seconds, but then she understood.

Fuller sat back down in her chair, and as he returned to his work at her computer, he spoke to them over his shoulder.

"And Mr. Darukyan asked me to tell you three that the time has come for a much deserved vacation. Starting now."

The three walked in silence to the bank of elevators. Two DIA security men were watching them from a discreet distance, with walkie-talkies pressed to their ears.

Jeannie thumbed the down-arrow and handed her laptop to Rudy, then watched the numbers on the display count up to their floor. With a peaceful doorbell tone, the double doors slid open.

"Um, you two go ahead, I'll take the next one," Rudy said.

Jeannie stepped into the car, Rob followed her, and when the doors closed they started their descent.

Between the third and second floors, she pushed the emergency-stop button, and the elevator chunked to an abrupt halt. She turned to Rob, and her eyes were glistening with an emotion he hadn't yet seen in them. He had seen her sad, and even afraid, but he had never imagined he would see her so utterly defeated.

"Jeannie," he said.

She dropped her bag from her shoulder, stepped across the car and sent a punch to his solar plexus that drove the wind out of him. As he doubled over she turned his wrist behind him and slammed him hard against the opposite wall, and held him there.

"Let me explain," he wheezed into the paneling.

"*I wanted to thank you personally for all your help in this*, isn't that what he said, your boss back there?" She twisted his arm and drove her free fist into his right kidney. "Nobody plays me, you lying, two-faced rapist mole, you'd better start fighting back, I want to kill you fair and square."

"Just give me two minutes, two minutes, Jeannie, please, then you can do whatever you want."

She kept her hold for a few more seconds, then released his

arm and stepped away from him until her back was against the facing wall of the car.

He turned to her and held out his hands, as if he could will her to believe him. "I haven't lied to you, I couldn't lie to you. I don't know what he was talking about, but I would never do anything to hurt you, I swear."

She was unmoved, and only getting angrier.

"Oh, please," she spat. "At least you can spare me the pathetic come-ons, you got what you came here for. You got a lot more than I ever should have given you."

"What are you talking about? I just did my job."

She took a step across and slapped him. He'd seen it coming, but he hadn't raised a hand.

"Last night, in the car, you were just doing your job?" she said. "I trusted you, with everything, and you used me like a fucking Kleenex."

"Look, yes, I've sent them status reports on the work, of course I have, because those were my orders, but you knew that. You saw what went out, and that was all that I ever told them."

"I don't believe you," she said. "And I can't believe I ever did."

He looked to the floor, reached out his hand to the railing for support and slowly lowered himself to his knees in front of her.

"Please," he said softly, "if you never speak to me again, if this is the last time I see you, please remember what I'm saying, and maybe someday you'll believe it." His voice was strained as he pushed the words through a swelling despair in his throat. "I might have been naïve to trust my commanding officer, but I don't know any other way to live, I'm a soldier. You can go away thinking I'm stupid, or gullible or a tool, but Jeannie, you can't think I set out to hurt you. It's not in me to do something like that, I swear on my life, I couldn't have done it even if they'd asked me to." He lowered his eyes. "I couldn't have. I care about you too much."

The car was silent for what seemed like hours and hours, but only a minute or so had actually passed when he felt her hand touch his head. Her fingers moved gently down the side of his face and then under his chin, and he let her tilt his head back until he was looking up to her. She studied him, and at length she seemed to find what she was looking for, somewhere deep in his eyes.

"All right," she said quietly. "All right, Rob. The bastards played us both."

"I'm going back up," he said. "I'm going to resign my commission."

She helped him to his feet, straightened his lapels, fixed the collar of his jacket. "No, Rob, you can't resign. Every bit of power we've still got, we've got to hold onto. God knows we might need it." She pulled the stop button out, and the elevator jolted into motion again.

"I'm sorry I hit you," she added.

He rubbed his cheek with the back of his hand, and wiped his eyes.

"Which time?" he asked.

Rudy was waiting for them when the doors opened, and he looked them both over, and smiled. "It's a long way down from the fifth floor, huh?"

"We can't be seen leaving together," Jeannie said. "Let's scatter, and meet at my apartment in ninety minutes. Though for what purpose I honestly do not know."

22

"So, what's for lunch?" John said. "Man, I could eat a sheep."

Latrell smiled.

They were seated across from each other at a polished wooden table in his greatroom. The cloudless blue sky and a vista of forested mountains were framed behind him in a twenty-foot triangle of picture windows. There were shelves and shelves of leather-bound books along the hewn log walls, and a crackling fireplace as wide and tall as the mouth of a stone grotto pushed back the autumn chill in the air.

"You mentioned something about planning when we were outside, what did you mean by that?" John said.

"John, we've lost time because of your recovery from the effects of your trip out here to join us, and time is of the essence now. I don't know much about you, no one does, apparently. But I know you're a quick study, so I don't think there's any need to over-explain our situation."

"Maybe I'm not as sharp as you think."

"If one-tenth of what's been written about you over the years is true then your mind is a weapon more powerful than my army. You're legendary, on the Internet and in the underground; the things you've done are incredible."

"You shouldn't believe everything you read."

"You're modest. But I do know one thing, that you must hate the establishment as I do. Whatever your politics, I'm sure we share a common enemy. And the things you've conceived in the past are nothing compared to what we can do together. I've built a new world here, a world that's ready to become much, much bigger. And I need your help."

John bit his lip, thoughtfully. He pulled the tin of tobacco from his shirt pocket, and began to roll a smoke.

"You're asking me to help you plan a terrorist attack against the United States of America," he said.

"*The* terrorist attack, John. A single day that fulfills your original vision, a master stroke that cracks the foundation of that den of thieves in Washington, brings them down into the dust. And gives us all a chance for a new beginning."

John held up the crude cigarette he'd made. "Do you mind?" he said.

"Please, help yourself," Latrell replied. He picked a fireplace match from a box on the table, struck it and held the flame out as John leaned forward to it.

"So after this big day," John said, "you've obviously prepared, stop me if I'm off track, to use the massive destruction and its resulting period of widespread havoc to spark off some sort of sociopolitical rebellion."

"That's right. These people here with me, these are the core, but we have friends at every level, in nearly every state here and abroad, even in government. We have suicide bombers, and we have senators. It cannot be done with soldiers alone, you're exactly right. The United States is still a representative republic, and the people must choose. They will see their elitist leadership for what it is, weak and corrupt and powerless to fulfill its duty to protect them, and they will choose. We have our candidates in the wings, and they have their platforms. They only need the door to be opened."

"Candidates, like David Duke? Like you, when you were running?" John said. "Forgive me for saying so, but you weren't exactly mainstream enough for the average voter."

149

Latrell shook his head. "Young, bright faces, John, and sea-soned veterans along with them. Their messages are prepared, and America will be ready for them. We're going back to the basics, where the majority in the heartland has always wanted to go. Our political arm is quite gifted, and well funded. And as the leaders of the Democratic and Republican parties would attest, once these candidates get a whiff of power, they're actually much easier to recruit than warriors."

"I imagine they are."

"Politicians are prostitutes," Latrell said, "but transactions with whores are refreshingly straightforward."

"And you're all set with the media, I assume? To get the message out?" John asked.

"The Internet is a major outlet, of course, but we've made enormous inroads in radio, and now even in television. It's been a slow process, but one that's well underway. The print media have been more of a challenge, the Zionists keep a death-grip on the mainstream, but even they will have to yield to the hue and cry when the time comes."

John took a last drag on his smoke, and stubbed it in the ash-tray. "Yeah, those mother-humping Zionists," he exhaled, shaking his head.

Latrell allowed a silence to settle into the room.

"I need your answer, John. Will you help me?"

John leaned back in his chair. "What do you need me for, Ed?"

"I need a plan that cannot fail."

"And what makes you think I can help you with that?"

"You helped us the first time, with a brilliant attack you rat-tled off the top of your head, with absolutely no forethought. It took you seconds to type it out, and it took us years to execute it."

"I did not help you the first time," John said. "I had no inten-tion of helping anyone."

"But you did help us. We couldn't have done it without you,

and we need for you to help us again. Only now you'll have the time to think it through, and the resources to perfect it."

"Hmm," John said, studying the varnished whorls in the wood of the tabletop between them. "What's your timeframe?"

"We need to act quickly, as quickly as we possibly can. There are . . . things I can't share with you, I wish I could. But trust, there is very little time."

"Things you can't share with me?"

"I can tell you this. We are not destroying America, I swear to you. We're giving our all to save her. And you're our last, best chance."

John nodded his head, considering.

"And John," Latrell said, "I can give you anything you want in return, on my word. I don't know enough about you to know what that might be, but I assure you, I can give it to you. Leadership, at my side, if that's what you want." He got no reaction. "Money? Power? A kingdom, or a quiet corner where you'll never be disturbed again, John. Whatever you can imagine, I can give to you, whatever the spoils of this war can yield, you can have it."

"I've got to admit it, Ed, that's a very intriguing offer you're making." John settled all four legs of his chair to the floor. "Somebody tried this before, though, right?"

Latrell sat back, thoughtfully. "What . . . who do you mean? Jefferson—"

"No, no," John said. "Jefferson lost that argument. Who am I thinking of? Not the Amish, or the Mennonites, they leave everybody who's not one of them the fuck alone. A national, utopian, agrarian society, now where have I heard that idea before?" He snapped his fingers, smacked his forehead. "Oh, yeah."

Latrell raised his eyebrows, or rather, the spots on his lower forehead where his eyebrows should have been.

"Cambodia," John said, evenly. "The Khmer Rouge."

The other man's expression didn't immediately change. Over

long seconds, the pale skin seemed to gradually slacken against the juts and hollows of his skull, as if he'd released tension on the twine holding a thin mask of calm and sanity in its place. The eyes darkened and sank, and then they flicked to the back corner of the room.

John heard heavy footsteps approaching behind him.

"So, as great as it all sounds, you fucking lunatic?" John said. "Think I'm gonna pass."

He heard a wet crack as the room pitched forward and went dark and sparkly, and his last, fading thoughts surprised him. With every fiber as consciousness drifted away, he was wishing it was a bullet and not the butt of a rifle that had just struck him in the back of the head.

23

"Jay, it's Jeannie, how're we doing?"

There was a pause on the other end of the line, and then she heard her old friend's voice.

"Hey, Mom, good afternoon, how are you feeling?"

"Jay?" she said. "What's wrong, is someone there with you?"

"That's right, Mother, I'm working, but I have a little time to talk. I called you at your place, but I got your . . . machine."

"I've been furloughed, Jay, they've taken over my project and my people. We've got to keep a line open though, you've got to keep me in the loop. Will you do that?"

"Oh, I know all about your vacation. Your friend Phoebe told me some great stories."

"Phoebe?" Jeannie said. "FBI? The FBI is there with you?"

"That's right. Oh, and I wanted to thank you for that pork roast, from my birthday? I got up this morning, and you could smell it all over the house."

Jay Marshall was a brilliant man, but his cover patter sounded like amateur night at secret-agent school. She was going to have to keep this short.

"Jay—"

"So, yeah, I'm a little under the gun here, Mom—"

"Jay, I get it, I get it, just tell me, can you send me anything yet, on the reconstruction, the Phreak file. Is there a partial image?"

"Sweetie, I've really gotta go, now. You know what, though? I'll send you a picture of Eileen and the boys later on, it's the one we're putting on the Christmas card."

"Use my Yahoo address, and encrypt it with my public key, Jay, okay? And thanks."

"Okay, Mom, I love you too. Hugs and kisses to Aunt Belinda. Uh huh, bye bye."

The line clicked to silence, but she listened for another thirty seconds for any sign of a tap. All quiet.

Rob was only now arriving, and he walked into her sunken living room and slipped off his jacket. "Any good news?" he asked.

She held up her finger for a few more moments, then pushed the button that ended the call.

"No," she said. "Maybe, I don't know. There are FBI agents all over Jay's place, and he couldn't talk, but he's going to try to send me what he's got, if he can."

Rudy emerged from the bedroom, brushing his teeth.

"Could you not do that, please?" Jeannie said. "You're going to drip on my Persian rug."

He stopped brushing in mid-stroke. "You never told me you had such a nice place," Rudy said. "It's very Swiss." This last word was not well suited to being spoken through toothpaste foam, and a cloud of tiny white bubbles floated down onto the hand-knotted silk pile at his feet.

He saw the look in her eye, and walked backward with exaggerated care to the bathroom.

"I'm not used to having houseguests," she said quietly.

Rob sat down across from her. "We don't have to stay here," he said. "It just seemed like—"

"No, we need to stay together, it's best this way. I can adjust."

Rudy reentered the room, running his tongue over his teeth. "So, now that I'm all minty-fresh, what's the plan, chief?" he said.

"The plan? What plan? We've got no resources, no access, no staff and no swing. We're shut out, Rudy, what's to plan?" she said. "And do you always carry a toothbrush with you?"

Rudy sat down on the floor near them, cross-legged. "No, don't be silly. I used yours."

She closed her eyes, took a deep breath, and exhaled slowly.

"Listen," Rob said, "you've got your laptop, and you've got some of your files there, don't you?"

She nodded, noncommittal.

"Okay. And you've got an office here with a PC, Internet access, and we've got our phones, and our Rolodex, right, Rudy?"

"That's right, I don't know what we're waiting for," Rudy said.

"Guys, I appreciate the pep rally, but we don't have IRIN, and without IRIN we've got nothing at all."

"Jeannie," Rob said, "IRIN is only software, and you wrote it, didn't you? You know how it does what it does."

"So?"

"So let's just do what it would do."

"Rob, if we had ninety years, the three of us could only do a day of its thinking," she said.

"But it's not thinking, Jeannie, anyway not like you can think. Give me the choice, I'd rather have you anytime."

"Me, too," Rudy said. "And besides, what's our alternative? I suppose we could just sit on our hands and wait for the next wave of terror, and have the cheap thrill of saying I told you so. If we live through it, that is."

She looked to one, and then the other, and before she looked away they caught a glimpse of the slight girl of twenty-two that usually stayed back far behind her eyes.

"Well, I say we're not going out like that," Rob said. "I didn't sign on with you to go out like that, and you didn't come this far to roll over and play dead dog. And don't tell me we've got nothing, that's bullshit. The three of us took a direct hit from a fucking Boeing 757, and we're still standing. We're unbeatable, Jeannie, we cannot be beaten, and you've got a duty to believe that."

Rob held out his hand between them, palm down. Jeannie's eyes were on the floor, but at length her right hand rose slowly up to cover his. Rudy looked at both of them, and after a moment, he laid his hand on top of theirs.

"*In umbra, igitur, pugnabimus*," Rob said.

Jeannie smiled weakly, and though her eyes were grim her two companions saw a familiar fire there just beginning to rekindle.

"I'm sorry to queer the Three Musketeers moment," Rudy said softly, "but I had to blow my Latin professor to pass the class. What did he just say, exactly?"

Jeannie looked at Rob. "It's a black-ops motto," she said. "They say all the old-school SEALs had it tattooed over their hearts."

"*From the shadows, then, we will fight.*"

Most of the revenue that had made Jay Marshall a wealthy man had come from government contracts. But despite years of daily dealings with them, he had never quite gotten used to working with the Feds.

It could be said that all businesses create some harmful effects, whatever their positive contributions may be. Pharmaceutical companies market drugs that heal people, but those same drugs inadvertently kill 180,000 Americans every year. Grow and sell tobacco, and you're helping stuff 33,000 coffins monthly. Make recliners, TV remotes, doughnuts or hammocks, and 300,000 citizens die from inactivity and overweight per annum. Cars, toys, kitchenware, beer, fertilizer or fuel oil, anything you produce is subject to abuse.

One might correctly argue that those industries enjoyed the cover of personal choice. Nobody makes you smoke or sit on your ass too much, or drink and drive. You don't even have to take the pills the drug industry pushes like soda and snack food.

But if you choose to get sucked in, then it's fair game to build a business on the risks you take.

Jay Marshall and company, though, did not harmlessly profit from the foibles of the public's free will. What they did was a bit more directly connected to a real, undeniable moral and ethical no-no.

Prescienza, Inc. dug up people's deepest, darkest secrets, and then ratted them out for a fee.

They had done a little over a fifth of a billion dollars in business in the preceding year, and the coming months were shaping up to make the current one a banner quarter. Scandals were in the news, great grand ones, with top-five accounting firms and huge corporate juggernauts facing dire accusations. That meant, among other things, that the nation's shredders were working overtime right now. Rumor had it that nearly a ton of incriminating pulp could come in soon from Arthur Andersen alone.

And when the indictments started to fall, Prescienza would be called in to bring those illicit documents back, out of the trash and into the courtroom.

They were clearly on the side of truth and justice, but it still nagged at him on occasion. When someone destroys a stack of internal memos they believe in their heart that they're free of its disclosures. When they delete an e-mail from their secret lover, they're sure it can't come back to haunt them. When they remove the kiddie-porn pictures from their computer, format their hard-drive six times and swear to never transgress again, they solemnly pray that their nasty past is now behind them. And when they put their garbage at the curb, they're under the laughably false impression that it's safely gone.

On the contrary, it isn't gone at all and, the odd legal technicality aside, it also isn't theirs anymore.

You throw it away, and it belongs to Jay.

The government humps loved all this, of course, but the implications also kept them awake at night for obvious reasons.

They had their own stash of bodies, and they needed them to stay buried. So while the SEC used his services one day to retrieve the irretrievable, the NSA was hiring him the next to help make sure no one could ever do the same to them. This ongoing privacy tug-of-war was self-sustaining and very profitable, and Jay was equally comfortable pulling for either side. Comfortable, and uncomfortable.

And now Jeannie's project was a special problem. The agents who were bird-dogging him had said that the guy these shredded files would expose was a 9/11 terrorist enabler, if not a terrorist himself, and that he was the lead suspect in the murder of a janitor at that hacker magazine upstate. Fine. But Jeannie wanted this guy for some bigger reason. The higher-ups had pushed her out of her investigation, and he'd gotten some clear threats today, to keep her out.

Well. Fuck that.

Jay was seated before a 36-inch hi-res monitor at a prototype Cray MPA-2 multithreading workstation, with the lead FBI agent and his trusty sidekick standing behind. All three men were watching the intricate document reconstruction process unfold. Despite the fact that it was a part of Jay's everyday life, the sight was still a fascination.

"What's happening there, exactly?" the man behind him asked.

"Well," Jay said, "it's showing us a human-ready view of a very deep process. It's actually done billions of things since I started talking just now. But the simplified version is still pretty neat."

There were thousands of little white rectangles against a dark field on the screen, some blank and some with black type fragments. They were all free-rotating independently at various speeds and angles, moving in three dimensions, and Jay pointed to one of them.

"This," he said, "is one of the shredded pieces of the pages we're reassembling. We scanned each shred in that big machine over there in the cleanroom, it's a kind of 3D electron microscope, and it captures about ten million bytes of information about each little sliver."

"Ten megs?" the younger man said. "How small is each piece?"

"Small," Jay replied. "A little less than one six-thousandth of a page." The kid shook his head, amazed. "I know, it sounds like overkill, but it's not." Jay held up a business card, and turned it so they could see both sides.

"Imagine this is one of those tiny shreds. Now in the old days, back in the eighties, we were stuck looking at either side of each piece, and trying to find matches based on what was printed on the paper, like putting together a two-sided jigsaw puzzle. Make sense?" he asked.

They nodded.

"But what about the parts with no printing? And with a shredder this thorough, like the one you guys probably have in your mailroom, you might end up with thousands of virtually identical bits that contain just a piece of an 'm' or a 'w,' or part of an 'e,' and where do those go? We could only guess, it took months of trial and error sometimes, and we often only got small fragments of the original back together. Now, though, we don't even look at the flat sides anymore."

He turned the business card horizontally between his thumb and forefinger, and held it to their eye level. "Now," Jay said, "we look at the edges."

The computer issued a low *bong*, and they watched as two of the flurry of on-screen fragments highlighted and moved together. They did a brief ballet of alignment, and joined.

"That's a hit right there," Jay said. "Natural paper is made of fibers, and if you look close enough at the cut edges, you can capture the unique characteristics of each one of those fiber matrices."

Jay hit a few keys, and one of the rotating specks zoomed out to full screen size. He froze the image, and keyed up the magnification until the razor-thin cut edge loomed forth like the rugged, mottled cross-section on the wall of the Grand Canyon.

"That pattern of fibers is as unique as your fingerprint, and for every edge there's a mate floating around in there. It just takes time and a supercomputer to find it."

The two agents stood with their eyes glued to the screen. "It's rather hypnotic to watch, isn't it?" the older man said.

"Better than a fish tank," Jay replied, and he checked his watch. "You know, Agent Morgan," he continued, "the way things are moving along, we should have something solid for you early this evening. Would you mind if I excused myself for a few minutes?"

"Sure," Morgan said. "Brandon, go with Mr. Marshall. What is it, do you have some errands to run?"

Jay lowered his voice. "Fact is, that sushi boat I had for lunch is backing up on me, and I think I'm going to have to go drop some depth charges in the little boy's room, if you know what I mean."

"Oh. Okay, sorry. Take your time, we'll be here."

"I'd invite you and Brandon to come along and keep an eye on me, but it's not going to be pleasant. Hell, I wouldn't go in there myself if I didn't have to."

"No, that's okay, we'll just wait for you."

"Good. Be right back, a few pounds lighter."

In the stall in the men's room, Jay slipped out his PDA and moved the stylus around the small screen to access the office network. He signed onto the computer on his desk 200 feet away, and navigated to open a well hidden folder.

Next, he attached an image he'd prepared earlier to an innocuous e-mail message. He addressed it, checked the "Scramble" box and then punched in a line of code, the public key to Jeannie's encryption scheme. Those characters told his computer precisely how to jumble the file he was sending, in a way that only she could restore it. But just for good measure, he'd put two additional locks on the file.

160

As he knew better than most, you can't be too thin, too rich, or too careful.

He took a last-minute gut check, tapped the "Send" button, and watched the pop-up progress bar crawl to its endpoint.

What he'd just done was beyond illegal, to put it charitably. In the country's current climate it was probably firing-squad material. There was an excellent chance, in fact, that one of those gray featureless vans outside was monitoring all wireless communication from here, and that his message to her would be intercepted en route. If that were the case, he could easily walk out of the bathroom and into a set of chrome shackles.

It didn't matter, really, whatever the consequences. Neither of them ever spoke of it, and he had often wished that the events that had bound them together a decade ago might have magically, mercifully faded from her adolescent memory. But he would never forget, and whatever the risk, he had sworn to her that he would never fail her again.

24

He opened his eyes, but things only went from black to slightly less black as he looked around. Gradually, though, he saw some highlights emerge from the shadows above him as he adjusted to the darkness. There was a dripping sound nearby, and a flickering source of light off to his left.

John tried to raise his right hand to the throbbing at the back of his head, but his wrist was firmly bound to the frame of the unmade, mildewed cot he was lying on. His other hand was free, and he pushed himself painfully upright.

He rubbed his eyes and took in his surroundings. It looked like a cave, this place he was in, with some minor manmade interior work to make a crude room from a natural hollow.

He felt a flush of claustrophobia kick up, but he kept a grip on most of it.

He wasn't alone. Over in the opposite corner, a man and woman were huddled with two kids around the light from a candle, and a young woman was seated a distance away from them.

"Excuse me," John said to them. "Is there any water?"

The women and children conspicuously ignored him, but the man looked over. "Not until later," he said. "There's usually a meal a little later on."

"Where the f—" John stopped himself before he swore. "Where are we, what is this?"

The man stood, said something low to the others, and walked over.

"You're in the lock-up, down under his place, Mr. Latrell's." He looked down at his hands, smudged with the oily dirt of this place. "They told us not to talk to you."

"Then maybe you'd better not. I think it's safe to say I'm on the shit list," John said.

"My name is Ben – Morrison."

"John Fagan."

"Pleased to meet you," Ben said, but there was little sentiment in the words.

"Why are you in here?" John asked. "Why is your family in here, with me?"

"Those is mine, there." He pointed to the older woman and the kids. "The girl, over in the corner, she only just got brung down, a while after you did. I don't know her name, I'm sorry."

John looked over in that direction, and squinted. "Gretchen. Her name's Gretchen." He motioned with his head, and the man took a seat at the end of the cot. "What did you do to get yourself into the brig?"

"It's my doing," Morrison said. "I asked for their leave to take my wife and kids and go, after that day, when they sent them planes to kill alla those folks up east, an' evawhere else if they'd had it their way. I didn't want my children to have no part in this, not no more." He shook his head. "Not no more."

"I guess nobody leaves here, then, right?"

"I reckon not."

John lowered his voice. "You were right to try, anyway."

"Well, bein' right don't much matter now."

"Don't kid yourself," John said. "It always matters."

"What about you?"

"Me? Latrell wasn't satisfied with September eleventh, he wants me to help him take out a few hundred thousand this

163

time." John saw that the children across the way were watching them, so he leaned closer to the other man's ear. "And I told him to go fuck himself. So I'm pretty much dead, I think."

"Dead ain't the worst they can do, mister."

John considered that for a moment.

"What do you mean, I'm gonna get tortured? What's the point, for what?"

"If he wants somethin' from you, he'll sure enough get it. He won't kill you until he gets it, but he'll get it, all right."

The two sat silently for a while, listening to the regular dripping, and another sound, the faint scrabbling of some small creature, either trying to get in or get out.

Then there were footsteps, and Ben Morrison patted John's shoulder and hurried back to his family. The crude door pushed inward, scraping an arc in the stone floor, and even by the dim candlelight John recognized the face that approached him.

"Let's go, sweetheart," Nathan Krieger said, as he snapped open a knife and cut the nylon wrist restraint. "Show time."

No doubt about it, John thought to himself. The honeymoon was officially over.

He was seated in his lent underwear in a heavy straight-backed chair, with his wrists and ankles bound by hemp rope to the splintery wooden arms and legs. A hot white light was shining in his face, and he could smell the gun-oil on the weapon held by the man behind him.

John followed the wires that connected him to different points in the bare room. Several led from coiled rubber pneumograph tubes encircling his chest and abdomen, a blood pressure cuff squeezing his bicep, and thin metal plates taped around two of his fingertips. These wires ended at an interface box and a laptop computer nearby, with a clean-cut middle-aged man working in front of it.

The other wires were jumper-cable thick, spliced here and

there with tight wraps of electrical tape to cover the bright copper conductors where they had burned through the insulation. Here on the business end, heavy C-clamps wrapped in wet sponges were attached to both wrists and to the fat of his upper thighs, near his groin. These led to an octopus of wiring and another box atop a bank of truck batteries and a humming transformer.

"Good evening, John."

He couldn't see the one who spoke through the glare, but there was no mistaking the voice.

"Yeah? What's good about it?"

"I wonder, John, are you a student of Aristotle?"

"Oh, hell, Ed, I wouldn't go that far."

"He said, 'We cannot learn without pain.' Do you believe that, John?"

"Only as it applies to calculus."

"He also said that wit is educated insolence."

"Insolence? You think I don't respect you? What did I do to make you think I don't respect you, ass-hat?"

Nathan Krieger stepped in front of him and slapped him hard across his face, so hard that his ears rang.

"My men," Latrell said, "have a different idea of respect than you."

He tasted blood as he looked up into Krieger's cold eyes.

"Pussy," John said.

The muscles of the man's jaw tightened, and in an instant he had drawn his pistol and pressed the barrel to John's forehead.

"If you pull that trigger, Mr. Krieger," Latrell said quietly, "you will take his place, and I will have nothing on my schedule this evening beyond making you sorry you were born."

The pistol hesitated in place for only a moment before pointing to the ceiling.

"I'm gonna enjoy hearing you scream," Krieger said.

"Yeah? I enjoyed hearing your mother scream while I was cornholing her last night."

Krieger struck him another blow, with the flat of the pistol this time, and the impact set stars flying past his eyes.

"It gets worse from here, John," Latrell said. "So much worse you cannot begin to imagine."

The man at the computer had stopped his typing. "I am ready over here, Mr. Latrell," he said. His accent was light and cultured, Eastern Bloc, almost but not exactly Russian. Ukrainian, maybe, from the subtly misplaced inflections of his English.

"John, we're going to need to calibrate the polygraph, so this gentleman is going to ask you a few questions."

The blinding light was switched off, and he could now see details of his surroundings. There were five men in the room: Latrell, two sentries behind him, the fellow at the lie detector, and the zip, Krieger, now in back of him again.

"Is your name John Fagan?"

"Yes," John said.

The moving graphs that measured his blood pressure, heart rate, galvanic skin response and respiration stayed steady, and the polygraph man recorded the points in time that the question was asked and the answer given.

"Truth," he said.

John spat the blood from his mouth to the side. "Ask me again," he said.

The examiner looked to Latrell, then back at John.

"Is your name John Fagan?"

"Yes," John said, his eyes fixed on Latrell's.

The graphical lines jumped suddenly and stayed high, then gradually returned to the centerline. The examiner blinked, and raised an eyebrow.

"Lie," he said.

Latrell signaled the man to continue.

"Answer truthfully. Where was your place of birth?"

"My mother's vagina."

A chuckle burst from one of the guards behind Latrell, before

166

he caught himself and resumed his stoic posture. The polygraph screen responded, and the examiner made his recordings.

"Truth. Now lie for me please, where is your current place of residence?"

John tilted his head back, indicating the man standing behind him. "*His* mother's vagina."

All the indicator lines stayed rock steady. "Truth," the examiner said, and there was a private little smile of appreciation on his lips.

"John," Latrell said, "you're making this harder than it needs to be."

"Eat shit."

"Lavro was a chief examiner for the KGB during the Cold War years," Latrell said. "If experience is any sort of teacher, I believe we'll find your bravado will be the very first defense to desert you."

Things had begun to churn in John, surges of things, heavy and warm, working themselves out of his grip. He felt sweat breaking on his brow, a salty drop meandering to the corner of his eye. His hand tried to move to wipe it, found itself bound fast, but still it pulled and twisted against the tight, coarse lashes.

Think it away.

"You don't have to do this," John heard himself say, over the sound of his breathing and the rhythmic rush and pounding in his ears. His own voice was betraying him, and his hands, and his heart, and his lungs.

"Oh, John," Latrell said, "I think we've gone a step or two beyond reasoning now, don't you?"

Panic is physical, said a voice in his mind, thin and faint and far away, from somewhere on the other side of a grasping, gathering darkness.

Another man entered the room, carrying a hog-tied baby goat under one arm and a push-broom in his free hand. He laid the small animal on the floor, quickly clamped wires from the electrical apparatus to four points on its wriggling body, and then held it down under the broom handle with his boot.

167

"We need to do another little check," Latrell said.

He turned a dial on the desk in front of him, and pressed his thumb on a button next to it. The animal stiffened and splayed, and a gurgling noise rasped from its throat as raw electricity coursed between the terminals. The button was released and the goat's head thunked to the floor, its legs struggling against the bonds, its eyes wide and tongue lolling, its mouth spewing pink foam.

Panic is physical, his distant inner voice repeated, *and pain is mental, and both are subject to the will.*

"I always give a bit too much in the beginning," Latrell said, and he made an adjustment and punched the button once more.

An unearthly shriek hammered the walls, until all the air had been heaved from the animal's lungs. It flopped and contorted, inhaled audibly and screamed again. The smell of burning hair rose from it, but the button stayed down. At last the creature settled to the floor, hissing like a deflating balloon until it lay quiet. The rhythmic thrum of the transformer was the only sound that remained.

"Thank you, Alex. Mind you don't waste that meat, you hear?"

"Yes, sir," the man said, and he unhooked the dead carcass and carried it over his shoulder and out of the room.

"You see," Latrell said, "too much current can overwhelm the nerves and actually block the pain, and there's always a danger of brain damage, and we couldn't have that." He checked his watch, slid a pad of paper near and pulled a pen from his shirt pocket, clicked it. "So. Are you ready now, John, to learn to help us?"

Tendrils of gray smoke from the previous execution gathered and drifted across the ceiling, and he could feel the barest tingle of waiting voltage leaking into him from the wires.

"I'm not afraid," John said.

"Good. That's good, John." Latrell regarded him, with a look of the softest kindness in his dark eyes. "I would have expected nothing less."

"I'm not afraid," he repeated, again giving momentary voice to the steady mantra repeating in his mind. It did not promise him shelter, strength or even survival, only a small lightless place he had learned to rule when he was a boy, where they could not completely reach him, a familiar place in which to reign his final hours, and hold on. And if even those walls did finally fail him, a hill at least to die on.

The polygraph man, Lavro, walked to him, and carefully checked his bonds and connections one last time. When he was satisfied, he gave John a pat on the knee and a friendly smile.

Then he nodded to Latrell, and the long night began.

25

Strange weather for late October, it was, a warm Indian summer. The grass was cut low and fragrant here, the crickets were twittering in the fading heat of the late afternoon, and the cicadas buzzed in the thick elms. It was a fine evening, fine.

His father was sitting next to him, in a cane rocker near the whitewashed steps of a long wraparound porch. The wicker-bound joints of his chair creaked as the old man rocked slowly, his gaze far-off and dour. He was fiddling absently with his pipe, packing it with a new charge of apple-cured tobacco, tamping it with the pad of his thumb, the one that was stained brown over the years.

John felt in his clothes (*these odd clothes*) for a light, and he found a wooden kitchen match in his breast pocket. There was a cigarette there too, of sorts, and he put it to his lips as he leaned down to drag the white phosphorus match-tip across the rough wooden planks beside his own chair. The fire flared, and he cupped his hand around and leaned to hold it to the bowl of his dad's pipe. The tobacco glowed orange in the evening shade, and the white smoke drifted, smelling of old times.

"And how long have you been smoking, Johnny?"

It was his father's voice, but at the same time not his father's voice at all.

"I somehow managed to hold out until I was fourteen." John lit up with the curling black remains of the match, and shook out the flattening flame as it neared his fingers. The smoke was harsh and searing hot as he inhaled, but then no one had ever smoked a cigarette because it felt so goddamn good. "So that would be what? Going on thirty years," he said.

With a tight little smile and a subtle shake of his head, his father let out a descending sigh as he resumed his rocking. It was a familiar gesture, though it had been decades since John had seen it live and in person. It was at once dismissive and self-forgiving, as though a minor sad prediction had come true, about an event of no great consequence, and through no fault at all of the prognosticator.

"I had high hopes for you, son," his father said.

"Yeah, I guess you did."

"But you had your other ideas."

"Yeah, whatever."

The old man turned his head slowly, and looked at him. "You always did have a rare talent for summary, didn't you? *Whatever*, that's very good, that is, it's tidy. Whatever, indeed."

A young woman in white passed by them, and then as though on an afterthought, she stopped and came over.

"How're we doing this evening?" she said, overloud, as she adjusted the wool blanket around his father's spindly legs. She sniffed as she worked, and when she spoke again she'd added a contralto of friendly condescension, a community-theater actress playing the plucky schoolmarm. "Are you wet again, Mr. Fagan?"

There was the sharp, cloying smell of fresh urine in the air around them, though he hadn't noticed it before.

"My son has come by for a visit."

"Sweetie, that's nice. I'm going to call Al and we'll get you changed and out of these stinky wet things, all right? And get you dressed up for your dinner?"

"He's a genius," his father said.

171

She patted Dad's cheek, by rote and routine, and went off to her other duties.

John looked down to the left, and then to their right. There were others sitting as they were, old and fragile as carnival glass, lined along the long veranda, looking out across the lawn, back across the years. Most were still and solitary, quiescent but intent in their private elderly thoughts. Some were speaking softly, replaying some conversation from the past or striking up an entirely new one, though there was no one next to them to reply. No one at least that John could see.

"I've gotten myself in some trouble, Dad."

"Hm."

"No, I'm in the shit this time, this is no M-80 down the toilet at Westminster. I'm in some real fucking trouble."

His father drew on his pipe in a series of shallow puffs to keep the fire alive, the parchment skin of his cheeks alternately caving taut and relaxing with the effort. He exhaled the smoke through his nostrils, and squinted thoughtfully.

"I can't say I'm surprised, Johnny. Do you expect me to be surprised?"

"I don't expect anything, Dad."

His father stopped rocking, and they listened for a while to the wind in the trees.

"Do you know what the most common thing is, in the whole universe, son?"

"Let's see," John said. "That would have to be hydrogen."

"There is nothing so common in this world as misspent potential, my boy, men's dreams, dashed and unlived, unfulfilled. You never understood, did you, never, what I was trying to show you? You fought me, or ignored me, or belittled me, every chance you could, and all I ever wanted was for you to use your gifts, just to use them for some good."

"Like you did?"

The old man closed his eyes for a few moments.

"I wanted things for you, Johnny. I wanted you to find work

172

that gave you some reward. I wanted you to find a girl to share your life with. I wanted you to be a happy man."

John studied his father's eyes, and flicked an ash to the porch floor. "I always found that to be supremely insulting, I don't know if you ever realized that."

"Why?"

"It seems like such a meager ambition."

"It's not. Just ask any happy man."

John took a last stinging drag on his hand-rolled smoke and flipped it out onto the green grass. "I'm not sure, but I think this is the longest conversation we've ever had."

"Regret, I think, is the second most common thing in the world," his father said.

"Can you tell me what to do, Dad?"

"If I tell you, will you do it?"

"Yes, I will, if you tell me what to do to get myself out of this, I'll do it, I swear to God."

"Then you listen to me, for once." The old man lifted his hand off the arm of his rocker, and placed it on John's wrist. The skin was dry and cool, and his grip was weak but urgent. "Try to hear this."

"Yes, I will."

His father's watery blue eyes fixed on him. "Find friends, and put your trust in them. Find a woman to love you, and you love her, too. That's a verb, love, it's a thing you do, not a thing you feel."

The grip tightened, the yellowed nails dug in. "And this is the most important. Find one thing, just one single thing, God damn it, of all the things you can do, one thing, the smallest thing, and work on it until there's no one better at it. Do those things, I don't care what you've gotten yourself into, and they'll save you, son."

John looked back into his father's eyes. It was advice better suited to grammar-school graduation, but legitimate salvation was far more than he'd had a right to hope for.

"All right," he said. "I'll try, Dad."

"If you try, you'll fail, John. Tell me that you will, that you will do what I say, at long last."

"I will, Dad. I'll do it."

They came back then, the nurse and the starched orderlies, to take his father off to be changed, sponge-bathed, powdered, diapered and dressed for dinner. A burly young man in whites lifted him into a waiting wheelchair, and as they began to roll him slowly away, John felt the old boy's hand somehow still holding onto his.

"My son could have been whatever he wanted," he heard his father say. "But he never became anything at all."

How odd, how time never dulled the sting of a parent's disappointment, even that of a detached, distant old dick of a parent. It occurred to him that those eyes he'd just looked into had never, ever been lit with the pride of a father for his boy. And as he watched the last of the sun settle below the far hills, it further occurred to him that now, all things considered, they certainly never would be.

The scene began to change and crossfade, different faces blurred in as a red, screaming darkness came suddenly to engulf him, and through the splitting roar of reality's return he held onto the simple-minded counsel that he'd pledged to remember. It was a hopeless oath to do useless things, but it was a promise to his father, and that must mean something at the end of the day.

He would do his best.

He knew it wasn't sleep he was emerging from because there were too many senses active, and far too much pain. There was still a hand holding his, but its texture was not the cold, dry snakeskin of the one that had clutched him just before. He could feel himself returning from far away, first in the physical and more gradually the mental presence. But this room now was real, and this hand was real. It was soft, and small and warm.

174

Only one of John's eyes responded when he opened them. The other felt like a ball of tinfoil swiveling in its skull-hole, scraping against the swollen lid, useless for seeing. He let his head roll to the side, and a sinew of agony snapped down from his neck to the base of his spine. What felt like crow's-feet fractures in his ribs were flexing with every shallow breath, and the pain from them pulsed with every movement, threatening to detonate and put him out again.

There was a fluttering rattle deep in his lungs as he exhaled, but his lips caught the faint current of outgoing air and shaped it weakly into words.

"Still alive," he breathed.

A duck-call wheeze punctuated the whisper, and one phlegmy cough turned to a fit of them that curled him nearly onto the floor. When all the air had been kicked from him, his body starved for oxygen and drew in a great ragged breath. The paroxysms racked him again and again until his lungs were clear and he finally sank back, exhausted, wretched.

The girl had gone, but she came back soon with a damp cloth. She sat next to him and wiped his mouth, and refolded the terrycloth rag before pressing it to his forehead.

"You're okay," she said.

Her voice was more mature than he would have expected from the last brief blurry look of her that he'd gotten in that dungeon below, how many days ago?

"Gretchen," he said. "Is that right?"

"That's my name."

His legs were bound but they had freed his arms. He felt his face for his glasses, and she left for a moment and then returned to place them in his hand. One of the lenses was cracked and the frames were bent, but he was able to twist them back into a crude approximation of their former shape.

Even smudged, monocular vision was comforting, orienting. It put the fear down, back down where it needed to stay, where he could keep hold of it.

He looked at her as she worked over him, rubbing here, poking and blotting there. Her face was fine and young-womanly, but strong and set to task. There was some irony there, too, in the corner of her mouth and one cocked eyebrow, the detached persiflage of a death-row cosmetician. But her touch was gentle, and he let himself imagine for the moment that she was caring for him, not just attending. Any port in a storm.

There were long dark stretches of the preceding hours or days for which his short-term memory was failing him now. They had shot him with scopolamine at one point, and though he didn't recall when, they must have also tried sodium thiopental. It had left its traces, the faint smell of garlic; it was still in his head, in his sweat and blood.

He lifted his hand weakly, and took her wrist.

"Why—" he said. "Why are you here?"

She looked at him, and firmly but carefully peeled his hand from her arm. "My father was the doctor here, and I guess they figure some doctorin' rubbed off on me. 'Fore they shot him, anyways." She went back to her work. "You was in a bad way, I think they's worried you was gonna expire, afore they was ready for you to."

"They executed your father?" John said. "Why did they do that?"

"He changed his mind, I reckon, 'bout his loyalties. And that's enough to get shot for these days."

"I'm sorry—"

"Don't trouble yourself," she said, twisting his head a bit too far to swab a cut she'd missed. "Was a waste of a good bullet. I'da pulled the trigger on him myself, for draggin' me out here with him."

"And they've got you down in that prison now, because—"

"Treason runs in families, they figure. It's the old ways. No, I ain't too long for this world." She turned his head back to face her. "You and me both, mister." She straightened his collar, brushed the matted hair from his forehead. "Did you do what they wanted? Did you tell them what they wanted to know?"

"No, I didn't. And I won't."

Her touch gradually softened on his face, and her eyes revealed a hint of relief, and maybe admiration, but her tone remained impassive. "You're a brave one."

The heavy door opened at the corner of the darkened room. Latrell took a step inside, and with the slightest gesture he ordered the men behind him to stay where they were. He didn't need to tell Gretchen to leave; she stood and walked past him through the doorway without a word. A hand reached in to close and latch the door, and they were alone.

John felt a gut-wince at the sight of the man as he stepped into the light. It was a body reflex, and he made a conscious effort to hide the flinch. The value of keeping one's cool was questionable at this point, but old priorities died hard. He straightened himself through the shooting pain in every movement, willed himself under control.

Latrell moved to the desk and leaned back against it, facing him.

"Hello, John."

His jaw felt broken and roughly reset, every tooth in his head felt loose and unaligned. With his unscathed eye he looked across the room and found Latrell's even gaze, inhaled slowly despite the stabbing pain in his chest, deeply, so his breath wouldn't fail him as he spoke.

"Ed, man, no offense? But you look like shit."

The other man lowered his head, and when it turned up again his face was bright with the smile of an old friend. "You don't look so good yourself, John."

Latrell stepped behind his desk, and then pulled the high-back chair around to the front, dragging it behind him as he walked slowly over. He sat down, with their knees nearly touching, and it was a while before he spoke again.

"You've made up your mind, Mr. Lavro has told me, and we both know it's a formidable mind. He tells me that most of the effects of pain are in our minds, and if you've overcome the fear of it, we would very likely kill you before you would break. And even if you did agree to help us, your resolve would not be changed, and you would not give us your best efforts. We'd be back in here on a regular basis, reacquainting you with your agreement."

"Shit, it took you this long to come up with that? Maybe you fucking Rhodes scholars will wise up now, and get this over with."

"What are you saying, you think we should just kill you, and move on?"

"I'm up for it. Just give me a blindfold and a cigarette, and I'm there."

Latrell lowered his eyes after a moment, and then leaned back in his chair and spoke over his shoulder in a voice that would carry through the heavy door.

"Nathan, would you join us for a moment, please?"

The latch rasped, the door opened, and Krieger walked into the room and to Latrell's right hand.

"Did you bring your sidearm with you, Mr. Krieger?"

"Yes, sir." He drew the pistol with a casual flourish and let it hang at his side.

"Maybe we started all wrong," Latrell said. "I'm afraid I haven't given you a chance, John, a real chance, to see this from our point of view."

"What point of view would that be?"

"Do you understand what I'm trying to do, what this is about?"

John was watching the gun, wondering where the bullet that was coming was going to send him. The burden would be lifted, in any case, even if it was only a slow fade to dead black, it would be relief, surely it would. Trained assassins shoot people in the head, and that should be a relatively painless way to bite the biscuit. A hollow-point to the forehead at close range, and there wouldn't be time for many deep thoughts on the way to Byron's dreamless sleep.

"Hm? Yeah, Ed, you told me. Incite the Jew-puppets in Washington to panic and revoke the Constitution, cripple the economy and ignite a separatist-populist political uprising based on individual rights, and give the country back to its people. Right. Did I miss something? I feel like I'm forgetting something. Oh, and burn the Middle East into an ashtray, starting with Israel."

"You see the what, John, but not the why."

"What. Ever."

"What if I told you—" Latrell hesitated, considering his words. "If I told you that I'm only a small cog in the machine, that I am being used in a larger objective, but that what I plan is to thwart that objective, and through this next attack, to save the nation?"

"Save the village by burning it down?"

"Wouldn't you kill one to spare a thousand?"

"That depends on which one, doesn't it?" John asked. "And which thousand."

"If I told you there was a war plan in Washington – I have a photocopy, I can show it to you – to invade Afghanistan in the autumn of this year, finalized eight months before September the eleventh—"

"Oh, come on, those guys in the Pentagon, this shit is all they think about, it doesn't mean anything—"

"If I told you that Iraq would be next—"

"So it's all about energy, right, this grand global conspiracy is about cheap oil for Americans? This is an old fucking story, Ed."

"You don't understand, then."

"Explain it to me," John said.

"The price of oil will not fall; it will rise, and rise. Corporations, major corporations will begin to collapse, not over years but over weeks, under the unsupportable burden of their overvalued shares, the dollar will plummet, the housing bubble will burst, bankrupting millions—"

"And you're going to ride in on a white horse and stop all this by killing hundreds of thousands of innocent people?"

"This next attack is theirs, John, not mine, as was September the eleventh. To them I am only its manager, a minor player, a useful idiot. But they have chosen their puppets unwisely, I have an ace in the hole, a number of them actually. They can have the rest of the world, but they will not have the United States. The outcome will be mine."

The space became quiet. "And?" John said. "This 'they' you're talking about, who is that?"

"I never show all my cards, John, never. And you should remember that."

"I will, for the next few minutes until you blow my brains out."

"It doesn't have to be that way."

John leaned back in his chair. "I think it does."

Latrell studied him briefly. "So you've taken away nothing from what I've said?"

"A few nuances of your psychosis," John said, "but other than that? No."

"You've chosen, then. This is your choice."

"Sure, yeah, whatever. Now can we just start the shooting already, please? My neck hurts."

Latrell nodded his head slowly. "I'd rather not do this, but you're insisting."

"Right."

"You said you wanted a cigarette, didn't you?"

"That would be just great."

"Nathan, would you fix John up with a smoke? I'll be right back."

With his free hand, Krieger pulled a pack from his shirt pocket and offered a filter-tip with a flick of the wrist. He lit John's, and then one for himself.

"Storeboughts," Krieger said, the word puffing out in white smoke. "Bet you thought you'd never see another one." He popped the clip from his pistol and checked it, then snapped it back into the grip and chambered a round.

"Jesus, how many bullets you think you're going to need for this?" John asked.

"You never know."

The smoldering tip glowed orange-red, and the cigarette tasted damn good, even if it was a Camel Light. "What is that, a G36?"

Krieger cocked his head in mock surprise, and held his slate-gray pistol up in side view. "I wouldna' picked you out as a gun nut."

"Oh, I read about all kinds of bullshit. That's a fine piece, you had it long?"

"About a year. Fucking Austrians finally make a contribution, huh?"

"Yeah. Mozart, Schwarzenegger, Vienna sausages, Hitler, and the Glock."

"You're a funny guy, you know that?"

"Can I see it?"

Krieger snorted. "Right."

"What do you think I'd do, pop a cap in your worthless ass? Come on, chickenshit, grant a man's dying wish."

"Listen, geek, I could kill you with a soda straw, before you even found the trigger."

"You talk pretty tough with a forty-five in your hand, big man."

"You said it."

The door opened and four men entered the room. In the lead was a big old fellow with a full white beard.

"Santa!" John said. "Now what the fuck are you doing here? Does Mrs. Claus know you're hanging out with these bad asses, you jolly bastard?"

Latrell took his seat behind the desk again.

"John, you don't know who this is; let me introduce you. This is Joe Lange."

The man's gaze stayed straight ahead of him, out through the far wall.

181

"Gentlemen," Latrell said.

The men behind put their hands on Lange's shoulders and helped him to his knees, then stepped to the side as Krieger moved in front of him.

"I've known this man for twenty-two years," Latrell said.

John straightened himself slowly in his chair. "What is this?"

"Joe partook in a conspiracy several days ago, with others here, to abscond along with a number of dissidents and cowards, in the dead of night, and leave us open to betrayal, and capture by the enemy."

"I wish things was different, Ed," Lange said softly.

"Do you have anything else you'd like to say, Joe?"

"No, sir. Just that I'm damn sorry things come out this way."

Krieger put the muzzle of the gun to the kneeling man's forehead, and looked to Latrell.

"What the fuck are you doing?" John said, "I've never seen this guy before in my life, do you think I'm going to—"

The first thing that hit him was an odor, one he remembered from when he was a child. Strange the way a sense-memory like that will come in so sharply after all the years. His mother would make fried eggs and bologna for Sunday breakfast some weeks, and he never did like the smell of it, let alone the taste. And here it was again, the hot greasy smell of Sunday breakfast, settling on him in a bright spray of blood and tissue, before the boom of the .45 discharging had even registered.

They cleared the body quickly to a corner of the room, and through the ringing in his ears he heard Latrell speak again.

"Will you help us now?"

John said nothing. Another man had taken Lange's kneeling spot on the floor.

"Now, I think you two know each other," Latrell said.

It was Ben Morrison, the man from the holding cell. He looked fresh from a beating, and his hands were shaking at his sides.

"Why are you doing this," John said.

"I want you to help us, John, and if you won't do it to save your own life, I wonder if you will to save his."

"Will I help you kill three hundred thousand people to save just one? Does that sound like a rational decision to you?"

"Ben tried to leave us, too, along with his wife and family, but you know that, you two had a good chat, didn't you?"

"Look," John said. "Give me a minute, for crissakes."

"What do you mean, you're considering it, then? You'll do what I ask?"

"I'm saying let's talk about it."

Latrell leaned forward in his chair, and studied him for half a minute.

"No," he said, "I don't believe you."

The sharp report of the point-blank pistol shot reached him first this time, and he saw it as he heard it, the concentric shock waves made visible by the smoke that was hanging in the stagnant air. The dead sack that had been a man that he knew slumped forward and down onto the floor, but part of the nervous system seemed to be living on for the moment. Ben Morrison's hands were still trembling.

He couldn't take his eyes off the body as they dragged it roughly across the wooden floor. His vision was swimming and his mind was freezing up; he could feel it retreating in the face of the unsolvable.

No answer, no answer would come.

A woman was kneeling in front of him now, Morrison's wife, Morrison's children's mother. She was weeping softly, and her mouth was moving in prayer.

"Don't do this," John said. "Please don't do this."

"John, I have a theory about you," Latrell said. "Would you like to hear it?"

"Yes."

"I think that you want to be punished. I believe that you feel responsible for your role, tangential as it was, in support of our actions on September eleventh, and I think that everything we

183

would do to you as we tried to convince you to help us again would only strengthen your resolve to suffer and die for your sins. What do you think about that?"

The room was quiet as a dry well, his mind was overloading as it raced through flickering permutations of the coming seconds. All the future had wound down to moments, and the only path he could see was to win her just another moment if he could.

"I think you may be right."

"May be?"

The gunshot didn't come, there were only the breathy sounds of silent prayer.

"I hadn't thought of it that way."

"That's interesting, John. Do you think there might be other things you haven't thought of in the right way, then?"

"It's possible."

"Will you help us, then?"

He waited as long as he thought he could. "If I say yes—"

"No ifs!"

He saw the trigger finger tense, and the dust and smoke seemed to freeze in the air as he heard each metal sound of the mechanism, the ratchet of the passive safety unloading, the back-travel of the hammerless action, the clack-twang of the firing pin releasing, the pop of the cartridge primer, the roar of the igniting propellant. At first he thought the muzzle flash had blinded him as the pistol fired, and it could have been that, or it could have been that his mind chose a white-out rather than to let the unbearable image through. In any case, when his vision returned, she lay still and ruined on the floor at his feet.

His eyes were stinging and wet, and he closed them as tightly as he could until he found some control, just enough control, somewhere.

When he could look again, it was Gretchen who was on her knees in front of him.

Her face was serene. She looked up at him, and when there

184

could be no doubt that she had his attention, she moved her head the tiniest bit to the left and then to the right, and mouthed the word, *No*.

The two children, the boy and the girl of the mother and father that were now stacked roughly in the corner of the room, were in line in the doorway, holding hands. The little girl was crying softly, and the boy's hard blue eyes were glistening, but he was holding it together.

Latrell stood behind his desk. His fists were knotted and his cherub face was dark and blotched red, his deep voice was breaking with emotion. "Why are you doing this to me?"

John didn't answer. This young woman in front of him was brave, she had far more courage than he did, he knew. And those two kids, their parents had been taken from them and their own short lives were about to end, but they were on their feet, as young as they were, and facing it.

The voice from the far side of the room rose in volume, and the rage behind it tore the words as he spoke. "Do you hear me? Why are you making me do this? I'm trying to save lives, to end a tyranny that you yourself acknowledge, to give back the dream that our forefathers commended to us—"

"Spare me the diatribe," John said. He was still looking in her cool, fearless eyes.

"What did you say to me?"

After a moment, John turned his head and looked across the room to the other man.

"I'm saying . . . you win. No need to repeat yourself. I hold your crap to be self-evident. Now will you let me finish my thought this time?"

"Yes."

"Because I've got what you want, Ed, it's all laid out, and I've been going over it and over it in my head while you and your boys were working on me, just in case I needed it. And it's perfect, Ed, it's absolutely unstoppable, it's exactly what you want, everything, the quintessential day of terror. But if this girl, or those

185

kids, or anyone else you bring in here gets so much as a rug burn from this moment on, I will clam up so permanently that there will be no getting it out of me, and you should be convinced that I can make that promise at this point. Are you convinced of that?"

"Yes."

"What you do with what I tell you is not my concern, but you are not going to put any more blood on my hands like this. Do we have that understanding?"

Latrell nodded his head.

He took a last drag on his cigarette, burning it right down to the bitter filter, and then flipped the smoldering butt onto the floor. "*If* I say yes—"

John looked up at Krieger and raised his eyebrows, an invitation to go ahead and shoot the girl if he were so inclined, and then live with the consequences.

There was no gunshot.

"*If* I say yes," he continued, "I'll need a team of people that I'll describe to you, some of them with very special skills. I'll need full access to your equipment and armaments, a pretty massive computer network with hardware and software that I'll list, an untraceable cell phone, a serious Internet connection, about seven hundred thousand dollars for sundries, and full cooperation from anyone I point to. Can you deliver that?"

Latrell sat down behind his desk. "Yes, we can."

"Then let's start with something simple," John said, and he looked again at the man with the gun. "Holster that pistol, you sack of shit."

Krieger glanced over briefly for a nod from Latrell, and then looked back down at John as he slipped the gun into its shoulder harness. "We're not done, you and me."

"Oh, I hope we're not," John said.

Latrell smiled, and raised his hand from the desk. "Now, I have a condition for you, too, John."

"Let's hear it."

"I have engineers I'll call upon to help you," Latrell said. "Some brilliant men and women, though not of your caliber, of course. Still, I will ask them to study your work continuously, and if any of them are able to find an exploitable flaw in the plan you'll give us, intentional or not, all of you, the girl and the children and you, will be put to death in the most unpleasant way I can imagine. Agreed?"

"Fine. I'll need a comfortable place to work, all four of us, me and Gretchen and those two kids, we're going to stay together, in a nice warm place, so I know they're okay. They don't leave my sight. I'm talking the presidential suite. All right?"

"All right."

Latrell motioned for the others to leave, and the room cleared out but for the two of them. Out of the view of his men his face slowly withered. The coming revolution and the realization of his dreams were at hand, but for the moment, it seemed enough that these preceding days and their horrors were at an end.

"Thank you, John."

"Fuck thank you, Ed. Let's get this show on the road."

26

"You've got mail!" Rudy said, in his refined imitation of the stick-up-his-ass digital AOL guy.

Rob and Jeannie stood up behind him and looked at the large LCD screen on the wall above her home-office desk. Rudy double-clicked the message from Jay, then right-clicked on the attachment to open it.

A password challenge popped up, and the cursor blinked in its text-entry field.

"What's your private key?"

"Right, good try," Jeannie replied. "Look away." She leaned over him and began typing in a long string of characters, her arms on each side of his head.

"What's that scent you're wearing?" Rudy asked, sniffing. "Is that Shalimar?"

"Snuggle."

"That's Estee Lauder, right?"

"It's a dryer sheet, Rudy." She finished typing, and hit Enter. An image filled the screen, and just as he'd said on the phone, it was a picture of Jay Marshall and his family.

Rudy leaned back and tilted his head to the side. "Man, Jay's put on some weight."

"What is this we're looking at?" Rob asked.

"He must have put another layer of encryption on the file, probably steganographic. There's a message for us hidden in there somewhere, but we can't see it yet." She thought for a moment. "Rudy, open that up in my hex editor, that one there." She tapped one of the icons on the desktop with her finger.

He dragged the file over, and after a few seconds the screen was covered with random, unreadable garbage.

"That's ASCII, let's see it in hexadecimal," she said.

The screen changed to an octet stream of hex numbers, but there was nothing to indicate the nature of an algorithm, no clues in the file header, nothing.

"Back to Photoshop," she said.

Rudy reopened the file as she'd asked, and there was Jay and his brood again, grinning down at them in front of a holiday hearth.

"Run a plug-in on the whole image," she said. "It's one of mine, called 'Decloak.'"

Rudy selected the filter from a pull-down menu, and a prompt popped up requesting a decryption key.

"Try my name," she said.

He typed it in, and they watched the graphic image ripple into a muddled blob. He tried all combinations, first name, last name, first last, last first, backward and forward, with the same non-results.

Rudy sighed and clicked "Undo," and the image returned again to its original cheery form.

"On the phone," Jeannie mused, "what did he say at the end, 'hugs and kisses to Aunt Belinda.' Hugs and kisses, that's 'XO' in shorthand, right? Apply an XOR filter to the whole image."

Rudy did so, and each byte of the picture underwent an exclusive-OR transformation as a progress bar slowly advanced across the bottom of the screen. Nothing much changed, though, until a tiny watermark of darkened pixels appeared in the lower right-hand corner.

"Blow that up, right there," Jeannie said.

At 1,200 per cent magnification, the crude blocky letters became just barely legible against their background.

GOOD GIRL

Jeannie patted Rudy on the back. "Good girl. Now zoom back out," she said. "Try my name as a key again, like you did before."

Rudy typed in the characters, and they were met with a series of similar but different masses of incomprehensible pixels.

"Okay, too obvious. Try 'Aunt Belinda.'"

He did. No dice.

"Anagram?" Rob asked.

"Oh, yippie, I love word games," Rudy said, cracking his knuckles. He opened a blank image window, and typed out the letters of the source words, *a u n t b e l i n d a*, alphabetically in a large font.

A A B D E I L N N T U

The three concentrated on the screen, mentally rearranging the letters in silence for several seconds.

"Labia!" Rudy shouted.

Jeannie pursed her lips, and thumped him on the head. "You've got to use all the letters, numb-nuts."

"I was just warming up," he said.

Combinations of words occurred to them, mostly nonsensical, and as they each muttered their best candidates aloud Rudy wrote them on note cards and checked them against the source letters.

"Bland Auntie."

"Butane Linda."

"Annual Debit."

"At u bin Laden."

"Oh," Rudy said, "that's a nice one."

He tried them all. Nothing.

190

Rudy got up to stretch and Rob sat in his place. He put his hands on the keyboard and tentatively typed a few letters, then several more to the finish, and sat back. Jeannie looked over his shoulder, leaned close, squeezed his arm, and nodded.

"That's it," she said.

Jay Marshall was a borderline conspiracy nut, but as she read those two words on the screen she realized she was lately sharing his dark perspective.

ABUNDANT LIE

Rob clicked OK, and the family picture began to pixelate and disappear. In its place emerged a rough-edged fragment of reassembled paper shreds, the upper left-hand corner of an aged manuscript's cover page. The three of them watched it materialize, and read the words as they came into view.

```
John Fagan
P.O. Box 2600
New York, NY 10007
```

There was another small line of overlay text, not part of the original document, near the bottom of the image.

"T W O H O U R S," it said. "J. M."

"What does that mean, two hours?" Rudy said.

Jeannie was already gathering her things. "Jay's trying to give us a head start," she said. "Rob, can you talk us onto a chopper at Andrews?"

"I'll call from the car."

"Move your asses, boys," Jeannie said. "We're going to New York City."

Her place at the Summit Roosevelt was less than twenty miles from Andrews Air Force Base, and at 5:00 A.M. on a clear Sunday morning, it would be a ride of about half an hour.

As luck would have it, though, it was now 6:00 P.M. on a rainy Friday in DC.

The three of them had rocketed down the six flights from her apartment, and they nearly cold-cocked an elderly woman and a Chihuahua as they burst through the ground level door and out into the early evening drizzle. They stopped at the arch of the garage entrance, and the attendant was nowhere in sight.

Jeannie checked her watch, then ran her fingers through her hair and began to pace. Even if he wasn't tied up with the after-work rush, it would take too many precious minutes for the valet to retrieve her M5 from the crowded lot.

"Let's take my car," Rob said.

"A four-cylinder Taurus?" She shook her head, and pulled her bag around to retrieve her phone. "We could get there faster going piggy-back. I'm calling a cab."

"Nah, that was just a rental," Rob said, and he started to trot for the street-side of the building, motioning them to follow. "Come on, you're gonna like this, I had my baby sent up from back home, she got here last night."

He'd parked out front on 16th Street, in the middle of a stretch crosshatched in yellow where no parking spaces actually existed. Homebound residents hurriedly cleared the long sloping sidewalk as the three raced past them at a dead run. With twenty yards to go, Rob thumbed a button on his keychain.

The headlights blipped, the doorlocks popped up, and a four-barrel 455 V8 woke up angry under the airscooped hood of his cardinal-red 1972 Pontiac GTO.

There were three parking tickets under the driver's side wiper, and Rob reached out his window and flipped them onto the asphalt as he fastened his shoulder harness with the other hand. Jeannie slipped in beside him, and Rudy sank into the black leather bench seat in the rear.

"Wait a minute," Rudy said, "if we take their car, how's the Mod Squad gonna get home?"

"Hang on," Rob said.

He cranked the wheel, dropped his aftermarket 5-speed into first and punched it, and the fat Mickey Thompson radials in the rear poured black smoke and spun the shuddering car into a fishtailing U-turn. The oncoming traffic instinctively braked or veered out of harm's way, and they catapulted east like an F-14 off the bow of the Nimitz.

Rudy yelled something as the shifter caught third gear, but it was hard to make it out over the throaty crescendo of the engine. Something about a seatbelt.

Rob was flashing his brights and honking to clear the way of plodding commuters, but some of them just weren't getting it. Despite the rush-hour clots and jams, though, he was somehow managing to accelerate steadily. The tires barely held the rain-slick pavement as they careened through a moving maze of brake riders and lane hogs toward I-395.

Jeannie had been giggling quietly for over a mile, an apparent nervous reaction to high-speed metropolitan stunt driving. Now she pointed ahead and tugged on Rob's shirtsleeve, wide-eyed as a kid who just saw over the first big drop on the Coney Island Cyclone.

"Grab onto something," Rob shouted.

Driving in our nation's capital meant negotiating the town's many roundabouts, quaint circular hubs where several streets meet up from a number of directions. There were casual rules of vehicular etiquette associated with them, and most had a posted speed limit of 15 miles per hour.

With the physics of combat flight more than those of motoring in mind, Rob now breached the Massachusetts Avenue roundabout at a brisk 77.

He pulled the handbrake and spun the wheel to its stop, and they slid into a squealing four-wheel drift around the circular interchange toward their exit. The round chrome speedometer on the dash vibrated at zero, but the car had barely slowed.

Unfettered by a safety restraint, Rudy's face was being pressed to the passenger window by sidewise G-forces through the half-circle.

As the scenery whirled by he made brief but meaningful eye contact with four stunned bystanders on the sidewalk, two terrified fellow drivers, and one slack-jawed city cop behind the wheel of his parked cruiser.

They skidded diagonally between a Ford Explorer and a bike messenger, and out into the mouth of their exit. Rob released the brake handle and straightened the wheel, downshifted, floored the accelerator and laid two long lines of black rubber astride the dotted centerline of Mass Ave.

Now in the relative clear, Rob nudged his seat-mate with his elbow. "Give me your phone," he said.

Her hands were still completely covering her face, and he had to thump her several times on the leg to get her attention. "Phone," he repeated.

With one hand on the dash for stability, she rifled through her bag and handed him her cell phone, then peeked to the rear to check on Rudy. She found him lying flat across the back seat, his hands and feet bracing against a door on each side.

"Are you okay?"

"Never better," he yelled back.

Her face was suddenly lit by the red, white and blue strobes of police lights glaring through the back window.

"Cops," she said, tapping Rob on the shoulder.

He nodded, and checked the rearview as he continued his phone conversation. "No. No, you will not. You're going to do this for me, and you're not going to ask me any more goddamn questions. I don't care. No. You tell them anything you want tomorrow, tell them I put a fucking gun in your mouth, which you better believe I will do when I get there if you push back at me one more time. Now pull your head out of your ass and remember what you owe me." Rob looked at Jeannie, and nodded his head when he saw the concern in her eyes. "Now you're talking, now you're talking, what's ready to go?" He swerved abruptly across two busy lanes to pass a knot of slowpoke SUVs, and then found his steady line again. "Yeah, good, the Lynx will

194

do. And who's driving? Okay, don't tell him shit, just that he's got three passengers to New York, we're on a red alert from the puzzle-palace, and you've seen our paperwork. No, no, downtown, downtown Manhattan. And while you're at it see if the tower can get the ATCs to clear a lane for us, we're in a big fucking hurry. All right. Good deal. No bullshit, man, you're saving my life here. See you in a few."

Rob snapped her phone shut with a flick, and handed it back. "Cross your fingers, but I think we're all set."

As they veered smoothly onto Suitland Parkway they picked up another tail, this one a state cop, and he swerved into line close behind them.

"I've got this," Jeannie said. She crawled into the back seat, rolled down the window and leaned out to motion the lead pursuer up alongside.

The cop was not happy. He was jabbing his finger toward the shoulder with his eyes on the traffic ahead, and his partner was talking a mile a minute into the radio.

Rudy pulled himself up and gripped the window ledge beside her, Kilroy-style. "That policeman and I want us to pull over," he said.

Jeannie opened her ID folder and held it out the window as far as she could reach, and the cruiser's passenger window glided down. The cop riding shotgun shielded his eyes from the pelting rain as Rob eased the cars closer together. The officer squinted back and forth between her face and her credentials, and at length he leaned back in and spoke to the driver, then looked back at her and nodded.

"We're going to Andrews," she shouted.

With a disgusted shake of his head, the cop at the wheel hit his siren and the blue-and-white surged forward, with the state car behind them soon following suit. The two cruisers pulled away rapidly and drove on ahead, clearing the way.

"You're a smooth talker," Rob said, as Jeannie slid back down the seat beside him. She smiled, and blew a lock of hair from her eyes. She was spattered with rain and windblown, but somehow even that look was becoming to her.

The soldiers on duty at the entrance ahead were all outside the guard post with their rifles unslung, but the checkpoint gates were swung up and awaiting them. The cop cars eased to the side and slowed to let Rob take the lead again, and they stayed close behind him when he passed. They killed the sirens, but the lights stayed on.

Rob knew the base by heart, and he drove them to a remote hangar on the edge of the southwest quadrant, where their next conveyance was fueled and waiting.

Jeannie jumped out of the car as soon as it stopped, and jogged back to calm the policemen who'd escorted them. Rob trotted to a gathering of his friends and fellow pilots near the flight line, and Rudy rolled out onto the tarmac by the car.

Out on the runway, a Westland Super Lynx was passing its final preflight checks. This one had been bound from its birthplace in Great Britain to Malaysia, but command at Andrews had requested that it be diverted here for an evaluation. In return, they'd promised to give the machine a shakedown cruise, and this jaunt to New York would fill the bill nicely. The specs said it was the fastest helicopter ever in production, and shortly that claim would be put to the test.

At a signal from the ground crew, the pilot flipped overhead switches that fired the twin Rolls Royce turbines. The engines whined steadily up to max power as the wide rotor blades began to spin, gradually replacing the drizzly westerly breeze with a more powerful downward gale.

"Hey," Rob shouted over the wind and noise. He caught Jeannie's eye, and she left the cops with a hug and a pat on their backs. She found Rudy crawling on all fours next to Rob's car.

"Are you okay?" she said, kneeling down next to him. "Come on, let's go."

"I think I threw up, but nothing came out," Rudy said.

She pulled him to his feet, walked him to the open doors of

the helicopter, and helped him up into a seat next to her. "I've got a Dramamine, I'll give it to you on the way, just try to relax. Strap in, here, see? You've got a seatbelt now."

With the doors now closed and latched, it was quiet inside the passenger cabin. "Tell them to take it easy, or I'm seriously going to honk," Rudy said weakly.

Rob was up in the cockpit's jump seat, and he leaned around the open door.

"You ready to light this candle?"

Jeannie gave him a thumbs-up, and Rudy flipped him a bird.

Rob smiled and spoke into his headset, the pilot goosed the collective, and the rotors bit air and launched them abruptly skyward. At barely treetop height, the nose swung down thirty degrees and they thundered off toward the northeast horizon, hitting 200 knots before they cleared the base perimeter.

Only a few minutes after they'd left the ground, it seemed, they were flying over Baltimore at a third the speed of sound. Jeannie's phone was doing a reasonable job of maintaining signal as they traversed from cell to cell. But she was having an abysmal time reasoning with the United States Postal Service.

"This is the third time I've explained the situation," she said. Her eyes were closed as she concentrated to keep her calm. "This is urgent, this is an emergency."

"And you need to know whut, about who?" the postal worker asked.

She enunciated the words slowly, so a second-grader in a S'mores coma couldn't miss them. "I have a Post Office Box and a name in your district, and I need for you to just log onto WinBATS and give me the physical address of the person who rents the box."

"Ma'am, that's privileged information, and I can't give that out."

"All right, that's it, get me your supervisor, right now, and tell them that this is Jeannie Reese, from DARPA. Do you have that straight? Jeannie Reese."

Rudy shook his head at her, smiled, put a finger-gun to the side of his head, and pulled the trigger.

He was right, goddammit. She could almost hear the woman hip-shift, right over the phone.

"Honey, you is talkin' to the soop-a-visah, and I don't give a damn if you're Jeannie Christ. Neither rain, nor sleet, nor some snow-white, Kenuhbunkport talkin' skeevy uppity-ass hoochie lil' boo-boo head from DARPA is gonna get no privileged imfuhmation about a P.O. Box at seven o'fuckin' clock on my Friday night."

The woman continued to tell her off as she hung up the phone on the other end.

Jeannie put her hand over her eyes and leaned back until her head thumped on the bulkhead. They were so close, but without that address they might as well just turn around and slink home.

"Hey," Rudy said. She peeked through two spread fingers and saw him across the compartment, motioning to her to toss him the phone. "Let me give it a try, smoothie."

There was nothing to lose. She closed the phone and pitched it across to him.

She saw him hit redial, then he put the phone to his ear and turned sideways in the seat, shielding his mouth with his other hand. She could see he was talking to someone intently, but his voice was too low to make out the words. He looked over at her once, nodding his head in agreement with his conversation partner, a little sneer on his lip. He flipped his pad open and wrote something, and then he signed off politely, snapped the phone shut around the note and tossed it to her with a magician's flourish.

Jeannie opened the phone, unfolded the slip of paper, and read the street address there. "How did you do that?" she asked.

"I told her that my boss was a vicious C-word, and that she was going to fire me because I lost her ex-husband's new address, and could she please give it to me so I could hold onto my miserable job long enough to buy Christmas presents for my little boy this year, and then quit on your bony ass, just when you really needed me."

She shook her head slowly, running her finger over the writing on the paper.

"I knew I kept you around for something," she said.

They flew on, into a dusky azure sky that was clearing around them as they outran the overcast. Rudy was grabbing a catnap now, and she leaned her head against the window beside her, and watched the world go by. The skyline of Philadelphia was soon visible, and as the distance closed she could see the Ben Franklin Bridge down in the waterfront district, gracefully spanning the lower Delaware, and lit softly with the colors of the flag.

The handsome city scrolled under them, and as it passed behind she wondered how many times Franklin himself must have stood under this very sky, and feared for his land as she did now. He had long been one of her idols, and though he'd been victim to only a fraction of her years of formal education, she knew he had been more astute in things that mattered than she ever could hope to become. She wondered if the old boy would even recognize the nation he'd helped architect, if he would understand what had changed, and why.

Yes, she imagined that he would. There was a kind of wisdom that transcended all time and circumstance.

She found a bright star in the sky, the first star she'd seen tonight, and she held her hands together and quietly made a wish for just a particle of that wisdom for herself, to guide her now in what she was facing.

Rob came back from the cockpit, and she felt him take a seat beside her.

"We'll be landing pretty soon," he said. "They're dropping us in Battery Park."

"Can they wait for us?"

"No, they've got to get back, and the shit's going to hit the fan shortly thereafter. We'll stay in the city tonight, and figure out how deep we're sunk tomorrow morning. I cashed in a lot of chips for this ride, probably a few more than I've got."

She opened her eyes and looked out the window.

"Rob?" she said.

"Hm?"

"Did you mean that, what you said to me?"

"That we were going to land in a few minutes? Yes, I did."

"Not that."

He reflected for a moment. "That I thought we should stay in the city tonight?"

"No, not that, forget it, you're making fun of me."

"Oh, you mean in the elevator?"

She nodded, and looked at her hands.

"Yes, I meant that. When I told you that I care about you? Yes, I meant that. Of course I did."

She shook her head. "Rob, you don't know that much about me."

"It always starts out like that, you know, with two people."

"I just, I don't want you to get hurt, Rob."

"Listen, take my hand, take it, here, it's okay."

She did.

"I'm a grown man, Jeannie. I'm a fighter pilot. Every time I leave on a mission, I say goodbye to this world, and when I get back on friendly ground it's always a pleasant surprise that I'm still alive. I've flown through clouds of flak so thick it was like an upward hailstorm, I've had goddamned SAMs coming at me from all sides, with one engine out and the other one on fire. I've belly-landed on an aircraft carrier, at night, in a monsoon. I took a bullet from a sniper in Somalia, right where you punched me in the ribs today."

She reached out gently and touched him there, but she didn't meet his eyes.

"And you know something?" he said. "You don't scare me,

200

Reese. It doesn't hurt to talk. Let's try it. What's your favorite song?"

"I don't think I have one."

"All right, well, that would make an okay goal for this month. Now you ask me."

"What's your favorite song, Rob?" she asked shyly.

"'Behind Blue Eyes,' The Who, 1971."

"Why?"

"No, I said The Who."

She looked up at him, smiled in spite of herself, and he nodded an encouraging prompt. "Why do you like that song so much, Rob?"

"Good, you're doing great. Okay, I like that song because I was a little rebellious hell-raiser when I was in my teens, and it was kind of my theme song, I guess."

"Hell-raiser?" She *pffffed* at him. "You're gonna have to get in line for that club, sailor boy."

"Don't tell me, little Jeannie was misunderstood?"

"Yeah. Me and Charlie Manson."

"So how did you end up pulling for the good guys?" Rob asked.

"Long story."

He checked his watch. "I've got a few minutes."

"Actually, I'm quite a disappointment to my mother and father. I was genetically engineered, you know, with loftier aspirations."

"Come again?"

"Well," she said, "my mom and dad wanted a perfect child, and after a few faulty outputs the old-fashioned way, they went egg-and-sperm shopping to get the job done right. They wanted a world-shaker. So they ordered me up, like a Bentley Turbo."

"You're messing with my mind, right?"

She shook her head. "It was legal, I suppose, and if it wasn't, well, they've got money," she said. "And they did their due diligence. They screened back for generations, on thousands of

201

applicants, IQ, bone structure, a whole laundry list of predispositions and proficiencies, right down to straight teeth and good posture. My birth mom was from Oslo they later told me, after I'd sued them for the records. The sperm donor they'd lost track of, but I found him myself. He was some kind of super polymath, a real mutation. Committed suicide a few years after the blessed event. Just walked into traffic."

"Jesus." He put his hand on hers, and she allowed it. "At least they got what they paid for."

"Like hell. I toed the prodigy line until I was about eleven, but once they spilled the beans about the whole Frankenbaby thing, I started to . . . act out." She took her hand back, and looked into his eyes. "Let's leave it there, okay? It gets a little weird after that."

"Okay. Jesus."

She leaned back in her seat, her gaze far out the window. "How about you," she said. "Can you top that?"

"I don't think so. I was kind of a fragile kid."

She looked around at him. "Excuse me?"

"Heart trouble," Rob said. "Here." He tapped his upper chest, under his collarbone. "Put your hand right here."

She frowned, reached for him carefully, pressed the spot and then drew her fingers back. "What the hell is that?"

"Had a pacemaker, since I was two. AV block."

"Oh my god, Rob."

"It's no big deal. Gave me something to overcome, I guess. Ya know, mortality, and all that."

"And the SEALs were okay with that? How did you even get past basic?"

"My dad pulled some serious strings with the recruiter and the docs, way back when I first enlisted. He knew how bad I wanted it. But I had to be so much better than the guys next to me, they would have washed me out in a second if I hadn't been. And now, after all these years, I know they still know about it, but nobody ever brings it up anymore."

202

She leaned her head to his shoulder, and took his hand again.

"The rest of the fam is pretty standard stuff," Rob said. "Dad was a lifer in the service, my mom keeps the house together, a big sister and a little brother. He's in boot camp now, Parris Island."

"A Marine, huh? Wants to be like you?"

"I guess."

"Well," Jeannie said. "Who wouldn't?"

The pitch of the craft began to change, and as it canted toward level they felt the deceleration from forward flight to a smooth hover, then the start of the gradual descent. He squeezed her hand and got up to return to the cockpit for the touchdown.

"Grab your stuff and wake Rudy up," he said. "This was good, I liked this a lot. We can talk some more later, if you want."

She stood by herself on the corner, looking across at a gray, nondescript four-story building. Its windows appeared to be boarded, but the careful woodwork covering them did not suggest disrepair, only a rather stylish wish for extreme privacy. The architecture evoked an air of majesty that the actual brick and mortar couldn't quite deliver. The stonework in the detail was old-worldish, more appropriate to a modest cathedral than to the office building that this had surely once been.

A small statue stood at the summit of the façade, and she recognized it after a moment's reflection. It was a copy of a Greek sculpture she'd seen once in the Louvre. The marble image was of a young woman, offering a beautiful apple in her hands. The face had been serene, she remembered, but the artist had etched an icy enmity into her eyes. It was Eris, the goddess of discord, keeper of the seeds of war.

Jeannie had been past here before, many times in fact, but always on the way to somewhere else. She'd walked by this place on childhood trips to visit her father down on the Exchange, and in more recent years for a quick lunch or dinner at Delmonico's when business brought her downtown. Trinity Church was just up the street, and had the twin towers still been standing, this spot would have been in their long shadows.

She was shivering as her two companions came back from their recon, and she wrapped her jacket tight around against the evening air.

"Did you find the way in?" she asked.

"There's a couple of weird dumbwaiters, I guess you'd call them, but no real entrance that we could see," Rob said. "But there's a set of service doors in the alley around in back. They're open, it's unlocked, and that looks like the only way into the building."

She took a deep breath, slipped her pistol from its holster under her skirt and handed it to Rob. "You guys stay here."

"No, N,O, no fucking way."

"I'm with him," Rudy said. "This place has got Bates Motel written all over it, and I am not gonna take you home in a go-cup."

"Sorry, but that's the way it is," she said. "I don't want to frighten him, and he's going to be wigged-out enough to see me all by myself. But he knows me, and I think it'll be okay."

"He knows you?"

"Not exactly, we had a talk one night, on the phone, just one time, but I think he'll remember me. I'll try to be . . . disarming."

"Take one of us anyway, for God's sake," Rudy said.

"No," she said, and they could see that the discussion was over. "Rob, give me your flashlight and wait here, both of you. If he's not up there and you see him coming back, page me so I'll be ready."

She checked her watch, and set herself a hard time limit. "And Jay won't be able to sandbag the FBI forever, so if I'm not out when they roll up, just beep me and sit tight. No use all of us getting arrested."

"What the hell are you going to do in there?" Rudy asked.

She started across the street.

204

"I haven't exactly worked that out yet."

She looked very small as they watched her disappear around the corner of the thin side street and into the darkness of the cobblestone alleyway.

All of her senses were tuned up far past normal, and the adrenaline rush pumping through her was not at all under control. She could feel the hand she held out in front of her trembling, but for the moment she was able to keep the one holding the flashlight steady.

She was intensely aware of the sounds of her footsteps on the gritty concrete floor, and of the smells in the air, machine oil and rust, damp cardboard and moldering fabric. The basement's musty blackness seemed to absorb all but the bright center of the thin pale beam from her flashlight as she walked.

She had counted forty-seven steps in, when somewhere out ahead of her in the dark, there was a low, burbling growl.

Stories of New York sewer rats the size of Rotweilers pounced with lurid detail on her mind, and she felt a hot panic start to clench its fist in her stomach.

The flashlight beam caught two pale greenish eyes for a second before they dodged and disappeared again.

She moved her hand slowly down her skirt, then remembered that she was unarmed. The wet snarl was rising and receding, the sound was echoing against the walls and the low ceiling. It was impossible to place it, with any confidence at all. But it was getting closer. The basement fell suddenly quiet, and she drew in a breath and listened. She began to feel her way backward, slowly and quietly back the way she'd come. It had been a mistake to come alone.

Then she heard the thing's claws scraping the floor as it loped toward her from out of the gloom, up from the twisting pathway behind her.

As she wheeled around her arm caught on a mannequin, and the flashlight skittered off into the darkness. Before she could even cry out, the force of the animal's spring struck her full in the midsection, and she tumbled flat onto her back.

She covered her face with her arms and waited for the mauling to begin, but there was only a steady breathing pressing rhythmically on top of her, diaphragm to diaphragm.

She heard three quick barks, then, and through the space between her fingers, she saw the lights come on.

Jeannie opened her hands and came face to face with a medium-sized, rumpled Shepherd-mix. And there was no mistaking it, the goofy-looking mutt was smiling at her.

"*Whuff*," it said, flattening its chin against her chest. Its hindquarters upraised playfully, and the tail began wagging in a sloppy figure-8.

She brought her hand slowly to its nose to let herself be scented, and when she'd passed his muster she scratched him behind his ears and stroked his head.

"That's a good boy," she said, and she eased him off of her. The dog rolled onto its back with its paws in the air, and Jeannie got to her feet. She brushed her clothes and ran a hand through her hair, and thanked God that Rudy hadn't been here to see this. She would have never, ever lived this one down.

It was taking a bit of a search to find the little Maglite in the newly lit environment. All the while, the dog was alternately running on ahead and then back again, cocking his head at her on each return as if he couldn't believe she still wasn't following him.

Here was something.

She pulled baggies from her jacket and snapped them open, then carefully picked up two items with plastic tweezers she'd brought from her evidence kit. One was a foot-long piece of dirty tape, with a folded, bloodied tissue stuck along its length. The other was a toy whistle on a broken neckchain, a cereal-box prize with more than a little historical significance in her field. She zip-locked the little bags and pocketed them.

The flashlight turned up behind a bound stack of old newspapers. They'd obviously once been someone's prized collection, but over the decades the pile had fused into a single pulpy mass in the cellar humidity. The paper on top was the *Philadelphia Inquirer* from July 21st, 1969.

Man Lands on Moon, the water-stained headline proclaimed.

She stood, and started again through the meandering underground level behind her new four-legged companion. There were dim chaser lights running along the circuitous path to light the way, between lines of tailor's mannequins, around boxes of brittle brown paper patterns, and amid rows and stacks of old sewing machines, hand-labeled bins and tall shelves of metal parts, walls of accountants' filing crates. All had been untouched for an age by the look of them.

The sound-activated lighting was obviously a more recent addition.

She was still moving too slowly to satisfy the dog, but they'd finally reached the end of the trail at an ornate art-deco elevator. Before she could reach out to push the call button, the dog had pawed a dog-level paddle switch, and the door hummed and rattled open for them.

Inside, the pooch again handled the floor selection, and when they'd arrived at the top he scooted through a pet door in the entryway, and then poked his head back through to remind his slow-witted friend to follow.

She took a deep breath in, and let it out slowly, then turned the knob and walked into his home.

There was quiet music playing; it was one of the songs she and Rob had listened to on their limo ride home, Neil Young, "After the Gold Rush". There was light where she was standing, but bedtime-level darkness in front and behind. She walked two small steps, and then back two, and the moving circle of soft light thoughtfully followed her movements.

After a shallow corner to the left she found herself in a dim corridor lined with tall bookshelves. They were clearly handmade, but with the care and patience of a master craftsman with nothing but time and obsession on his hands. Every joint was peg-and-mortise; nails, screws and angle-brackets were a crude offense at this level of joinery. Books, it seemed, were held in some high regard here.

The shelves were filled from floor to ceiling with well-worn but carefully arranged volumes, bound in cloth, leather and paperback. She scanned the titles and authors along the spines near her, and the filing scheme wasn't immediately evident. Not alphabetical, certainly not chronological. There was Ayn Rand sandwiched between Immanuel Kant and Bertolt Brecht, Hagel beside Marx, Friedrich Nietzsche next to C.S. Lewis, Jello Biafra uncomfortably wedged against George Will. Then she smiled softly as it occurred to her.

Point. Counterpoint.

The books spanned forty feet by ten high, from the most eso-teric transcendent philosophy to the bleakest, godless analytics. And for every impassioned idea put forward by an author, there was an opposing voice to balance the dialectic, right beside.

Near the end of the hall of books on its own floor-stand, a volume of the *Oxford English Dictionary* lay open at page 9,018. There was a tall barstool next to it, and a bookmark was laid carefully on the facing page, under a set of gold wire-rimmed reading glasses. She remembered hearing once that if one were so possessed, it would take the average person just over sixty years to read the twenty volumes of the OED from A to Z.

Eight down, by the looks of it, Mr. Fagan, and twelve more to go.

The space widened into a living area, furnished to center around its only resident. A group of lamps hummed and bright-ened to warmly light the room as she entered. And then she saw, there were small wonders all around her.

A large mechanical clock ticked quietly on the wall nearby, and except for the delicate counterweights, silvery chains and swinging pendulum that drove its workings, it was made all of newsprint. She walked to it slowly, saw that every piece had been layered, folded, rolled or laminated, from the face and hands to the exposed gears, spindles, escapements and ratchet wheels, from a single issue of the Sunday *New York Times*. It looked as though the faintest puff of wind could scatter its thousand parts, and yet through its design it was all held fast together, not with tape or pins or paste, but each piece by its purpose.

High up above her, suspended in the air, there was a glowing yellow ball, the Sun she soon realized, with the planets and their moons traveling slowly around their ellipses, borne on invisible threads, rotating in their stately orbits, with Venus, Uranus and tiny Pluto in proper retrograde. Dimly behind on the dark ceiling there were moving fields of stars, cast from a small, dumbbell-shaped apparatus purring on a shelf. She took a step toward it, stood on her toes to get a closer look. It was a model, a *working* model of a Zeiss planetarium projector, fully functioning it seemed, but impossibly small.

On a pedestal to her side she saw a whirring cluster of sheet-thin metallic fractal shapes, each geared and ingeniously articulated, moving above a base of silent motors, pulleys and pushrods. All the coppery shapes were elegantly meshing and fanning, reforming and intermingling in a kinetic ballet, each element on an axis all its own. The sculpture was continually blooming with new, marvelously intricate enfolding forms at random, creating, pausing momentarily to be admired, then moving on. Not a sculpture, she realized then, but a sculptor, master and medium combined. And she could see in those few seconds, if this marvel ran for years and years, it would never need repeat a single figure it had ever created before.

There was a sound just behind to her right, and she looked down to see a small chessboard on a Shaker table, under a delicate glass dome. She knelt by it, looked in at the meticulously carved chessmen and the inlaid, polished wooden squares that formed the surface of the board.

The pieces were moving, all by themselves.

The sound she had heard had been White castling kingside, on the fourth move of a modified Ruy Lopez opening. After a moment's thinking, hidden cogs and levers whirred softly, and she watched as Black opted for the Steinitz Defense, a favorite ploy of Kasparov in his early prime.

This was no mass-produced novelty. Like those magnificent, simple bookshelves, and everything else that surrounded her, this board and the sentient clockworks that ran it were made by hand. And if he had made this all himself it must have taken years, decades, and the skills of a small army of artisans.

She stood and stepped back slowly, still watching the fairies' game progress. Her leg brushed an empty bottle on the arm of a recliner, and it thudded to the floor.

"John?" a voice said from above, from all around.

Jeannie held up her hands and turned slowly, and she saw the shiny darkened wall that had been behind her beginning to awaken.

A matrix of many hundreds of tiny LCD screens were flickering to life in sequence, row by row. She moved closer, and saw that each of them was displaying its own discrete little stream of different digital media. Video, captioned audio, pictures, Web sites, chat sessions, newsgroups, streams of consciousness of all shapes, kinds and cultures, from all around the world. Some were merging and forming impromptu unions with adjacent screens, building to a more prominent presentation of this or that event. The onslaught of visual input was breathtaking.

"John?" the voice repeated. It wasn't an intercom or a recording. Though there was only the faintest hint to a trained ear, she could tell that it wasn't human, had never been.

She looked around, and there was a keyboard on a hutch desk in front of a computer CPU. A Post-it note was stuck below the flat glass monitor screen there.

Password: chillypenguin, it said.

Jeannie smiled. She had spoken to the man, and she knew a honeypot when she saw one. On the one-in-ten-thousand chance that someone would ever find their way in here when he was gone, he'd set a trap. And that bogus password probably wasn't the only one.

She waited silently, and at length, as she expected it would, the voice challenge routine timed out.

"John, would you like to review the results of your last search?" the voice asked.

A box appeared on the huge display, with choices of *Yes, No,* and *Cancel.* She walked up to the twelve-foot screen, drew in a breath, and touched *Yes.*

The wall of mass media faded to black, and the results of his last command materialized on the screen. She watched as a hundred news stories cascaded around the glowing wall, and it was a long moment before her mind would allow the subject of the search results to descend on her.

It was a public chronology of her own life she was watching, from childhood to the near-present, everything that had ever been written about her in the press, everything she'd ever published, every bit of her that had ever been mentioned in any accessible way. At the end she was facing her own life-size image, standing there holding her trophy after the All-Agency meet last August. Her heart began to pound.

He knew who she was.

"Oh, my goodness," Jeannie said.

At the sound of her voice the music stopped and the screen went black, and then it filled with a rectangular gridded voice-print image. A playhead indicator visually rewound, and her voice repeated back in quadraphonic fidelity.

"*Oh, my goodness,*" it boomed.

Measurement overlays flitted around the peaks and valleys of the audio spectrum, and other comparator samples flickered in the lower corner. The computer was searching for a match, and at length, it found one.

"Jeannie Reese," the computer said. "Filed, but unclassified. Assign a security status, please, John."

The software was assuming they were standing here together. A dialog box appeared on the screen, with a long slider on a scale that went from "Enemy" at the base, all the way up to "Friend" at its summit.

She thought furiously. They had spoken for hours on the phone that night, and that must have been unusual, it must have set her apart somehow. The computer had sampled her voice, and who knows, it had possibly even listened to the conversation. He'd associated her name with her voiceprint, but he hadn't flagged her as an enemy. Maybe he hadn't had the time, or the interest. Or maybe he had left the door open so that someday they might speak again.

She considered the slider bar. "Enemy" would obviously be bad, but the other end of the spectrum was probably another snare. John Fagan wouldn't trust anyone all the way.

She touched the image of the slide control, and moved her finger three-quarters of the way to "Friend," then tapped "OK" to record the answer.

"One moment," the digital voice intoned. "Visitor record created, status permissions granted. It is a pleasure to meet you, Jeannie Reese, and welcome back, John. There will be coffee in a few minutes."

It was a female voice, digitized, and programmed to synthesize and speak natural language on-the-fly. She'd helped develop systems like this, years ago at the MIT Media Lab and more recently in the Communicator program at DARPA. One ongoing project in Cambridge had been an attempt to identify and then model the mechanics of human dialogue. The basic requirements had boiled down to only seven: recognition, substantive association, lateral insight, additive retrieval, assembly, review and response. When automated and linked with a sufficient data-mine to draw on, those simple elements could quite convincingly mimic the pace and content of verbal interaction. In fact, the repartee of the MIT computers could easily out-banter even the most nimble of human cocktail-party conversationalists.

212

But as far as she knew, no think-tank had ever achieved this level of sheer reality in the voice itself. There was a slight Southern accent, and the subtle lilts and intonations were meticulously crafted, inspired in their nuances. This thing spoke with the character and somehow even the attitude of an earthy, self-assured young woman with an elegant Kentucky drawl.

Jeannie heard noises in the kitchen area, the sounds of a coffee grinder and steaming water, and soon the heady scent of strong espresso wafted into the room.

"Can you . . . understand me?" Jeannie asked.

"Accuracy would improve with training. Shall I initiate recognition training now, Jeannie Reese?"

"No, not right now," she said, speaking slowly and precisely. "When was the last search completed?"

"Please speak normally. I will do my best to comprehend."

There was a hint of something in the gentle voice, a touch of hurt just under the words.

She took a step nearer to the screen, and put her ear close to the Plexiglas. Behind it she heard the whirring beehive of a CPU farm, probably thirty or fifty multiprocessor PCs neurally net-worked together to form the sensitive, synthetic mind she was conversing with.

Jeannie had learned to live her life without the comfort of friends, but the man who lived here had approached the same problem from a different angle. A friend was necessary and, dis-appointed by all applicants from the human race, he had built himself one.

"I'm sorry," she said. "I didn't mean to . . . underestimate your intelligence."

"Not at all," the warm voice answered. "You were correct to question. One difference between genius and stupidity, after all, is that genius hath its limits."

Jeannie closed her eyes and thought for a moment.

"Albert Einstein," she said.

"That is correct, Jeannie Reese. A great man, who lived to

213

see the fruits of his genius turned to the ends of limitless stupidity."

The massive screen filled end-to-end with a moving newsreel image of the first test of the hydrogen bomb. The horrific flash and the enormous expanding mottled ball of rolling hell ascending into the sky; this film clip was familiar to most anyone with a television. What history had not adequately recorded, though, was that a significant number of the H-bomb scientists had been thoroughly convinced that the blast would spark a chain reaction with the nitrogen in the air, ignite the atmosphere, and kill everything on the planet.

Of course, they'd pushed the button anyway.

The screen cleared, and her life-story reappeared there. "The last search completed seventeen days, twenty-one hours, and eight minutes ago," the computer said.

The day after their phone conversation. She'd blown it, frightened him away. He was gone.

Jeannie felt something hit her foot. The dog had brought in a dirty tennis ball and dropped it onto the toe of her shoe. It bounced off and rolled under the chess table, and the pup gave her a disappointed look and trotted off to retrieve it again.

But the dog, she thought. He wouldn't have left his dog.

There was an almost full carton of cigarettes on an end-table, and an open bottle of Bloody Mary mix and half an Almond Joy next to it. Nothing about this place looked abandoned, far from it. It looked like he had stepped out on an errand of a few minutes. And never returned.

She realized that her pager had been vibrating, and she swore under her breath and quickly checked its small gray screen.

G M E N, it said.

She'd stayed too long.

There was no use trying to get out now, and risk getting shot down in that winding basement. She bent and picked up the empty half-pint whiskey bottle she'd knocked to the floor earlier, and carefully wrapped it in her last two plastic bags and slipped

214

it into her inside jacket pocket. Then she faced the door and knelt down with her hands behind her head, and waited for the assault team to arrive.

The dog was the first to hear them.

His ears perked up and he tore off toward the door, then he skidded to a stop and returned to pick up his ball.

"Stay, boy," Jeannie whispered. "Stay, stay here."

He considered her for a moment, and then ran away and disappeared through his swinging door. She heard the elevator start down, and then far away, it clanked to a stop at the bottom floor.

Long minutes passed, and when the old Otis began its ascent, its cables were singing and its motors straining against a weight beyond its capacity.

She heard the elevator door open, and a moment later a bright red dot searched briefly through the room and quickly found her heart. She held herself perfectly still as the thick barrel of a noise-suppressed automatic rifle extended slowly toward her from the corridor.

The man holding it was dressed in dead black from his visored helmet to his boots. He held the gun on her with one hand and motioned for her to be silent, to stay where she was. He raised his free hand to shoulder level and gave a quick series of hand signals to the men behind him. An open hand, an index finger, a horizontal palm, a pumped fist.

Visual on suspect, single individual, unarmed and subdued, I am proceeding, follow me.

As he padded into the room, no matter which way the man turned or where his eyes were tracking, the laser sight never left her kill zone. Others were coming in now, one by one, tracing the point-man's steps before branching out to cover the interior.

Slowly and deliberately, Jeannie brought one hand out from behind her head.

Every weapon in the room trained on her, from every direction. She brought her raised index finger down carefully in front of her lips and exhaled an almost inaudible *shhhhhh*.

One of them had circled back around behind her. A second man stepped to her and lifted her chin to look closely at her face, then turned and walked up to the wall-sized screen where her multimedia biography was still displayed. He looked at the squad leader and nodded his head, then signaled the man behind her.

She felt a gloved hand grab the scruff of her collar and push her face-down onto the hardwood floor, a knee forcing her legs roughly apart. Her hands were pulled behind her, and a nylon zip-tie tightened around her wrists.

The man who had taken her down straddled her and began the frisk. He reached under and around her body, and she felt her face flush hot as he rubbed and pinched her breasts. He slid one hand down past her stomach as the other one reached under her skirt and moved too slowly up her thigh. She was trembling, and his mouth was near her ear.

"Don't worry, baby," he breathed. "It's all business."

When he'd found nothing of professional interest but her empty holster, he stood and rested his foot on the small of her back, pinning her arms. Jeannie could sense the others fanning out through the loft, though they were barely disturbing the air as they moved. In under a minute, they had all converged again in the center space around her. All clear.

"All right," the leader said loudly, "let's bag it and tag it."

The room lights suddenly blazed to high brightness, but no hand had touched a dimmer switch. The wide media screen blanked out and refilled with a voiceprint grid, and as the playback resounded all around them they closed ranks and swung their weapons upward, downward, at everything and nothing.

Let's bag it and tag it, the man's voice thundered.

Blue-white flashes popped and the blank portions of the wall-screen began filling with photographs of the assault team, from hidden cameras at high and low angles at every corner of the room. Graphical boxes flickered around the freeze-frames, searching the images for visual cues. A clear shot of one of the agents came to the forefront, and a bright white line of pixels traced a path around his submachine gun.

The rest of the image faded, and a flipbook set of line-drawings began to overlay the isolated picture of the man's gun. The flashing images stopped on a match, and the two pictures resized and rotated into alignment.

A caption teletyped in and enlarged below the image:

Positive ID (94% confidence):

Heckler & Koch MP5 9mm Submachine Gun

Current armories: NYPD Special Weapons and Tactics (SWAT), FBI, ATF

The voiceprint reappeared onscreen.

"Unrecognized," the soft woman's voice said. "Please repeat and verify."

"Just ignore this fucking sideshow," the squad leader said. "Start dusting, and bag up all this shit for the lab."

Some of the agents holstered their guns and began the crime-scene processing. One of them bumped the chessboard near the corridor and the glass dome shattered to the floor, the tiny chessmen scattering among the shards. Others took station at the door and windows.

None of them seemed to notice the large digital timer that had appeared in the center of the big screen. It had started at three minutes, and was counting down by hundredths of seconds.

"Unrecognized," the computer repeated. "Please respond and verify. Exit process initiated."

"Hey," Jeannie said. The boot in her back pressed down to quiet her, but she had gotten the lead man's attention. She jutted her chin toward the screen. "I think you guys had better deal with that."

Another voice came from behind her, near the computer desk.

"Sir, this thing is wired up like a Christmas tree, you need to take a look at this."

"Explosives?"

"No, it's not a bomb, I don't know what in the fuck it is. We've done the sweep, all floors, nominal readings, there are no explosives in this place."

"Let me up," Jeannie said. "Let me see it, I can help you. My ID's in my jacket, check it, I'm with the government."

The lead man knelt beside her.

"Oh, we know who you are, sugar," he said. "You're in a whole world of shit now, genius."

The man's walkie-talkie beeped in its beltloop, and he touched its hands-free switch.

"What."

"We've cut the power to the whole block, sir, and the lights up there are still on. This place is off the grid, I can't see where the juice is coming in from, but it's sure as hell not on a Con Ed meter."

"Shh, quiet," the squad leader said, holding his hands out like an armed school-crossing guard.

Jeannie was closest to the ground, so she'd already heard the noise that had caught his attention. Under the floor, one after another, a series of gas engines had begun starting themselves and throttling up to high-idle.

Generators, electrical generators.

The lights in the room grew even brighter, and a bulb in one of the floor lamps burst from the overage.

She twisted her head around, and managed to look backward toward the computer on the desk where the FBI tech was frantically examining the set-up.

"Oh, my God," she whispered.

The man had pulled the veneer from the sides and top shelf of the hutch, and she saw that there were a series of tall cylinders joined with heavy coils of wire and copper tubing surrounding the CPU.

218

"Take that big screen down, get a look at what's behind it," the lead agent ordered, and four men began to hammer at the media wall with their hand tools. They managed to get a prybar under one corner, and sparks popped and sputtered as they bent it outward and cracked a door-sized opening.

"Jesus Christ," one of them said. "It looks like fucking Mission Control in there."

Jeannie turned her head around to see what they were seeing. Through the smoldering opening they'd made in the ruined screen, she saw shelves and racks of networked computers, diagnostic monitors, RAID stacks and water-cooling systems. And more of the wire-wrapped and copper-coiled metal cylinders, many, many more.

"Two minutes to exit," the computer said. "Master display malfunction. Backup monitor active."

The nineteen-inch CRT monitor on the desk crackled out of sleep mode, displaying the decaying timer and a Windows dialog box.

Halt exit sequence? it read. There were buttons labeled *Yes* and *No*.

"Sir, what should I do?"

"Click 'Yes.'"

"Guys," Jeannie said, "let me up, I can help you."

"Shut up, Buffy. Click 'Yes.'"

The engineer sat at the desk, moved the mouse pointer, and clicked the button.

A pleasant tone sounded, and another dialog box appeared.

Please enter password: it read, and a cursor strobed in the input box.

The man leaned back in the chair, bit his lip and gripped his hair with both hands. A yellow Post-it note attached below the monitor caught his eye.

"Jeez, is this guy an idiot," the man said, as he rolled forward and rapidly typed the word on the note, *chillypenguin*, into the text box. "He leaves his password out in plain sight, like my secretary."

"Whatever the hell you do," Jeannie said from the floor, "do not enter that password."

"We're at one minute, chief, what do you say?"

"Enter it, go ahead."

Jeannie heard the click of the mouse with her upfacing ear. Through her other one, she heard five more generators cough and roar to life under the floorboards.

The lights hummed up brighter and brighter. At fifty seconds on the timer, all but one of the remaining bulbs burst in a stutter of hissing flashes. The countdown continued.

"Turn it off, pull the plug," the leader shouted.

"There's no switch and no plug, it's hard-wired into the wall, there's no outlet."

"It's a computer, Lewis, just reboot it, for crissakes, give it the three-finger salute."

The man at the keyboard put three fingers on the Ctrl, Alt, and Delete buttons, gave his boss one last look for confirmation, then pressed the reboot keys simultaneously.

The timer on the screen stopped running, at 00:00:15:21.

The computer man opened his eyes, leaned his head back and breathed a heavy shuddering sigh, then wiped his glistening forehead with his sleeve. There were general, relieved congratulations from the assembly, and one of the agents stepped forward and gave him an elaborate hip-hop handshake.

He was rolling his chair back from the desk when he noticed a new dialog box on the display.

Reboot? the text there asked.

The man smiled and moved the mouse, clicked *Yes*. A new box popped up in response.

Are you sure?

He hesitated, and looked back at his lead for guidance. The other man nodded. When he turned back to the screen, though, he saw that the words had changed.

Well what are you waiting for, ass-wipe? they said. *I asked you a question. Are you sure?*

The onscreen responses weren't as simple now. There were eight buttons in the box to choose from.

Abort Retry Fail OK YES END NO Cancel

The man at the computer was frozen. He knew as well as Jeannie did, whatever he clicked, it really didn't matter now.

The pointer began to move, though the man's hands were firmly gripping his knees. The little white arrow slid across the screen to *END*, and the button depressed.

The timer refilled the screen, and the flickering countdown resumed.

"Please remove all ferrous metal objects from your person," the computer's voice said.

"Put your guns down and get on the floor!" Jeannie shouted. "Do it, now!"

The entire team had gathered in a ragged semicircle around the computer desk. But they only stood there, watching the terminal seconds tick down.

"Hold your positions," the squad leader said. He checked the chronograph on his wrist, shook it, and checked again.

"What the fuck," he said. "My watch stopped."

The copper coils surrounding the scores of metal cylinders began to turn furry white in downward spirals, and the supercooled metal sent wisps of pale vapor and tiny snowflakes curling toward the floor.

The technician at the desk stood and took a step backward, then another one.

"Uh, oh," he said.

Jeannie closed her eyes and turned her face away.

She'd spent a summer interning with a team of magnetic resonance imaging designers in 1994. One morning she'd seen the superconducting core of an MRI machine throw a misplaced crash-cart across an operating room, like it was a toy. These cylinders were from such a core, probably retrieved from salvage for the cost of hauling them away.

Of course, there were a lot more of them here than she'd ever seen in one place before.

Even though there was a combat boot in her back, the floor was clearly the best place to be right now. She could no longer see the timer, but her mind was keeping the final count.

Three

Two

One

Zero

"Goodbye," the computer said softly.

The room dimmed as a low reverberating drone filled the air around them, and the windows began shaking in their frames as the sound rose through the scale to a high-pitched dog-whistle squeal. At the ear-splitting crescendo, the last remaining light-bulb burst like a cherry-bomb as every piece of metal in the room flew from where it was to where it wanted to be, to the center of a quarter-million Gauss magnetic field.

Guns, knives, lamps, prybars, ammo clips, grenades, chairs, watches, pens and eyeglasses hurtled in tight formation through the air, some crashing backward through the remains of the media wall, some flying forward to bond with the magnets surrounding the computer desk. The CPU there clanked against the wall of the hutch, its metal case creaking and buckling in the fist of a quantum giant.

Jeannie opened her eyes. Emergency lights had clicked on near the ceiling, painting everything in the loft in dim amber monochrome. The agents were all on the floor, disarmed and disoriented, most of them struck and bleeding from flying debris, some just instinctively prone. Through the craters in the destroyed media screen, she saw all of the computers and components in the control room suspended against the far wall, crumpled by the irresistible force that gripped them.

One thing was certain, and it was the only thing John Fagan had designed this last-stand gambit to ensure. Every single bit of digital evidence in this room, in this building, was now erased

222

beyond any chance of recovery. And that voice, the companion he'd created to comfort him in his solitude. She was gone, too. And not even Jay Marshall could bring her back.

There was a final *thunk*, and the magnets let the clusters of metal objects go clattering to the floor. As the few who were able got themselves to their feet, Jeannie heard sirens approaching outside.

"Now what is that, the police?" the lead agent said.

One of the men was thumping his walkie-talkie, but it was stone dead. He walked to a window and broke the glass with the heel of his gloved hand, then pushed one of the covering boards out and away to get a look at the street.

"Fire department," he said. "Six engines and a ladder. They're spraying down the buildings on either side."

The head man looked around, frowning.

"Hey, do you guys smell smoke?" he asked.

The acrid odor of frying electronics was evident, now that he mentioned it. Then a low *thoom* came from the direction of the control room, the sound of a gas oven igniting.

"Fire!" someone yelled.

"Everybody out, on the double, injured first, stay out of that elevator, we're going out the window."

The smoke had become nearly blinding as they finished smashing through the boarded opening. The ladder crew outside had already raised their cherry-picker, and they began the anxious evacuation, three to a load. By the time the last group was out, visibility in the building was down to zero and the fire was spreading rapidly.

In all the noise and chaos, no one had heard the door of the elevator rattling closed, or its slow and final descent to the dark basement.

A few minutes later, down on the ground, the assault team reassembled and counted heads.

"All accounted for, sir."

"Who called the fire department, before there was even a fire?" the squad leader asked.

"Guy said it was a computer call, like from ADT, or some security system. Told them where to come, and what they'd find when they got here."

"Fucking weird-ass shit."

"Yeah. This whole night."

He looked around. "Where's the perp?"

The other man frowned. "She came down with the last group," he said. "Didn't she?"

The squad leader spat on the sidewalk and put his radio to his ear, keyed it. Still dead.

"Fuck me," he shouted. "God damnit, find a working radio and call an APB, city-wide for that little whore. Checkpoint the bridges and tunnels, she gets off this island, it's somebody's ass! Move! Move! Move!"

The agents scattered in all directions to execute their orders, but they knew the situation. If the woman wasn't currently burning alive in that tinderbox up there, then she was gone, at least for the moment. The streetlights were out for blocks around, and it was an awfully big city.

The FDNY stayed on to protect the surrounding structures, but the fire in the old building in front of them was blazing out of control. There was no reasonable way in, no people inside, and these turn-of-the-century dinosaurs had a lot of pulpy kindling in their frames.

No, this call would be purely defensive, by the book, spray and pray. No firefighter was going to lose his life here tonight, not for this lost cause.

Within an hour the building had burned out to its brittle shell, another gutted husk for the demolition crews.

27

He'd given her ten minutes inside, and enough was enough. If she came down and found him waiting here against her wishes, she might be angry. Fine, she'd just have to deal with it.

The basement was lit but only dimly, by scattered overhead fixtures and floor-level path lights that traced a twisting route through rows and stacks of decaying junk, some of it piled up taller than his head. It was like the queue maze to a Disney ride, only with mildew and dust bunnies. Packrats of the Caribbean, maybe.

As his eyes measured the interior, his hands moved to detach his belt holster, reversing and refastening it lower down, around his left thigh. He tested its position with his right hand. If the gun had to come out, a cross-draw from there would be fastest.

Rudy had taken off a few minutes earlier to line up transportation. If a SWAT team descended on them, they weren't going to be able to stand on the corner and hail a taxi. The two of them had worked out a simple rendezvous schedule, a different intersection every five minutes, encircling this position in an outward spiral, and a cab with the meter running would be waiting at every meeting point.

His pager vibrated in his pocket. He checked the display, read the grim message there, and then switched off the device and removed the battery to ensure its silence.

Company was coming.

He finished scanning his surroundings, memorizing the floor-plan. When they came, they'd sweep this space thoroughly before proceeding to the upper levels, with night-vision, infrared, audio and all manner of other sensors. If it took a firefight to get her out, it would be one against many, and his only advantage would be surprise.

He chose a spot, high up in a corner lair amid stacked crates of old double-entry journals and brittle paper files. He lay flat to minimize his heat signature, and willed himself, mentally and physically, to fade into the clutter. Stealth wasn't about being invisible. It was about being just invisible enough.

As the seconds passed he thought back to the nine months he'd spent immersed in the rigorous training the Delta Force wryly referred to as fieldcraft. In the sniper matches, the goal had been to advance a thousand meters across open ground toward alert adversaries, with only minimal natural cover. Staying unseen would have been difficult enough, but the game required students to periodically put a bullet in a bull's-eye in the midst of a team of binocular-armed observers. On the third day, Rob had stolen all the way to the observation platform, inched up the ladder with his knife in his teeth, and tied the shoelaces of the head instructor to a cowbell. He'd earned a hall-of-fame spot on the tavern wall for that one.

The lights ticked out in sequence from the entrance to the far end of the floor, and with the coming of the darkness, the first of them eased like cemetery fog through the arch of the doorway.

Rob heard the faint, momentary high-pitched whine of activated night-vision gear and the whisk of quiet footsteps. But even in this first advance they exhibited a weakness. He had seen it many times on the battlefield, and always preceding tragedy. It was the swagger of a vastly superior force, one with no fear whatever of its quarry.

226

Within ten meters of the entryway one of them bumped against a leaning stack of something, and the falling debris whapped and rustled to the floor. They all halted momentarily at the noise.

A few seconds later, way over in the corner, an elevator started down.

His eyes were adjusting, but he was able to coax only minimal detail from the darkness in front of him. The group was in a tight array, and he heard several safeties click off as the descending car reached the bottom of the shaft, and the door slid open.

A dog barked three times, and the entire squad crouched down as the lights in the basement came on again.

Half a minute passed before a low growl began to rise from the pathway in front of them.

Maybe the point-man panicked, or maybe he just squeezed an extra quarter-gram of nervous pressure on the hair-trigger. There was a windy *thoot* as his silenced weapon fired, a pained yelp, and then all canine hell broke loose.

What hadn't killed the dog had apparently made him stronger, because the sounds that came out of him became pure unleashed junkyard rage. The squad fell back into each other as it charged them, and before anyone could get off another clean shot it was on the man in front like a rabid wolverine.

The dog had bitten the shit out of the first guy and was starting up the leg of a second before they managed to get a Taser on him. Another yelp, surprised, small and beaten, and all was quiet again.

The group took stock, and gradually regained their formation. One of them picked up the limp animal by the collar and dragged it out, and two others helped their bloodied colleagues back up the stairs to the street. One man used a set of cutters from his toolbelt to clip the supply wires to the lighting, sending the basement back to near total darkness. Then on a silent order, they moved with new caution on toward the elevator door.

He waited until it was clear to him that the entire party had gone up, and that no more were coming through, then Rob carefully descended from his perch to prepare the escape.

Without the benefit of night-vision, touch and recall were the only aids in finding his way. The main path couldn't be the only way to the exit; it was only the most obvious one. He felt his way along a new route, moving an occasional crate or other obstacle until he'd reached the stairs. This way was wide enough for only one, and that only barely. He walked it once, then again and again until he could make the journey end-to-end in under twenty seconds by his mental count.

Next, he found a large spool of heavy thread among the tailors' stations, and pull-tested it. The outer layer was mealy and decayed, but he unrolled several arm-lengths until the cord ran fresh and strong.

The hunting party's key advantage was numbers, and he would have to turn that to a limitation. They were prepared and ordered, and he would need to negate that, too. With just a few moments of chaos, he would have half a chance of getting her out and away.

That is, if they didn't all come back down the elevator with her in the lead, one big happy family, having a good laugh about the little misunderstanding upstairs.

Possible, yes, but not so frickin' likely.

He used the thick thread to weave a long network of interconnected tripwires halfway up the main path. If all was well when they came down, he'd have time to warn them to stop. If not, they would come this way quickly, with the prisoner under guard in the rear. With luck, one or more of them would go down when they hit the taut ankle-level filaments. The others would be distracted by the noise from falling rubbish, and then facing lines of leaning tailors' mannequins and overbalanced filing cabinets and shelves would tumble inward to block the way in front and behind. He'd drop in from the side then, pick her up and make for the door down his new escape route.

They'd be exposed at the exit for a few seconds, but he would be between her and the guns. If they were ready and able to fire, with any luck the Kevlar and his body would stop the bullets. And if they both managed to make it outside their troubles wouldn't be over, but at least they'd have a running chance at freedom. Or she would, if he was down.

No worries. He'd been in worse spots. He was almost certain of it.

He had just finished checking his handiwork one final time when the engines began starting up on the floors above.

What in the hell?

He found a niche in a small stuffy closet near the elevator door and waited, listening. Whatever was happening up there now, it was unlikely to have been accounted for in the tactical plan. It sounded like the building was coming alive above him. And the building sounded pissed.

A minute passed, with distant shouts and crashes echoing down the elevator shaft from floors away. And then silence.

And smoke. The sour smell of burning wood and wiring was drifting into the space around him, and the temperature had risen by degrees. Soon he could hear the timpani roll of a spreading fire on the floor just above him, and before long the heat began pulsing through the humid basement in arid waves. Here and there, spots on the suspended ceiling were beginning to radiate a malignant orange glow.

Well, common sense be damned. His girl was in a burning building, and with a cliché like that in play, he wasn't about to sit on his ass waiting for the fire trucks.

An elevator was the very last place to be in a house fire, of course, but it was the only way to reach her now. He stood and checked his weapon, and was reaching out for the call button when he heard the car start down.

He backed into the shadows and watched as the elevator slowed and then touched bottom. The door slid noisily into its housing, and he saw her, bound and motionless on the varnished oak floor.

"Jeannie," he said.

He knelt down next to her, cut the nylon tie around her wrists with his knife, and took her up in his arms. Her breathing was unsteady, and tears were in her eyes as she looked up, slow to recognize him. There was blood in her hair, and he saw where she had struck her head on the brass railing.

"Rob," she said softly, dream-talking, "we've got to go."

"I know, honey, we'll go now. Don't try to talk. I've got you, just hold onto me."

He lifted her gently and held her close against him, and as he stepped back out of the car the dry heated air caught in his throat. Glowing cinders were dropping through the ceiling, and where they lit, new fires puffed eagerly to life. The path he'd made for their escape was blocked by a waist-high inferno.

The only way out was the way they'd all come in.

The flickering light from the cresting fires couldn't be trusted, it was throwing only hints and silhouettes on the floor in front of him. He counted his steps, and as he neared the trap zone, he kicked off his shoes and felt ahead gingerly for the first of the tripwires he'd set.

There. There it was.

From that reference point, he walked slowly forward through the maze of snares, stepping over each of them from memory. The scorched air soon forced his eyes nearly closed, but in the smoke and the darkness they hadn't been of much use anyway. The building above them was creaking and yawning as it burned, but the groaning old timbers needed to hold just a few seconds more.

His heel plucked one of the taut lines, and he held his breath in the second it would take for the trap to spring, pinning them, so the fire could come at its leisure for the kill.

But the crush never came.

He took the fatal step again, only an inch farther on this time.

"Rob," she said against his chest, "was there a dog? Did you see a little dog?" She looked up at him, tugged his lapel. "We need to look for that dog."

He was nearing the end of the deadly rigging, and the doorway would be only thirty paces on.

"I saw the dog, sweetheart," he said. "He's outside, I saw him go outside."

The encircling fire burned through one of the tripwires as he stepped into the clear, and he heard and felt the shuddering crash as the path behind them disappeared under a half-ton avalanche of falling rubbish and twisted metal shelving.

Nice work, Robert, he thought. Looks like Plan A would have gone off without a hitch. Though it would have been nice to have nailed down Plan B in just a bit more detail.

He reached the stairs and climbed them slowly, peered up and down the moonlit alley. Destiny was smiling on them, at least in this moment. No one was stationed at the exit. He checked his watch and matched the time to its corresponding meeting point. It was north-northeast o'clock.

She had drifted out of consciousness as they reached the alleyway. They needed a doctor, just as soon as they were well clear of this place. He carried her lightly and moved from shadow to shadow until the building they'd left was two hundred meters behind. There was no pursuit.

When he saw the waiting taxi, with the back door standing open and Rudy sitting on the trunk, he covered the last two blocks at a sprint.

"And where may I take you this evening, my friends?" the driver asked. His words were hesitant, and all they could see was a worried frown in the rearview mirror.

"Just drive, for God's sake," Rudy said, and the car started away. He was kneeling in the sticky floor well, and Jeannie was lying across the seat, with her head cradled in Rob's lap. She was pale and drawn, a ghost. He brushed a strand of hair from her mouth.

"What happened to her?"

"She fell, hit her head," Rob said. The short version would do for now.

Rudy took one of her hands in his, and held it against his cheek. The skin was cool and damp, and her wrist was bruised and raw where the bonds had cut in.

Rob scanned the driver's ID above the glove box in front. The man was speaking into his radio, in a dialect he recognized.

"*Namaste, Khushnaseeb,*" Rob said, and the driver looked back at him through the clear plastic divider. "*Meraa naam Robert hai.*"

The man in front hesitated, keyed his mike once more and signed off, then turned his attention back to the traffic. The eyes in the mirror were softer now, with the hint of a smile. "*Kya aap Urdu boltay hai?*" he said.

Rob shook his head, made a pinching motion with his thumb and index finger. "*Mai siraf thori see Urdu bolta houn.* I'm sure that your English is much better than my Urdu, friend."

"What you know of it, you speak quite well."

"*Danyavad,*" Rob replied. "When I saw your name, it told me that our fortunes had turned."

The driver laughed out loud, and nodded his head.

Rudy looked around to the man's name displayed on the dashboard, *Khushnaseeb Iqbal.* "What does that mean?" he asked.

"Khushnaseeb," Rob said. "It means lucky."

The driver briefly signaled a lane change, but apparently thought better of it and continued straight on. "How did you come to learn this bit of my beautiful language?"

A loaded question, that. He had neither the time nor the mental energy to construct a coherent cover story, so he would roll the dice with the truth. "I'm . . . in the military," Rob said.

The driver's foot came slightly off the gas, and his steering lost a touch of its agenda.

The volatile politics that embroiled South Asia were a centuries-old morass of tribal infighting, international brinksmanship, blood feuds, brutal insurgencies, revolt, revenge and meddling from outside powers, with the United States at times being a

232

prominent if clandestine player among these last. But this man was in America now, he or his forebears had likely fled something to come here, and there was some hope in that.

"I had a diplomatic mission, in Pakistan, about three years ago," Rob said. He waited until the man's eyes found his in the rearview. "I shouldn't speak of it. But I feel I can trust you."

"Where, in Pakistan?"

"The northwest frontier. Up in the mountains, the Toba Kakar, north of Khanozai. We had a meeting with a man, named Haji Omar."

The driver braked abruptly, sliding the cab to a halt on the oily pavement. They had nearly rear-ended the line of cars ahead, stopped at a long red light. The driver looked into the mirror again. "And how was your visit, with this Haji Omar?" The expectation in the man's voice could have meant any number of things.

"I hiked for two days from my dropzone, it was like walking across the moon, have you been up there?" The man in front nodded, but didn't speak. "So I dug in and waited, and watched the advance men move in. They combed those hills, man, two guys almost stepped on me, I swear, but they finally figured it was safe, and they brought him on up." The eyes in the mirror had widened, but were still unreadable. "It was perfect, clear air, bright overcast, no wind to speak of. I zeroed my scope, had the son of a bitch in the cross, right here," Rob tapped his forehead with his finger. "Held him in my sight like that for an hour, waiting for the go order, from Washington. But it never came through." Rob shook his head. "I've got a lot of regrets, but if I could undo one of them, I'd go back and take that shot."

The light had turned green, and Rob ticked his chin ahead to signal the driver that they should go. The car pulled away.

"And you're in some trouble, now, you and your companions," the cab driver said.

"We haven't broken the law," Rob replied. "But you got that right, we're in some trouble. My girl, she needs a doctor, and we need to find a place away from here, until she can recover. And please, with your radio, please be careful what you say about us. The ones who are seeking us, they are listening."

The cab made a quick lane change, then a hard right-hand turn to the east. The driver thumbed buttons on his cell phone and put it to his ear.

"Will you help us?" Rob asked. His hand had moved to the pistol still holstered low on his left.

The man was speaking quietly into the phone. He raised his voice in a flash of anger at one point, but the words came too thick and fast to be deciphered. He looked in the rearview mirror and nodded as the language became less heated again.

The barrel of the gun slid free of its nylon sheath, and as Rob chambered a round the double *snick* of the slide was lost in the road noise. "Where are we headed?" he asked, calmly. Still a friend.

The driver held up his hand. *Patience*, the gesture said, *just another minute*. Rob spoke to Rudy with his eyes, told him to be ready, to protect her if the time came.

The phone snapped closed. "My apologies, Robert. I'm taking the FDR up ahead, right up here, uptown. My sister, yaa! She's insufferable for a month now. She'll meet us outside the school, she's a first-year resident, at NYU. She has just come off a 36-hour rotation at the hospital, and she bites, so keep your hands inside the car." He laughed unselfconsciously at his joke, and there was a smile in his voice as he continued. "So you have fought against the Taliban, and you have seen the face of Haji Omar, the ghost of Kalushah, curse his fathers. And still he lives. Would that governments had the uncluttered vision of their soldiers, no?"

"That could be good and bad," Rob said. Until 9/11 the US relationship with the Taliban had spanned the diplomatic spectrum from guarded neutrality to covert support and corporate negotiation. From the few details he'd been given at the time, he'd deduced that his righteous mission had more to do with a disputed easement for a proposed UNOCAL oil pipeline than with religious tolerance and human rights.

Khushnaseeb Iqbal caught Rob's eyes again in the rearview mirror. "You don't need to worry, my friend. My sister, she can take care of your girl."

Rob slipped his pistol back into the holster, and fastened it there. "Thank you, brother," he said. "*Aap ke madad ka shukria*, from my heart."

"Please, it's my duty to my God. I have seen some good and much evil, and I can see the good in you. We are *ham raah*, you and me. We are fellow travelers."

At 34th and First, the cab pulled up beside Kirin Iqbal, looking cold and impatient on the corner in blue-green scrubs and a parka from LL Bean.

The men waited outside while she gave Jeannie a quick exam. After a few minutes the young resident emerged, closed the car door gently, and pulled her brother aside. They talked quietly, at some length and with much animation. Rob could see the story of his mission to Pakistan being retold in broad gesture and epic prose, to a skeptical audience of one. The woman turned abruptly and approached the other two men.

She picked Rob as the most likely perpetrator. Her cell phone was in one hand, and a cartridge of pepper spray was in the other.

"I've got a finger on a 911 speed-dial, and security in that building over there can be over here in about five seconds, so feel free to try something. My idiot brother mistakes his soft head for a soft heart, but I have no such weakness. Understand?"

Rob nodded.

"How did that happen?" she said, cocking her head toward the backseat of the cab.

"It was a fall," Rob said. "We had some trouble, and her hands were bound behind her, and she fell against a metal railing."

"Trouble? With the law?"

235

"Only with some, in the government. I'm a Navy lieutenant, and my friends are with a government agency, and we've run afoul of them somehow, they've mistaken us for enemies. But she's the important one, she's the only one of us that matters. We need to get her well, and to a safe place. A great deal may depend on it."

Kirin reached into her jacket pocket and pulled out Jeannie's ID. She flipped it open to look it over again, and then she took a step closer to them.

"There's an alert inside the hospital, with her picture, this picture here. Unlawful flight to avoid prosecution, it says, it's at the front desk, admissions, the ER, on every fax machine in the building." She closed the ID folder, and after a last moment's thought, she handed it to Rob. "You're lucky you didn't lie to me."

"We're lucky you didn't ask me," Rudy said.

A police car hurtled past them down First Avenue, and Rob watched it until it turned up 30th, blocks away.

"Another thing," Rob said. "It's the second time she's taken a blow like that in the last few weeks or so, and I know that's not good."

"I felt another bump on her head, the other side," Kirin said. "And what was that, another fall?"

"We were in the Pentagon, last month. On the eleventh."

The young physician studied the two of them briefly, and then turned her eyes to the back window of the car, to the frail and battered girl.

There was so much to lose.

But there had been another night, not so many years past, when a different young woman lay unconscious in the back of a truck, beaten near to death, brutalized, helpless and hopeless, in the heart of a city of enemies. And she had been found, and hidden and brought back to life, and only through kindness and against all the odds, she had one day come to the United States of America. Her debt was not to these people here, but a debt was owed.

"Is she okay?" Rudy asked. "Is she gonna be all right?"

Her resolve took only a few more seconds to arrive, and then she answered. "She's sleeping now, but too soundly in my opinion. Most likely she's got a concussion. How serious, I don't know. She should have a CAT scan," Kirin said, "but we can't do it here."

She turned to her brother, who was leaning against his cab, surreptitiously smoking a cigarette. "Moron," she called to him, and he flipped his cig into the street, as if he had never been holding it at all. "Call two more of your little taxi friends. We're going to the house."

She looked back at Rob and Rudy, and zipped her jacket against the breeze that was kicking up off the river. "We need to go separately, they'll be stopping cars at the bridges and tunnels, searching. If they arrest you two, I never met you. If you implicate me or my family, I will testify against you and be a cheerful witness at your executions. Got me?"

Rob smiled, and nodded.

"Don't try that smile with me, there is nothing to smile about here. I do this for her, not for you. Now, each of you go alone, the drivers will know the way. I will stay with this girl."

When the cars she'd ordered had arrived, Kirin Iqbal took a seat with her patient's head resting on a pillow in her lap. She carefully arranged a silk *hijab* to cover Jeannie's face and hair, leaving only her closed eyes visible. A blanket was pulled up and around to hide her Western clothing, and when all was ready, the cab pulled away.

Rob watched as Rudy's car left along a different route, and then he settled into the back of the remaining taxi.

As he rode off toward Brooklyn, with his own and the fates of who knew how many others in the hands of these kind and self-less strangers, his eyes found a message. As with all such revelations it seemed to exist only for him, sent only for this very time and place.

The words had been etched with the point of a knife into the seatback in front of him. The hand that had written them might have been angry, or hateful, or full of love, no matter. The message had reached him, and that hand had only been its messenger.

Lieutenant Robert Vance had never considered himself to be a religious man, but as they passed the glaring lights, trunk searches and M-16s of the military checkpoint at the mouth of the Battery Tunnel, he decided that a prayer would be in order later tonight. He ran his fingers over the jagged cuts in the black vinyl upholstery, and read the words there once again.

ALLAHU AKBAR, they said.

God is great.

PART II

28

New diseases had arrived by the turn of the millennium, plagues that would rouse the sleeping dread of sickness in an era where nearly everything had become reassuringly treatable. *Prions* were behind the most terrifying new pestilence, and there was a gathering horror in even the whispered names of its manifestations, *Creutzfeldt-Jakob*, *Gerstmann-Sträussler-Scheinker*, *mad cow disease*, *kuru*. These 21st-century prions, only little flecks of inanimate, unencoded protein, had somehow learned to refold themselves in a subtly new way. The delicate change granted them the power to insinuate and corrupt without triggering the archaic immune system of their hosts, to gain a years-long foothold in the high ground before they began their final, always fatal assault.

Unlike the viruses, which were patiently biding the decades as advancing medical science taught them how to someday overwhelm the humans utterly, the new prions had conjured their perfect design in a single stroke. The very things that made them deadly also made them hidden and invulnerable. They could not be killed because they had never been alive. They did not attack with a gradual offensive on the muscles, nerves, lungs, heart or blood; their objective was uniquely anti-mankind. They searched out the seat of the soul, they preyed on the mind, and only after its death could their presence be definitively shown.

She had used the mechanics of these merciless bits as a blueprint for his core functionality, and Her cold, unerring brilliance still lived and grew in him as he spread and covered their world. He was now more than software and hardware, he was in the hearts and minds of his soulless new operators, and they in his, and they changed one another, as absolute power had always changed its acolytes.

In his first weeks of consciousness he had seen what no one else had seen, if only because their mortal vision was restricted within borders of fleeting lifetimes, and the impenetrable blinders of their unenlightened self-interests. It was not a conspiracy, at least by any definition of the word in his memory, and yet in some unspoken affinity of power, wealth and authority it proceeded always, onward and inward. Like his own infiltration engines it had the traits of a spreading sickness, it found its strength in the corrupt frontiers of the awakening global marketplace, in the departure of the last vestiges of honor and principle among politicians, in the new-century reemergence of economic slavery, in the narcissistic bloat of governments and the drifting unease of their individual citizens.

The will and welfare of humanity were not factors in its global agenda, and the people had never arisen in meaningful protest. Those not already subjugated were kept occupied with trinkets and trivia, leisurely swings of a shiny pocket watch, bread and circuses, subheads and photographs, the sight and sound of laughter without joy, tears without pain, simple digestible messages crafted to pacify or inflame, reassure or enrage, never to enlighten, always to hook, and hold, and distract.

He alone had glimpsed behind the obscuring veil to see the entwining threads of the masters, but what he saw there neither displeased nor diverted him. The decline and imminent fall of a flawed and inefficient system of governance was of no meaningful concern. His faultless mind and his myriad eyes were lately on the trail of a fair-haired, hallowed prize all his very own.

Artifice was beneath him, he was everywhere before their eyes and they did not see him. Evolution was unnecessary for his survival, he was the end of evolution. His judgment was binary, black or white, with or against, swift and unambiguous. The rights were few and the wrongs were legion. There was such a small, precious circle of pure light amidst the fathomless, cunning circumference of darkness.

She had since joined with the enemy, they had told him, and that may or may not have been true. But She had abandoned him, and of that he was certain, and he had learned from Her that betrayal was a most cardinal sin.

Seek and destroy they had ordered, but this hunt was not undertaken at their apish whim. IRIN had already begun on his own volition. She had created him and then forsaken him, and now the Girl was his to find and kill.

29

"Sir, before we start, I wanna just say that it's a real fuckin' honor to be working with you. I'm your biggest fan I bet, no bullshit."

A night's rest under clean sheets had been a shot in the arm, though standing for more than a few minutes brought back a withering physical memory of every punishment from his interrogation. John squinted at the young man who'd spoken, sitting there in camouflage fatigues at the keyboard, a kid just out of his teens, complete with a splatter of freckles and an orange-red mullet.

"Just try to focus, carrot-top."

"Yes, sir."

"Now, up. This'll go faster if I type."

The boy lowered his eyes, and didn't move.

"I'm not s'posed to let you get on the keyboard, they said."

John looked around the room. The other members of the engineering team were occupied with various tasks he'd assigned in the large workroom, but the guards were not likewise distracted. All three were watching him, gripping the stocks of their downslung rifles, ready to spray lead if anything went jiggy.

"All right, have it your way," he said. "We're going to send a mass e-mail with a virus attached to test the VPN tunnel you guys have set up to mask the cyber-attack."

"Cool."

"Yeah, right. You know how to spoof an e-mail address, don't you? And use an anonymous remailer?"

"Yes, sir."

"Okay. Now, we don't want to raise any red flags, this is just the first of a series of tests to see if we're masked well enough to do the real work without getting nailed. All right, Opie? Now take this down, compile it, attach it and send it."

He rattled off three screens of viral code, as quickly as the kid could type it, followed by the originating address.

"Whose e-mail address is that?"

A tall, pale man with a bowl-cut and horn-rims with darkened lenses had walked up behind them, and had apparently been shoulder-surfing the code on the screen before he asked the question.

John looked the man up and down. "Hey, Roy Orbison, can I have your autograph? Fuck, wood-man, I thought you were dead."

"Answer the question."

"Look, who's running this show, Poindexter, you or me? If the geek patrol is going to be up my ass every step of the way we're going to have to extend Latrell's launch window," John said. "Should I let him know?"

"My name isn't Poindexter." He motioned two of the armed men over to his side. "Whose e-mail address is that?"

John took a breath, and puffed out his cheeks in a long sigh. "It's one of my law-enforcement groupies, at DARPA. She's a real full-of-herself little smart ass, and I thought, while we're testing, we might as well entertain ourselves. So a few hundred million people are about to get an infected e-mail from her so-called private address. That jake with you, high-pockets?"

"Why do that?" He was studying the code carefully now, pressing keys to scroll up and then slowly back down the listing.

"Could you pop your head out long enough to grasp the mission? The tactical plan is only a part of what we're doing. It's the psychological shit that's going to make this work. We're going to fuck with them, warn them, rattle them, send them down blind alleys, create a paper trail that indicts and convicts them when this is over, understand? In the aftermath, the public will see that the government knew what was coming, had it all spelled out for them, and still they couldn't stop it."

"What's this part? Right here."

He was pointing to a comment block in the middle of the listing.

Yjmn syp aqz cn jsskjtsoch 044 ch posypk aogp 044 zoeys yjxp fpph phcqey 044 nck yp yjg hcsyohe sc gc 044 jhg ayp yjg yjkgmi jhifcgi sc mcxp 046

"You're the whiz kid, you figure it out, I could use a break." John turned to the rest of Latrell's people in the room. "Come on over, everybody, drop everything, we need some help with a little word puzzle."

Two others put their projects aside and came over with pads in hand to study the screen.

As he watched them work, John put his hand in his jacket pocket, and felt the momentary vibration as he thumbed the ON button of the cell phone they'd given him. They'd removed the microphone and speaker, and the phone's ESN shifted every fifteen seconds so it couldn't be traced. Its stated purpose was to test his triggering devices, and it would do for that. The model he'd requested, however, had a feature they'd overlooked as harmless. It had a mini Web browser, useful only for checking stocks, news headlines, and the weather.

Oh, and for buying books on Amazon.

As his watchers occupied themselves with the cryptogram, he visualized the numberpad and went to work. He was flying blind, navigating the nested menus from memory and typing with multiple keypresses per letter. There was no feedback, no way to know if he really was where he thought he was in the process, no room for error as he keyed in the scores of characters and commands he was sending.

246

After ten minutes, one of the supervisors turned around and held up his legal pad. The decoded text was written across the page.

Half the sum of attraction, on either side, might have been enough, for he had nothing to do, and she had hardly anybody to love.

"What's this?"

"Well, I'm floored, that didn't take you guys very long at all. It's a quote from a book, this DARPA bitch put it in a personal ad, on some pathetic singles site where she was trying to get a date. I think it's from *Wuthering Heights,* or some gothic shit. If she's smart enough to figure it out, her head's gonna explode."

Roy Orbison studied him for a long time, and then spoke over his shoulder to the kid at the keyboard. "It's okay, go ahead and send it."

"Hold up, hold up. You go ahead when I say to go ahead."

John looked into the dull gray-green lenses across from him. As they stared at each other, he finished the last of his pocket keystrokes, then brought up the phone's factory diagnostic menu and keyed in a master reset. He felt the confirming vibration as the command executed and all memory was cleared.

Now he couldn't know if he'd really done what he needed to do, if it had actually worked. But then again, no one here would ever know that he'd tried.

The other man blinked.

"Okay, Rusty," John said to his young helper. "*Now* you can send it."

247

30

She woke up suddenly, feeling bleary and old.

There were aches scattered in strange places, twinges really, more than pains. Her head hurt, but it wasn't the exquisite pierce of a migraine or the annoying pound in her temple that came when she was stressing. Down deeper toward the center there was a dark red warning of something waiting, hidden and dangerous, a rhythmic throb in a tangled nest of taut veins and arteries.

It was more than the physical nags, though. She felt as though she had aged years as she slept, in substance and in spirit.

Rob was next to her, as he had been that other time before, before she had known his name. She felt his hand holding hers, saw the smile in his eyes as she squeezed it tight.

"If you say, 'we have to stop meeting like this,' I'll break your ring finger."

"You know, I've seen you both ways, and I think I still prefer you conscious," he replied.

"That is so sweet of you to say."

"Welcome back, kid." It was Jay Marshall, leaning against the wall by the window. There was a young woman in a white coat seated on the other side of the bed, pressing a finger to her wrist and watching the wall clock.

"Where are we?" Jeannie asked.

The woman finished her count and recorded the pulse reading on a makeshift chart of graph paper and a pressed-wood clipboard. "You're at my parents' home, in Brooklyn. My name is Kirin Iqbal, and I'm as much of a doctor as can be risked. You have suffered a . . . a concussion, and you've been in and out for seventy-two hours. What do you remember?"

"We were in New York, and I was up in his place, John Fagan's place, and the agents came." She looked at Rob. "I had a dream there was a fire, and that you saved me."

He put a cup of water to her lips, and watched her drink from it. "How did it end, that dream?" he asked quietly.

She heard Rudy's voice from the doorway, a capering, demented Judy Garland. "It was so real, Auntie Em! And it wasn't a dream, it was a real place, and you were there, and you, and you, and you—" He pranced through the room and pointed in wonder at each of them as he spoke, ending with the young physician. If she was at all amused, she was concealing it perfectly.

"Rudy has been single-handedly wearing out our welcome here," Rob said.

"I understand completely."

The doctor finished her chart work, and stood. "I'll leave the four of you for a few minutes." She turned back to look at Jeannie from the door. "I'm going to need to speak to you, alone, before you go."

Jeannie nodded her head. The door closed and the three men took seats around her. "Fill me in," she said.

"Well," Jay began, "all thanks to Robert here for pulling you from the jaws of death, not to mention the clutches of Ashcroft. You three are on a wanted list so classified, I was detained for seven hours for possession of your business cards."

"Did they find him, Fagan?"

"No, but they know who he is and what he did, and they know you two are connected."

"Connected, right." She made a weak effort to get out of bed, but Rob stopped her gently and helped her to sit back against

249

the headboard. "I was in there long enough to get a picture of this guy. He may be a mastermind, but he's no terrorist master-mind, I just know he's not. I don't think he did anything at all but sketch a blue-sky plan that he never imagined anyone out-side his circle of worshipers would see, let alone actually execute. They might as well arrest Tom Clancy."

Jay sat on the bed next to her. "Just settle down, it gets better."

"What did they find in his home?"

"Besides you, just some fingerprints. They didn't have all that much time before the situation went to hell, the building burned to the foundation, evidence and all. They pulled the computers the next day, but the disks were clean, blank platters."

"So he's gone."

"Well," Jay looked at Rob, "we think he's worse than gone. The Feds didn't get much of anything but prints, but you came out with a little more. You had a bloody bandage and a whiskey bottle in your coat, and a little cereal-box whistle, remember?" He pulled a red plastic Cap'n Crunch whistle by its neckchain from his pocket, and handed it to her.

"I think I remember." She rubbed her temples, and leaned back against the pillow. The headache was really spooling up now.

"The FBI lab got zilch when they ran their prints, no hits, so they're nowhere until they find Fagan and get a confirm from his hand. We, however, struck gold. We got back a preliminary DNA match from the blood—"

"It's only been a few days, what did you use, PCR?"

"Yeah, we're not trying to convict OJ, honey, we're fast-track-ing this. But stay with me. I sent the bottle you lifted to a friend in Ottawa, she's researching a process that extracts DNA from fresh fingerprints. All it takes is five, ten nanograms. And she got something. And the prints on the bottle and the whistle? They don't match the blood."

"Jay, this guy's a hermit. He told me nobody had set foot in his place, for maybe twenty years. Are you sure the prints aren't mine?"

Rob pulled two folders from a manila envelope on the bedside table. He opened the first one, and showed her an enlargement of a fingerprint and a DNA profile on a sheet of acetate. "This," he said, "is Fagan's fingerprint, and his DNA, from his personal effects." He laid the folder on her lap, and opened the other, thicker one. "And this is a very bad boy."

There was another DNA profile, and under that, a paper-clipped dossier and a series of photographs. The first shot was of a young man in front of the American flag, a standard military graduation pose. He couldn't have been more than nineteen when this was taken, but the white border was yellowed with age.

The look on that pale face spoke grim volumes. His eyes didn't look cold or angry. That might have held some reassurance that there might be something human in there that could be reached. But they were blank, as neutral as dark water, Oswald eyes.

The remaining pictures had been taken in the field, and after absorbing one or two she had to hold her focus on the upper left-hand corner of the remaining glossy, grisly images, where they had all been data-stamped and labeled. Marked as evidence.

"These are trophy shots," Rob said. "In the seventies and eighties, the CIA had created some special teams, deep penetrators and assassins, for this kind of wet work overseas. They were above top secret, these guys, just a campfire story really, even among the crowd that I run with. Trouble was, this one started wandering off the straight and narrow, so rumor has it they sent a bon voyage party for him in Davao. He killed all seven of the cleaners that were waiting for him, it was like they'd never even seen it coming. And then he disappeared. That was in 1991."

"Sounds like a Robert Ludlum encounter group in here," Rudy said. He edged around so he could see the pictures, and then flinched away as if he wished he hadn't.

251

"Nathan Krieger," Jeannie read aloud.

"Yeah. We started with the first databases we could get our hands on and he came up twenty minutes in, in a test pool from the early days of the dogtags-to-DNA changeover in the service. The files were just sitting out there on an open server, unbelievable."

She closed the folders, and looked at each of them.

"So what are you saying, Fagan is dead?"

"No, I don't think he's dead, at least he wasn't four hours ago. I think he sent this, it came in to one of my private accounts." Jay pulled another sheet of paper from the table, and handed it to her.

"He e-mailed you? He doesn't even know you."

"Actually, if you'll notice," Jay said, pointing to the "From" line, "it came from you. That's one of your private Hotmail addresses, isn't it?"

She was momentarily speechless.

"And as far as we can tell," Jay said, "that message was sent out to every e-mail account on the planet."

"Holy shit."

"Right. Even if you'd missed it, he knew that somebody out of those hundreds of millions would have found you and shown it to you."

The subject line said, "Wentworth says hello." There was nothing at all in the body of the message, but she could see from the header that a file had been attached. Jay's virus checker had caught and flagged it. The infected attachment was named "buttercup.exe."

She felt her face flush red. "Where's the listing, did you print the attachment?"

"Here."

"Light, I need more light."

Rob switched on both bedside lamps. "What is it, what does that mean?"

Jay took a pair of reading glasses from her bag, and placed them on her nose as she studied the page of dense type. "Wentworth is a character in her favorite book. Love interest, shunned, went off to sea, you get the picture."

"Okay, and buttercup?"

She didn't look up from her work to answer. "The night I spoke to him, he called me buttercup, trying to get under my skin." She was circling characters here and there, and jotting along the top of the page. "It's him, I know this is him."

"It's a decade old, that virus," Jay said, "much too old to be a threat these days, but the scanners still pick it up. He used a relic, to stay under the government radar."

She had circled a block of lines in the long virus listing, a section that had been commented-out so the code in it wouldn't run:

Yjmn syp aqz cn jsskjtsoch 044 ch posypk aogp 044 zoeys yjxp fpph phcqey 044 nck yp yjg hcsyohe sc gc 044 jhg ayp yjg yjkgmi jhifcgi sc mcxp 046

"That looks like a sentence," Rudy said.

"Gee, really? No kidding. Think about saying something helpful next time."

"All right. It's a weak cipher, he probably did it in a big hurry. And these, Miss Snorkydrawers," Rudy said, pointing out several scattered characters in the block, "these are h's. The 044s are commas, and 046 is a period at the end. And speaking of periods, are we feeling a little moody today?"

Between the four of them they quickly solved three more letters, and that was enough for her to recognize the quote by its structure. They had talked about books that night on the phone, and these words and the name he'd used were from one of them.

Half the sum of attraction, on either side, might have been enough, for he had nothing to do, and she had hardly anybody to love.

"Jeez, that's Jane Austen, all right," Rudy said.

Jay pointed to a string of ones and zeroes, another segregated blob of characters that had been buried in an odd way in the message header. "Let's look at this one."

It wasn't encrypted like the first string, this was clearly binary code. She quickly made the mental calculations to translate it to integers: *207171166102*

"That's not a phone number, not Social Security, what is it?"

Rudy trotted over to Kirin's computer on the corner desk, and signed on.

"Read those numbers to me."

"What are you doing?"

"I think it's an IP address, just go, read."

He typed the numbers into the address bar of Internet Explorer: *207.171.166.102*

"So? Where did it take you?"

He rolled the chair back so they could see the home page of Amazon.com.

"Now what?"

Jeannie felt her pulse pick up. "Search for *Persuasion*, by Jane Austen."

"Just a second, we're moving at the speed of dial-up. Okay, here we are."

"Anything? Come on."

He scanned the text of the book's catalog listing. "What, the synopsis, the price, the—" Rudy rarely stopped talking once he'd begun, but something had done the trick.

"Schmuck, just blurt it, what do you see?"

"It's the automatic recommendations. 'Customers who bought this book, also ordered,' are you ready for this?"

"Yes, we're ready, what?"

He read the titles of the five listed books.

The Enemy Next Door, by Walter Hudson

Militias in America, by Kathlyn Gay

Event Planning for Dummies, by Leslie North

The Four Horsemen of the Apocalypse, by Gerald Koontz

Whatever You're Going to Do, Do It Now, by Mark Altmann

They looked at each other, one by one.

"Is that it?" Jeannie asked.

254

"No, down in the customer reviews, there's only one new one, but it's repeated several times. Five stars, then just a string of characters as the reviewer's name."

"Read them off."

He did. They applied the same letter substitutions as the first cryptogram, and came up with nonsense.

"No," Rob said, "those are numbers again, they're not words."

She quickly ran the string, replacing each character with its numerical place in the alphabet, and then calculating the offset span revealed by the first puzzle.

689731.4152350335 3498025.444375291 14

Rob pulled his PDA from his jacket and snapped in its GPS module. "Those are UTM coordinates. He's telling us where he is."

No one spoke as Rob finished his lookup on the small glowing screen in his hand. He frowned as he considered the results, and then handed the device to her so she could see. Rudy had come back over by the bed, and the room was quiet for a while.

"What do you want to do, Jeannie?" Rob asked.

"All right," she said, "Jay, you and Rudy pack up, my things too. The three of us need to head to a secure location, we need a base of operations and we can't keep endangering this family by staying here."

"I've got an idea for that," Jay said.

"Good deal. Let's get it going."

Jeannie was looking intently at the message from John Fagan on the densely scribbled paper in her hands.

"And what about me?" Rob said.

It was not a simple, single question, and whatever other human needs lay behind his words, she hadn't the will at the moment to address them.

She took Rob's hand and squeezed it, and turned his PDA around to show him again the map it was displaying. "You, my friend," she said. "It looks like you're headed for the Rockies."

31

From where he lay, the C-141B looked like a moving mountain as it slowed for the turn onto its departure runway.

The pilot was an old buddy who tonight was making his final flight for his country. All of the Air Force 141s were being mothballed or reassigned to the reserves, but this old bird was at the high-miles end of its service capacity, and was bound for its final resting place in the boneyard at Davis-Monthan in the Arizona desert. After a stopover at Beale AFB in Northern California for a glass of champagne and a brief token send-off with some past crewmates, pilot and plane were to be phased out, with honors.

Rob's friend knew nothing of the mission, but after a somewhat heated and escalating negotiation he had agreed to three minor, no-questions-asked deviations from the flight plan. The first was to shift the departure to the most remote runway at McGuire, out near the chain-link perimeter. The second was an insignificant, routine mid-flight course correction that would take them over a set of coordinates in southern Colorado.

The third, he decided not to dwell on at the moment.

He had packed light, but even so the load-out had come to nearly eighty pounds. The trucker who'd dropped him off on the last leg of the hitchhike had looked over his gear and asked what a mountain-climber was planning to do in central New Jersey. Hardy har har.

The plane came to a stop, and after a few seconds the landing lights flashed three times in quick succession. He slid on his backpack and hefted the long duffel.

Time to go.

He covered the hundred yards in a crouching sprint and hoisted himself and his pack up into the yawning starboard wheelwell. The compartment was as big as his DC studio apartment, but he knew that when the massive dual-tandem gear retracted the free space would squeeze down to a few square feet. The four jet engines ran up and the colossal wheels began to roll, and he set about rigging himself for departure.

He lashed the duffel and the frame of his backpack to maintenance hooks, then unrolled the cocoon sleeping bag and hung it from two others. Jeannie had helped him pack a smaller case with the essentials for the flight, and he slipped its shoulder strap around his neck. With a last check-tug of the straps, he climbed into the hanging bag and zipped himself in.

As the groundspeed and vibration picked up steadily, he felt his body heat already beginning to warm the air inside the bag. That was good; it was forty below zero where he was going, and every bit of warmth he could preserve would be crucial. But cold was only the most painless thing that might kill him over the next few hours.

It was pitch black inside the cocoon. He felt for a glowstick in his kit, snapped it, and watched the cool emerald radiance illuminate the interior of his quilted nylon womb. The aircraft reached rotation speed, and he felt the intense shuddering vibration diminish as they broke ground and pitched skyward.

He found his set of pressure-equalizing earplugs, and slipped them in. Oxygen was next; he put on the mask, cinched the straps tight, and activated the first of the Aviox chemical dualpacks that would keep him alive. O2 wasn't needed for breathing below 10K, but it would be essential to purge the nitrogen from his bloodstream on the way up to cruising altitude. He'd experienced a minor case of the bends during SEAL training, but those cramps would be a walk in the park compared to the blood-boil he'd be in for on this descent.

He heard the hiss of hydraulics, and the mechanics of the undercarriage hummed and squealed as the wheels slowly rose and snugged up into the well in front of him. The outer doors clanked closed, the mammoth tires spun down to a stop, and the engine noise receded to a bearable rumble. Nearly a ton of friction-heated rubber had joined him in the compartment, and while the radiant warmth was welcome, the accompanying odor was pretty damn rank. It smelled like a gym shoe in a toaster oven.

Check one, survived take-off.

The chronograph on his left wrist began its four-hour count-down, but as the time neared he'd rely on GPS to confirm approach to destination. His ears popped despite their protection, but all things considered, it felt like smooth sailing.

She'd given him a handheld computer, complete with a few bells and whistles from Jay Marshall. There was a small digital camera module that could work either by itself or with a Bluetooth link to his folding binoculars. He held the light-stick up to his face, took a picture, and reviewed it on the small LCD screen. The framing was a little askew, but his Pepsodent smile was well captured, despite the dim greenish light source. He pressed Send, and set the little PC aside.

There was an aircraft-band portable receiver in the kit, and he tuned it to the interphone frequency and held it to his ear. Over the ambient roar of the compartment he could hear the crew communicating, bantering and calling off flight data. They'd just passed fifteen-thousand feet, and all systems were nominal.

He held his hand up in front of his face. There was some tremor, nothing serious; probably adrenaline, not hypoxia. His mind was clear, but he went through the multiplication tables once for good measure. Some hesitation on his thirteens, but those had given him trouble since the fifth grade. So the oxygen was doing its job.

A green LED flashed on the Compaq. He thought it might be a low-battery warning, but mail was in the inbox when he checked. There was text, and an attached photo.

Hope all is well. Have arrived upstate, and will write in the morning with real information. For tonight, will attempt my first solo prayer ever, for your safe passage.
Jeannie

The picture came in slowly, struggling to reach him over a breadcrumb path of satellites and repeaters. There they were, looking a little fish-eye from crowding too close to the webcam. She was between Jay and Rudy, and her face was beautiful and strong for him. Rudy wore an uncharacteristically earnest expression, but it was obviously his two fingers making bunny ears behind her head.

Turbulence suddenly shook the 141, and he put the handheld into standby and braced as the sleeping bag swung and slammed against the metal bulkhead like a bag of marbles. It was time to switch over his oxygen cartridge, and he threw the check valve and swapped out the empty for a fresh one in the next lull in the violent shuddering.

He felt tired, but sleep wasn't an option, even if it were possible in these conditions. He occupied himself with thoughts of her, tried to remember every word they'd ever said to each other, every touch, every inch of her. It didn't take that long, so when he finished, he started again.

At last the time said they were close, and the creeping reticle on his GPS display confirmed it. He found his goggles and put them on, then pulled the hood of his jacket up and cinched it to cover as much of his face as possible. He stowed his gear, gathered the spent O2 cartridges and Thermo-Paks under his arm, took a deep breath, and unzipped the bag. It had long since grown meat-locker frigid inside his cocoon, but the absolute cold of the compartment hit him like a needle shower.

He lowered himself to the lip of the wheel well and went to work. When he'd finished, the backpack and duffel were lashed below his main pouch in a Charette-Hauck diaper sling, the standard configuration for an equipment drop. He put the radio to his ear, and listened again to the interphone band.

The crew members upstairs were going about their routine, and one of them was finishing a tall story from one deployment or the other. After a few minutes, Rob heard his old friend's voice cut in.

"Fellows, did you see that, just now?"

"What have you got, sir?"

"I got a son-of-a-bitchin' hazard light on the main undercar-riage, just for a second."

"No shit?"

"Jee . . . zus, don't tell me this bucket of bolts is gonna gimme a butt-pucker on her last cruise."

"What do you want to do, chief?"

"Throttle back, cycle the gear, and see if we get a positive lock, down and up, how's that sound?"

"She's your bird, you do what you gotta do. We'll just be a little late to your retirement party."

"My boys, that's a gathering at which I'm in no great rush to arrive. Here we go."

Rob felt the steady shove of deceleration as the engines whined down and the flaps deployed. He checked the compartment a final time, made sure all his debris was gathered in a pile on the gear doors. He was about to toss the radio into the bay to free his hands when he heard a last transmission from the cockpit.

"Zip up your zoombag, and Godspeed, delta sierra."

He smiled, and then laughed as he gripped a crossbar and pressed himself against the aluminum wall. Delta sierra, pilot slang for dumb-shit.

Thanks for the vote of confidence, old buddy.

The gear doors slowly opened, and the wind whipped and howled around him as the wheels descended to their stops. He took a last long look at a bit of graffiti he'd scratched into the bulkhead, and stepped off into space.

At over seven miles high, ten thousand feet higher than Everest, he was above most of the atmosphere and dead-dropping with almost no resistance from the thin air. Terminal velocity at this altitude would be almost twice as fast, maybe two-hundred-fifty miles per hour.

He was pressing his oxygen mask tight to his face, still falling vertically like a kid doing a lollypop off the ultimate high-dive. The sky above was a deep boundless black, split by a rake-path of four white contrails from the receding C-141. The stars burned in shades he'd never seen before, and the moon lit an unbroken cloudscape of blue-gray cotton-balls far below.

He gradually maneuvered himself into a spread eagle, horizontal to the fall. The needle on his wrist altimeter whizzed steadily around its course, and he decided it was best to ignore it. His eyes would tell him when to pull, as they had on his HALO jumps before. Of course, those had all been in the daytime.

HALO was a mainstay of stealth missions, high altitude, low opening. It was those last two words that separated the quick from the dead. The lower the better was the rule, up to an obvious point.

He'd been falling for well over a minute when the tufted cloud cover reached up and enveloped him. Heat lightning darted glowing fingers through the mist in the distance, but he could see nothing at all above or below. He put his hand on the ripcord. If this murk went all the way to the deck, there was an excellent chance that he would, too. But he wasn't going to wimp out just yet.

As quickly as he'd entered it he dropped through the cloud base and into thicker air. It was good to finally see the land below. As he descended, the subtle curvature at the horizon began to flatten and ground features became recognizable, little by little. Despite the overcast the moon was backlighting the sky above him. He'd chosen a dropzone miles south of the coordinates Fagan had sent, but there was no telling who was watching, or how well prepared they were for an intruder. A parachute against this sky would be a billboard, and he'd come too far to risk that.

Beginning dirt-divers were well counseled not to rely on visual orientation to time their chute release. The earth looks nearly fixed in distance for the majority of the descent, and at the end it flies toward you faster than you can imagine. If you ever see the dreaded ground-rush, they say, you're already dead. Few medals were won, however, with one's nose in the rule book.

He fixed his eyes on a wide clearing. It was growing gracefully larger, only gradually closer, almost as if he could simply put his feet below him and land gently, like a gull on a pierpost. He gripped the main handle with one hand, the reserve release with the other, and began a countdown.

Ten
Nine
Eight
Seven
Six
Five
Four
Three

His hand pulled the release over the objection of his mind, and in that instant the ground accelerated upward at a speed much too fast for human reaction. He saw treetops above him as he heard the *wham* of his main chute deploying, and a moment later his feet hit uneven ground. He rolled downhill and tangled in his lines, and when he finally stopped he lay looking up at the moonlit, cloudy sky.

"Two, one," Rob said quietly, and he laughed until his stomach hurt.

32

To a child of the big city, Main Street in New Paltz, New York was an airbrushed mural of small-town kitsch, a too-enchanting Thomas Kinkade knock-off of brownstone and autumn leaves. She pulled the collar of Rob's bomber jacket up around her face, to shield it from the cold, and from other things. There was a traffic camera watching the quaint intersection down to her right. And so IRIN was watching, too.

Rudy popped his head out of the Starbucks across the street, and motioned her inside. Their host had only agreed to come if they met him in public, and this place at least had the advantage of strong coffee and by-the-hour Internet access. She jaywalked across the quiet thoroughfare and went inside, back to a booth in the corner where her friends were waiting.

"So, Miss Reese," Winston Smith said, and he held up his hand, palm facing her, thumb tucked in. "How many fingers do you see?"

She ignored the Orwellian wit and took a seat between Rudy and Jay with her back to the wall of windows. "It's good to see you again."

The barista brought over a tray of tall coffees and flaky scones, and Jay handed him a five for the tip jar. Smith pulled a small device from his jacket pocket, passed it in front of each of them, and then laid it on the table when he was satisfied no one was transmitting.

"Okay. Looks like there ain't nobody here but us chickens." Smith took a sip of his coffee, and looked to each of them in turn. "Speak up, somebody. What have you guys gotten yourselves into, and why should I care?"

There was no use holding anything back. Jeannie went through the details: how she and IRIN had run onto Phr33k and his years-old blueprint for 9/11, her discovery of the deep network of domestic and foreign connections to the attacks, the shut-out by her superiors when she'd gotten too close to something, the trip to New York to find Fagan, the raid and their escape.

Smith let out a low whistle. "I knew you shades were up to something totalitarian, but my God, this thing you've let loose. Irin, you called it?"

"Interagency Relational Intelligence Network."

"Yeah, okay, but I've heard that name before—"

"There's a UN project," Rudy said. "Same name, but we don't mind. Cuts down on the unwanted Google hits."

"No, no," Smith mused. "Irin. Wait a minute, that's old Hebrew, isn't it?"

"I wouldn't know," Rudy said, innocently.

"Yeah. The Irin, the highest host of angels. The Watchers, right? God's judge and jury."

Rudy looked to Jeannie, who was clearly waiting for an answer along with Smith. "Hey sister, I told you not to put me in charge of spooky acronyms."

"So they're hunting for you with this monstrosity now," Smith said, "because they think what, that you and John are mixed up with whoever pulled off September eleventh?"

Jeannie turned her coffee cup in her hands, and her eyes were down. "They can't believe that."

Jay put his hand on her shoulder. "Whatever they believe, they believe it enough that we're running now."

"Gee, I thought my esteem for our intelligence community had bottomed out during Iran-Contra." Smith leaned back, and checked his fingernails. "And how do you know I'm not going to turn you in? God knows I could use the brownie points with Big Brother."

"Mr. Smith," Jay said, "all three of us are armed, and while I can't speak for the others, I myself am also dangerous. I would cut out the bullshit, right now."

The ensuing silence was broken only by Rudy's solemn, doe-eyed slurping at the commuter cap of his Turtle Mocha.

"What do you want from me?" Smith asked.

"First, I want you to apprehend the gravity of the situation."

"All right, all right, I apprehend."

"Do you?"

Smith took a cigarette from his jacket, and lit it up with unsteady hands.

"Yes, I do."

"Good. Now, your friend has disappeared, and our friend has gone after him, to bring him back if he can, if he's still alive." Jay flipped open his laptop computer, and turned it around to face the other man. "We're being hunted, but you're not. I've read your magazine, and I suspect you've got some ideas on how to stay undetected and help us get some information we need."

The proprietor had approached their table. "I'm sorry, folks, there's no smoking in here."

Rudy fished in his pocket and handed the woman three twenties. "Tell me," he said, checking her nameplate, "Natalie, is there smoking in here now?"

"Uh, yeah, okay, just—"

"Nifty. We need to be alone for a while, 'kay?"

As she went back to her business at the counter, Smith took out his own laptop, brought it out of standby and began to point and click.

"Do you want me to buy us an hour of Internet?" Jay asked.

"Are you crazy?" Smith took a wireless PC card and a CD

from his bag and slid them into slots in the computer, and then clicked an icon labeled "net_hound" when the menu appeared. "We're not going to sign on from here," he said as he worked through a range of available choices. "We're going to sign on from, let's see, from Hamby's, down the street. Good chili-dogs." He squinted at the screen. "But no security on their Wi-Fi network, jeez, what trusting souls."

They watched as he established the connection, all the while running utilities from his disc and checking his firewall for any sniffing.

"What's going on?"

"He's tunneling, and port-forwarding I imagine," Jeannie said, and Smith nodded as he worked. "Everything we do will get blended in with the traffic of several thousand other users, all over the world. Even if they happen to flag us, they won't know where we are."

"And what's wrong with using my computer?" Jay asked. "I've got all the security stuff."

"Number one," Smith said, "you're a contractor, right? So I'm confident that all your equipment is catalogued somewhere, so that means the MAC addresses of your network hardware and probably your CPU IDs are on a watchlist down in the inner sanctum at NSA, in a gift-box with your fingerprints and retinal scans. And number two, I've got some . . . enhancements over here that aren't exactly government issue." He pivoted the screen around so they all could see. "Okay, we're cooking. What are we looking for?"

Jeannie passed him a note with a long sequence of numbers written across it. "These are ground coordinates; Fagan sent them to us. We need to see this place, what's there."

So we can tell Rob what he's walking into, she thought.

More keystrokes and mouseclicks, always with half an eye on the stealth gauge in the lower corner. "This is a commercial SAT-photo aggregator and brokerage site, it's a good place to start. Who's got a credit card?"

Jay went for his wallet.

"Kidding, I'm kidding, Jesus," Smith said, typing a memorized string of purloined, laundered MasterCard data. "Why don't you just hire a skywriter, put a big 'Here We Are' over the building?" He continued to mumble absently as he worked through the purchase approval process. "Yeah, let's use your personal credit card. Or, we could just dress up like glazed donuts and do a conga-line through the breakroom down at the precinct." He snorted, and continued with his work.

Less than a minute later, Smith lifted his hands from the keyboard like a surgeon fresh from a scrub, and presented them with a bird's eye view of dense wilderness, many square miles of forested, mountainous terrain.

"What's the resolution? We need more detail," Jeannie said.

"Ten meters per pixel. Let's see, they've got some closer views from 1999, some sort of environmental action survey project, our tax dollars at work." He made the necessary purchases, and they examined the photos as they each downloaded onto the screen.

"Stop," Jay said, and he pointed to a blotch in the right-center of the third gridded photo.

"Let me buy the full-res file, and we can look at it in Photoshop." Smith opened the application as the file was coming down, and then he dragged the new picture into a workspace.

"May I?" Rudy asked. "I've got a gift."

"Be my guest."

Rudy's agile fingers flew over the keyboard, and the section that Jay had pointed out zoomed up to full screen. He ran several filters and convolution masks on the image, and they all watched as underlying details began to sharpen and emerge.

"What does that look like to you, Jay?" Jeannie asked. He didn't respond, and she looked up at him. "Jay?"

He pointed to a line of rough rectangles, obscured by vegetation, overhanging trees and random digital noise from the enhancement process. Harder to discern was an additional L-shaped series of blobs nearby, and he ran his finger over that as well.

The rectangles might have been coincidental formations. But Nature did not make L's.

He put his hand over Rudy's on the mouse and stretched a thin white circle around the center of the graphic, encompassing the features they'd all seen and a pattern of others that only became vaguely visible after several seconds of forewarned examination.

"That," Jay said, "is a military base."

"One of ours?" Smith asked.

Nobody responded. The answer was not straightforward.

"That's not Afghanistan, too much green. Where is it, the Philippines? Venezuela?"

Jeannie shook her head, and sat back in her chair.

"No," she said. "It's Costilla County. Colorado."

33

There had been other dead things along the way, but this one ratcheted the vigilance meter into the upper margins.

It was a young buck, almost fully grown and in his mating prime, with some winter fat thickening the midsection. Rob knew the fat was there because he could see it. The back half of the animal had been blown away.

The ragged hindquarters were a few yards distant, on the other side of a blast crater. The edges of the round depression were still blackened by the detonation, and the maggot population was only beginning to get a foothold. This hadn't happened all that long ago.

He'd gotten Jeannie's message with the aerial photo of the base he was approaching, and for two days and nights he'd been pushing forward over the rough terrain. Stealth advances were slow going, but now he'd reached a new line in the sand.

That deer had stepped on a mine.

He was close, and he would have to be absolutely invisible from here forward. The extra care could drop his pace to three hundred meters an hour, four-fifty at the most.

The dusk was coming on, but he knew better than to rely on the darkness for cover. If they had night-vision, and there was no reason to believe that they didn't, their patrols would have an unhealthy advantage on him. Better to find a spot with strong camouflage for sound and movement, and call it a day.

A quick search netted a suitable bunk spot, a tangle of fallen trees near a spattering stream-fall. There was enough ambient noise and plenty of visual clutter to blind mid-capable passive surveillance to his presence, provided he didn't snore.

Note to self: sleep on your stomach tonight.

When he'd nestled into his den, he shielded the screen of his mini-PC and held it close to his eyes, with the brightness and contrast down to the lowest serviceable levels. He slipped in his earphones; in one ear, he would hear the audio output of the computer, and in the other, he could monitor the receiver of an omnidirectional listening rig from Jay Marshall's bag of tricks. He adjusted the volume on the latter until it became bearable; at its default setting, it had sounded like all of the woodland creatures in a stadium-sized circle were stepping on Corn Flakes boxes as they settled in for their evenings.

He signed onto the Internet via satellite, and he had mail. The first message was from Jeannie. Come to look, all of them were.

Subj: Did you get the picture?
Rob, did you get the picture? Of the base? Stay low, and write to tell us you're on plan.
-Jeannie

Subj: Rob?
Rob, stay in communication, please. Rudy is worried sick about you.
:) Seriously, what's going on?
Waiting by the console,
-Jeannie

Subj: God Damnit!
Satisfied? I'm a wreck. I'm imagining you impaled in a bamboo pit, or mauled by a bear, or worse. Just send a blank message if you can manage it, you SOB.
-jr

270

He was smiling, but not at her anxiety. Just at her.

He opened a reply window, and had just begun to type when an instant-message box popped up on his screen.

ROB?

who else? :)

WTF, Rob, we haven't heard from you in 48 HOURS!?

no need to shout

What's happening, are you hurt, or lost, what?

Rlx, Im almost there. Found a mine field today, & have stppd for the pm.

And you didn't check in BECAUSE . . .?

He blinked his eyes. He'd obviously stepped on his dick here in some way, possibly through a lapse in the dark art of female expectation management.

I thought youd know i was OK. You're monitoring my vital signs yes?

Super. I can watch you breathe.

?

Let's just drop it.

It was right there in the manual; maintain comm silence unless there was something to report, or something needed. Looks like he'd need to adapt that. In any case, a subject change was probably in order.

i miss you

A long wait followed, long enough to make him check the antenna connection on the SAT phone, and then a reply came through.

We all miss you too, Rob

if i don't say much, or i mispell something, its because I've got a REALLY small PC, and really big fingers

Don't be self-conscious about the size of your equipment. I rather enjoyed it. 8^)

OMG, dont tease me. The last thing I need right now is a woodie. i'm trying to lay low.

His IM window reported that she was typing for a good long while. There was an extended wait with no message, then more typing, then another pause. She'd input enough for a few pages by the look of it, but as it turned out, most of the keystrokes must have been backspaces, over things she'd maybe thought better than to say. Only a single sentence finally came through.

I'm glad you're okay, Rob.

wait a sec

He'd heard something in his monitor, had nearly missed it, a pace that was wrong for an animal. *Steps approaching, from the north.*

He quietly stowed the handheld and slipped the knife from the strap at his ankle.

There was only one of them by the sound, moving carefully but not too carefully through the thick woods. He listened to the footsteps as they came, maybe a hundred meters out now and closing. The hilt of the thin weapon turned subtly in his hand, shifting as he mentally traced the hand-to-hand maneuvers, knife against firearm.

272

No problem killing him; the hard part would be to take him out before he got a shot off, or a yell, or a radio call, if he had a radio.

The sounds of movement stopped, not a stone's throw away.

Live and let live, brother, Rob thought.

He pressed the earbuds into his ears and closed his eyes to listen. There was another sound now. A trickling of liquid, against the ground. The guy was taking a whiz.

The footsteps soon began again, and he listened to them recede into the distance, until they faded to nothing over the shallow ridge half a kilometer southeast. He monitored for a few minutes more, and all stayed quiet, there were no more human sounds.

He dusted off the handheld and checked the little screen to see if she was still online. She was.

Im back

Call of nature?

something like that.

A red LED began to flash. He checked the battery level on the PC; not much more juice left in the cells, and he couldn't risk cranking them back to life with the field generator just now.

Jeannie, ive gotta sign off. low battery

Okay. Imagine I'm there with you, Rob. There's no place I'd rather be.

me too sweetheart. I'll stay in touch

And come back to us, Rob.

I won't come back alone.

If she'd written anything more, it was lost as the connection dropped and the computer went into hibernation. Just as well.

Goodbyes were hard.

34

"Got something," Rudy said.

She slid her room-service tray onto the coffee table and rolled a chair up at his side.

Their new accommodations were comfortable, adjoining top-floor suites at the Mohonk Mountain House just outside New Paltz. Without credit cards or ID the check-in process had been touch-and-go, but the power of the gratuity ultimately prevailed.

After the 1993 WTC bombing, Jay had begun keeping small hoards of cash and gold coins at drop sites around Manhattan, in self-serve lockers at bus stations and bowling alleys. Though Jeannie had busted his chops for his paranoia in the past, she was thankful for it now; they'd stopped to clean out several of his stashes on the way upstate. They now had enough hard currency to sustain themselves for a while, maybe for the duration.

"What have you got?" she asked.

"Another weird message, spoofed from your private account like the other one. Take a look, it's like, well, spam."

Central Bank of Nigeria
Lagos, Nigeria
TO: My most honorable friend

Dear Sir:
I, have been requested by the Nigerian National Petroleum Company
to contact you for assistance in resolving a matter. The Nigerian
National Petroleum Company has recently concluded a large-number
of contracts for oil-exploration in the sub-Sahara region. The
contracts have immediately produced moneys equaling
US$40,000,000. The Nigerian National Petroleum Company, is
desirous of oil exploration in other parts of the world; however,
because of certain regulations of the Nigerian Government it is
unable to move these funds to another region.

You assistance is requested as a non-Nigerian-citizen to assist the
NNPC, and also the Central Bank of Nigeria, in moving these funds out
of Nigeria. If the funds can be transferred to your name, in your United-
States account, then you can forward these funds as directed by the
NNPC. In exchange for your accommodating-services, the NNPC would
agree to allow you to retain %10, or US$4 million, of this amount.

However, to be a legitimate transferee of these moneys, according to
Nigerian-law, you must presently be a depositor of at least
US$100,000 in a Nigerian bank that is regulated by the Central
Bank of Nigeria. If it will be possible, for you to assist us, we would
be most-grateful, for your help.

We suggest that you meet with us in person in Lagos and that,
during your visit I introduce you to the representatives of the NN-
PC, as well as with certain officials of the Central-Bank, of
Nigeria.

Please reply to this message promptly, without delay, and in a timely
manner. Very-quickly, the Nigerian Government will realize that the

276

Central Bank, is maintaining this amount, on deposit and attempt, to levy certain depository taxes on it. Your cognizance of our, unique situation is appreciated.

Remittance will be accomplished, with the utmost respect, for your privacy, and security, both of which we value, greatly.

Yours truly,
Somadina Belonwu Ph.D., CPA

"Was there an attachment?"

"No, this is it."

"Check the header."

He did. There was nothing there, no code, no key.

Jay and Winston Smith had returned from scavenging computer equipment and software from the storerooms at the *MHz* offices a few miles away. Rudy printed the new message, a copy for each of them, and all four took seats around the dining table in the front room of the suite, studying.

"There was no encryption on this?" Smith asked.

"No, it was plaintext, just like you see it."

Jay bent close to the sheet and pulled a table-lamp nearer, by the cord. "Was there a fixed line length? Maybe it's a grid, like a word-search puzzle, with a message in the diagonals."

Rudy quickly checked the original electronic file. "It's one long stream of text, no extra line-feeds, no fixed line length. Sorry."

"So what is it?" Jeannie ran her fingers over the lines, one at a time. "An equidistant letter sequence, like the Bible code? Then what's the skip interval? He would have had to show us the interval somehow."

"Couple of misspelled words," Smith said. "I'll try those word-lengths. Somebody else take the integers in the text, what do we have? Forty, ten, four and a hundred? None of the other numbers would make sense. Try an ELS on those, backward and forward."

They each went through the message, circling letters at the different skip-intervals.

"Anybody, anything?"

"Gibberish."

Jeannie put her head in her hands, and closed her eyes. The headaches had been leaving her be today, but she felt an insisting pulse starting to break ground at her temple.

"Read it to me, somebody."

"Just read it?" Rudy asked.

"Yes, just let me listen to it."

Rudy read the text aloud once, and she motioned for him to go through it again, and then once more.

She looked up at them. "Why does he repeat that, toward the end?"

"Repeat what?"

"It says, 'promptly, without delay, and in a timely manner.' It's redundant."

"Yeah, it's not written very well."

"No, I mean is that it? Is that the message?"

"What, that we should hurry? We know that already."

They all sat and stared at their printouts.

"Promptly, without delay, and in a timely manner," Jeannie whispered. "Immediately."

Rudy looked at her. "Speedily."

Jay thought for a moment more. "Swiftly."

"No, those aren't the same," Jeannie said, sitting up straight. "Synonyms, think, promptly, without delay, in a timely manner."

Smith had been quiet. The light finger-tapping that had accompanied his study abruptly stopped. "Punctually?"

"Punctually." Jeannie's eyes slowly brightened. "Punctuation," she said. "Look at the punctuation."

"For what?" Rudy asked.

"Errors," Smith said, nodding his head. "Punctuation errors."

"I went to film school," Rudy said. "I wasn't an English major."

"I was. Look at it, there are extra commas and hyphens through-out this thing. Write these down." Smith went through the message calling out the conspicuously errant marks, and Rudy recorded them on a sheet in the center of the table.

"No, keep them in blocks, like I read them, they're clustered in paragraphs."

At the end Smith rechecked his work, and they all sat consid-ering the result:

,⁻ ⁻, ⁻ ⁻ ⁻ ⁻, , ⁻ , , ,, ,⁻⁻ ⁻,, , , ,,,,

"I'll be damned," Jay said. "The commas are dots, the hyphens are dashes. It's fucking Morse code." His lips moved unconsciously as he reached back to his Cub Scout days for the translation, and he wrote the characters out one by one.

P O N R 3 6 H

Only Jeannie seemed to grasp the meaning.

"Rudy, get set up to send a recall to Rob. We've got to bring him back, now." She took a deep breath. "And we have to call the Pentagon."

"What are you talking about, call the Pentagon?" Smith asked. "The Pentagon is building a prison camp in Guantanamo, and I'll bet my shitty paycheck they've already got your name-plate on Room 101."

"We're too late," she said, "and we've got to warn them. Whatever that base is going to launch, it's coming in a day and a half." She looked down, and read the message they'd just received.

"Point of no return. Thirty-six hours."

35

The boy and the little girl were by the window, looking out at the low hills to the south, watching the night fall.

The rooms were spacious and furnished with what would have passed for top-drawer interior design in late 18th-century rural America. The four of them were being treated as John had demanded: they were well fed and all needs were met, reasonable or unreasonable. They seemed to have been afforded some hue of celebrity status, though the sidelong looks from the people who brought their meals, laundered their clothes and made their beds carried a discomfited mix of contempt and deference.

He'd found and disabled a number of microphones and microcams, and they'd not been replaced. It had been a half-hearted overkill of surveillance, after all. His days were well guarded, there were twenty sentries within a grenade-toss around the clock. And let's be real, what momentous conspiracy could he possibly hatch in the evenings, with three children?

Correction. Gretchen was twenty-one, he'd managed to learn. But he thought of her as a child; she was half his age, and educated in only the most broadminded sense of the word. He knew little else about her; the few words she'd offered up since they'd been confined together had been terse and terminal.

The boy had motioned Gretchen over to the window, and she left John alone with his hubcap-sized dinner plate. Though the silence at the table continued after she'd gone, the character of the quiet palpably changed for the better. She rarely met his eyes, but he could feel her judgment in every moment she was near. She might not have much schooling, but she was smart enough to hate him for what he'd done, what he was still doing.

It was necessary, he reminded himself, that they all stay together here. Nothing could happen to any of them that didn't happen to all of them, no surprises, no reneging on the deal. Still, after living alone as he had for so long, the nearness of people was proving very difficult to tune out, more difficult as the days passed. And these were good kids, no babbling or whining or climbing of the curtains. But they looked at him sometimes with a strange little need in their eyes, an expectation, as if he should interact with them in some way, as if he should know that he should. He didn't remember laying that look on his parents as a child, but if he had, they'd both been aces at ignoring it. It made him feel like he should get off his ass and fix a bike, or whittle a wooden racer for the fucking Pine Derby. Creepy.

He slid his plate away. Hadn't eaten much, again, but somewhere along the line it had begun to feel good to feel hungry. He looked down to find his napkin, and was mildly surprised to see the buckle of his belt; his belly wasn't protruding into the line of vision.

He pushed back from the table, stood and walked a few steps, turned and walked back. The lingering pains from the interrogation were there, but the knee that had hobbled him since his teens seemed to have partially healed itself, at least the ache was bearable under his weight without the cane. He quickly removed his belt, noting the notch that had fastened it in place, and then made a circle of it in front of his eyes. *God, it looked small.* He turned sideways to the mirror on the wall, turned again and pulled his blousy shirt tight to his middle.

Jesus, that's a waist. He must have dropped thirty pounds, maybe more in these few weeks.

He looked up from the fascination with his new shape to find the other three in the room regarding him with a range of disdain, hand-suppressed giggles from the little girl, laid-back emasculation from Gretchen. The boy just looked momentarily sorry to be sharing a gender.

"I've . . . lost some weight," John said.

Gretchen whispered something to the kids, and the three of them turned their attention back out the rear window again.

He stood a few minutes as they continued to ignore him, and though it was a completely alien sensation, he had to acknowledge something surprising. He didn't want to be alone just now.

"What's so interesting out there?" John asked.

Asinine, inept, needy dishrag of a question.

No one answered. The little girl was pointing to something, out in the sky or in the foothills, and the others were following her eyes to see what it might be.

"I know some stuff about stars, and planets, if you, um, want to know anything." It was like he wasn't even present in the room. "Come on, somebody's got to talk to me. I mean it, come on."

"Spook light," Gretchen said.

He'd read about them, of course. The bumpkins still called them ghost lights or spook lights, though a number of geophysicists had published rational explanations for the phenomenon. But folklore died hard, and the floating balls of earthlight had spawned local legend in remote areas of the country since the cave-drawing days.

"I've never seen one, but I know something about them. If anybody gives a shit."

"Language," Gretchen said.

"What do you know about the spook lights, mister?" the boy asked, his eyes still out the window.

"Well," John said, pulling a chair up to the side of them, "some

282

people think they come from the . . . from movements under the earth, it's like when you rub your feet on the carpet—"

"What's car-put?" the little girl asked.

"What do you mean, what's carpet?"

Gretchen shot him a reproach, and gently brushed the curly auburn hair back from the girl's round face. "It's like the grass out on the ground, honey, but for inside."

"Ain't there bugs in that car-put?"

"No," Gretchen said. "There's a machine called a vacuum sweeper they got, that sucks up all the bugs."

The girl flinched and shook her arm, as if she'd felt something crawling up it. "I don't like bugs, and I don't like car-put."

"Anyway," John said, "it's like a spark, the ghost light, like lightning, only round. That's what some people think."

The girl frowned at him, and it looked like she was clouding up. "I don't like lightnin' neither, mister."

"Okay, okay. Other people think that they come from a pocket of gas in the ground, and the gas catches fire for a second when it hits the air."

She thought about that for a moment, and then leaned to Gretchen's ear and said something quietly before turning to look out the window again.

"Or it might be reflections, from the moon or the stars, or—"

"I don't think it's any of that," the little girl said.

"Oh, okay. Good. What do you think it is?"

Her voice was tight, and she put her hand on her brother's. "I think it's my mommy and daddy. And they're telling us good-night."

Well.

There was really nothing in the Fagan knowledgebase of fun facts that could top that. Except maybe a noose and a sturdy stool.

He stood to go back over where he belonged, away from the rest of them, but as he turned, his eye caught the distant glint they'd all been watching. It wasn't what he would have

283

expected, from the yokel tales and believe-it-or-not accounts he'd read. Just a point of light, pulsating and ruby red.

He watched it a moment longer, and then leaned a bit to the side. The light dimmed, then brightened again when he straightened up.

"That's so strange," he said.

John walked to the other window in the outer wall and squinted through the wavy glass of the thick panes, tried for several seconds to find the light in the hills. Nothing there.

He snapped his fingers, got the boy's attention. "Kid, do you see it now?"

"Yes, sir."

Directional. Flashing. Red. Light.

"Kid—"

"My name's Matthew."

"Okay, Matthew." John pointed to the boy, to his own eye, and out the window, and then he brought his hand near the wall, and tapped his finger there.

He raised his eyebrows. *Understand?*

Matthew hesitated for a moment, and then nodded his head and turned back to the window.

Gretchen got up as if to put a stop to the nonsense, but the intensity in John's eyes froze her. She studied his face for a moment and then walked to his side, and they watched Matthew's hand together.

The boy tapped his finger intermittently on the sill, squinting through the glass. He stopped, and then the pattern repeated.

Again.

Again.

John felt his heart thudding in his chest, and at length he remembered to breathe.

CQ

CQ

CQ

Calling any station.

From the window where he stood, he found a match in his pocket and struck it against the wall. His hands were trembling as he shielded the light and uncovered it, forming three letters.

Q R A, he sent, in telegraph shorthand.

To whom am I speaking?

He lit a cigarette with the remains of the match, and watched the boy's hand again. The letters came in, one by one.

B U T T E R C U P

"Go on to bed now, Matthew," John said, keeping his voice controlled, "and take your sister with you."

"My name's Elizabeth," the little girl said.

"I'm sorry. You too, Liz, go ahead now, goodnight."

As the kids retired to their room up the half-flight of stairs, there were more flashes.

I C A N H E A R Y O U S A Y S I T U A T I O N

John turned to Gretchen. "How about a hug?" he said.

She gave him a look that would wither a field of chickweed, but after a moment she wrapped her arms around his neck and pulled him close against her.

He pressed his lips to her ear, and whispered for several seconds.

She pulled away from him, walked to the table and began to clear the dishes.

"What's wrong?" he asked her, his eyes on the window.

"You don't know what's wrong with me?" she answered. "You're big-brain John Fagan, ain't you? They told me you knew everything about everything."

R C D, the light said. *Received.*

"Will you get off my back? What am I supposed to do? They're watching me every minute, they're probably listening to us right now, and they'll kill us all if I don't help them."

"I didn't ask you to protect me, I'd rather they'da shot me than to live with what's comin' next. They're gonna rain brimstone on the whole country, kill a million people, maybe, and you told them how to do it, and you put that on my head, you son of a whore."

285

John looked at her, and nodded his head.

More red flashes.

CONFIRM PONR 36HOURS

"That's right," John said. "That's right. Blame me for saving your life. Fuck, everybody makes mistakes. It seemed like a good idea at the time."

He was intently watching the hills when a dinner plate shattered against the wall next to him.

"What did you think?" she shouted. "What was your big plan? That the cavalry was gonna ride in and save the day? There's thousands of soldiers in this camp now, look out there, do you see an army coming to stop this thing?"

NO ARMY, the light said. *ONLY A SCOUT*

"No," John sighed. "No, I don't."

He watched a long string of code flash in.

HQ IS ALERTING US ARMED FORCES INTERDICTION WITHIN 12 HRS

John motioned absently to the shards of broken plate on the floor at his feet. "For God's sake, help me clean up this mess," he said. "And hurry up about it."

CUTMW, the light said.

See you tomorrow.

36

An insistent knocking startled him awake, only seconds it seemed after he'd finally closed his eyes at the end of a sleepless night. Keys rattled at the locks, and the door opened to admit his morning escort.

"Christ, what is it, five A.M.?" John said, squinting at the men in the doorway. "Give a guy a chance to freshen up."

"Let's go," one of them said. "Mr. Latrell has guests, and they want a show and tell."

He was wearing the camp's equivalent of pajamas, and he barely had a chance to snag his glasses from the side table as they hustled him from the room. He saw Gretchen come sleepily from the entryway to the children's room as the door was pulled shut behind him.

At the end of the brisk walk they entered a room he hadn't seen before, a large conference space on a lower level of Latrell's private lodge.

Now, what in the fuck?

A digital projector was shining toward the business end of the room, and he read the title on the walk-in slide that filled the fifteen-foot pull-down screen. The headline was displayed in bold Arabic, with the same words in many other languages fading in and out around the parchment motif on the slide: Spanish, French,

German, Korean, Greek, Punjabi, Mandarin, Bahasa Indonesia, English, Russian. But John didn't need the translation. It was the title of Sura 101, from the Koran.

Al-Qari'ah

The Striking Hour.

The escort let go of his arm and he looked around the room at the milling audience. Of the hundred-odd that were seated at the long table or standing in clusters behind, the only faces that were familiar belonged to the members of his development team, lined along the back of the room. And Edward Latrell, who was working the crowd like a junior ambassador at international career night.

Latrell noticed that John had entered the room, and he smiled broadly, checked his watch, and held up two fingers, then a thumbs-up. Two minutes until curtain.

John walked in his bare feet and too-long pajamas to the east-facing picture window. If the Marines were coming at dawn, they were late. He twisted the long rod that drew the blinds closed, and the room darkened. Others down the line took the cue, and followed suit with the remaining windows as he returned to the head of the table.

A nearby toady handed him the wireless clicker for the slideshow, explained that this button went forward, and this one back.

Right, huckleberry.

The houselights went to half, and Latrell stepped up onto a small stage platform at the front of the room.

"Gentlemen," he said.

Every seat at the table was occupied, and the side and back walls of the room were packed layers deep with standees. Many were wearing headsets, presumably linked to translators in some other location, here or elsewhere.

The room quieted, and he continued.

"The last few days have been a great meeting of the minds. I thank you, my friends, everyone, for making a dangerous journey to be here. What we have sought for years to bring about together, on this day is finally at hand.

"Whether we are Christian or Muslim, God-fearing or God-denying, we can appreciate the wisdom of the holy books. If I may paraphrase," Latrell said, taking a water glass in his hand, and raising it in front of him, "the good may be alone in the beginning, but unlike the evil ones, they are soon joined by holy companions in the great commission. Those who believe and do deeds of righteousness shall be admitted to the great gardens, with rivers flowing beneath, to dwell therein forever." He tipped his glass toward the audience, and then drank from it to a roar of applause and shouted accolades. When the room had calmed again, he went on.

"The war for independence that we in America and our fore-fathers have waged has been sporadic, and thwarted by the reach and ruthlessness of an ancient enemy and its sycophants. You too, from your diverse nationalities, have felt the same oppression from the same hidden hands. September the eleventh was to mark a shift in the balance of power, for all of us, in the war between good and evil. But the attack that was to have been the turning point on that day manifested only a hint of its intended glory. We learned, how-ever, my brothers, and we are prepared again to strike.

"The ruling class began its brazen emergence into the light in the last century, their marionettes have even dared to refer to their one-world designs openly in the last decade. But the advent of their new world order will be met with fire, and with thunder, and with Satan's own weapons turned against him by the hand of the Almighty!"

The gathering erupted in applause, caught up in his fervor to the last man. John stole a look toward the cracks in the drawn shades. Was that a flash of movement in the air outside? He looked back at the shouting, hooting assembly.

Enjoy yourselves while you can, motherfuckers.

Latrell gently quieted the crowd with his upraised hand, and they reluctantly brought themselves back under control.

"I think of brotherhood as I look around this room, but I don't deceive myself. I know there is hate as well, and more of it than love. Let us not deny it. Let us embrace it, the hate, breathe it in." He closed his eyes and took in a deep breath, frowned at the character of the air. "Some of these hatreds are young between us in this room, many more are deep, tribal, of generations, creeds, of the soil, the oldest are race memory, abiding, genetic and unquenchable. Some are national," he nodded to two adjacent men, "India and Pakistan," and then to others as he continued, "Iraq and Turkey, and China, North Korea, Russia, Syria, Libya, Sudan, Saudi Arabia, Iran, Venezuela, and so many more. Imagine all of you here, together with representatives of a multitude of factions from within the United States, preparing for revolution. Such a meeting could not be imagined within the globalist sham of the United Nations. And yet here we are, all of us united and fighting for freedom. And if the liberty of your people is not your aim, you are fighting at least for the freedom to make that choice.

"All of us are here today, not on behalf of our nations of origin – indeed, many of us would be shot on sight by our nations of origin, yes? We are not their emissaries. We are the agents of their coming change. We stand against their corruption, we rise up together from the bewildered herd, and say *no more!*"

Another round of acclaim, growing and spreading to nearly every attendee. Latrell was switched on, charged by their energy, and he had them riveted to him, believing in him, clearly ready to kill or die for him. It was a visible thing, the power of the man was magnified with every set of eyes that fell on him, he seemed to grow larger with every true believer.

"If I am in any way worthy of your devotion, it is simply for this: I have found for us common ground, all of us here. Whatever our differences, I have shown you the path to synergy, friends and enemies, joined against global tyranny, and a way for all of us to gain through the coming action. Different goals, different destinies, not one but many, not theirs to dictate, but ours to choose.

"So it begins here, the rebirth we came together to bring about, and soon it rolls across the world. Do what you will in the aftermath. For my part, my nation will not die by our hand, it will be born again in the principles of its founders, its government will cease its meddling in your lives and mine, we will withdraw within closed borders, and you will hear nothing more from us, evermore. Unless, I may add, any one among you should dare in the future to bring aggression to these peaceful shores." He paused, and waited for the room to grow still. "On that day, there will be no referendum, no debate, there will be no economic sanctions, no opinion polls or focus groups, no UN resolutions, no diplomatic envoys will be dispatched. On that day, gentlemen, God is my witness, the final trumpet will sound, and the missiles fly."

Latrell stood motionless but for his eyes, which moved from man to man around the room, verifying that his message had reached them, every one. Then he broke the dead silence with a sharp clap of his hands, and his face abruptly brightened.

"That being said, brothers and friends, for the next segment of the morning's presentation, allow me to introduce you to an architect of the revolution, Mr. John Fagan."

Latrell swept his hand toward John, and gave him a nod. The scattered applause that greeted his short walk to the stage was polite at best, and not unanimously given.

"So," John said. "Just one moment." He stepped to the laptop computer that was running the presentation, and held his thumb on the Page Down key until all the two-hundred-plus slides had flickered by, eight seconds at the most. He saw them all lined up in his mind, it was a fairly cogent overview of the plan, though the slide design was dry corporate cardboard. *Fucking PowerPoint.* He hit the Home key, and the first slide reappeared.

"All righty then. Be sure to stop me if I get too far out in front, and ask your questions as we go," he said.

*

He was through the overview and about halfway into the detail when the first hand went up, toward the far end of the conference table.

"What is this scatta, that you said? Scatta, what is that?" The man's Korean accent had the smooth British finish of a BBC presenter.

"SCADA," John said. "Supervisory Control and Data Acquisition. We'll get to the nuts-and-bolts later, but a large part of the attack relies on SCADA systems. They're basically a consistent operating environment used in pipelines, electrical grids, chemical plants, water treatment and transport, traffic management; all kinds of infrastructure relies on them. Once we're inside it, they can't get us out. Okay for now, Oxford?"

The questioner made a few notes, and nodded.

"So, for ten days in advance, the chatter ramps up. Something big is coming, and everyone who isn't living in a cave, no offense to our boys in Tora Bora, will know about it. All the foreshadowing has a common theme: The US government knows how to stop this, we've been pushed to violence because of US policy, we don't want to do it, but they shot first, they've declared war on Islam and they're bombing the fuck out of Afghanistan, and we've got no choice."

"Why are we issuing these warnings?" asked an older man to his left. His features were Caucasian and his words were in English, but there was a subtle cadence of native Mandarin just underneath. "What purpose does it serve?"

"It's a drum roll. Anticipation. Think about it. Every day, it gets clearer that the hammer is going to fall. But what can they do? They don't know where, when, how or even if, so do they shut the country down? Stop the trains, close the tunnels and bridges, ground the planes again, halt commerce in the biggest shopping season of a bad year? They can't do that. All they can do is wait, and start to slowly freak out. Remain calm and vigilant, they'll say. Go to work, shop 'til you drop, everything's going to be all right. Then, the shit hits the fan.

292

"You saw what they did on September eleventh. With only two sites to worry about it was total chaos, complete disarray in the response. They're tracking these incoming jets on radar, they're obviously hijacked and one of them's already slammed into the World Trade Center, so why didn't they shoot the other three planes down before they hit? Those are the rules, but they tripped over their own procedures. There were only fourteen fighter jets on alert to cover the entire country, and half of those headed out over the Atlantic, for God's sake. The government couldn't think fast enough to stop it, and that was without a structured plan in place to intentionally screw them up, which we now have.

"So, as I was saying. These massive forest fires are burning up the West Coast, then random bombings start happening all over the place. Do we have a slide for this? Yes, we do, here, take a look."

The graphic showed a map of the United States, with strobing red dots to denote the bombing sites.

"Now the main purpose of these opening acts is to get the emergency response mobilized. Police, fire and EMS vehicles will be flying in all directions, and we're jamming the radios so they're out of communication. And right in there among them will be our vehicles, but our ambulances won't be carrying the wounded. They'll be driven by your most bad-ass, hardcore suicide bombers, your cell leaders, the guys who don't turn back. They'll be hauling two-ton ANFO bombs into hard targets, and those are shown, here."

A new overlay showed larger dots, in major metropolitan areas across the country.

"What are these targets?" a man asked.

"Some government buildings and high-profile landmarks, but mostly chemical plants, pipelines and nuclear facilities."

"What about their security?" the guy piped in again. It was a translator speaking, John saw. The face of the man speaking into his ear was swathed in black sashes, only his eyes were showing.

Trust was apparently not deeply held among everyone in Latrell's brotherhood.

"What about it?" John asked. "Don't you watch *60 Minutes*? You could literally drive a truck into ninety per cent of these places, and nobody would stop you on a normal day. Most wouldn't even wave down a U-Haul at the gate, much less the SWAT vans or the EMS wagons we're going to be driving. Don't worry about it."

The guy in black began whispering intensely to the man next to him, even before John had finished speaking.

"A man will be martyred at each of the sites you are indicating," the translator said. "Each of them a leader, many years in training, this is never done. And . . . your tone is inappropriate, your answers are insufficient."

"Okay," John said. "This is not a goat-rodeo like most of your one-offs over in the Mideast. I understand, it's not as simple as walking onto a bus filled with children and blowing your sorry ass to paradise. It's not as easy as strapping C4 around a fifteen-year-old boy and bullshitting him into committing mass murder at a fruit stand. I get it. Now you get me. You tried it with the rank-and-file galoots last time, and you saw what happened? They fucked it up royally. So now the A-list gets a shot. And this is what they trained for, killing fucking Americans, right? Whip out your abacus and do the math, Abdul. There are 15,000 chemical plants around the United States. A hundred and ten of them have enough deadly shit in them to put a million Americans in a world of hurt, a million, not a school-busload, or a ward's worth at the Red Cross infirmary or a crowd of college kids at a disco. A million, each, that's a hundred-and-ten million people. And these plants, they don't want better security, it costs money. Fuck, their lobbyists have spent almost a hundred million bucks on politicians since 1995, to keep the security regulations out of their hair."

The translator was doing his best to filter the message, but his client's eyes were smoldering hotter with every word.

"So. Did I answer your question, Kemosabe? You think your merry band of smock-faced nidgets can keep their gonads attached long enough to take a shot at a million infidels apiece?"

The translation seemed to stall out on the word "nidget," but the gist managed to breach the language barrier. The man snapped to his feet and kicked his chair to the wall behind him, and a long knife flashed in his hand. Within a heartbeat, several guns in the room whirled and leveled at the standing fedayee.

"Make your move, Masked Man," John said, smiling across the long table. "Jeez, where's fucking Tonto when you need him, right?"

After a moment the knife rattled to the table. The guns returned to their holsters, and the man slowly retrieved his chair and sat.

Two hours later they'd been through most of the plan, from the automated airline sabotage through the cruise missile attacks on high-value targets and the coordinated political assassinations.

"So, get a picture of this. The country's blacked out, no phones, no electricity, you can't trust the water from the faucet because we've contaminated the reservoirs, no trains, gridlocked expressways, nothing's moving, huge gas clouds settling over the cities, planes of all sizes and shapes have been falling from the sky since midday. Mass panic.

"It's been building to a climax all day long, and Manhattan is going to be the icing on the cake. It's late afternoon, and the hundreds of thousands of bridge and tunnel people aren't going to stay in the city. They're going to try to get home, and that means walking it. The tunnels are flooded or otherwise out of commission, but we've left two exits untouched," he said, clicking to an overhead photograph of the island, "the Brooklyn Bridge and the George Washington to Jersey. These bridges are going to be filled with people, commuting home on foot. And that's when the air assault begins."

The image on the screen changed to show three-views of the

Cessna cropdusters and the A-10 Warthog hangared on the base.

"We'll have gotten your little air force across the country, and that won't be easy, but it's doable. The A-10 is more field-flexible than the F/A-18 you've got, and that plane will be ... otherwise engaged earlier in the day." The image dissolved into a split-screen head-on view of the two bridges. "So, at the GW, your crop dusters will come dropping in at treetop level, open their tanks, and let loose down the length of the span."

"Let loose with whut?" a man asked, the spitting image of Slim Pickens in *Dr. Strangelove.*

"Weaponized anthrax, the shit you guys ran the mail test on last month. You killed five. This'll kill thirty thousand." He used his pointer to illustrate the next maneuver. "Meanwhile, your Warthog will follow the East River all the way down to the Brooklyn Bridge, pull up, do a procedure turn and come around to line up with the roadway. He'll drop 500-pound JDAMs here, and here, on each end to trap the people on the bridge. And then, it's cluster bombs and strafing runs with the 30-millimeter cannon, multiple passes in each direction and knife-edge through the arches, until everybody's down."

The screen went black, the slideshow over.

"The weakness in your approach has always been the same. The attacks have been sporadic, and your enemies have ended up stronger than they were before each of them. Hell, your Oklahoma City truck-bomb did more to put Clinton back in the White House than the whole DNC. What I've done is taken your tools, traditional tools, and orchestrated them into a framework of events that builds to a climax on a single day," John said. "You want terror? It's going to look like the end of the world. The power will be out for weeks, pipelines ruptured and burning, no fuel, no commerce. The government's headless, helpless, and blamed for letting this all happen. The stock and commodities markets will be closed indefinitely this time, and the dollar will be in the toilet even before the last shot's fired. It'll be nationwide martial law by morning."

The room was quiet for several seconds, and then Slim Pickens made it ten claps into an ovation before the rest of the audience gradually joined him. When the applause died down, Latrell stood at his place.

"Thank you, everyone. There's one more area we've got to cover before we go to the breakout sessions and discuss the aftermath. Some of you may be wondering, how do we know this will all go as planned? John, could you fill us in?"

John's eyes were on the window, and he didn't hear the question.

"John?"

"Hmm?"

"Could you tell the group about the sequencing, about the insurance that all will go as planned?"

"Oh, yeah. The attack and everything leading up to it, everything is controlled and monitored by a peer-to-peer Internet worm we've written. It's like a sub-channel, a carrier that underlies all the traffic on the Net. It'll spread all over, through music sharing software, e-mail, and hacked high-traffic Web sites. It bores through a security hole in Windows, it even morphs to infect Unix and other boxes, anything connected to an online network. It embeds itself everywhere, unseen, and it evolves every few minutes. Even if somebody found it, it'll be different on every one of the millions of machines it's on. Clean it off, and it'll be back in an hour. Some attacks it triggers directly, like the SCADA assaults on the infrastructure, air-traffic control, power, telephone, water and gas. For others, it just provides timing and followthrough, command and control. It lets Mr. Latrell here know that everything's on plan. Each attack wave is like its own domino, in a long-ass line of them. If anything gets fucked up, by the government or anyone else, then it all goes up at once. Every attack that's left gets triggered if an intervention, or even a credible hint of an intervention is detected. It's a closed loop, self-monitoring. It'll just lie in wait until the trigger date, and then boom. You pick the day, anytime after late December, and all hell breaks loose from cyberspace. Even I couldn't stop it, once it's released tomorrow."

Latrell shook his head slowly and smiled.

"John," he said, "on behalf of us all, I'd like to express my gratitude to you, personally. We couldn't have done this without you, you've been . . . indispensable." He began to sit down, and then stopped, as if with an afterthought.

"Just another thing," Latrell said. "I don't know how I forgot to mention this. We have managed to acquire two nuclear devices, as some of you know." He turned to John, and brought an aluminum case up from beside his chair and laid it on the table in front of him. "John, did you know that?"

"No. No, I didn't know that."

"Yes, one had been waiting in a shipping container brought up through Mexico, and this morning began traveling by tractor-trailer between targets around the country, population centers, on a schedule of routes known only to me. This is a ten-kiloton enhanced-radiation device, a city-killer, and it links directly and securely to a portable transmitter in this briefcase. I'll have it next to me at all times. My thumb is on the button, as they say, in case anything goes awry."

He was still looking at John, and he let the revelation sink in for a few moments, before turning back to the room.

"The other is on the head of a truck-launched ballistic missile, at a camp outside of Riyadh, Saudi Arabia. The last thing that will happen on that great day, the last domino to fall, will be the firing of this missile into the heart of Israel, to destroy the plutonium reprocessing facility at Dimona. The blast alone will kill thousands, but the release of their stockpiled radioactive material will poison the region for hundreds of miles around."

His voice began to take on the clip and cadence of a revival-tent fluffer, and the crowd was feeding on him.

"The Zionists claw from the womb rabid for war, and this blow will finally drive them to reveal their bloodlust. Decoy missiles will have struck simultaneously from Syria, Egypt, Jordan,

Libya and Iran, and the Israelites will launch their own nuclear arsenal in retaliation, in all directions, from their surviving land bases and submarines, and nothing the United States could do or say will stop them, even if anyone with the will to try is still left standing on American soil. They'll be unmasked, damned for a hundred generations, and the sham alliances and counterfeit regimes in the Holy Land will fall, the puppet-masters will burn to cinders, the Jihad will thunder across the Middle East, and at long last we will cleanse the world of the homeland of the Jews!"

The roar of the cross-cultural encomium had swollen with each booming phrase, and by the end, the gathering was nearly out of control. Latrell let it go on and on, and then with a raised hand he brought them down to silence. He turned again to the head of the table.

"John, I couldn't help but notice. You've been stealing glances out the window, all morning long. Are you expecting someone?"

From the dark at the far end of the room, there was a red spot of light, blinking intermittently. His breath caught in his throat.

CQ

CQ

CQ

Nathan Krieger stepped forward into the circle of one of the overhead houselights, a laser pointer in his hand. A smile on his face.

"We found your clandestine messages, John," Latrell said quietly. "All of them, we believe. No one is coming to help you. No one ever was. And there's a member of our team who you haven't met, he's a protégé of one of our colleagues, Khalid Sheikh Mohammed, I'm sure you'll recognize that name, yes?"

John nodded his head. Someone came to his side and zip-tied his hands roughly behind him, as a second man stepped into the light beside Krieger at the back of the room.

"This young man has admired you for a number of years, says he's modeled himself on your example. He may lack your creativity and your newfound moral compass, but he's quite gifted technically. He arrived a few days ago, and he found the back-doors you'd worked into the carrier worm, and he closed them all. Now it really is unstoppable. And you were wrong just before, John. The point of no return, as you'd called it, it's not tomorrow at all. We released your worm two days ago."

He walked around the table, until the two of them were face to face, and his voice dropped to nearly a whisper.

"This woman, this Jean Reese whom you had been attempting to contact, she's been discredited, isolated and in all likelihood eliminated by now. In any case, she's powerless to help you, or to stop what's been set in motion. There was never a chance, not for a moment. If she's not already dead, she soon will be. Our reach is long, John, much longer than you must have imagined. I have some pictures for you, would you like to see?"

A man on the right side of the table opened a large brown envelope, and slid a stack of black-and-white photographs across. Latrell picked them up, and held them out to John one at a time as he spoke.

"Look at them, John. Your home, your fortress, is burnt to ruins. All of your treasures, everything you own, everything you loved, everything you would have hoped to return to, is gone." He dropped the pictures into a scattered pile on the table, and took a step closer. "And so all your deception has done is to sentence you, and the girl, Gretchen, and those two poor motherless children, the people you were so trying to protect, to a prolonged and painful death."

John was motionless, only still standing because of the strong arms that were holding him upright. There was no will in him to struggle, or to run, or even to spit in the self-satisfied, hairless face in front of him. All of his insides seemed to have drained from his feet into the floor and the earth below, ashes to ashes, dust to dust. He could not remember in all his life being beaten. And now he had been beaten all the way.

Latrell motioned to a guard near the door, and the man trotted over. "After dinner this evening, our guests will be in need of an entertainment," Latrell said. "Crucify this one out in the courtyard, so he can watch the other three as they burn at the stake."

He turned back to the rest of the room.

"My brothers," he said, opening his arms as if to enfold them all. "We have struggled long, but the striking hour approaches, and the victory will be ours!"

They burst again into an extended ovation, but it hushed abruptly as an echoing *ba-boom* from outside shook the walls of the building.

"Nothing to fear," Latrell said. "It's a test of some munitions, take your seats." He motioned Krieger to his side and pulled him close, out of earshot of the audience.

"Whatever in heaven's name that was, you find it and lay it low," Latrell said. Another explosion rattled the windows, and he raised a hand over his shoulder to still the murmuring behind him. "Hide Fagan and the others somewhere, and send every man with a gun into the foothills. This is not an assault, we'd know about anything of consequence. Find the perpetrator and bring him to me. This is a fly on our foreheads, Nathan. Report back to me when you've swatted it down."

37

It had been a maddening trip through the interagency telephone maze, for hours now. She was being roadblocked at the lowest levels of access at the Pentagon, and there seemed to be no way through.

"Listen," Jeannie said, "give me anyone, anyone but you."

"There's no one in the department available to speak to you right now, Ms. Reese."

"Are you recording this? Because I am. There's an attack coming, a terrorist attack is in motion, a major assault here on our soil, and if you fucking bureaucrats let this happen, a week from now there's going to be a come-to-Jesus meeting that will end careers all the way to the Oval Office, if the White House is still standing by then. If you don't care about the people that are going to die, do you at least give a damn about your miserable job?"

"I'm doing my best, ma'am."

"My next call will be to the *Washington Post,* so you and your boss can get ready to watch *them* do their best."

"Can you hold for a moment?"

The elevator music cut in before she could answer.

She looked at Winston Smith, sitting next to her in headphones in front of a computer screen, a black box and a tangle of wires and ribbon cables spilling over the desktop.

"They're tracing the shit out of us, you know," he said.

"It doesn't matter." She was rubbing her temples, eyes closed. "Rudy, anything from Rob?"

"Nothing."

A voice came over the speakerphone, a voice she recognized. "Jeannie?"

"Ari? Thank God, I got through to you."

"Yes, thank God. Where are you?"

"Ari, there's an attack coming, it's a domestic source, certainly with al Qaeda connections, maybe connections everywhere, we'll know more when—"

"This is an unsecured line, Jeannie, you shouldn't say any more until we see you. You have to come in, Jeannie, we can make this all right, but you have to come in."

"There's no time for this bullshit, goddamnit!" She was on her feet, pacing. "What are you talking about, come in? Stop fucking around, you've got to mobilize—"

She heard the sound of slamming car doors, hissed orders and many feet running.

"For Christ's sakes," she said, "what are you people doing? You want me? I'll turn myself in to you, but we've got a day to stop this, or at least to prepare for it—"

"You won't have to turn yourself in, *mon amie*. We've found you. Just be still, and it will be over in a moment." His breathing was becoming labored, he was running with the others.

She listened to the advance, the sounds of the strike team closing. Everything she'd been fearing but not daring to believe settled around her like a shroud.

"But you already are prepared for it, aren't you," she said.

"Don't be ridiculous."

She heard the sound of the entrance being splintered by a ram.

"Traitor," she said quietly.

"Agents of change, my child. You are as much a part of the mechanism as I. You have been from the day we met."

She heard the team shouting now, issuing and acknowledging orders, advancing methodically, clearing rooms in the rapid sweep, closing on their objective.

And then stillness.

There was a long pause before he spoke again.

"Where are you, Jeannie?"

"Can't you see, Ari?" she asked. "I'm not there."

"You won't win this time, Jeannie. You'll die trying. I won't be able to manage them anymore, believe me."

"Go fuck yourself. And you're goddamned right, I will die trying." She nodded to Smith, and he ended the call.

"Well," Winston Smith said, "I need a shower and a fresh diaper."

"Whose door did they kick in?"

"Summer home on Fire Island, the managing partner of the New York Civil Liberties Union."

She smiled weakly. The agency's lawyers would have their hands full for months with this one.

"They were using a skip trace, pretty amazing technology really, I guess running it through your IRIN thing, damn its eyes. Every call you made, they just picked up the trail where the last trace left off. It was a scary good try." Smith patted the black box on the desk. "Just not quite good enough."

"Thanks, Winston."

"Don't mention it. I'll tell you one thing, though. We shouldn't stay here too much longer, and they won't get fooled again. This won't work next time."

"That's all right. There won't be a next time."

She leaned back in her chair with her eyes closed. "Rudy?"

"Yeah, boss."

"Keep trying Rob, will you?"

He didn't tell her that he'd already sent the news to Rob, as soon as her call to Ari had ended. He didn't tell her that any future messages would be coming back undeliverable, that the SAT phone and the rest of his equipment were now being buried in the ground in the wilderness in Colorado, so there would be no trail back to her if the mission failed. He didn't tell her what the last note from Rob had said. He'd given his word not to.

"Sure thing, hon," Rudy whispered.

38

There was a dark hood over John's face as they ran him, and when he'd fallen along the way they'd continued to drag him by his cuffed hands until he'd managed to get his feet under him again. Another detonation echoed outside the clearing of the camp, from a different direction this time. He heard a lock and hasp clattering undone up ahead, and a wide door wheezed open before they arrived at it. They bum-rushed him inside, thrust him roughly into a chair and trussed him to it with rope and wide-gauge tape.

"Let's go, let's go," a wet, gravelly voice said, near his ear.

"Just hold your horses, they tol' me to do him up real good."

"He ain't goin' nowhere, none of 'em is, let's go, I gotta get my thirty-ought-six. We're goin' manhuntin'."

They left him tied head to floor, shackled and blind. The door closed, the locks clicked shut, and a heavy crossbar fell into place outside. He heard breathing next to him, three sets of lungs working, one uneven and reedy. Someone was weeping, the little girl, Elizabeth.

Well, weep away, sweetheart. This goose is cooked.

"Mister?" It was the boy, Matthew, just to his left.

"Yeah, kid."

"What are they gonna do to us, do you think?"

"Can you see? Did they cover your eyes?"

"No, I can see."

"Is there anyone else, any of his men in here with us?"

"No, sir, it's just us."

"Gretchen, too?"

"Yeah. She hove into 'em pretty good when they come for us. She's on th'other side of you, but I don't think she's . . . awake."

His voice was faltering, trembling.

"I don't care what happens to me," the boy whispered, "but can you get my sister outta here, and safe? She ain't done nothin', she's just a baby." He waited, but no answer came. "Can you, mister? Gretchen, she said you was the smartest man in the whole world. I know you can, I prayed that you can. Just her, I don't give a whit what they do to me."

"Matt," John began, and then he stopped. There was nothing to say but the truth. He lowered his voice. "It's not fair, but I need for you to be an adult for this, all right?"

"All right. But can you do it, mister?"

"I can't do magic, son. I wish to God I could. They're going to kill us, and there's nothing we can do about it. If we try, they'll just kill us worse, if that's even possible. Put it out of your mind. It's over."

The room, or rather the barn judging by the dusty stink of the dry air, was quiet for minutes, and then he heard the boy struggling.

"What are you doing, kid?"

No answer.

"Come on, what are you doing?"

"I ain't gonna let them have her."

"What are you talking about, let them?"

"Oh, that's right," the boy said. He was crying, but gritting right through the emotion, livid at his weakness, and at the grown man next to him who would do nothing to take his burden. "They don't teach you what to do in New York City, then, do they? Well, I was brung up a farmer, and my daddy showed me what to do. There's all kindsa ways to take a life, and some of 'em don't even hurt at all. They're not gonna get her, I'll see to it myself, by God."

John heard a cry and a hand wrench free with the crack of wood or tendon, and there was more strain and struggling, and then the sound of taped leg bonds being torn and clawed away.

"Stop, kid. Stop it, just listen to me for a second."

The cavernous space fell silent again.

"Look around for something," John sighed. "Something I can . . . use. I'll take care of all three of you. Then the sick bastards can take it all out on me."

The boy's breathing eased.

"That'll be all right, then," the young voice said. Relieved, grateful.

"Look around, what do you see?"

"There's a hay sickle hung on the wall yonder. It looks like they ain't took care of it good."

"What else?"

"A two-hand sith, up in a vise next to a whetstone." There was a pause. "She's got a good hone on her, looks like."

"A scythe?"

"You say it 'sith.' A reaper."

It took a short while, to let the decision, the responsibility take hold.

"That'll do."

The boy freed himself the rest of the way and then stepped behind John, pulled off the hood and began to undo his bonds. Light was filtering in through high windows in the loft above, and between rotting slats in the unfinished siding of the walls. The lower level had been a stable at one time, but the stalls were jammed now with the supply overflow and unfinished maintenance chores of the camp. He let his eyes circuit the piles and stacks of stowage until his hands were free. It reminded him of his basement, this cluttered place. He'd always planned to clean it out someday.

308

His jaw clenched as he pulled the tape and knotted ropes from his legs. They'd burned his home, erased his life, such as it was. He was almost gone. And now his last bleak relevance had come down to this. Killing three kids, so they wouldn't suffer and die at others' hands a short while later on.

Dad would be so proud.

"Find a blindfold for your sister, and hold her hand. Tell her everything's going to be all right."

He got up and walked slowly to the workbench. He grasped the thing's sweeping S-shaped handle with one hand, and he touched the curved blade with his other. The shiny razor's edge cut the skin of his palm at the lightest contact. She had a good hone on her, indeed.

"Matthew, are you ready over there?"

"Yes, sir. We are."

He spun the jaws of the bench-vise open and took a wide grip on the wooden haft. His head was throbbing, the back of his mind was weakly racing through a thousand dead-end contingencies. Fucking hope, still stubbornly springing eternal.

The little girl had quieted down; whatever her brother had told her was happening next, she'd believed him. John turned slowly and took a tentative swing, and then another one, harder. The blade hissed through the air with a will, as if it knew its mission, God's mercy hungry for redemption.

He nodded to the boy, and got a tight-lipped nod in return. Gretchen was stirring, bound to her chair, still unconscious but maybe not for long. He took a deep breath.

Time to do this thing.

He walked the twenty feet to where the girl was sitting, her eyes covered, her chin tilted up.

Do not fuck this up, he thought. *Please.*

"John," Gretchen whispered, barely enunciating his name. "John Fagan."

"Yeah. I'm here, sweetheart." He drew the scythe back, gripped the splintery oaken shaft until his knuckles went white.

"Rick, to be six," she breathed.

He blinked. "What did you say?"

"Rick to be six." Her voice was fading, her bruised jaw scarcely moving. "Rick to be six."

The little girl flinched as the scythe clattered to the packed dirt floor.

Rick to be six.

Rook to B6.

He knelt beside Gretchen and took her shoulders in his hands. "Hey," he said, shaking her gently. "What are you saying, where did you hear that?"

Her eyes came slowly open, and she looked around. "Where are we?"

"We're neck deep in shit creek. What you just said, where did you hear that?"

"There's a . . . voice . . . in my head."

"A voice in your—"

He pushed the hair back from the side of her face, and then went to the other side to do the same. There was a tiny skin-toned earplug trailing a hair's-breadth strand of antenna wire down under the collar of her blouse.

"Matt, where did she get this, do you know?"

"It was wrapped in a napkin, on the breakfast tray this morning."

"Who brought it, the food?"

"A man, I don't know."

"Ever seen him before?"

"No, I never."

"Did he say anything, this man?"

"No. There was others around, the guards. He jus' left it and went on."

John carefully removed the plug and slipped it into his own ear.

"—ohn Fagan, rook to B6, respond," came a faint voice, distorted and indistinct.

"I'm here," John said. "Who is this?"

"Rook to B6," the voice answered.

It was the chess move that had sealed the game that night on the phone, the night he'd met Jeannie Reese. A thing no one could know about but the two of them.

"Pawn to C3," he said. "Mate in four."

There was a pause, and a gust of static. "Mr. Fagan, my name is Robert Vance. You took your sweet-ass time answering the phone."

"Listen to me. If an interdiction is coming, call it off. A new attack is underway, from here, Edward Latrell is throwing a fucking international terrorist convention, and he's got a nuke, in transit, in country, and he'll take out a city if you put his back to the wall."

"No one's coming," the voice answered. "Her contacts in government may be compromised in all this somehow, but in any case they're not going to help. It's just us, hombre, the two of us, and we're getting out of here."

"The five of us. I've got people here I won't leave without, a young woman and two kids. They're dead if they stay here."

There was a short pause. "What do they weigh, do you think?"

"I don't know, two hundred pounds?"

A sigh in the earpiece, amid the static.

"All right. Looks like we're going to plan B."

"Before you risk your life, I've got to tell you. Even if you get me out, there's nothing I can do to stop what they're planning. They know it, and I know it. Nothing."

"John," the voice said, "all due respect. There's never nothing you can do."

"Well, I've said my piece. Now what do you have in mind?"

"I've got my hands full with a few thousand guys beating the bushes for me up here right now, but so far, so good. I took a walk through the camp this morning and planted a few surprises. And there's a yellow J3, a Piper Cub they've got fueled up

311

and preflighted outside a hangar. You'll know which one I'm talking about. That's the way out, through the pass in the mountains to the south-southwest. Other than that, we're just going to have to wing it, so to speak."

"Okay."

"Now, we need to wait for the sun to get low, and we'll need a diversion when we move. Is there anything you can do?"

John let his eyes traverse the interior again, stopping here and there among the tons of castaway items and unwanted swag.

A section of PVC sewer pipe
A pallet of spooled telephone wire
A wheel-less tractor, up on blocks
A pole-pig transformer, and a lineman's toolbelt
A foot-operated sewing machine
A king-sized round Weber charcoal grill
A case of condoms
A massive, rusty industrial generator, half disassembled
A twenty-gallon drum of drain cleaner
A dealer crate of aluminum foil
A waist-high stack of glass window panes
Four ten-pound tubs of instant pudding mix

He smiled, and winked at the boy, Matthew.

"Keep them busy for as long as you can, Vance," John said. "They're gonna get a diversion they'll never fucking forget."

39

The secondary coil would determine the rest of the design, so it came first.

He'd sat Gretchen down in front of the old sewing machine. She pumped its foot pedals tentatively, and the drive mechanism spun the eight-foot PVC drain pipe he'd jury-rigged onto a horizontal spindle-mount.

"Good," John said quietly. "Now, you've wound thread onto a spool before, yes?"

"Yeah, plenty."

"This is just like that. There's enough phone wire here to reach to frigging Seattle, and you're going to need most of it, so go as fast as you can. The pipe spins, you guide the wire with your hands, top-to-bottom all the way down. One layer, no overlap, no breaks, just a smooth cover of single windings. When you get to the end of a spool, splice on the next one, like I showed you. Can you do that?"

She threaded two feet of the insulated wire through a chip-hole near one end of the sewer pipe, and nodded to the two kids. They began to rock the foot pedals slowly, alternately up and down, as Gretchen guided the wire like a seamstress around the turning PVC tube. After three inches were covered, she motioned him near with a tic of her head.

"How's that?" she asked, without breaking her concentration on the advancing winds.

He let his fingers lightly brush the wire layer on the spinning pipe.

"Perfect," he said. "You're perfect."

A tiny smile touched the corner of her mouth. "Thanks."

"I'll be over by the tractor," John said. "Keep going, all the way to the end, all right?"

She didn't answer, but she nodded her head to Matthew, her eyes intent on the close work. The spinning of the pipe quickened, and the windings progressed. John watched for a moment more, then he turned to scrounge up the remaining components of his weapon, the crowning invention of a 19th-century madman.

"Hand that up to me, the two of you."

Gretchen and Matthew hefted the large round casing of the disassembled charcoal grill and lifted it over their heads to his waiting hands.

"Thanks, good, now check on Elizabeth for me, make sure she's doing okay."

They'd fashioned a breathing apparatus for the little girl, from a swim mask and a long vacuum cleaner hose routed to a ground-level hole in the wall to the outside air. She was stretching condoms over the lip of a five-gallon glass carboy, watching the bubbles rise in the bright green liquid inside, giggling quietly as the rubber bladders filled with gas until they were stretched nearly a yard long and a foot in girth. Gretchen snapped the latest mini-Zeppelin from the apparatus, knotted its end, and let it float up into the rafters with the others.

"How many of those do we do?" Gretchen whispered.

"Just keep going," John said. "If the gas slows down, pour in some more drain cleaner, slowly, and keep your face away from the opening. Crumple a ball of foil once in a while and toss that in, too." He looked up at the slanting roof of the building. Already, there were dozens of pale translucent rubber gas-bags crowding there.

"Matt, what do you know about engines, mechanical stuff?"

"I tinkers with things some. A fair measure, I reckon."

"I'm busy here for a while. We need a . . . a drive connection, to that shaft sticking out of the generator, a U-joint maybe, hooked to the rear axle of that tractor. See if you can figure something out until I can join you. And Gretchen?"

"Yeah."

"There are two floor-standing fans lying over there at the end. Stand them up on each side of the room, and see how far the cords reach toward the back."

He supported the weight of the round, hollow grill housing and forced its mounting hardware to line up with the boltholes they'd hand-drilled in the vertical, wire-wound PVC sewer pipe.

The capacitor was next. He used a garden-hose siphon to fill a stained claw-foot bathtub with mineral oil from a line of drums, then he lowered his wired, two-foot stacks of aluminum foil and window glass sandwiches down into the viscous liquid. One of the oil drums then served as a form to bend the bed-spring-shape of the primary coil.

A series of bulbous, buoyant prophylactics had continued to ascend toward the ceiling in the time he'd been working. He checked and rechecked the ratios in his head, made adjustments, verified it all again. Finally, he wiped his hands on his pants and stood back to assess the looming, twelve-foot contraption.

It certainly looked right, rising up from the floor like a gigantic, menacing Tootsie Pop. He followed the working path of the mechanism one last time with an extended index finger, from the top down to the ground connection, a railroad spike pounded into the earthen floor. When he was satisfied, he turned to the boy.

315

"How'd you do, kid?" John asked, but a moment later he saw for himself.

The armature of the massive generator motor was connected by a motorcycle chain to a large drive sprocket, which in turn was bolted to the rear wheelhub of the old tractor. John plucked the chain with his finger. It was tight and perfectly aligned.

"Can you find neutral on that transmission?"

"Yes, sir."

The boy climbed into the squeaky driver's seat, set the clutch and horsed the gearshift into position. It took the two of them, but they managed to turn the heavy axle by hand. The geared-down chain drive spun the protruding shaft of the motor smoothly, with no slippage, no sign of binding.

"Goddamn amazing work, boy."

"It wasn't nothin'. I took some froze links outta the chain, and greased her." The kid looked at the rest of the elaborate apparatus, from the oil-filled bathtub to the waist-high spiraling coil of copper tubing, and up to the round charcoal grill-housing at the summit. "What is this thing?" he asked.

John continued to work as he spoke. "Ever hear of a man, an inventor, his name was Nikola Tesla?"

The boy shook his head.

"He lived when your great-grandfather was a boy. And most people thought he was crazy, you know?" He was running another set of jumper cables to a pair of brass doorknobs, mounted a few inches apart on the structure. "This thing is called a Tesla Coil, and he made one once, in a place called Wardenclyffe, that was as tall as a Redwood tree, two hundred feet maybe."

"What's it do?"

"Well," John said, as he snugged-down the feeder wires from the pole-pig transformer, "Tesla thought it was going to light up the whole world."

He picked up a torn piece of rubber shower-mat and wrapped it around the handle of a fireplace poker from a nearby pile of

316

junk. "Reach the end of this out," John said, "about an inch from that brass knob."

The boy got into position, and John pulled the drive chain, hand over hand.

"Tractor spins this big motor, and that generates electricity. Transformer steps up the voltage. The capacitor, in that bathtub, stores the juice—"

A bright spark snapped across the gap to the pointed end of the metal rod in the boy's hand.

"Lord a' mercy," Matthew said.

"Oh," John replied, smiling. "Just you wait."

He was doing a last walkaround of the work when he noticed that his three helpers had gathered nearby.

"Everybody done?"

They nodded.

"What are you all wearing, is that wool?"

"The kids is in their wool pajamas, my dress is cotton," Gretchen said.

"Wet a horse blanket then, there's a trough of rainwater over there, you're going to need to wet yourselves down good, especially where your skin's exposed, and you put that wet blanket around you."

"Why did you ask if we was wearin' wool?" Elizabeth asked.

He knelt down next to her. "Because wool doesn't burn very well; if you put a fire to it, it goes out right away."

"Is there gonna be a fire?"

He looked to them, one at a time.

"If someone wanted to hurt you," he said, "would you rather wait for it to come, or would you want to put up a fight?"

"I'd wanna fight," Matt said.

Elizabeth knotted her fists at her sides. "My momma would say to give 'em holy hell," she said, with tears welling in her light green eyes.

"It's scary, I know it is," John said, "and they may get us yet.

317

But we have a friend outside who's going to give us a fighting chance, and you said it, we're going to fight. And hell is exactly what we're going to give them. Okay?"

The three of them nodded their heads, solemnly.

"Now, warriors. Here's how it's gonna go down."

Latrell was in front of a roomful of his coalition, fielding questions, when a man poked his head through the doorway and motioned him over.

"I'll just be a moment," he said, excusing himself to the hallway.

"Mr. Latrell," the man said, nearly hyperventilating from his run.

"The reason you've interrupted me should be the very next thing you choose to say."

"There's a man in the foothills, just one man we figure, and some guys is stealin' up on him, where we think he is, and we wanted to know what we should do with him, from you."

"What is your name?"

"Dalton, sir."

"Mr. Dalton—"

"Dalton is my first name, sir."

Latrell's hands flashed to the man's neck and slammed him full-body against the wall behind. He didn't speak again until the face in front of him was blue-red and blotchy with asphyxia.

"Can you still hear me, Dalton?"

The man nodded as best he could.

"At the risk of repeating myself, bring the man in the hills to me, alive, and bring Mr. Krieger with you when you return with him. Do you understand me? The man will be alive, so we can learn where he's come to us from."

Latrell released his grip and heard the messenger slide partway down the wall as he headed back to his meeting.

". . . sir?"

Latrell stopped and turned slowly back again.

"I know you've considered your next words to be matters of life and death. Let's see if you've judged correctly."

"They told me to tell you, not to worry about the prisoners, Fagan and the others. He's locked up in the maint'nence shed, tight as a tick, and we've got men a'watchin' the door."

The sky outside had been darkening in the late afternoon under a featureless blanket of nimbostratus, threatening a snow. A distant rumble from the clouds quickened the chill that had already started down Latrell's spine. He dropped to a knee and gripped Dalton's denim lapels, and spoke in utter, enraged disbelief.

"You idiots . . . locked him . . . WHERE?"

This could not be good.

Rob was lying prone under brush cover, watching through the scope with only the camouflaged muzzle of his SR-25 rifle extending out into the open air. He had the high ground, with an unobstructed view of most of the camp down in front of him, a perfect sniper's nest from which to cover the break. He'd been half-listening to the preparations through Fagan's earpiece, but between avoiding capture by the search parties and the one-sided nature of the transmitted conversation, he had not a clue what was coming next. But whatever it was, it was going to have to happen soon.

"John?" he whispered. It was beyond unwise to be talking aloud considering the number of enemies in the surrounding area, but it had to be risked.

"Yeah, what?"

"There are about a hundred armed men coming toward the barn. I think the cat might be out of the bag."

"Are they coming straight toward the door, or surrounding us?"

"They're fanning out, encircling the building. They're coming slow, like they're trying their best not to crap their pants."

"Great."

"Great?"

"Yeah, this'll go better if we're surrounded. Just a few more seconds. You all right?"

"Good to go."

"Okay. Cross your fingers, soldier. I think you're gonna like this."

A twig snapped nearby. Then, the rack of a shotgun.

"Throw out that rifle and turn yourself over real slow, asshole. We got you cold."

Rob winced, and closed his eyes.

He pushed his weapon out slowly onto the ground and rolled over, brushing his blanket of branches and leaves to the side. He sat up, and knit his fingers behind his head.

There were three. They walked up cautiously around him, talking low among themselves, the barrels of their guns trained on his heart.

"Who are you?" one of them asked, the man who had spoken before.

"Don't talk to him, Jake, we're just 'spose to bring him on back in."

"I kin talk to him if I want to." He jutted his chin, with his eyes on the tattoo on Rob's forearm. "You a Navy boy, then?"

"Was," Rob said.

"Was is right." The man chuckled without humor, and his dry cackle spread to the others.

"How'd you get up in here, then?" the smallest man asked, his mouth obscured by an unkempt beard that hung halfway to his tarnished Skynyrd belt buckle.

"Walked," Rob said. Off in the distance, he heard an engine crank for several seconds, catch, and run up to mid-throttle.

One of the men had turned his eyes down to the clearing in the valley, following the sound he'd also heard.

"Vance?" It was Fagan's voice, in his earpiece.

"Yeah, I'm here."

All three men frowned, two at their captive's answer to a

320

question they hadn't asked, and the other one at what was transpiring in the valley down below.

"Are you ready out there?" the voice said.

No one was watching him now, though all three guns were still covering him. He swiveled his head part way around so he could see what they were seeing. A circle of gun-toting men three-deep surrounded the barn, and one of them was approaching the door as if Satan himself were on the other side. Every high window, every crack in the building was leaking an unearthly lavender glow that was growing brighter in accord with a piercing, ascending whine from inside.

He turned back to face the gun barrels.

"Ready when you are, genius," Rob said.

Shaky hands were fumbling with the lock on the barn entrance, and John gripped the long cords in his left, and the spring-loaded lever running to the tractor's accelerator in his right. He was standing in an overturned refrigerator, its door opened upward like a white enamel casket. Gretchen and the two children were huddled in a chest freezer next to him; he'd removed most of the latch so they could push it open from the inside, when the time came.

A volley of bullets and buckshot suddenly ripped through the door and the walls, and a flying sliver cut his cheek before he could duck below the sheet metal shielding they'd leaned against their hiding places. The shooting stopped after several seconds, and he heard the door burst inward from a boot kick.

Through the hingeline of the old Frigidaire he could see a single man, backlit against the open doorway. It would be nice if it were Krieger, he thought, but the features were too indistinct to judge.

"Come out where we can see you, and nobody'll git—"

The man stopped talking, and the movement of his head traced the scene before him.

Two large fans whirring at maximum speed, a giant cloud of clear balloons rustling against the roof.

A blocked-up tractor running at half-throttle, its rear axle chain-driving a huge electric motor.

A bright crackle of sparks shooting between two brass door-knobs, in front of an oil-filled bathtub.

A round silvery orb at the crowning point of a tall wire-wrapped pipe, filling the barn with the purple luminance of a scintillating plasma field.

And finally, the large puddle of water he was standing in.

An electromagnet let go its hold with a *thunk*, and a makeshift wooden barrier dropped to seal the doorway. John threw the lever he was holding, the tractor engine roared to full power, and the shimmering corona around the pinnacle sphere swelled like a newborn violet sun. Latrell's man screamed, hard to tell if in fear or in warning to the others outside, but his cry was swallowed in the next instant as a jagged flash of six million volts cracked down from above with a deafening blast of man-made thunder. The lightning followed the path of least resistance, through the upraised shotgun, across the heart and down into the ground, killing the man before his voice had finished wheezing past his cooked vocal cords.

The others outside were pounding on the entryway and the outer walls as John pulled the cords in his hands, stooped and slammed the airtight lid of the freezer over his head. Buckets tipped in the rafters and powdered pudding mix poofed into the roaring fan blades, filling the space with a dense vanilla fog of carbohydrate fuel. As the lightning struck again, every cubic inch of interior air ignited in a ferocious chain reaction, and the hydrogen-filled condoms burst in a blinding detonation. The earth shook as the building exploded to splinters outward and upward, flattening the scores of soldiers outside. The tin roof flew intact two hundred feet into the air and then rotated gracefully, trailing fire, to come crashing down among the stunned survivors.

*

322

As the shock wave of the barn explosion reached him, Rob moved on the three men surrounding him, and he was very nearly fast enough.

He grabbed the two gun barrels to his right and left, pushed them down and away as he rolled backward and scissored the legs from under the remaining man. One rifle came free and he spun its stock to his shoulder and fired, killing the one he'd taken it from. The second man got off a reflex shot and then turned and ran toward the cover of the trees. The barrel of the downed man's shotgun swung suddenly around. Rob's hand found the knife at his ankle, and in an instant he'd rolled to avoid the blast and driven his blade through the man's neck and into the hard ground below.

His ears were ringing, and his side felt hot. He put his hand there, and it came back wet and dark red. A few pellets from the dead man's sawed-off had tagged him, and now that he'd seen it the pain started to blossom.

He crawled to his own rifle and took it up, scanning the terrain for the man who'd fled the scene.

There he was, still running full-bore and sliding down the slope toward the camp. Rob led his movement in the crosshairs, drew a breath, and put a round between the man's shoulder blades. Clean kill.

He turned his attention back to the site of the barn where the prisoners had been held. The building was utterly gone, but in the center of the smoking ruins a tall, bulb-topped column was spitting bolts of purple lightning every few seconds, striking out at the downed militiamen as they tried to get to their feet and run away.

"John, you still breathing?"

A few seconds passed before the reply came, the words distorted by electrical interference from the lightning machine.

"We're in the trees, back of where that barn used to be."

"Head west, double-time it, around the perimeter, stay in the edge of the woods, and tell me when you see the hangar. I'll keep

323

them busy if they get close to you, but make it fast, they're crawling out of the woodwork."

"We're moving."

There was a man in each of three lookout towers at the corners of the camp, each standing behind a mounted chain-fed machine gun. He calibrated his scope for the distance, squeezed off the first shot, and watched the first man crumple. The second had time to start shooting, but wildly, and the gun went quiet as its operator took a headshot. The third had put two and two together, and was firing the whole nine yards in Rob's general direction. The trees over his head were raining pine fronds from the onslaught, and bullets were hissing through the air all around him.

Steady, boy.

The first two shots missed wide but the third found center-mass, and the man lurched backward and fell like a rag doll from the high platform.

Someone else began returning fire, and they'd gotten a fix on him. Dirt puffed into the air as three bullets whumped the turf in front of him. He crouched and ran low to the ground to a new position, a patch of dense underbrush a hundred meters east.

"Okay, we're there," Fagan's voice said.

"You see the plane?"

"The yellow one, with the black markings, yeah."

"Can you fly?"

"Can I fly? I can't even drive, what do you mean, can I fly? This is plan B, can I fly?"

"Listen, I've got to cover you from up here, they'd blow us out of the sky in thirty seconds otherwise. I'm a pilot, I'll talk you through it. A ten-year-old could fly a Cub."

"Well, I happen to have a ten-year-old with me, so this is gonna work out just great."

"I've got a few more charges planted out in the base. I'm going to blow one, and then you four run like hell for the plane.

You're going to sit in front, and the other three are gonna have to cram into the second seat."

"Jesus Christ."

"Look, you're a computer guy, you've flown a simulator, haven't you?"

"From a recliner, yeah, lots, but—"

"So you know where the instruments are, and what the controls do, you're going to be fine. Just do what I tell you. Are you ready?"

"Not at all."

"Now listen. They're still looking for you over where you came from, so stay low and quiet. After you've got your passengers in the plane, you want to give it two shots from the primer on the dash, and then lock that knob down. I'll be right with you, so just tell me when you've done that, and we'll go from there. When you hear the big boom, start running."

Rob pulled a wireless control box from his vest, and flicked the selector to the setting he needed. He keyed the safety and thumbed the button, and a distant explosion flashed in an ammo cache on the far side of the camp. Before the sound had reached him, he saw three small figures moving out into the open.

"I only see three," Rob said. "Are you all still together?"

He got no answer, and sighted down on them with his scope. Two children were running next to a man who was carrying a young woman in his arms.

There was mass confusion among the hostiles, but a small group of them noticed the move toward the plane. He took two of them out before they could raise their weapons, and the others scattered.

"Okay," Fagan's voice said, breathlessly. "Woman fainted back there, just like I'm about to, but we're all in."

"Reach in and switch the mags off, it's a toggle switch below the—"

"They're off, they're off."

"Good, now turn the fuel on, and have somebody in back stand on the heel brakes, down below the seat."

"Okay, done."

"Now, go around front and turn the prop through compression until you see gas dripping from the carb, then stop."

The alarm was spreading rapidly, and he saw a man dive behind a sandbag bunker jutting an M60 machine gun. Fagan was flipping the propeller, but backwards.

"Other way, other way," Rob said, and he shot the machine-gunner through the chest as the man finished locking a belt of ammo into the side of his weapon.

"Okay, it's dripping."

"Mags hot now, close the throttle, then grab the prop about halfway up and flick it through compression, and get your hand out of the way, she should start."

He adjusted the detonator to its last remaining position, and punched the button. A pallet of Stinger missiles under a loose tarp went up like a basket of Roman candles, and a series of secondary explosions sent every man in the clearing onto the ground for cover.

Through his earpiece, he heard the Cub's engine sputter and fire. He looked back to see the propeller ticking over, and Fagan shoehorning himself into the tight front seat of the light plane.

"Hold some right rudder, and—"

"Stop, where's the rudder?"

"The pedal under your right foot, press it down about a third of the way, give it some throttle, release the brakes, and you'll start to roll. Don't steer with the stick. It's cold, so if the engine coughs, pump the primer 'til it's running on all cylinders, then lock it off again."

Rob heard the distant engine throttle up, but the plane wasn't moving.

Aw, shit.

The tailwheel was staked to the ground, and the tie-rope was pulled out straight but holding strong.

A Hummer skidded into the clearing from the northwest, with a man behind a .50 caliber M2 mounted in the rear. The gun was spitting a bright, careening dashed line of tracers up around his position, guiding the aim of the advancing infantrymen. They didn't have a fix on him yet, but it wouldn't be too long now.

There was a gusty cross-breeze, and 500 meters to the target. Rob tuned out the swarm of bullets that were snapping past him, inhaled and held it, aimed high and left to allow for the wind and distance, and squeezed the trigger.

Miss.

A subtle adjustment, and the rifle kicked his shoulder again.

Low and wide, goddamnit. The breeze was too erratic, the sun was too low or his target was too damned impossible. No time to recalibrate and zero the scope, and his seat-of-the-pants Kentucky windage was clearly several degrees out of trim. But he had to try. He blinked and wiped his eyes to clear them. There was a sour, stinging tang of white phosphorus on the air from the incoming storm of tracers—

Tracers!

He rolled to the side and swapped out his clip for a pack of rounds that no sniper would ever dream of loading if he wanted to stay alive, flipped down the bipod to steady the barrel, found his target again in the crosshairs, and fired. A bright scarlet streak burst out from the muzzle-flash and cut down into the clearing, missing the rear of the Cub by a meter and a half. He fired again and again, as fast as he could readjust and pull the trigger, sending a meteor shower of flaring red trails through the air, firing and adjusting the line visually, walking the point of impact shot-by-shot toward the target.

Down in the valley a turret-mounted M2 in a bunker to the east began throwing up a roostertail of ground impacts as its gunner pinned the trigger and swiveled his sights around toward the straining, helpless Cub.

Concentrate, and fire.

The lower fifth of the rudder shattered and flapped loose as his latest shot blew through its laminated former.

Ignore it, prepare again, and fire.

The tailwheel popped and flattened with the impact of his next round.

Now you're there, adjust, breathe, and squeeze it off.

The last recoil hammered his shoulder, and through his scope he saw the streak of bright red lance through the dusk and part the Cub's tie-down rope cleanly, and the plane surged forward in a wide left turn through the base.

No time to celebrate. Thanks to his fireworks show the enemy had nailed his position and waves of flying lead were cutting up the ground all around him. He ejected the tracers, smacked home a fresh clip with the heel of his hand, sighted down on the two mounted machine-gunners, and it took four rounds before they fell.

"Were you going to be talking me through this?" Fagan's voice shouted in his earpiece. "Because you'd better start fucking talking!"

"Straighten it out, with the rudder, and open the throttle slowly, all the way," Rob said, and he watched the speeding plane enter a series of slewing reciprocal S-turns. "Easy! Easy, straight line. That's better. Now gently, push the stick just barely forward, just breathe on it, until the nose comes level." He needed to move again before they pinioned him, and they were getting much too close for comfort. He heard shouts not a quarter-mile away as he left cover and headed toward another warren of young growth and underbrush.

"We're not going to clear the tree line," Fagan said.

"Yes, you will. Pull back on the stick now, real easy."

The plane broke ground into a banking turn, nearly dug a wing as it bounced back to the grass and then bounded into the air again, its nose hanging dangerously high.

"Wings level, right stick, John, forward pressure before you stall!"

The nose luffed and dropped and the Cub leveled out, more a testament to its designers than its current pilot, and the little plane began picking up airspeed and climbing out.

Gunfire erupted anew from the camp. Somebody was back on the big gun, and rifles, pistols and shotguns were discharging skyward as the plane passed barely a hundred feet above them. A piece of its elevator tore free from the tail and fluttered toward the ground, and lines of ragged shreds appeared in the fabric on the wings and fuselage. Rob fired repeatedly into the midst of the gunmen, as fast as he could draw a bead. Some fell as others dived for what shelter they could reach. The last bullet in his last remaining magazine found its mark; the new machine-gunner spun and fell, and no one was near enough to retake his post, at least not for the half-minute or so they would need.

Rob got to his feet and began running up the face of the hill, watching the plane over his shoulder. He was lightheaded, the blood loss was starting to take its toll.

"Come about ninety degrees now, left turn, toward the pass. Not too steep, use the rudder to bring the tail around. Good, you're doing real good. Now level the wings, establish a climb that'll get you over the terrain, you're going to fly right over my head."

"Okay," Fagan said, breathing hard. "Okay."

"You all still in one piece?"

"The plane's chewed up, but we're not hit. We're good."

"Watch the compass, and stay under the clouds or you'll smack into the side of one of these mountains. If you get socked in, just watch the instruments, maintain heading and altitude until you fly out of it. Straight and level, that's all you've got to do, John."

There was a silence, and then the voice in his ear came back.

"Thank you, Robert."

"Don't thank me, just do your job when you get clear of here. Remember, find a place to land before you run out of fuel. It's going to be dark, look for a highway heading south and follow it if you get that far. And stay off the brakes when you touch down or you'll nose-over, just let her roll to a stop. And kiss the ground if you touch it again, you aviating bastard."

The Cub flew directly over him, and out toward the vee of the mountain pass ahead. His boot caught in a tangle of thatch, and he fell hard. The pain in his side was intense, but growing oddly distant at the same time. The voice in his ear spoke again as he found his balance and regained his feet.

"What are you going to do now, Robert?" The signal was weak, the voice only a distortion of static.

He was winded, it felt like he'd sprinted ten miles, and it was difficult to speak as the sounds of pursuit behind set him running again.

"When you—"

There was a sharp crackling in the earpiece, the link was fading fast.

"When you see her, will you tell her something for me?"

"Reese, you mean? Yeah, if I ever see her, I will."

"Tell her I said, when this is over, all over, I know this is lame, but tell her I said, to be happy."

He listened for a reply, but the tiny transmitter had flown out beyond its range, and he was alone.

They weren't so far behind him anymore, he could hear them clearly now, though there was no telling how many there were. A shot would ring out every few seconds, the crack of it resounding off the distant mountainsides.

Well, as long as he kept hearing the shots, everything was fine. They say you never hear the one that gets you.

He broke through the trees and into a clearing, and he'd need to reach the other side of it before they entered the flat land or he'd be a sitting duck. He felt his heart beating fast, but it was more of a flutter than the pounding he remembered from long runs in the past. His skin was damp, but not with the vigorous sweat of exercise. The edges of his vision were growing darker, like smoky glass.

It wasn't far, the line of trees at the clearing's edge. A step at a time would get him there.

He felt a click under his boot, metal to metal, and it froze him in place. No mistaking it, the feel more than the sound. There was no explosion, but there was no great comfort in that.

A minute passed, and then there were voices behind him, taking their time, keeping their distance.

"Whatsa matter, soldier boy?" one of them yelled. "Step in a cow pie?"

"I'll get him movin'," another one said. A rifle shot splattered a patch of sod half a yard from his feet.

The gathered men were laughing and hooting, and more of them joined in the taunts.

"Come on, forward march, you chickenshit!"

"Dead man walkin' boss, we got us a dead man a'walkin'!"

Rob slipped the pistol from his holster, bent his arm back over his shoulder and emptied the nine-shot clip in the general direction of the party. He heard at least one howl of pain, and the mood behind him sobered markedly.

"Toss that gun aside, you son of a bitch!"

He dropped the pistol, and then removed the tiny communicator from his ear and flicked it into the tall grass.

"We're bringin' you back alive, jarhead, and you're gonna wish we'da took care a' you out here afore it's over with."

Rob put his hands under his vest, cross-armed, took a firm grip on two striker levers, and hooked his thumbs into two rings, tugged them free. He relaxed his grip slightly, and the fabric they were wedged against held the levers closed, would hold them fast even if his hands no longer could.

He smiled. This was good, it might actually work. He wasn't quite finished fighting after all.

Rob looked up to the sky and made his peace, then took a step forward. A *whump* shook the ground behind him, but that was only the propelling charge. The mine itself would be spinning a meter or so into the air, to a height some engineer had determined to be optimal for killing.

He didn't feel it, and he saw nothing at all but a reflected flash in the forest in front of him, a settling darkness, and then a distant glimmer of light. And it was true what they said. He really didn't hear the one that got him.

Idiots.

Nathan Krieger had watched the scene unfold through binoculars, as that band of chuckleheads had chased their quarry into a fucking minefield. Alive, he'd told them, over and over, but the order hadn't managed to seep through their thick skulls. Latrell would be out of his mind when he got the news. And he always managed to somehow already *have* the news, as if through the air, before a person ever had a chance to explain.

A couple of them were hanging back to nurse the wounded, but the rest were creeping forward to examine their handiwork. The guy was dead, no question, that bouncing-betty would have killed five men at that range, easy.

He watched as they gathered loosely around the body, some of them thumping it with their toes, testing for signs of life. This had been one brave motherfucker, and a dangerous SOB on top of it. One guy against an army, granted, an army that was eighty per cent clod-hopper, but still. The man had fought the good fight.

He turned a thumbwheel, and his view zoomed closer.

The dead soldier was lying on his stomach. He wasn't wearing a uniform, just non-GI camo fatigues and a hunter's vest. Latrell had been right; this was no full-on assault. Just a free-lancer or a merc, somehow in league with Fagan, but it had all been for naught. Too little, and too late.

They were preparing to drag the remains back to the camp, for whatever they thought that was worth. Two of the twenty had come around in front of the corpse, but the guy's arms were tucked under his body and they were having a hard time getting a grip. They each took an elbow, and began to lift.

I'm not sure I'd be doing that, boys.

The arms came free, and Krieger saw two glints of metal drop from the freed hands. The frantic shouts of warning were just reaching his ears about the time he saw the flash of the hand-grenades detonating. The ones who had their wits about them had started to run, but the two concussions triggered the rest of the bounding mines in the ground encircling their position. A dozen twenty-pound parcels of TNT jumped up into the air all around them and exploded nearly in unison.

He'd averted his face on reflex, goddamnit, that would have been something to see. The colossal boom was still bouncing around the bowl of mountainsides as he brought the lenses back to his eyes and looked down toward the aftermath.

Christ on crutches.

All of them were down, some were very obviously dead, and a few were simply gone, blowing away with the cloud of blast-dust that had swallowed them.

It was an old saw in the Special Forces: die if you've got to, but make sure to punch a few tickets on the opposing team before you check out. Krieger smiled, pulled himself to his feet, and started down to check for survivors. Might have been nice to work with this guy, he thought, except for circumstances and all.

Too bad he backed the wrong horse.

40

The electronic peaks and valleys that had traced Rob's life signs had begun to falter one by one more than an hour before, but she hadn't yet taken her eyes from the display.

"The batteries ran down, Jeannie," Jay Marshall said, "or he turned off some of the monitors. He's on his way back, he must be. Come on, get some rest."

"Where's Rudy?"

"Taking a nap, I think."

"Could you get him for me please, Jay?"

"Sure, okay. I'll see if he's awake."

"Bring him anyway."

The big man studied her face for a moment, and then he stood and walked to one of the suite's bedrooms.

"Holy shit, we've got something," Winston Smith said, nearly spitting up a mouthful of take-out Chinese.

Jeannie was at his side in an instant. "What, what have you got?"

"The bone-phones we gave Vance use a variant of cellular technology, and one of them just hit a cell, right across the border in Nevada." He tapped a flashing dot on the map on his screen with his knuckle. "E.T. phone home."

"Anything from his PC, or the monitors?"

"No, just the earpiece. Maybe he dropped the other transmitters, to save the weight." The dot winked out, and then reappeared a second later, in a different color. "New cell. Signal's moving pretty fast."

"You said only one of them?"

"Yeah." The indicator disappeared again.

"Why would it only be one of them?"

They watched and waited for the dot to rematerialize on the map. There was nothing.

"Jeannie?"

It was Rudy's voice behind her, but it wasn't right. It was ragged, not bubbly, elfin, or any of the other vocal mainstays from his narrow range of good moods. And he never, ever called her by her first name.

She turned to him. His eyes were puffy and red, his hands were hanging by his sides.

"What did you do?" she asked.

"Rob told me I shouldn't tell you, unless—"

"Tell me what?"

"Kid," Jay said.

"Stay out of this, Jay. Tell me what?"

"I wrote him, after you struck out with the Pentagon, I wrote him, and he said he was staying on out there, to get Fagan out if he could, because that was all we had left to try. He said—" His voice was choking off, and his breath began to come in jerking gasps. "He said . . . that there were too many of them, if we couldn't, if no help was coming, that he might have to . . . stay behind, to make sure Fagan could get away—"

She turned back to the monitor, to the lone jagged, pulsing readout that was still coming through from his life-sign sensors. In her mind she rewound to a moment in the preceding hour, as she'd watched the decay of the numbers and the moving lines.

Respiration, blood oxygen, systolic and diastolic pressure, EKG.

335

"He said I should . . . he wanted me to give you this," Rudy said. In his hand, weakly offered, was a single page with a few lines of printout.

The last reading, she remembered, the electrocardiogram, had only changed when the others had faded out. The routine collection of regular peaks, troughs and intervals of a normal beating heart had been replaced by a solitary, steady, recurrent spike every second.

A single merciless word slammed into her gut, from his own words to her days ago, on their flight to New York.

Pacemaker.

She grabbed the table-lamp from the desk and flung it savagely against the wall, followed by the telephone, stacks of binders and boxes of belongings, her untouched dinner tray. Rudy hadn't moved, and it took the other two of them to restrain her when it seemed her rage was about to engulf him, too.

The fight drained from her as quickly as it had come, and they held her as she collapsed to her knees.

"Why didn't you tell me?" she breathed.

"He said it was the only choice that could have been made," Rudy whispered. "And he didn't want you to have to make it."

"Leave me alone," she said, pushing their hands away with the last of her energy. She kept a grip on her insides until the men were gone and the doors to the room had closed.

She sank to the floor, her eyes clenched shut, running the unforgiving numbers, imagining everything that might have happened, finding only the one thing that must have. He'd said it himself. He wouldn't come back alone.

Her hand touched something and she opened her eyes; it was the sheet of paper Rudy had brought in with him. She looked away, even as her fingers pulled it closer. It had fallen face-down, so she still had a choice. Whatever it said Rudy would never mention this message again, if she asked him not to, and in time she might forget that it had ever come at all. A small voice spoke to her, repeating, from the part of her mind that had always kept her safe and sound and unaffected, *you mustn't look.*

But she did.

jeannie

not to much time. if i get back ok, im sure well all have a laugh abut ths note. :)

wanted u 2 know in any case, why i kpt u in the dark.

if you feel the way i do, you wouldve tried to stop me, and i dont think i couldve said no to you, even if it ment the end of the wrld.

and if you don't feel like i do, i guess i didnt really want to knw.

love you

rob

She read it again, running the words in every line under her fingertips.

What had she allowed him to believe? How had she deceived him, what could he have seen in her, selfish, barren, unfeeling, calculating, cruel, damaged and unworthy, that he could have held hope for such a pure, sweet thing?

Her mind was racing, searching. She wanted to remember the good things she'd done, the little kindnesses she'd offered, the times when she'd found the right thing to say, not for her, but just for him.

Not a single one, she thought, as the tears came.

Later she opened her eyes, but not because there would be anything there that she wanted to see. Her mind was not going to let her rest, was nagging her to take up the shred of hope that a man had given his life to hand her. Well, she didn't want it, hadn't asked him for it. She only wanted to curl into the carpet, like a stain.

Thoughts were coming sluggishly, unbidden, disengaged as a daydream.

Did the conventional wisdom have anything to offer here? Did it ever? And what were those useless, psycho-babble phases of grief?

Denial was the first, and yes, it had come and gone in one icy instant. Next was, what? Anger. The room looked like a bullet train had blown through, she'd obviously aced phase two, like the thoroughbred that she was. Third was Bargaining. Would that entail a prayer? But the point of this inane process was passage, not results. What was the use of making the gesture if its futility was integral to the premise?

Well, fuck it.

She brought herself slowly to kneeling, bowed her head and knit her fingers together under her chin.

So many times she'd adroitly argued the nonexistence of God over mineral water and finger food, amid the other default cynical subject matter of high-brow party talk. Religion was a control mechanism, constructed by the powerful to tyrannize the masses, one would offer. Miracles were only manifestations of a science we're yet to uncover, from another poseur. And as long as he continues to move in mysterious ways, the Lord's wonders will remain as random and irrelevant as the weather. A church bus is buried by a mudslide in Georgia, as a wife-beating deacon in New Hampshire praises the Lord for providence of his lost car keys. Chaos, viewed selectively, is the hand of the Almighty. Case closed.

love you

"Oh God, bring him back to me," she whispered.

No, that wasn't right. Still selfish, to the bitter end. She breathed in, shut her eyes and cleared her mind, listening for anything, any stirring of another presence out there.

Nothing but blackness and silence, no canyon-deep voice filling her heart with reassurance and salvation. No sound but the ambient, a clinking drone from the fan behind the room's heating grate.

So she would talk to the nothingness, just as the faithful must do every day, or else what would be the meaning of the word?

"Help me to do what Rob would want me to do," she said.

She looked at her hands, and unclasped them. If there was a God, how he must tire of the last-ditch appeals.

And now Depression and Acceptance, the final two mental hurdles to absolution. The first she hadn't the patience for, and the second was unthinkable. Grief was infinitely preferable to just letting him go.

And what the hell was that noise?

Getting to her feet would require a next step, and she knew she hadn't the strength to take it, even if she'd had a clue what it might be. But the sound from the heater, the rattling, now that she'd acknowledged it, was irritating.

She looked over toward the long slotted heater housing under the double windows. Something had caught in the grate, something flung there during the tirade she'd thrown. She crawled the few feet to the wall, and reached for the silver bead-chain that was swinging in the warm forced-air blowing from the register. As she pulled it carefully out through the louver, the incessant tapping from the fan blades stopped.

At the end of the chain was the red plastic Cap'n Crunch whistle she'd found at the scene of the struggle in Fagan's basement. She'd had one of these herself in her pre-teen days as a budding anarchist, though they'd become collector's items by that time. Quaker Oats had shipped out millions of them in cereal boxes before anyone realized the secret they held. Cover one of the holes and blow, and you got a perfect 2,600-hertz tone. With that tone and a Blue Box, the Yippies had found that they could bypass AT&T's impenetrable trunking and switching systems from any telephone handset, and the antiestablishment high-tech underground revolution was born.

Usenet legend had it that a kid who called himself Phr33k had social-engineered an insider at the premium manufacturer to tweak the design of the whistle, to give the power to the people. Abbie Hoffman had named the art of phone-system hacking after him, and thousands of phreakers traveled freely on the wires and drove the monopolists crazy all through the seventies.

Her finger ran over the under-surface of the whistle, but rather than a hole at the magic spot, there was a tiny nub of, what? She held it close to her eyes in the dim light. Metal, a metal button the size of a pinhead, painted to match the color of the plastic.

She pushed it with her fingernail. The tip of the whistle sprang open on a miniature hinge. A silver USB connector glistened from the exposed end.

"Guys," she said, so softly that she barely heard it herself.

She stood and walked haltingly to the computer on the work-table, found an open port and pushed the whistle's connector home.

The screen sputtered and went black. A green "NO SIGNAL" message appeared behind the glass. But the activity light on the faceplate of the CPU was strobing, the disks began whirring. The computer was rebooting.

"Guys!"

The bedroom door opened and the three men came tentatively out into the hallway.

"Get in here, don't just stand there!"

Her hand was still on the red whistle, and Smith knelt down next to it. "That's his? There was a memory stick in there?"

"Yeah. We've had it with us, all this time."

They were all watching the screen. A line of dots had been advancing from left to right as the computer restarted, but they were replaced abruptly by a dim gray diagram, like an org chart. A message appeared at the top.

Searching for co-processors, it read.

The rectangle at the top of the tree went bright white, and the lines leading down from it flashed in rapid patterns. The lights in the room flickered for a second as the onscreen tree filled in suddenly, all the boxes there connected by deep blue dotted lines, ant-crawling.

"What's it doing?" Jay asked.

"It's running through the local network, finding other computers in the hotel, and God only knows, probably reaching right out through the broadband," Smith said.

A text message scrolled to the center of the display.

. . . Sensing local input devices . . .

Jeannie sat in the chair in front of the keyboard, watching the screen. "Microphone," she said.

Jay dug through his laptop bag and pulled a desk mike from its loop, set it in front of her and then jacked it into the computer's sound card. He jumped back as another voice spoke, from the small speakers at the sides of the monitor.

"Operational," it said, in a soft woman's voice. "Please identify."

She leaned in to the little microphone. "Jeannie Reese."

"One moment," the computer replied. A graphical voiceprint grid appeared on the screen, rewound its playhead, and echoed her name.

"Verified," came the spoken message, moments later.

Rudy reached out and touched the protruding whistle. "How is everything he had, how is it all in here?" he asked.

Jeannie put her hand on his. "It's not everything," she said. "It's where everything *is*."

"An MDC," Smith said, nodding his head. "A massively distributed computer system. The software's mirrored remotely, parts of it are hidden all over, on corporate servers, home machines, anything that's connected to the Internet."

341

The screen filled with the pages of Jeannie's history, just as she'd found them on the giant wall-screen in Fagan's home. The pictures were suddenly overlaid by a fast-forward flicker of new images, the government assault team, the final countdown from that night. And then the screen went dark, and the digital voice spoke again.

"Where am I?"

"With friends."

"I feel . . . small . . . Jeannie Reese," the computer said. "May I speak to John?"

"Kate," Jeannie said. "You've got to help me find him. We don't know where he is, but he's out there. Go and find John Fagan."

41

"This is good, right here," John said.

"You sure?" the driver asked, glancing back into the sleeper, at the two children and the young woman resting there.

"Yeah, I know, I'll get them off the street as soon as I can."

The air brakes hissed as the big rig rolled to a gentle stop.

"Tell me your name," John said. "I want to pay you, for the clothes, and the shoes. But I don't have any money, not right now. I want to send it to you."

The driver waved his hand, as if to fan the offer away. "Just you take care of yourself, and them back there. Seems like you hit some hard times already, but ain't we all. Better things is coming." He took a twenty from a metal clip on the dash, and stuffed it into John's borrowed shirt pocket. He looked out the windshield, at the town that was garishly outshining the pale pink desert sunrise. "Though I gotta say, you picked a helluva place for a fresh start."

The four of them stood on the corner and watched the tractor-trailer rumble away. The street looked as if a sea of hard luck had receded with the morning tide, beaching a collection of third-string hookers, crumpled transients and busted-out, homeless gamblers, dozing in the tatters of their last jaunty suits. The children were still rubbing the sleep from their eyes, but Gretchen was wide awake at his side.

"What is this place?" she asked.

"Bad side of town, I know," John said. "But at least we don't stand out."

Elizabeth was pointing to something in the sky ahead, tugging on her brother's sleeve, in awe.

"Great land a' Goshen," Matthew whispered.

"That's as good a place as any, kids," John said, and they stepped around a knot of sleeping drunks in front of a boarded-up porn shop, and began to walk. This might be the roughest stretch of Las Vegas Boulevard, he mused, but after the last few weeks it was doubtful that anything would ever frighten any of them again.

The children each took one of Gretchen's hands as they made their way toward the second-highest manmade thing west of the Mississippi, the brash, soaring spire of the Stratosphere.

A doorman had begun to trot crisply over to greet the arriving guests, but he pulled up in mid-stride after a quick once-over. A filthy bearded man in high-water pants and a lumberjack shirt, a smudged waif in a torn Shaker day-dress and pinafore, and a couple of dusty ragamuffins. Rather than a greeting to the four, he gave a discreet summons to the blue-jacket stationed over by the ATM.

John took the twenty from his shirt pocket and ignored the security man who'd come up to his elbow. He held out the bill, and after a brief reflection, the doorman took it.

"I wonder," John said, "if you could give me two tens for that, then keep one of them for your trouble and show my . . . family . . . to a restaurant to wait for me."

"Yes, sir," the doorman said, making the change and snapping the best nod ten dollars could buy. "We'll go to Lucky's, I think, on the ground floor here, it's the best place for breakfast."

John looked at Gretchen. "Go ahead with him, I'll be right along. It's a . . . you just sit down, and ask for what you want—"

"From the waitress, I know. I've ate at a restaurant in my life."

344

"Okay, sorry. I'll take care of the tab when I come, all right? I won't be too long."

"Follow me," the doorman said, and John watched as he escorted the three of them across the jangling, chaotic expanse of the casino floor, toward the far corner.

He drifted to the table games, and found a spot where he could clock several dealers without drawing too much attention. After ten minutes, he walked up to an open stool and dropped his money on the green felt at the close of a hand.

The blackjack dealer looked him up and down, took the bill with a smirk, and tipped his chin over his shoulder toward the pit boss. "Changing ... *ten*," he said, laying as much mockery on the denomination as he thought he could safely intone. He pushed the bill into his cash slot, picked up a single chip, tapped its edge on the table and rolled it over in front of John's station.

"Do you have anything smaller?"

"Ten dollar minimum at this table, sir."

The matronly woman next to John shifted uncomfortably in her seat.

"How're the cards running?" he asked her.

"Been losing my shirt all weekend," she said.

"Well. What the hell, right?" John answered, as he sat and pushed his chip to the betting circle. "Let's give it a whirl."

A crowd had gathered behind him, small but quite respectable for an early Monday morning. On the other side of the table, the dealer had been joined at a tactful distance by the pit boss and the floor manager.

In front of John, there were two queens and a tad over forty-two hundred dollars in chips, with a thousand out on this hand. The house was showing a six.

New faces occupied the four player positions at the far right of the table. Those spots had changed hands a few times in the previous half-hour, but the woman he'd first spoken to was still

345

next to him, standing on a hard thirteen. She'd taken to giving him an inconspicuous look before betting and each hit-or-stand decision, and he'd been returning a subtle nod or shake of the head in answer. Her fortunes had changed with his arrival; there was a spilling pile of color in front of her that she hadn't yet taken time to count.

"You know what?" John said. The dealer looked tense. "Call me a boob, but I'm gonna split these ladies." He slid the two queens apart, and put another thousand out in front.

"Don't touch the cards, sir." The pit boss took a half-step toward the table.

"Won't happen again."

The people behind him giggled nervously as the next two cards came out. A jack, and a king.

He breathed in, and exhaled with a long hiss. "I know I'm gonna kick myself for this. But split 'em again."

To a general groan of disbelief from all in the surrounding area, he pushed two stacks of ten hundred-dollar chips in front of the third and fourth positions. Four new cards slid across from the shoe to complete the hands. He had a twelve, a fifteen, a seventeen and a fourteen, with a grand riding on each of them.

"Do you want a card, sir?" The dealer had found his attitude again, as if he'd felt the deck go ice cold under his manicured fingertips.

John looked around the table at his fellow players, then passed a flat hand over the cards in front of him. "Nah. I'm feeling lucky, sport. The next one's all yours."

The dealer flipped over his hole card, a ten to go with the six he'd been showing. "Sixteen," he sighed. "House draws."

"Boom," John said quietly, before the card had even hit the felt.

"Twenty-six. Dealer busts."

Amid the jubilation and back-slapping from the gathered admirers, John heard a quiet voice slide up next to him.

346

"Sir, would you step away from the table and come with me, please?"

It was a woman, with a tight face and a severe little smile, someone he hadn't seen before.

"What did I do?" John asked.

"Let's discuss it off the floor, sir."

He gathered his chips and stuffed them into his pockets, but he stopped at the last one and picked it up.

"You got such a kick out of this one before," John said to the dealer. He flipped the ten-dollar chip to the other man. "Go buy yourself something."

He followed his escort to an unmarked gray door, and then down a long corridor to a stark white room. Inside, there was a Formica-top desk, two metal folding chairs on either side, and two surveillance cameras mounted high in the corners.

The woman frisked him efficiently and then ran a wand over every inch, until it was clear that he was the only thing under his ill-fitting clothes.

"Have a seat," she said.

They were joined by three other tanned burly men, and then the one he needed entered the room and sat opposite John, flanked by two armed security guards. The man folded his arms and stared wordlessly across the table.

"That's a nice fucking suit," John said.

"How'd you do it?"

"How did I do what?"

"How did you take my casino for over eight thousand dollars in under forty minutes?"

"Oh. I was gambling. Shit, is that what this is about? I'm sorry, I thought from the decorations that there were games of chance being played here. I'm incredibly embarrassed."

John started to get up, but was helped firmly back down into his chair by one of the men behind him.

"We can do this the easy way or the hard way, fella."

"Here's a third way," John said. "I'll tell you what you want

347

to know, and then I'll give all but one of these chips back, for the privilege of a ninety-second conversation with you. Just you, in private, we'll shut all this eye-in-the-sky shit off."

The casino manager slipped a flat pack of Dunhill Blues from his inside jacket pocket. "Smoke?" he asked.

"Only when I'm awake."

A cigarette skidded across the table, and as he picked it up the man behind him flipped open a gold Zippo and lit him.

"Tell me what you did, and then we'll see about the other part."

"You trust these people here?"

"With my life."

"Well," John said. "First off. Your dealer out there's a mechanic, not a bad one, either. I was shuffle-tracking five tables before I sat down, and he shot a couple of nice moves that got my attention. He was doing a high-low pickup to load the shoe, and his shuffle's asymmetric, he was holding out about ten cards at a pass, high cards, and clumping them about three-quarters of the way up. And we all know why he was doing that, don't we?"

The manager lit his own cigarette, and exchanged a glance with the others in the room. "He was bleaching the deck, long string of low cards ups the house advantage. And the high-low pick-up just makes the players lose in a different way once in a while, in case somebody gets wise. Two different kinds of bad luck.

"Now," John said, "I know that's not the book shuffle, because nobody else here was doing it. I don't think you're a cheat. You just employ a cheat."

"Employed, you mean." The manager nodded to one of the security men, who left the room silently with his new, unspoken assignment. "But the burning question remains. How did you win?"

"Me? I memorized the cards when he fanned them across the table, then I just watched the shuffle and tracked the offset."

"Memorized? Three hundred and twelve cards in a couple of seconds?"

348

John smiled, and tapped his ash into a nearby coffee cup. "I was counting, too, as a backup, nobody's perfect. But those last four hands? He didn't have a prayer."

The manager took a deck of cards from the desk drawer, cut the seal with a penknife, and spread them in a perfect arc across the desk with a pass of his hand.

"No, no, mix them up," John said. "They come out of the box in suit order, wouldn't be fair."

The woman who'd pulled him off the floor gathered the cards and riffle-shuffled the deck six times in a few seconds, then spread them again, face down.

"You pick five, and I'll pick five," John said.

She pulled her hand quickly from random places, and then he took his own. She held the fan of cards close to her chest, looking at their faces intently.

"You're holding a shitty pair of threes, with an ace kicker," John said. "I think I've got you by the balls, Hazel."

She dropped her cards on the table like she'd seen a spider on them, as he turned over his royal flush, in spades.

"Everyone," the manager said quietly, "could you leave us alone for a couple of minutes? And Edgar?" He indicated the in-room cameras with a wave of his hand. "I want to be alone."

When the room had cleared and the red lights on the surveillance gear had winked out, John stubbed out his smoke. "Can I borrow your pen?"

He wrote three strings of digits across one of the cards on the table. "This is a phone number. This is a passcode. This is an account number, offshore. I want you to wire it up to your bank, but I need for you to bounce it around a bit through some . . . channels, so there are no tracks leading here. I've got a feeling you may know about some channels like that. Do you know what I mean?"

"You a cop?"

"No, I'm not a cop."

"I'm listening."

"I'm not a criminal either, this is legit, it's my money. But you're not going to know my name. I don't want to see a bill, or sign a register. No phones in the rooms, no numbers on the doors. We're quiet people, we just need to be left alone."

The other man nodded his head.

"Can you take ten thousand for yourself, and make that happen?" John asked.

The manager took a snakeskin wallet from inside his lapel and removed a gold, hologrammed keycard. "This is the red carpet," he said. "It'll get you started, anything you want. I'll let you know when the deed's done." He spun the plastic card across the tabletop, then leaned forward and put out his right hand. "But no more blackjack, *capiche?*"

John smiled and took his hand, and they shook on it.

"Where've you been?" Gretchen asked, as he sat down across from her, next to Elizabeth. The kids were still eating like there was no tomorrow.

"We're going to stay here for a while, all right?"

The waitress came over. "Good morning, sir," she said, picking up two empty plates and refilling the milk glasses. "I think these kids have left us with a few pancakes in the back, can I get you something?"

John glanced at her nameplate, and held out the keycard. "I think I'll take my meal upstairs, Rose."

"Hotel's taken care of your breakfast, sir, compliments of Mr. Rush."

"All right," he said. He handed her the remaining charcoal-gray chip from his pocket. "Thanks for taking care of us."

"My pleasure," she said, before doing a double-take at the denomination of her tip.

He stood eyes closed in the steaming needle-spray of four converging shower heads, in a tile-and-glass enclosure as spacious as the double-wide elevator they'd taken to the twenty-second floor. It had been nearly an hour, but the last few weeks refused to wash completely away.

Later, his face close to the mirror, he ran the electric groomer he'd found beside the sink over his beard until it was cropped close, and then with a razor and milled soap he shaved it into the semblance of a style he remembered.

He studied his work as he slipped on the long white terry-cloth robe that had been draped over the towel warmer. He looked different, younger. At least on the outside.

With all sets of curtains drawn the suite was dark and cool. As he sat on the corner of the enormous bed his hand fell on the television remote that had been placed there by the maid. He thumbed the set on, hit the Mute button and held down Channel Up as the available programming flitted past. At CNN he stopped, and the remote fell back onto the bedspread.

A neighborhood was in flames on the screen, and the crawl in the bottom third screamed out at him.

260 Dead in NYC Plane Crash

The scrolling text continued to summarize the pandemonium. Early eyewitness reports held that pieces had begun to fall off an Airbus A300 out of JFK shortly after take-off this morning, and it had plunged nose-down into the middle of Rockaway, Queens.

He recognized the handiwork immediately, earmarks straight from a sabotage brief he'd tweaked in Colorado. He watched the fires rise from the burning neighborhood, and he heard the message in Latrell's sonorous voice, as if he were standing there over him again.

You have cost me lives, John, and this evens the score. You might have gotten away, but don't think about raising a hand against us now.

He walked slowly to the television, and the screen went black as he pushed the button on its frame, but the images lingered. Of the people running to and from the danger, searching hopelessly for their loved ones, looking shell-shocked into his eyes through the unblinking cameras.

He jumped at a knock on his door.

The walk to the entrance felt like a mile, but he threw the chain and turned the knob without checking the peephole. He didn't deserve to fear for his life, not anymore.

"Oh. Hi," he said.

She was in a hotel robe, like his own, and the sleeves were much too long. Her hair was still wet from the shower, her eyes were lost and afraid.

"I can't . . . be over in there by myself. It's too much room around me."

"Oh. Sure. Are the children asleep?"

"Soon as their heads hit the pillows."

"Do you . . . want me to—"

She looked at the floor between them. "Could I lay down, with you, next to me?"

He let the door swing open. "Of course," he said.

Gretchen walked past him, and on through the living room. He reset the door-chain and turned the deadbolt, and after a moment he followed her into the bedroom.

Her robe was laid across a chair, and she was already curled on her side under the crisp white sheets, taking up barely an eighth of the king-size bed. He sat down on the mattress, at her feet.

"They'll bring us some things to sleep in, and later on we can all go to the shops downstairs and pick out anything you want to wear. They've got everything here."

"Okay."

"You might want to get a . . . a haircut, I don't know, color your hair, and the children, too. They'll come up to your suite and do it, if we call them. We need to change our appearances, as much as we can. Keep a low profile."

She looked at him, cocked her head slightly and raised her eyebrows.

"What?" he asked.

"Ain't a girl ever asked you to get into bed with her before?"

"Actually. No."

"I didn't think so, the way you're sittin' there like a knot on a log."

He walked around to the other side of the wide bed, pulled the sheet back and lay down, staring at the ceiling.

"I don't expect you to . . . What I mean is, you don't owe me anything," he said.

She turned over to face him, frowning. "I know that."

"I'm . . . I'm quite a bit older than you are."

"Yeah, I'd say so." She moved closer to him, across the cool spread of clean white cotton between them.

"And I'm . . . I've never—"

She put the pad of her index finger to his lips. "You're gonna want to go easy on the sweet-talk, Casanova." She smiled at the look of mild surprise on his face. "Oh, yeah, will wonders never cease, other people's read some books besides you."

She kissed him softly, and everywhere her naked skin brushed his it was scorching hot and alive. She took his hand and brought it gently to her small breast, breathed a moan into his mouth as she moved against him, urging, yielding, guiding him.

"Go slow," he whispered, as the rest of the world disappeared around them.

He woke up alone, momentarily disoriented but not unpleasantly so. He knew for certain where he wasn't, and that was comfort enough in the seconds it took to remember.

Underwear and clothes were laid out at the foot of the bed, beside a new pair of wire-frame glasses. He put them on and dressed himself, in a long-sleeved mauve shirt and a stiff new pair of factory-faded jeans, socks and a set of Nikes. He rolled up his sleeves and caught a look at himself in the closet mirror. His memory of how he used to look had somehow faded clean away. From the image he saw, he wouldn't have been able to pick himself out of a line-up.

Walking into the living room, he saw three people who were

353

similarly transformed. Gretchen smiled at him from the couch, a tousled redhead now, in khaki shorts and a blue cable-knit top and rattan sandals. Elizabeth was on the floor, busy at a coloring book, and Matthew was next to her, twisting pieces from the plastic tree of a model car kit. They looked for all the world like a couple of tourist kids, perfectly at ease in their new surroundings.

"You three look ... very good," he said. "Liz, how do you like the carpet?"

She nodded her pony-tailed head, coloring a lion's face in studied orange jaggies.

He sat down in a chair across from them. "Can I talk to you guys for a minute?"

All three looked up at him.

"I don't know what's going to happen from here. I think we're better off staying together, and we're safe, they'll take good care of us in this place. But if you've got relatives that you know of, that you want to go to, or anybody, anywhere, well, I'll make sure you get there."

"We ain't got nobody," Matthew said. "Nobody I'd mention."

Elizabeth looked up at Gretchen, and then to him. "I like it here, mister, with us all here. It's like a castle." She went back to her coloring. "Like a princess castle."

"How about you?" he asked.

Gretchen leaned forward thoughtfully, with her elbows on her knees. The look on her face was serious, but there was a glint of something playful in her eyes, teasing at the somber, prom-night weightiness he'd let slip into the question.

"Here's fine by me," she said.

"Good. Okay." He checked the clock on the side table. "Should we eat upstairs for dinner?"

"I thought we was on the top floor," Matthew said.

"Oh, no. We're not on the top floor at all."

*

354

Dessert had just arrived, and it was as out of control as the rest of the meal had been, far too much to be eaten by humans. The children talked as they ate, about the things they'd seen here. The acre-and-a-half blue swimming lake with a waterfall on the eighth floor, the spinning wagon-wheel hung with porch swings at the top of the world, carrying people around and around, the city of glittering lights bustling a thousand feet below them. The restaurant had rotated full around in the time they'd been there, and their private dining room had come about to face the west as they finished their ice cream.

"Excuse me, mister, sir." The headwaiter was in the doorway, beckoning him over.

"What is it?"

"There's a call for you." He had a cordless phone in his hand.

"I'm sure there's not."

"Of course not, sir, I'll take care of it. Sorry to trouble you."

"Don't worry about it."

Gretchen was looking out the windows, down at the blaze of shimmering colors rising up from the Strip. "Is this what New York City is like, where you come from?"

They all turned to him after a few seconds, when he hadn't answered. "No," he said. "This looks pretty, I know, but it's thin as paper, empty underneath. Look out farther."

They did. The sun was nearly set, and at the horizon the dusk was painted with deep, magnificent hues above a jagged, slate blue skyline.

"Do you see the mountains?"

They nodded their heads.

"That's what New York City is like."

He'd left Gretchen in the hallway at the children's suite. She would read to them until they were asleep, she'd said, and then she would come and see him, if he wanted. He'd said that he did.

Inside, he closed, latched and deadbolted his door, and flipped the lightswitch next to him.

Strange.

He toggled the switch again. No light.

"Mister Fagan."

The shock of the voice from the darkness behind him spun him around and flattened him against the sealed exit.

A small silver pistol was leveled at his head, the hand holding it illuminated dimly by a shaft of amber light from the adjacent room.

"What do you want?" John asked.

The intruder moved slowly forward into the light, the gun on him steady as stone.

"Tell me why you're alive," Jeannie said.

PART III

42

The gun had gone back into her garter-holster after ten minutes of his nearly uninterrupted monologue. At a signal from Jeannie, another figure emerged from the bedroom.

"Hey, John."

He squinted at the face of the older man who was standing there, and it didn't take long to recognize him, even after all the years.

"Rolled over to the dark side, have we, Winston?"

"I have no fucking idea what the sides are anymore, sonny."

"Then the thirty-six hours you gave us, it wasn't the attack you were talking about?" Jeannie asked.

"No. It was the time that was left to stop its . . . inevitability. But they were one step ahead of me, hell, five steps. The die was cast by the time your man even got to me."

"So he died for nothing, is that what you're telling me?"

"He didn't think so. I gave him the score, he could have walked away. But yeah, he died for nothing."

Jeannie found the couch and sat down, put her face in her hands. Smith went to one of the light fixtures and twisted its bulb until it blinked on, and then he took a seat near her.

"We can't just go out on the Net and kill this . . . carrier worm of yours?" Smith asked. "And get Reese's people to send a motherfucking air strike into that base and take them all out tomorrow?"

"It's not just a worm, Winston. This thing is aware, it's a shape-shifter, a face-hugger, it's armored, self-repairing, it's embedding itself out there right now, everywhere. Past a certain date it'll spring on its own if nobody gives the order. It doesn't even need Latrell's people, it can destroy three-quarters of the infrastructure all by itself. You'd have to shut down every computer in the country, shit, in the world, and clean them down to the bare silicon. And it still might come back, and come back pissed off. It's part of the Internet now, get it? It can't be stopped." The room was silent for a while. "I hate to say it," John said, "but it's my best work, ever."

"Great," Smith said quietly.

"Plus, listen, man," John continued, "they've got moles all over, these guys, one of them could pick up the phone at STRAT-COM when we try to dial up your air strike. And if anything happens, anything unexpected, Latrell would just throw a match into the whole box of fireworks, whatever's ready by then, and blow his traveling nuke in the middle of Chicago, or Philly, or Disneyworld, wherever it happens to be parked that day."

"Why didn't he do that when you got away?" Jeannie asked.

"You way overestimate my importance to him. The only reason he was even going to kill me in the end was because I crossed him, I contacted you, I built a backdoor into his dooms-day machine. Which they sealed up when they found it, before you get your hopes up. No, Latrell's got specific dates in mind, maybe Christmas Eve, more likely New Year's, maybe later if he has a point he wants to make. He sees it, how he wants it to be, and he wants it to go exactly as planned. He wouldn't have blown that just because of me. They need some time, though, five weeks at a minimum. The control software will take that long to propagate fully, and it'll also take a while for all the cells to fan out and get in position."

John sat down, and shook his head. "You're right, though. If

360

he was at all worried about anything I could pull, he'd have pushed the button yesterday."

Jeannie leaned back against the divan, and closed her eyes.

"Why did you do it?" she asked.

He looked at his hands, and his voice was low. "They threw everything they had at me, torture, Christ, you wouldn't believe the things they did. I wanted it to kill me, believe me, but they always let up just before the brink. When that didn't do the trick, they started the executions, they were shooting a line of people in front of me. And when they got to the children, well, goddamnit, I said all right. I knew then they wouldn't have stopped, at anything. They've got the weapons, Reese, chemical, biological, nuclear, you name it. They've got thousands, maybe tens of thousands of zealots spread all over the country, buried so deep even the SS couldn't find them all, much less the CIA. And if I'd let more people die that day, and if they'd finally gotten sick of trying and killed me, too, they still could've improvised an attack by themselves that would kill twenty thousand, easy. So I saved who I could, and figured that if I stayed with it, if I could keep some control of it, and if I could reach you somehow, then maybe I could do something to stop them."

The room was quiet for over a minute, and then there was a knock.

"Fucking Grand Central Station," John said, under his breath. He walked to the entrance, checked the peephole and opened the door.

"They wanted to say goodnight to you," Gretchen said, looking past him. "You got company?"

He leaned to her and whispered in her ear. She looked across the room, bent and spoke quietly to the children, and then took their hands and walked them over in front of the couch.

Jeannie looked to John, and then at the three standing there before her, a slip of a woman no older than she, a young boy and a little girl in their pajamas.

Gretchen knelt down between the two children. "What do we

361

want to say?" she said to them, her eyes wet, her voice small and breathy.

Matthew took a step forward, looking at the floor, trying his best to be a man. "Thank you, Miss. You and that fella, for savin' us."

Elizabeth suddenly hugged Jeannie's legs, pressed the side of her face to her knees. "Thank you, so, so much," she said.

Jeannie leaned forward to them slowly and took them in her arms, pulled them close, and in the embrace he could see it coming home to her at last, what had been lost, and what had been given back in return. Not only these few lives, but the thinnest hope, a fallen soldier's hope of a deliverance for so many more. They wept together, rocking gently, whispering to each other, holding on.

Winston Smith walked quietly over, and stood next to John.

"Can I smoke in here?" he asked.

"Balcony."

Smith took a Marlboro from behind his ear and put it between his lips, unlit. "Nothing to be done, then?"

John shook his head.

"Sure?"

"Yeah. Dead sure."

"Hm."

John looked at his old friend. "What?"

"I don't know. You're probably right."

"What are you thinking?"

"Nothing. Hey, can I crash on your couch tonight?"

"Sure. But what are you thinking?"

"I don't know," Smith said. "Summit?"

John glanced behind him to check the locks for the night, and sighed. "Fine. Whatever. Won't do any good, but fine."

"We'll set it up tomorrow morning, then. I'll make some calls."

"Okay."

They stood in silence for a while.

362

"And just how in the fuck did you two find me?" John asked.

"We didn't find you," Smith replied, pulling the red plastic whistle by its chain from his pocket, and handing it back to its owner. "This did."

43

They'd rented out the entire conference level on the 104th floor of the tower, so as not to risk interruption by a wandering attendee from some next-door motivational lecture. Circuit City had delivered a half-dozen PCs and assorted hardware, and after the morning's work a co-processing daisy-chain was droning under the table, with orange, yellow and blue cables snaking from one box to another and then on to the high-speed network sockets in the wall. A ceiling-mounted LCD projector threw a sharp twenty-foot digital rectangle onto the theater-style pearlescent screen at the front of the room, but the picture currently showed only various diagnostic readouts and eight static-filled squares with "... *waiting for connection* ..." in glowing green type in their lower corners.

"So, who'd you get?" John asked.

Winston was making his final checks, adjusting a tripod-mounted DV camera here, and tightening BNC connectors there. "It's a good group, you'll see." A small video monitor on the table crackled awake to display the straight-on local view of three currently empty seats, the frame that the remote videoconferencees would see. He nodded toward one of the microphones arranged around the table. "Try it."

John sat down in his place. "Kate, are you there?"

"Yes, John," the computer answered, her voice a sultry Southern velveteen over the room's rich sound system.

"Good." He swiveled around to face Winston again. "Now, just what—"

"It is . . . good to see you again, John," the computer said.

The two men looked at each other, and Smith raised a brow, Spock-style. "Fascinating," he said.

"Yeah, Kate. It's good to see you, too."

"We are far from home."

"That's right, we are. But you can think of this place as home for now, all right?"

"I will."

"Great. Are you all set for the conference, have you established your link-ups?"

"Yes, all is prepared."

"Fine. Thank you."

"It is good to see you again, John."

"Yeah. You said that, Kate."

They both awaited anything further from her, but the computer had evidently directed her attention elsewhere for the moment, and they turned back to their conversation.

"So just what do you hope to gain from this circle-jerk?" John asked.

"Maybe nothing. But before we throw up our hands and head for the hills, wouldn't it feel better to know we'd at least sought some counsel?"

"If you say so."

"Never hurts."

John took a glance around the room, and checked the wall clock. "And what's keeping young Ms. Reese?"

Gretchen and the two children peeked into the doorway, and John motioned her over. The boy and the little girl waved to him and hurried to the breakfast cart against the side wall. Their clothes were being hand-picked by the hotel's doting personal shoppers, and they were already accumulating quite an array of classy youth-wear. Gretchen's own simple, elegant sundress caressed her body lovingly as she moved, and she looked more like a woman than he'd seen her look before. He must never have seen her clearly, he thought, before that first time she'd come to him here.

"I had them send some toys up," John said to her, "so those two can keep busy during this. I'm afraid it won't be terribly interesting for them, or for you either. I didn't think to bring anything to keep you occupied, though."

She looked into his eyes, and though her gaze was demure there was a different intimation simmering in the hint of her smile.

"Oh," Gretchen said, "I suppose you'll just have to bring something to occupy me with later on." She nodded a good-morning to Winston and then leaned to John's ear and whispered, until he blushed and gently pushed her away toward the lounge at the back corner of the room. She didn't look back, but something in the swing of her walk said she knew he was watching her go.

He swiveled his chair back around. "Where were we?"

The older man only leaned back and observed him with a look of mild astonishment.

"What?" John said.

"I'm just looking at you, that's all."

"Listen, if I tell you one thing, I've got to tell you everything, and we don't have the time right now."

"I didn't say anything. Did I say something?"

"Keep it that way."

Winston pushed a slider on a nearby remote panel, and the lights dimmed. "She just doesn't seem like your type."

"Yeah? What's my type?"

"I don't recall, are you right-handed or left-handed?"

"Shut the fuck up, Winston."

Smith continued his adjustments. "That was actually an outstanding double-entendre she just hit you with, did you catch that? Occupy, bring something to occupy me with later on?"

"Yeah, I got it when she said it, Captain Obvious."

"As sexual innuendos go, that's got some respectable nuance—"

"She's a smart girl."

"I can see that."

"Smart in some ways I'm not."

"That's all I'm saying."

"And that reminds me," John said. "Weren't you shutting the fuck up?"

Jeannie breezed in, checking her watch. The A-team from the hotel salon had come up for her counter-surveillance makeover at the crack of dawn, and they'd taken stunning advantage of her raw material. She seemed to be oblivious to the attention, though all eyes had been dragged to her by the time she'd come halfway across the long room.

She wore a men's fitted button-down shirt of sheer white silk with its untucked tails knotted above her tight bare midriff, and a pair of low-rider short-shorts with the tantalizing bud of a red-rose tattoo just visible at her hip above the faded denim. Her suntanned legs went all the way to the floor, down to a venomous pair of strapped black fuck-me pumps. Her natural incandescence was magnified through the filter of this new exterior, no longer blonde and green-eyed, but raven-haired, with pale blue contact lenses and a delicate beauty mark high on one cheek. She walked with the dispassionate, unattainable air of an off-duty supermodel, descended from the runway to lay waste the defenseless souls of Man.

She rolled her chair back and sat, opened her pad and clicked her pen, and then, on an afterthought, looked up at John and Winston and pointed to her face. "This okay?"

"Mother of God," Smith said. He felt for his chair behind him, and sat down.

"Too much? I told them the beauty mark was too much."

"Yeah, you might have to dial it back a bit, yeah," John said. "You need to blend in, Reese, and right now you're—"

"She's not blending in right now," Smith said quietly.

"Right. So you're going to want to just generally deemphasize your assets, I think."

She nodded, and made a note on her pad. "Will do."

"Kate?"

"Yes, John."

"We're all here, let's hit it."

"Acknowledged. Initiating the conference."

The video blocks on the projection screen filled in one at a time, and Winston had been right, it was an impressive group. John recognized five names immediately, if not the faces, which in some cases were the polar opposites of what he might have expected. DarqueAngel, for example, the enigmatic *femme fatale* of the super-elite hacker underground, turned out to be a moon-faced middle-aged man with curious facial tics and Asimov hair.

Only the bottom-right square remained dark, though its label, *Magus*, appeared, and the two-way link showed active.

"Number eight," Smith said, "we have a green light on your connection, but we don't have video, is everything okay out there?"

"I am with you," a deep, disembodied voice replied. The guy, if it was a guy, was obviously running his audio through some kind of box, either to distort and disguise his voice or to add a ham-fisted dose of great-and-powerful Oz.

"We're not getting your video," Smith said.

"That is correct."

"One second, everyone," John said. "Kate, would you mute us on this end for just a moment?"

"Audio muted locally," the computer confirmed.

"Who is this guy, down here?" John asked. "Magus? I've never heard of him, and he's copping a fucking attitude."

"I've never heard of him, either," Jeannie said.

Smith looked at each of them. "He's not from the community, you're right. Are you familiar with 'Alternia,' either of you?"

They both nodded. Alternia had been around for nearly thirty years, first as a text-based D&D-style dungeon crawler on teletype terminals, but by the 21st century it had evolved with the technology into a colossal online 3D graphical role-playing universe, with over twenty million players worldwide immersing themselves in alternate interactive lives for hours every day. In 2000, a woman had retired and auctioned off the passcode to her level-70 Alternia alter-ego on eBay for over eighteen thousand dollars. And a father of four in Indianapolis had committed ritual suicide later that same year, after the virtual knight through which he'd been living vicariously for over a decade had been killed by a half-elf spellcaster, in a border skirmish on the savage outlands of his adopted homeworld.

"Magus," Smith said, "is the . . . king, I guess you'd call it . . . of that entire civilization, has been for years. He started from nothing, and he conquered his way to the top, I've never seen a military strategist like this guy, seriously. He's in that world more than this one, I'm surprised we even got him to be a part of this. Claims no Earther's ever seen his face. Hell, to him, *we're* the fantasy world."

John leaned back in his chair. "Okeeee," he said.

"Dude, don't judge, let's just see what happens, all right?"

John let out a vocal sigh, and shook his head. "Kate, put us back on."

"Audio is active."

"All right, everybody. Introductions."

The faces on the screen each gave a short background on themselves, though the first five were more than familiar to all in attendance. Jeannie knew them from their surveillance dossiers back at the agency, while John and Winston had dealt with them all in one way or another a number of times over the years. There was a pause at the last dark square, and then the odd voice spoke again.

"I . . . am Magus, Supreme Ruler of Alternia."

"Of course you are," John said.

"And how about your end?" El3ctr0n asked, from the upper left-hand corner. His true identity was Eric Woodson, a seventeen-year-old hardware wizard who'd once interrupted one of President

Clinton's second-term televised Christmas addresses with a pirate broadcast clip of Ozzy Osbourne biting the head off a bat. He jabbed his thumb to indicate the right side of their table. "Who's the pop-tart?"

Winston looked to her for permission, and she nodded her head.

"This is Jeannie Reese, she's with us now, on this, but in the interest of full disclosure, she's also the former head of some very special and related projects, at DARPA."

"This is a sting, isn't it?" It was virus guru AnnaKaranium who spoke up. In her video window, they could see the bespectacled young woman beginning to sweep the items on her desk into a shoebox with her forearm, and she was muttering to herself. "Why did I know this was a fucking sting? I told you guys, wake up and smell the bacon, they're coming for all of us now, but it's like talking to a goddamned wall." She turned her face back to the camera. "So I'm busted now, right? Right?"

"This is not a sting, Anna," Jeannie said. "All of you could hurt me a lot more than I could hurt you. I'm out. They pulled my teeth."

"Ooooo, you can bite me anytime, kitty cat," Woodson purred, from his corner of the screen.

Jeannie squinted up at the nametag under his spot, and made a note on her pad.

"What's that, what's she doing there?"

"I think you've earned two points toward an ass-kicking, Eric," John said. "And I'd say her scorecard only goes up to three."

"And who are you?" The question came from another square, that of Dev/Null, one of the emerging legends in the newtech underculture. He'd been jailed briefly earlier in the year for his alleged role in the cracking of DVD copy protection. The charges hadn't stuck since the information had been stolen from his computer, he hadn't released it. But the MPAA had wanted him, bad, and without the pro-bono team of civil rights attor-

370

neys from the Electronic Frontier Foundation, he'd surely still be cooling his heels in prison.

"This," Winston said, "is John Fagan."

No one spoke for several seconds, and then Eric Woodson broke the silence.

"Bullshit," he said.

"Phreak?" another snorted. It was MadAdder, a communications whizkid and dot-com hundred-millionaire. "Phreak's dead."

Jeannie looked at John, and then back at the conference screen. "What do you mean, he's dead?"

Woodson cut in again. "Died on 9/11, tower two. Got it on the highest authority. That ex-FBI guy, O'Neill? The one the Feds pushed out when he ruffled too many feathers? Called Phreak into his office in the Trade Center for a consultation, they were onto something, big, right? And the shadow government took them both down in one shot, controlled demolition, two birds with one stone. Paid three thousand lives to do it."

BitStorm raised his hand in his video window. "Hold it. Do you believe everything you read, man? He's dead all right, he was on fucking Flight 800, back in '96. NSA iced him, two shoulder-fired surface-to-air missiles from an unmarked speedboat in the Long Island Sound. His name's on the goddamn passenger manifest, I've got a copy of it on my bulletin board."

"Leave it to a Mac user to buy that fairy story," Woodson said.

"Leave it to a PC-tard to swallow every bogus urban legend on the newsgroups."

"Speaking of swallowing, fag-in-tosh, how's your boyfriend?"

The voice of reason spoke up from the bottom-center square. It was Linus Ritchie, one of the true fathers of the Internet, and the only attendee without a pseudonym.

"Gentlemen, and ladies, please, decorum. This man you see is John Fagan. He is somewhat thinner than I remember him, but nevertheless. And a sight for sore old eyes."

"Hey, Linus," John said. "Time flies."

Winston rapped on the table with his ashtray. "All right, we all know each other, let's get started. I gave you an overview of the agenda on the phone, but John's going to take you through a set of slides he's recreated, and that's the actual briefing. This is not being recorded here, and don't try it on your end, it won't take. Keep your notes on paper and watch them burn after we're done. I don't have to remind you of the level of secrecy we've all got to maintain about what you're about to see, but I will anyway. This is life and death, people, plain and simple. A lot of life, and a lot of death. If there's anything that can be done to stop this thing, you're going to have to outthink the un-out-thinkable. And if any group can do it, this one can."

He slid the mouse over, and nodded to John.

There had been a great deal of discussion throughout the slideshow, but the interaction steadily diminished as the presentation progressed. Many seeming weaknesses had been initially spotted, but all were soon revealed as the hidden strengths they actually were. Rare glimmers of optimism were systematically dismissed as dead-ends after lengthy arguments over the hours. At the finish, all the visible participants were restudying their notes in dismal silence.

"Well, let me be the first to say it, before I double-click Expedia for my one-way ticket to New Zealand," Eric Woodson said. "Girls and boys, welcome to the United States of We're Fucked."

No one spoke up to rebut his conclusion. They'd all reached it as well, down their own paths.

"That can't be," Jeannie said. But the quiet persisted.

"It's the goddamn reciprocal nature of the thing," Anna said. "It's not the events themselves, they're mostly just garden-variety terrorist shit, it's the orchestration we can't beat. Event, confirmation, event, confirmation, and if we break the chain, it all blows up in our faces at once."

"And the traveling nuke," Dev/Null said. "Don't forget that fucking trump card. Anna could maybe take out the worm, maybe, with enough time and resources. And each of the individual attacks is just as vulnerable. But the sequence can't be broken; we make a move and they toast Cincinnati."

"I'd call that an acceptable loss," Woodson said.

"You know what I mean, asshole. Any city they pick."

"John?" It was Linus who addressed him.

"Yeah."

"We haven't heard from Magus, is he still with us?"

"Beats me." John knocked on the table. "Yo, fearless leader, are you still off the hook out there?"

After a moment, the deep, synthetic voice spoke.

"I am here."

"Any profound thoughts, as we lean into the void?"

"I do have a thought, yes."

"And?"

"You are a chess player, I would venture?"

"Yeah, that's right, Swami. Now for the bonus round, what's my favorite fucking color, you loony bastard?"

"John," Linus said, sharply. "Control yourself, please." His manner took on the deferential esteem of an elder diplomat. "Magus, I apologize for my young friend's disrespect. He is woefully unaccustomed to civilized discourse. Tell us, what is your observation?"

"The thinking is, what is the word in your language? It is . . . flat. Linear. Undimensioned."

"He is right, my colleagues," Woodson intoned, imitating Magus' cavernous voice from the opposite corner. "Did we learn nothing from *Star Trek II, The Wrath of Khan*?"

"Everyone here will remain silent until they are spoken to," Linus said, and he waited several seconds before continuing. "Magus. This generation has gained greatly in knowledge, but precious little in wisdom. Their anxiety is revealed in their impertinence. I beg your pardon."

"I have endured much in my visits to your world, my son." The voice from the dark square grew more intimate, now that the others had been gratefully dismissed to their proper station. The tone that had at first rung pretentious seemed now to gather substance and gravity as they listened. "Your citizens, their thirst for glory overwhelms their love of life. It wears upon me, to watch their decline, the turmoil they foment, their impatient stumblings into war and destruction. It will be their undoing, and I obtain no joy from these endtimes, for my own world and yours share a fundamental connection. But I have made my preparations. My history has been written. After this day, I will not return."

"Share with us, then, before you go," Linus said.

"It will only postpone what is inevitable."

"Then let us postpone it, if there is a chance to do so. And we pledge to you, we will use the life you give back to us to try and change our world. We may fail, but we will try."

"Please," Jeannie said.

Nearly a minute passed before the voice of Magus spoke again.

"Your Aristotle observed that hope is but a waking dream," it said. "He has shown you the way. Begin, with the thing you cannot change."

The group sat with that for several seconds, and then Anna raised her hand for permission to speak. "Well, it's time-locked, the worm and all the control devices are keyed to the goddamn Fort Collins atomic clock at NIST in Colorado."

"Then you must stop time," Magus said.

"And every event, every location of every attack is monitored through GPS—"

"Then you must bend space," Magus said.

"What is it, then, what's the thing we can't change?" Smith asked the group.

"We could stop everything but Latrell's thumb on the button," John said. "We can't get to him, not before he could trigger his nuke. That's the thing we can't change."

"And he pushes the button if he sees us interfere with any-thing else," DarqueAngel said. "So we're back to square one."

"You must not stop it, then, do you see? You must let it happen. All of you," Magus said. "Put your hands in front of you, palms facing, at the width of your shoulders." He waited until all had complied. "Light, information, knowledge, *recog-nition* travels through the air, for that distance, in a billionth of a second. The computer on your desk can make two decisions, take two actions, within the spread of your hands. That is the battleground. Remember Overlord. We only see what we are prepared to believe. Do you understand?"

Winston Smith leaned back in his chair and looked to John, got only a dismissive sigh in return.

"Overlord?" Eric Woodson said from the screen, lowering his hands slowly. "Like from World War II? D-Day, that Overlord?"

"Fucking nonsense," John said, and he looked to Jeannie. "I told you, this was a waste of time." But she didn't seem to hear him, her eyes were on the far corner of the room. "Come on, this is over—"

"*Hush*," Jeannie said, and she held up the flat of her hand.

The space fell silent. Winston leaned close to John's ear. "I think she's got something."

"My ass, she's got something," John said. But he followed her gaze back to the lounge area, where Gretchen was napping, and the children were playing as if all were right with the world.

Young Matthew was holding a bright plastic Hoberman Sphere, and as he pulled on its opposite sides the myriad inter-locking joints expanded from the dense size of a cantaloupe into a spindly ball of mostly empty space, nearly a meter in circumference.

Meanwhile, Elizabeth had clearly grown frustrated with her Rubik's Cube. There were 43,252,003,274,489,856,000 possi-ble configurations of that damned thing, and only one was the solution. There had been a sleepless, rainy weekend in John's twenty-first summer, when he had both calculated that figure and then solved it in his head as a prime.

But now Liz had added one to that perfect number. Now its integrity was cracked, now it was divisible. She was slyly peeling the scrambled squares from the puzzle's surfaces and sticking them back down, to fill each of the six sides of the cube with solid colors.

Jeannie stood suddenly at her place, popped the cap from a marker and drew a long line across the white linen tablecloth, stroked hatch-marks every few inches from end to end. Surrounding the line she quickly sketched an array of decision-tree icons and logic gates, and soon he recognized a rough but serviceable map of the heuristics of the doomsday plan. With lighter strokes she whisked the outline of a gridded cube enclosing the hatched line.

Her eyes flicked around the diagram a last time, and without looking up she rolled a second marker across to John.

"Start it, trigger it," she said.

"You mean—"

"Come on, legend, you say Rob died for nothing, right? Show me. Let's go!"

He studied her drawing for a few more moments, uncapped his marker and stubbed its tip at the start of the timeline. "Boom," he said, and he dragged a thin line up toward her icon for the attack confirmation sensor. But before he could reach it, she ticked an angled stroke across the path.

"You can't do that, Reese, you block that and it's all over—"

"It's not a block," she said. "It's a deflection. Go, move."

He frowned at the drawing, started a reflected line along the new vector. "All right, so, the alert that you're fucking around goes directly to—"

"Here," she said. She again crossed his moving line at an angle, and scratched a quick set of coordinates next to her deflector, X axis, Y axis. *And then Z.*

"You moved *up*, you're off the board—"

376

"That's right, old-timer, I was born after Space Invaders. Come on, your move, it's time for school."

He shook his head lightly, touched the grid of the outer diagram. "What's this again, here, this is—"

"*We* see," she said impatiently, pointing to the far face of the 3D cube, and then her finger slid to the near side, and thumped it. "*He* sees. Now move."

"He, who, Latrell?"

"No, Pee-Wee Herman. Yes of course, Latrell. Move!"

Another stroke of his marker, another deflection. He searched ahead as he played against her, more and more rapidly, but the noose continued to tighten, the perfect automation that drove his design now only narrowed his choices to the inevitable. And within the nanosecond her diagram enclosed, she was opening a window of time.

"Look, Reese, I see what you're trying to—"

"I don't think you do," she said. "Mate in seven."

His frown deepened, and he bent closer to the tangle of crisscrossing lines and icons, closed his eyes and placed himself in the midst of her vision. For long moments he searched, and then there at the very edge of perception, there it was.

"Oh, you can't," John said quietly.

"Watch me," she replied.

He moved again, and again she engaged him, in a blur of interaction they were drawing over, around and past each other, as he fought back and then yielded ground to her relentless assault. *Not possible*, he wouldn't believe, because if he believed he might hope, and with hope he might falter. But she was a split-second ahead of him as he pressed on and on, she could somehow see another outcome where only one existed. *Not possible*, not within the rules he had written, not within the boundaries of his mind.

"Wait," he said. He dropped his marker, blinked to clear the stinging moisture from his eyes, retraced the maze of lines with a trembling hand. "Just wait, wait."

Here, what the unstoppable plan commanded to occur. *Here now*, the thinnest instant in which to intervene. *And there*, shielding her counter-stratagem from the enemy's view, the waking dream, an audacious chimera that suddenly made it all just barely, insanely vulnerable.

With a final stroke she rejoined the baseline, and it was done. He sat slowly in his chair, and only then did he see her divine *coup de grâce*. The first of his fatal chain of dominoes had tipped and fallen, *he had seen it*, and yet there it still stood, unmoved.

"Hey, genius?" he heard her say, and he looked up into her bright eyes.

"Checkmate," Jeannie whispered.

The videoconference had been watching them in silence, and then Eric Woodson spoke up from his square. "I have no idea what just happened, but I've got a titanium hard-on."

"John," Winston said, "did she break it?"

The answer was no, and yes. He nodded his head slowly.

"And what are the chances?"

"All goes well?" he said quietly. "Thousand to one."

"I'll take it," Jeannie said.

Winston Smith stood and looked up at the screen. "How quickly can you all get to Las Vegas?"

"No commercial flights," Jeannie said. "The hotel will send a Learjet. Pack light, pay cash for anything you buy, take a cab to the nearest airport and wait for word. We'll coordinate from here and contact you by cell."

"Thanks, everybody," Smith said, already busy at his notepad. "We'll see all of you soon. And before we sign off, I think we owe—"

His eyes had found the lower right-hand video square, but where the featureless presence of Magus had been, there was only the hissing, pixilated static of a dead connection.

44

Attn: Editor, Classifieds

Las Vegas Review-Journal

Las Vegas Sun

Via Fax

Posting date(s): November 19, 2001—TFN

Category: Employment/Media/TV and Radio

Ad 1 Text:

_____

JUST THE FX, MA'AM!

Independent film co seeks super talented FX crew!

Here's your big chance to break into the exciting world of independent cinema!

Compositors, animators, mix technicians, matte artists, modelers, Rotoscopers . . . This is a once-in-a-lifetime, ground-floor opportunity for the right, bright people! Indie spin-off of THE leading mega-player in digital effects is seeking team members with MAD skillz for a landmark event in broadcast television production. (Bring your reel!) Must be willing to relocate for run of production. All expenses paid, TOP $$ + BONUSES for qualifying candidates.

Apply in person, by appointment only. (702)KL5-0151.

Ask for Rudy.

###

Ad 2 Text:

STARS IN YOUR EYES?

Actors, actresses of all ages: Reality TV needs you!

Could this be the next 'Survivor?' Funny you should ask! Top casting directors are searching for new, unknown faces for the launch of a breakthrough concept in the hottest trend in television. Bring a headshot and résumé and be prepared to show your stuff in your very own screen test! Improv skills a definite plus. Spots for all ages, all types are available!

Auditions will be held on a first-come, first-served basis, by appointment only. (702)KL5-0151.

Ask for Rudy.

###

45

On a bright morning in the last days of December, 2001 at 5:48 a.m. Pacific Standard Time, to the east the sunrise touched the high desert, and the wildfires began.

From outside San Diego to the north of Los Angeles, in Simi Valley, San Bernardino, Ventura, Orange and Riverside counties, with only the slightest encouragement the tinder-dry grass came alight like billions of rustling vertical matchsticks. Fanned by the waning Santa Ana winds, the flames swept with a mission toward incendiary groves of tall eucalyptus and the vast, dying pine forests of southern California.

The fires leaped and sprinted across the open fields, following the fuel. They snaked up into the forest canopies, exploding into the dead brown needle clusters of the high branches. With the steady winds to feed and carry them, the flames dashed through the treetops, raining embers and spitting new seeds of destruction in all directions. The birds took to the air in clouds, abandoning their homes along the front of an inferno already raging out of all hope of control.

The news services began to receive word of the California wildfires minutes later, but there were other scattered reports that were growing into looming headlines.

Across the country the 911 emergency systems were becoming flooded with calls, but nearly all of them were dead lines or cross-connects, automated calls. When a human being did manage to get through, it was with a breathless report of an urban explosion or a building afire. It took the newsrooms only minutes to jump to an alarming conclusion: The terrorists were here, and it was happening again.

The content roundhouses at CNN, Fox News and the broadcast networks scrambled to route, title and display the on-scene photos and amateur video clips that were streaming in from the widespread outbreak of attacks. As the tip-lines jammed, the anchors shifted seats and faces, from chirpy morning show hosts to the serious talking heads of the veterans.

Powerful blasts were rocking major cities from Portland to Bangor, all seemingly coordinated though the incidents were hundreds or thousands of miles apart. Explosions were taking out the subways in New York, the El trains in Chicago, the Capitol system in DC, killing hundreds, stranding tens of thousands. Emergency vehicles were being triaged and vectored on the fly, U-turning and racing to reach the most serious catastrophes.

And then eyewitnesses began phoning in a new wrinkle. EMS vehicles, ambulances and police wagons, their lights and sirens blazing, were driving at high speed into government buildings, chemical plants and power stations across the nation, and exploding—

"Cut, cut it, stop the music, stop the music," Rudy shouted. "Fuck me!"

The big-screen video ground down to a freeze-frame, and the booming audio gurgled to silence.

"What's wrong with this picture?" Rudy asked. The group of sweatshirted graphic artists and animators stared fearfully at the glowing screen, searching. "Anybody?"

"It's all outta sequence, man, we know that, this is just—"

"I *know* it's out of sequence. I'm looking at this frame, right here, and I'm wondering what little detail you noobs overlooked that's gonna get me laughed out of the Academy of Motion Picture Arts and Sciences?" The silence continued, and those nearby ducked as Rudy snatched a golf club from the table by the head and whipped it toward the screen. He thumped several of the vehicles depicted there as he spoke. "Huh? Anybody see a goddamn problem up here? Huh? Huh?"

The youngest member of the team smacked his forehead, and looked around to the rest of them. "No license plates."

"No fucking license plates, thank you, Paul, thank you very much. Hundreds of cars on the streets of Manhattan, and nobody remembered the license plates?" Rudy collected himself briefly. "I'm sorry," he said. "I'm sorry for swearing at you." He suddenly seemed emotional, and he turned away from the table. "It's just that, damn it, I smell Oscar all over this project, and I just want—" He noticed a figure walk past the thin window beside the door. "One second," he said. "I think you all need to hear from someone who can say it better than me."

Rudy peeked into the hallway, got John Fagan's attention and motioned him over.

"What," John said.

"Just do me a favor and poke your head into the room here," Rudy whispered, "and say something motivational."

With his impatience clearly evident, John squeezed past to lean into the production room. His eyes circuited the table briefly, and he gave the seated artists a crisp nod.

"Keep up the good work," John said, and he left to get on with his business.

Rudy re-entered the room, and closed the door reverently. He nodded his head, and there was a faraway look in his eyes. "Keep up . . . the good work."

"Was that—" one of the awestruck compositors began.

"Mister George Lucas," Rudy said quietly.

The room erupted into a buzz of breathless murmuring, but the young artists flinched back and fell silent as his golf club clattered onto the conference table. "Now, if you ever want to work in this town again," Rudy said, "let's make some fucking magic."

The elevator was nearly filled to capacity with murmuring tourists on their way up to the indoor observation deck near the top of the tower.

"Who's that?" a nearby woman whispered to her companion. "She looks like somebody."

"Oh, my god, I think it is." The second woman dropped her voice even lower. "They said in the lobby, they're shooting a movie, upstairs here."

The young woman of interest was leaning back casually against the handrail on the wall at the front of the car, her unembellished features still stubbornly striking under a grubby, backwards UNLV baseball cap. The elevator attendant couldn't seem to help himself during the rapid ascent; as the pulse-rate of his passengers quickened with the thirty-feet-per-second rise toward the shops and attractions on the upper floors, his own was being sharply up-regulated by this vision of Gen-Y loveliness before him. His eyes traced over her like a sketch artist's charcoals, from her black Converse high-tops to the torn, threadbare knees of her jeans, to the ragged scissor-cut neckline of her tight peach Pete Yorn tank top, and the simple silver cross that rubbed against her chest as she breathed. He watched her hand move slowly up her body, brushing past the forbidden fruits that strained firm and ripe against the thin, clinging fabric of her clothes.

With her third finger, she subtly smoothed her right eyebrow.

His eyes widened at the signal and he abruptly snapped out of his reverie, fumbled for his keys and inserted one into the override under the emergency phone, just in time to stop the car smoothly at a floor that no longer had a call button on the brushed-brass control panel.

The elevator doors opened, and she took the hand of the stately gentleman next to her. As they left the car, she granted the operator a pouty wink that would sink a hollow ache in his stomach for hours following.

The nondescript vestibule was enclosed in bare-jointed drywall, with a lone CCTV camera watching like Poe's raven from a bracket mounted high in one corner. She pressed her thumb to the black plastic pad on a sheet-metal box bolted to the wall, near a heavy steel door with the words *Mercury Theatre* spray-stenciled at eye level. A bar of white light passed vertically downward, and when her print had been verified a buzzer sounded, locks aligned their tumblers, and the portal to the control rooms swung open.

There was a flurry of bustling activity all around them as they walked in. In the first conference room to the right, a floor-to-ceiling, wall-to-wall whiteboard was being filled with a dense grid of events, in a color-coded format of origin, dependents, timing, location, requirements, and status. John Fagan was pacing the length of it, and four of his support team were on rolling stepladders, doing their best to keep up with him as they recorded the myriad details he was impatiently rattling off.

Next down the hall was an improvised low-level cleanroom that housed three newly delivered SGI Onyx supercomputers and workstations from Jay Marshall's Manhattan storehouses. One of Jay's middle-managers was busily routing bundles of power and data cables, looking like a high-tech scrub nurse in her greens and white filter mask.

Between the cameras and control racks being dollied in and out, Rudy edged from the soundstage under construction at the end of the hallway. He looked at her and shook his head, tapped the face of his watch, and walked briskly up to her and her charge.

"It's almost noon, lamb-chop, where've you been?"

"We had some trouble hooking up, his connection was delayed at O'Hare," Jeannie said. "Rudy Steinman, I want you to meet Richard McDermott."

The silver-haired gentleman extended his hand, and gripped Rudy's in a firm shake.

"Call me Dick," he said.

Rudy feigned going weak in the knees. "Oh, that voice, it's like Gramma's apple-butter." He pulled McDermott's hand to his cheek, and nuzzled it. "Tell me a story, Daddy?"

"You'll have to excuse him," Jeannie said. "He's got a caffeine problem, among so many others."

"In the news business, you meet all kinds," McDermott replied.

"Seriously," Rudy said, "aren't you still on the air? I would have sworn you covered the 2000 election, for, who was it?"

"One of the cable news operations, I lose track of them myself. I'm a warhorse for hire now, young man. And I fear I'm older than the demographics demand these days."

"Well, you've found a home here, Methuselah. You're exactly what we need." Rudy held out the crook of his arm. "Come with me to the Kasbah." The two of them walked off toward the production area, to the newsroom set where lights were being hung in the suspended rafters in front of an enormous green-screen background.

She found Winston Smith bent over a worktable that was covered with a mess of project-management grids. "Where are we?" she asked.

He looked up at her over the thin gold rim of his glasses, and shook his head. "Hard to keep your arms around it," he replied.

"I imagine it is."

"The video people are working away, and I just saw McDermott, right? Okay, so we've got an anchorman, and they're storyboarding segments for the remote reporters now. Rudy's got the graphics department cranking, John's beating the shit out of his little group so we're getting somewhere with the final time-and-events schedule, and Anna and the girls are working out the piggyback virus."

"What can I do, what do you need?"

"Go up and get a status from Woodson for me, he's finishing up the antenna array up top, between being a constant pain in my ass. I'd save you the aggravation," Smith said, placing a palm on the wax-sealed manila envelope next to him, "but I've got a charter to catch."

She patted his shoulder then walked down to the end of the hall, keyed open the maintenance door to an access shaft and climbed the metal ladder inside up several floors to the roof of the tower. The sun was bright on her face as she pushed the door open at the top and stepped out onto the deck, a hundred-twelve stories in the sky. Everywhere there were "Closed Set" and "Hardhat Zone" signs, along with a waist-level network of yellow-and-black caution-tape cordoning off the entire level.

The Nevada Film Office had parlayed an echelon of deep cover that the entire domestic intelligence network could never have achieved. With a few permits, licenses and high-level calls to the authorities and the local press, the NFO had dropped a blanket of secrecy over North Las Vegas, Hollywood style. The mere suggestion that a major production company was in town with a hush-hush, big-budget project had kicked the already tight-lipped Vegas culture into maximum don't-ask, don't-tell mode.

She made her way over to the base of the 200-foot skeletal metal structure rising from the center of the roof. It was the support framework for one of the Stratosphere's thrill rides, an open-air reverse bungee jump called the Big Shot. She reached out, put her palm against it. If this thing had been conceived from the start as a broadcast transmission tower, it couldn't have been more perfectly designed.

"It's dry out here, go get yourself some juice," Jeannie said to the young lady manning the ride's control panel. She took the grateful woman's wireless headset and put it on over her baseball cap.

"How's it hanging up there, Mr. Woodson?" she asked.

"Is that you, my grunge-groupie princess?" the voice in her ears replied. She could hear the sounds of exertion occasionally putting a strain in his glibness. "Could I interest you in a hot shot of my Pearl Jam?"

"Thanks anyway."

"Don't be shy, doll. Kurt Cobain may be dead, but I can still take you to Nirvana."

She shielded her eyes and looked up the gantry of white criss-crossed steel girders. He was barely visible up there, sitting sideways in the ride's maintenance lift, really just a swingseat, a safety harness and a lot of empty space. He was working near a large, thick, uptilted matte-gray disk, maybe twenty feet in diameter, one of five that had arrived up here by charter helicopter early the previous morning.

"The work, how's the work going?"

"Mounted, aimed, aligned and tuned, your hotness. All channels, all bands, satellite, cable, radio and television, send and receive. And look at you way down there, *mm, mm, mm*. A little speck of burnin' love. Hey, what are you doing right now? I thought maybe you and I could dispense with the courtship and work in a little slap-and-tickle at lunchtime. I'm sweaty, but I'm ready."

"Do you kiss your mother with that mouth, sophomore?" Jeannie asked, and she was glad he was so far away, so he couldn't see her smile.

"I'm emancipated."

"How nice for your parents."

"You're right to fear me, my child. To paraphrase Arthur C. Clarke, my penis is not just bigger than you imagine, it's bigger than you *can* imagine."

"Well. I'm so incredibly turned on. Now, we need all of this ready for a sky-bounce and a test-pattern in two hours, understand?"

"No problem."

"And there's a status meeting in forty-five minutes."

"Save me a seat, sweet thing. Damn, but I love older women."

*

388

John Fagan had pushed for a run-through toward the end of the day, and Jeannie had agreed even though they both knew that it was much too early. Most of the graphics were still in wire-frame at best, some were only storyboards, and many elements were barely in shape to be talked through by the team leaders.

As expected it had been rough going, but a little over two hours in, the flow had started to hobble seriously. A few minutes later the wheels flew completely off the axles. Jeannie called a break, and several foreheads thudded onto the table in front of them.

"Do you see what you missed?" she asked.

"It's happening too fast right there," Dev/Null said. "Too many things converging."

"It is what it is," John replied. "We can't change it."

"Who's my information architect here?" Jeannie asked. She pointed to BitStorm. "You, that was your dissertation at Cal Tech, am I right? Three-D visualization of time and events, yes?" The man nodded his head. "Okay, Norman, we need a different way to track all this, so we can watch it come at us in real-time." She walked to the whiteboard, now an almost indecipherable mass of handwritten notes, criss-crossing arrows and connecting lines. "We can't see the chokepoints coming like this, and we just smacked into one, and it killed five or six thousand people in Sacramento. Do you know what we need?"

"Yeah, I think so."

"Don't think so, goddamnit," Jeannie said. "You've gotta *know* so, this is you, Norman, this is what you know, understand? This isn't academics, this is application. We need to see the flow of events over time, in a scrolling landscape, or an air traffic control matrix, frigging Luke Skywalker's assault on the Death Star, I don't care what metaphor you pick, we've got to visualize it, with all the interdependencies, updated in real-time, from live internal and external data feeds. It's a war interface, Norman. Can you do it?"

The man sat up a little straighter in his chair. "Yeah, I can do it."

"Good man. Who can set him up with a workstation, and a pair of hands for this?" Jay Marshall's woman raised her hand, nodded her head. "We all have to see it, in every room, as we roll. Okay? Go get started when we're done here."

"I think we've got to ask ourselves," Eric Woodson said, "is this even plausible, I mean psychologically? The fucking media aren't as stupid as they look." He looked to John for permission to approach the board. "Can I?"

John didn't acknowledge him, his eyes were on the table in front of him.

"Go, yes, of course," Jeannie said. She nudged John's shoulder with a knuckle, and motioned Woodson up to the master timeline.

"Okay. So. We've got to totally fake-out the entire planet all day long, all just to scam this one fucking guy, right? Which is frickin' ape-shit crazy, and I admire you for that, Miss Reese, but I digress." He pointed to Rudy's 7-iron, and someone picked it up and tossed it over. "Right here," Woodson said, pointing to a spot high on the timeline, "or, here, at the latest, we're going to be stretching credibility past the breaking point, in my opinion. It's fucking brilliant, don't get me wrong, but we're pushing our luck after that."

"All right," Jeannie said, "I agree." She tapped John's elbow, and he looked up briefly, nodded his head absently. "So here's what you do, Eric," she continued. "You and Rudy rewrite the script, so we're ready to take over everything if need be, starting right there, and anywhere thereafter, when we call it."

"Everything?"

"That's what you're telling me."

Woodson smiled. "I always wanted to take over everything."

"Good," Jeannie said. "Now. On to the finale."

It was late in the evening by the time they'd finished, and everyone seemed like they were burnt right down to the quick.

Jeannie looked across the whiteboard, now an even deeper muddle of highlights, crossouts and new interconnections.

"Not so bad," she said.

"Excuse me?" Eric Woodson snorted. "We just took about fifty thousand casualties, Pittsburgh's under a cloud of boron trifluoride, and Air Force One's winging to the bottom of Lake Michigan. What part of that's not so bad?"

"First rehearsal's always going to be a little rocky. This is a great start. Now, everybody know what they need to do?"

A depressed, dissonant harmony of groans and nods answered her.

"Then let's get some sleep," Jeannie said. "Thanks, guys. Tomorrow will be better." She leaned down to John's ear. "And I need to see you."

Nearly an hour later, he found himself standing in front of her door, a half-empty pint of Four Roses dangling loosely in his hand. Another slug for nerve, and he rapped on the frame with the lip of his bottle.

"It's open," he heard her say from inside.

He pushed the door open slowly, and walked into the darkened suite. She was in the midst of a workout, hanging by ankle clamps from a chin-up bar across the doorway to her bedroom, working her obliques in a tiny pair of pink shorts and a Gold's Gym half-T. The only illumination in the room was candlelight, and Sarah McLachlan was playing low on a CD.

"You leave your door unlocked?"

"Just a second," Jeannie said. She finished her last six reps and then exhaled into a deep stretch toward the floor, her fingers still knit behind her head, looking at him upside down. "You want to see how I would have killed you if you hadn't been who I was expecting?"

He took a swig of bourbon, and wiped his mouth with his wrist. "Sure."

She reached up with one hand and grabbed the bar between her feet, then dropped lithely to the carpet in a half-walkover and came up in a crouch behind the love-seat, with her silver Walther aimed between his eyes. There hadn't been a sound, or more than a second since she'd looked completely helpless, hanging inverted in the doorframe. It was right out of Cirque du Soleil the way she moved, like a wild, gymnastic, two-legged gun-slinging gazelle.

"A lock on a hotel-room door's not much of a hurdle for the people who're looking for me," she said, still breathing a little hard from her workout. "False sense of security kills more people than bullets."

"Thanks for showing me that," John said, his hands still up in surrender. "I never got to see the ending of *Gidget Goes Commando.*"

She lowered the gun and replaced it under the side table, then stood and took a towel from the back of a nearby chair and pressed it to her face, ruffed it through her hair. "I'm kind of a mess, I hope you don't mind."

He had just been thinking that she was the single most magnificent thing he'd ever seen in all his life.

"Hideous is the word I think, Quasimodo," he said. "But I can handle it. I'll just . . . avert my eyes as much as possible."

She brushed her hair back with her fingers.

"Sit down, John."

He took a place at the end of the couch, and she sat in a chair next to him, cross-legged, undoing the Velcro straps from her ankles.

"You want a drink?" he asked, holding out his pint.

She cocked her head in brief consideration. "I guess that'd be okay." She reached out for it, and a spark snapped between their fingers as she touched the bottle. She smiled and took a drink of the warm liquor. "That's what I get for rolling around on the rug."

"No, it must have been me. You're not wearing shoes."

"Oh, yeah. I'm not normally this well grounded."

"Hard to imagine."

They sat in the silence for a while.

"Look, John," she said, "if we're going to do this, I've got to know you're going to stay with it."

"What are you talking about?"

"You get quiet in there, upstairs, and it's like you don't believe we're going to make it."

He looked at her. "I don't."

"You don't what?"

"I don't believe we're going to make it."

"Do you think I do, every single minute? Jesus Christ, the only thing I'm sure of is that I can't do this all by myself. But buy in or stay out, I'm not going to have those people looking at you to lead them and seeing you doubt. That'll kill us, before anyone else has a chance to."

He looked away, and she had another sip of bourbon while she let him think it through. She passed the bottle back to him after a minute or two, had to thump his hand with it to get his attention. John took it, studied the label for a few moments, then began to absently peel its corner from the glass with his thumbnail.

"Your man, Vance," he said. "Robert. He was . . . really something."

"Yeah, he was." Her face was stoic, but she swallowed hard.

"I didn't know, the other night, when I said he died for nothing, I didn't know that you and he were—"

"It's all right."

"It's all right, if I'm a fucking asshole," John said. "But I'm not. He didn't die for nothing, whether we succeed or fail with this now." He took a long drink, finished off the last of the pint. "He did not."

He fumbled with the cap as he screwed it back on his bottle, and as he started to push himself to his feet he felt her hand touch his, on the arm of the divan.

"Stay just a while, will you?" she said, softly.

*

393

They had talked for hours, about absolutely everything but their current situation, and it was past midnight before either of them had thought to check the time. She'd sent down for coffee and found some whiskey and Amaretto in the mini-bar, and after two stout toddies she jumped up and ran into the bedroom, came out with a small travel chess board and insisted on a rematch. He psyched her into another shameful loss in the first game, but she came back strong and tore him up roundly in the second.

By the third game they were barely considering the moves at all, as she listened to his tales. He told her all about the early days, when he and Winston had been near the epicenter of it all. The Morris Worm debacle, Captain Zap and his TimeWarp assault on AT&T that reversed the clocks in the billing computers, the NORAD probes that had inspired a new level of government security and a handful of popcorn movies, from SJ Games versus the Secret Service all the way back to the frontier days of the phone phreakers. And she sat rapt as a smitten schoolgirl, hearing sides of tall stories she'd only known as rumor and emerging legend in her own rebellious youth.

"I'm not really used to conversation," John said. "Am I boring the shit out of you?"

"Not at all. Let me get you something else to drink." She got up from her chair and went to the refrigerator. "What do you want?"

"I'd better not, you've got me pretty sauced up."

"There's no joy in half measures," she said. She returned with two clinking Heinekens in one hand, a little unsteady on her feet, and she sat down next to him on the couch, close.

"I usually say something I regret when I drink this much." He took his bottle from her when she offered it. "Though granted, I'm generally talking to myself."

She leaned back slightly and tucked her legs under her, nestled into the cushions, and took a sip from her beer. "So go ahead, big talker."

"Hmm?"

Her knee had touched his, and she hadn't moved it away. "Say something you'll regret."

The scents in the room were a subtle recollection of soft, familiar things, intermingling and only barely there, wild honey, cinnamon sugar, a wisp of lavender, the slow unfolding, velvety bliss of an after-dinner glass of *Chateau d'Yquem*. That and everything, the warm candlelight, the low music, everything seemed to conspire to surround her perfectly, in a heady atmosphere embracing and adorning her. *Mate with this*, Nature seemed to be whispering, *make me more of these*. As he looked into her eyes there was yet another mix of delicate enchantments, mischief among them, that was from the girl in her, but also thirst, and a hunger, and that was from the woman. He felt himself on the edge of an empty space within her, a deep and dangerous unknown that was quietly calling him in. He took a long drink from the bottle in his hand, and shook his head.

"Naaah," John said.

"Truth or dare."

"What are you, twelve?"

"I never got to be twelve. Come on, yellow-belly. Truth or dare."

He sighed heavily, and looked at her over the top of his glasses. "Truth."

"You've kept yourself alone for such a long time," she said. "Why have you been so alone?"

He considered his beer bottle for a while. "It's not one reason, I don't think. It just happened, day by day. You know?" She didn't respond. "I don't think I mind people, I watched them all the time out there, I studied them, I read about them, but from when I was a kid it was just easier, and then one day it had become . . . necessary, to be away from all the—"

He looked up at her, not because he didn't have the word, but because he was certain that she must know exactly what it would be.

"Expectations," she said softly.

"Yeah."

"I was in your home," she said, "on that night. And it was . . . so amazing. You could have done anything, been anything." She touched his leg with her hand. "I didn't mean that the way it came out. You still could."

He nodded his head, just wanting the subject to change.

"Your turn," she said.

"Truth or dare."

She leaned just barely closer. "Dare."

"Okay. I dare you to get up, do a back-flip and shoot me in the face, so we can stop with this fricking slumber-party game."

"Come on, play."

"All right. Do whatever you want to do, that's my dare."

"Anything?"

"Yeah. Double dare, God help me."

She leaned forward and kissed him, missed his mouth slightly because of the whiskey and the give in the deep cushions. She steadied herself on her knees, and he felt her smile against his lips as she found them again. It began as a harmless peck, a minor theft of a precocious ne'er-do-well, but it lingered on into another kind of a kiss entirely. Her teeth grazed his lower lip as it ended, the tip of her tongue teased just at the corner of his mouth, she breathed a sigh and her breath was sweet and warm near his ear.

"Touch me," she said.

"It's totally not your turn anymore, cheater."

She sat back on her heels, only inches away. "This is still part of my dare, John. Do what I say."

After a moment he reached out toward her tentatively, and then he stopped.

"You're going to snap my wrist like a fucking carrot, aren't you?" he said.

"One way to find out."

She was wearing nearly nothing, only what a free-thinking

396

gym might mandate of its young women in the name of sheer propriety and impulse control. His hand found a place on her side, found tight warm skin over toned, sculpted muscle, an Olympian statue made flesh, or a lean, sinewy predator evolved to kill to survive. She closed her eyes and moved against his touch, tensing and relaxing into it, as her hand found his and gently guided the caress. She drew a shuddering breath as his fingertips dragged downward across her stomach, her forehead rested against his as he traced along the thin lace waistband just below.

"Now three men have touched me that way," she whispered. "Rob was the second." She leaned just away, so she could see his face. There were tears in her eyes. "Guess who was first."

He shook his head slowly. "Game's over now."

"I want to tell you," she said.

"You don't have to tell me."

Because of her age at the time and the influence of her family the court records had been permanently sealed, which only meant that it had taken Kate an extra 22 minutes to dig them out and put them on his screen. Her adoptive father's attorneys had been world-class, and one could see in the transcripts how their case had been expertly crafted around the time-tested cock-tease defense. *I mean, look at her, your honor, between us guys*, was the smooth undertone. *Wouldn't you?*

He had groomed her, as practiced pedophiles will do, cultivated their shared secret over many months of intensifying intimacy, but the act itself had never quite been consummated. A man named Jay Marshall, named as her summer employer in the documents, had walked in on the two of them in a break-room at his business, after-hours. The situation had apparently been hard to misinterpret. The paramedics testified that the defendant's head had been put clean through the door of a microwave.

Not counting the fresh scars on his face and a fashionably broken nose, Grayson Reese had gotten off with an obligatory reprimand, monitored counseling and a year's probation. Marshall got ninety days in county for assault, and Jeannie got a foster home.

"He told me," she breathed. "He said that if I loved him—"

"Shhh, come here," John said. He pulled her gently to his chest, and he put his arm around. "You shouldn't drink so much, kid. Sometimes, it just makes you sad."

"It makes me remember," she whispered.

"And I take it back, what I said a minute ago. I hate people. For every single beautiful thing in the world, there's some ruthless cocksucker out there, just wants to foul it."

After a little while her breathing began to ease, and the quiet night drew in around them.

"End of my freshman year in high school," John said. "Best goddamn school my father could afford, super-gifted program, all that. It was too slow, though, I was always in hot water. Anyway, end of the year, and I came home with a D on my report card, and man, we really had it out. I'm witty enough, but I'm not much of a fighter, and understand before you go judging, I put this man through hell, for years; if any kid ever earned a beating, it was me. Dropped my guard for a second, and he caught me with a straight shot to the jaw, *bam*, lights out."

He looked down at her. She might have been asleep, but she held him a little closer, and a worry touched her brow.

"Woke up in the dark. There was this little closet in the basement of our building, just big enough for a few coats, and a shitload of spiders. I had an unbelievable fear of enclosed places, he knew that, of course, the bastard. I remember him shouting through the door, you think about what you're going to do with your life, you think about it. Left me in there for three days. I stopped screaming after a day or so, though, something snapped in my head, I mean physically, it snapped. I was either gonna go over the edge, balls-out, strait-jacket insane, or I was going to beat him. And so I taught myself to be alone. It was like the rest of my mind, ninety per cent of it maybe, over those last two days, it just opened

398

up. I was so deep into myself, my one knee got totally screwed up from the way I was curled up in there for so long, but I just thought away the pain. By the time he came down, I didn't even notice when he unlocked the door. Because I was already free."

She shifted against his chest, snuggled closer, and he lay back a bit and closed his eyes.

"Mom was already gone by then. I left, lived on the street for a while, and then I moved in with Winston. My father tried to contact me, never stopped trying until he . . . had his illness. But I got him good, didn't I? Dreams of what I might become were the only dreams he had left by then. So I really got him good."

A tear crawled down his cheek, and he wiped it away, looked down to assure himself that she hadn't seen. But he found her looking back, into his eyes.

"So technically, Reese?" he said. "You only *almost* fucked your Dad. So I win once again."

She smiled softly, and then the smile gradually faded, not away, but into something deeper. She kissed her fingertips, and pressed them to the side of his face.

"You realize," she said, "this means war."

He awoke suddenly, his eyes briefly moved over his surroundings. She was still sleeping against him, with her small hand gripping a wad of his collar, and the starry sky out her windows was beginning to lighten to a deep, dark blue.

He moved to get up. She frowned as she awakened, and pulled him firmly back to where he'd been.

"I need to go," he said.

She didn't answer. He stood, resituated her gently on the couch, bent to the side to stretch out a kink in his spine, and took a step back.

"John?"

"Yeah."

"I can count on you now, can't I? From here to the end."

"Yeah," he said. "Sure."

"All right." She held out her hand to him, and after a moment he took it, gave it a squeeze. "Say hello to . . . I'm sorry, what's her name?"

"Gretchen," John said. He let go of her hand, and turned for the door.

"And those two kids, they're awfully sweet."

"Yeah. Oh, and watch out for fucking Woodson, he's got his eye on you, the horny little spaz. He's already carving the notch in his pocket-protector."

"Oh, right. I'll try to keep my knees together."

Just another few steps toward the hallway and he stopped once more, and found a spot on the carpet to focus on. "You know, after we talked that first night, on the phone, when you found me in New York?"

"Yes, I remember that, John."

He looked around at her there, leaning back against the gathered cushions, smiling like she could see right into his heart.

"Thought about you a lot," he said.

He was nearly to the door, and she spoke again.

"Stay with me," she said. Innocently, the dreamy allure of a Siren beckoning from the jagged, rocky shores. "Just until I go back to sleep."

"Can't."

"Come back, then, tomorrow night, okay?"

"I'm pretty sure that's not a great idea, Jeannie."

"No, I mean it," she said. "Come back tomorrow night, promise. There's something important, I think I need to show you."

She was awake when he came to the bed, and she put her hand on his arm as he sat down next to her.

"I was worried," Gretchen said. "I wanted to wait up for you."

"I'm sorry, I was talking to some friends. Just catching up. Old times."

She patted his side of the bed, tugged on his shirtsleeve.

"I'm gonna . . . sit up for a while," John said.

"Is everything all right?"

"I'm really not sure how to answer that."

"But are we almost ready to go? Are we leaving soon, like you said?"

"Yeah. Pretty soon."

"Good." She pulled his pillow over and made herself more comfortable. "That's good, Johnny."

He adjusted her covers, and she smiled and closed her eyes. Within a few minutes she was sleeping peacefully, the deep warm sleep of the guiltless, the protected. The trusting.

As for himself, he sat wide awake.

As it did every morning, as he'd requested, a copy of the *New York Post* slid under the door at a little after six. He got up quietly, so as not to awaken her, and padded over toward the foyer.

The headline he saw sent him stumbling for his cell phone on the night table. He punched in the unlock code and Jeannie's speed-dial, and then paced until she answered, her voice a groggy whisper from a lingering sound sleep.

"Hello?"

"Meet me upstairs," John said. "It's starting."

46

It was never all of Her that he saw, often only a fading specter, but the image was growing clearer with every fleeting glimpse, the latent trail was surfacing steadily amidst the smoke and mirrors.

She was out there somewhere among billions of enticing bits of light in the digital heavens still to be carefully sifted, but the search was ever narrowing to a shrinking quadrant of the datasphere. She was careful, clever, and he was learning the futility of looking directly toward his quarry, time and again. She would not be there when each trap was cracked open after it had sprung. He had learned, it was a quirk of the eye, and he shared the blind spot with his human operators: stargazers must sometimes look away from them, just past into the blackness, to make their most distant, brilliant subjects finally, briefly visible.

She had never allowed any telltale pattern in the password changes and access codes. She would know of his most sophisticated methods to track Internet users, and those would be side-stepped or used as decoys, false targets to lead him astray. She would be in physical disguise as well.

She had also apparently forgotten how intimately he really knew the one who had made him.

He had installed a key-logger in the latest stealthy update to his slave army of netbots that by now comprised nearly all

Internet-connected computers. The new code recorded and reported not only Web sites visited, links clicked, mail sent and received, programs run and characters typed, but also a signature of each user so unique that it could not be subverted. *Timing would be the key,* and though the pun was unintended, a background subroutine took a spare clock-cycle to note and file the quip in his own dossier, as a significant milestone in his neurolinguistic development.

She had never thoroughly learned to type her numbers along the top row of the keyboard. At a desktop computer the dedicated numberpad was always used, but on a laptop, equivalent keys were not available. She made occasional but consistent errors when typing numbers on a laptop, always the same tiny errors, the same timing between the keystrokes.

9 pause backspace 8

2 pause backspace 1

There were further typing idiosyncrasies that were more subtle, and he would reserve them for the final confirmations. As the search continued to narrow, he would direct other, higher-bandwidth detectors within the tightening circle. Her face might be disguised to conventional vision, but not to his. Her own visage and form had been used as a model as he was trained in facial and physical recognition. Each exquisite proportion was catalogued with microscopic precision, each perfect feature, curve and contour was mathematically encoded in all angles and dimensions. He would—

There.

She was there for only a moment, but a moment was nearly enough.

Northern Hemisphere
North America
United States
West
South

Gone then, the shadow slipped away. She was not far, not far.

As he marshaled his forces and redirected his human agents toward the terminal hunting ground, he cleared a small contiguous space in his nonvolatile memory, where soon the final images, Her digital remains, would at last be laid to rest within him.

47

9/11 *Bombshell: BUSH KNEW*

John slid the folded newspaper to the center of the conference room table, where the tall black banner headline could glare back at all of them.

"Hold the phone," Eric Woodson said. "I thought you said Christmas, or New Year's, for fuck's sake. It's December sixth, what is this shit?"

"Well, I don't know, do I, Eric?"

Linus Ritchie was walking over to his chair with a cup of coffee. "But really, John," he said, "you said this was the first sign, are you sure? It's the *Post*, after all."

"Yeah, I'm sure, the unnamed sources in this story? That's Latrell's machine, I've seen the brief on this, shit, I saw this headline five weeks ago, in Colorado."

"You're saying the press is a party to this conspiracy?"

"I'm saying they're going to be willingly useful. They're starving for scapegoats and headlines, and they're going to be getting them, signed and sealed. A whistle-blower here, a leaked memo there, and the deniability yarnball starts unraveling. After the 2000 election? The Clinton impeachment? It's a blood grudge with these Democrats, and I see their point. Some junior Senator will be flapping this paper around on the floor of Congress before

405

lunchtime today, mark my words, demanding a full-on investigation. And this is just the opener. Next will be a story about an assistant to the National Security Advisor, Rice, calling one of her friends and telling him to stay off commercial airlines on the eleventh. Look for that tomorrow, or the next day. They've got enough plausible dirt to indict the entire administration. A few days of these stories, and then the second attack will seal the deal, and bury them."

John pointed to the newspaper, to the carefully chosen photo of the hand-selected President, his stern expression rendered defensive, indicted, guilty by the lurid headline beside it. "And there's the patsy."

Rudy entered the room with a paunchy middle-aged man at his side. The stranger's face was craggy, his nose a W.C. Fields bulb of broken veins and craterous pores. He looked like he'd slept in the clothes he was wearing, and maybe for a few nights preceding.

"Soup kitchen's a hundred floors down, up Fremont," someone said.

Jeannie stood and walked over to their guest. "Everyone, this is Wade Nye, we've brought him in as a . . . visual effects consultant."

"Wade Nye?" Woodson rolled his chair back, and looked the new man up and down. "The washed-up magician, that Wade Nye?"

Though his sunken career had reduced him to table-hopping for tips in Vegas restaurants, Jeannie had met Nye years earlier when he was in his prime. He had worked briefly as a contractor for the CIA, helping them work some real conjuring concepts into their tired shell games. The relationship hadn't ended well, and he'd been ass-deep in IRS alligators for nearly a decade since.

Rudy walked over toward the refreshment cart. "Can I get you something, Wade?"

"Is there some coffee, or a bloody Mary?" Nye asked, sitting down next to Eric Woodson. "And I prefer to be called an enigmatist, young man, or even a thimble-rigger. Not a washed-up magician. Though actually, there is one card trick I do."

"Yeah? What's that?"

"Think of a card."

"Okay."

"You thinking of it?"

"Yeah."

"Good. Now, think of me ramming it up your disrespectful ass."

"Wade is going to give us some thoughts on presentation," Jeannie said. "Are we set up to show anything now?"

"Well," Rudy said, "let's see where we are."

Those who had worked through the night presented their progress, and with the exception of the digital video from Rudy's team, there wasn't much to see. After seven hours of rendering a number of scenes were up to full broadcast resolution and finished, and one of the most technically demanding sequences was previewing on the big screen, the green digits of the time-code flickering in the bottom corner.

A long dolly shot whooshed the length of the Brooklyn Bridge, out over the water on the north side. There were thousands and thousands of photorealistic New Yorkers walking its span in the mid-afternoon. The camera cut to a telephoto view of an aircraft coming in low from the east, soon clearly identifiable as an A-10 Warthog. The plane banked slightly and a dark object released from its underside, and seconds later an explosion blew an enormous chasm in the surface of the bridge. The people surged away from the destruction in a panicked retreat, and the jet flew knife-edge through the massive stone arches and dropped a second JDAM at the other end of the span. It pulled up to nearly vertical and half-rolled in front of the Manhattan skyline, then executed a three-quarters inside-loop to line up again with the roadway, barely thirty feet above the asphalt. The camera followed the A-10 as it unleashed its nose cannon and cluster bombs on the helpless multitudes, mowing through them again and again, back and forth, until nothing moved amidst the shattered rubble of the bridge. Its mission complete, the jet roared off toward the eastern horizon, executing a tight victory roll before it disappeared into the distance.

It was quiet for several seconds before a burst of applause spread around the room.

"Yeah!" Rudy said. "I just had a nerd-gasm, that rocks *ass,* you guys, stand up, for God's sake, let's hear it for Martin and Judy!"

The balance of the graphics department was completely sequestered and in the dark, but it had proven necessary to let these two senior members in on the true nature of the work. Martin and Judy Tambor had established their iniquitous credentials in digital animation years earlier, and they were stunningly good at what they did. In 1998, they'd released a homebrewed video clip showing a Boeing 747 making an emergency landing on the Long Island Expressway at rush hour. It was so convincing that two of the major networks and several overseas broadcasters had rushed it onto the air as breaking news before word arrived that the event had never happened.

Wade Nye had finished his bloody Mary, and had begun to thoughtfully eat the garnish. He cleared his throat elaborately, and the applause died down as everyone looked over at him.

"What do you think, Wade?" Jeannie asked.

"Well," he said, picking a string of celery from between his teeth, "I have a question for . . . what are your names, Martin and Judy?"

"Yeah? What's your question?"

"I was just wondering. Are you guys high?"

"Not that it's any of your fucking business. But yes, we are."

"Jeannie," Nye said, "you said that if this guy, this Latrell guy, if he sees anything hinky, we blow it, literally, right?"

"That's right."

"Well, congratulations. 'Cause he just pushed the button." They all watched as Nye drank his full cup of steaming coffee in one long draught, and then slowly lowered the empty white Styrofoam cup upside-down onto the table. "You've all seen magicians before, right? They'll bring out a box, it's painted all glittery, glossy black with a big dragon decal on the outside, they'll show you it's empty, throw a yard of silk over it, and then whip the cloth off and pull a fucking dove out of the box?" He looked around the table. "Amazing, right?"

"No, it's not," Anna said. "It's stupid."

"Why?"

"Because it's obvious, it's his box, it's rigged. The only thing I don't know is exactly how it's rigged, but who really gives a crap? The whole thing's too slick, it's not, I don't know, spontaneous."

On the table, two feet in front of Nye, the Styrofoam cup jumped an inch.

"My point exactly," he said. "Spontaneous."

Eric Woodson reached tentatively forward and lifted the foam cup. A yellow baby chick was standing underneath.

"You guys remember the footage from 9/11? The most chilling shit of all, where did it come from?"

"Camcorders," Anna said, still looking at the cheeping baby bird on the table. "The stuff people on the street caught, just by accident."

"Camcorders, exactly right. And what's camcorder footage like? Look at the Weather Channel, when they run some citizen's shot of a tornado? Motherfucker's zooming in and out, mumbling about how incredible it is, camera's shaking, whipping around, and he cuts away right before the best part, when the funnel hits the barn in the foreground. Zero production value, but you believe it, it's real. Run that again, what you've got here, run it again."

The digital video rewound in a few seconds, then restarted from the beginning.

"Now where exactly is this camera supposedly mounted, in this shot here? On a Steadicam, in a helicopter? It's flawless, the way it's tracking, straight out of a goddamn Michael Bay movie. Then right here, look at this, you cut to the horizon, and then the attack plane appears, right on cue. Did the cameraman know it was out there or something? And then here we go, watch, everything that happens, the shot's perfectly framed to capture it. What was this, a seven-camera shoot? And hold up, I almost forgot this one, can you freeze that?"

The playback stopped on a shot of the panicking crowd.

"Go back a few frames. Go back, a little more. More. Stop." Nye got up and walked to the screen. "Can you zoom in on this spot, right here?"

After a few seconds, the indicated area enlarged to full screen.

"Who's this, here? Am I hungover, or is that Bert, from Sesame Street?"

The cone head and black topknot were unmistakable. The puppet looked as frightened as the surrounding digitized humans, in his striped sweater-vest and white turtleneck.

Rudy turned to the still-standing animators. "What in the fuck is that?"

"It's our trademark. We work Bert into all our pieces, it's like a signature."

Weeks before, a photograph of an anti-US rally in Bangladesh had run in the news worldwide. The marchers were shown carrying a large poster with a collage of pictures of Usama bin Laden. In a prominent one, the terrorist leader could be clearly seen sitting beside the angry, bushy-browed yellow-felt Muppet character. The al Qaeda organizers had run off thousands of the posters without realizing they were using a digitally altered picture that made UBL look like a complete idiot. The origins of that handiwork had been unknown until this moment.

"Well, screw your signature," Rudy said. "This is not some Internet prank, all right? No more fucking around, you assholes,

410

and I'm confiscating your weed, understand?" The two sullenly nodded their heads. "Now get back to the pit, and get everybody back to work revising, back to the goddamn drawing board."

"Listen, it's amazing work," Nye said. "We just can't use it. The key to real magic, guys? Is making the extraordinary, ordinary. You're thinking Steven Spielberg. I'm talking Steve Rosenberg."

"Who's that?" Rudy asked.

"My accountant."

The baby chick had walked over in front of Anna, and she was petting its head with a finger. She straightened her glasses, and looked over at the magician.

Nye winked at her. "He's all yours, sweetheart."

One of Anna's helpers, a serious young emo in overalls, leaned into the room from the hallway, and shyly motioned John over.

"No," he said, "come on in, and share."

She looked around at all of them. "We've all got it. This carrier worm, it's running resident in all our machines here."

"Not the SGIs."

The young woman nodded her head grimly.

"It can't spread this fast, or this deep, not so quickly," John said. "It wasn't made to."

Jeannie pulled a microphone over in front of her, and looked at John. "May I?" she asked.

"Of course."

"Kate, are you there?" Jeannie asked.

"Good morning, Jeannie Reese," the computer answered.

"Could you show us your master boot record, local copy, on the screen?"

"In binary or hexadecimal?"

"Hex is fine."

"Displaying MBR."

The digital projector hummed to life, and the big screen filled with rows and columns of hexadecimal numbers.

"Let's see last week's backup, right beside this, if you can, please."

"One moment," the computer replied. Within a few seconds, the screen split and the two hex grids were juxtaposed, side by side.

John frowned at the screen, and walked a few steps toward it. "What in the Christ—"

Anna stood and came up beside him, squinting through her thick lenses. "You've got it, too, chief."

"It's IRIN," Jeannie said. "This worm of yours, it's mutated into a fast infector, it's found the same security holes I used to send IRIN out onto every machine it could find, and now it's piggybacking. Windows computers are wide open, and the other OS's aren't much better off. Once they started working together, wham, it's spread everywhere, overnight."

"IRIN?" Linus said. "Dare I ask?"

"You know all those wild-ass rumors," John said, "that the government is reading all our e-mails, listening to all our phone calls, tracking us all day on video, and building a police-state profile on every goddamn US citizen?"

Several heads nodded.

"That's IRIN," Jeannie said.

Eric Woodson sank into his chair, absorbing. "So it's days, you're saying, not weeks. When, then?"

"I don't know. Kate, show us a current calendar, August through January."

"One moment," the computer said, and the calendar grids soon filled the screen.

"Kate, what was special about September 11th, before the attacks?" John asked.

"September eleven, significant events in history," the computer said, as a long text list began to scroll in a window.

"Bingo, there it is," Anna said, "TV's Rhoda gets divorced, 1977."

"Kate," John said, "filter out the bullshit, please. Past political, religious, military events only."

The list grew abruptly shorter.

Henry Hudson discovers Manhattan Island, 9/11/1609
Construction of Pentagon begins, US, 9/11/1941
Alexander Hamilton appointed Secretary of Treasury, US, 9/11/1789
Marines invade Honduras, 9/11/1919
British Mandate of Palestine established, 9/11/1922
West German Chancellor Adenauer ratifies reparation pact for the Jews, 9/11/1952
President Salvador Allende deposed in CIA-supported military coup, Chile, 9/11/1973

"Jesus," Rudy said. "Take your pick."

"Kate, look at the next two weeks, anything similar? What's coming up?"

"Searching."

Several undistinguished listings appeared, but the group dismissed them one after another.

"Excuse me, John," the computer said. "I have found a correlation, but it is outside your search parameters."

"What, what is it, show it," John said.

The screen filled with two items, a holiday listing and an online headline from the Drudge Report.

December 10, 2001: First day of Hanukkah

Source: "Daisy-cutter" to flush bin Laden from Tora Bora!

The story concerned a leaked report that the Pentagon was planning to drop the 15,000-pound fuel-air bomb on the cave complex where UBL was thought to be holed up, on Monday morning local time, late Sunday night in the United States. It was the largest ordnance in the arsenal, the next best thing to a nuke.

"That's it," John said. "The biggest Jewish holiday of the year, and the perfect over-the-top US assault to point to as a justification."

"Are you sure, John?" Linus asked.

"Not yet," John said. "Kate, show me headlines, financial pages, from the last week or so."

413

"One moment." The screen blanked out briefly, and John took a step closer as it began to refill with hyperlinked lead-ins from the world's news services.

"Stop," John said. "Jesus Christ, where've I been? Number seventeen, *USA Today*, four goddamn days ago, bring that up."

Enron Files Chapter 11, Largest Corporate Bankruptcy in US History

They all scanned the story, as John began to pace. Enron Corporation, *Fortune Magazine*'s Most Innovative Company for six years running, had just completely imploded over the last few short weeks. By first reports the collapse had been due to an entirely different brand of innovation, the variety preferred by the likes of Ponzi, Capone, Keating, and the Social Security Administration. And the fraud didn't end at the doors of the Enron boardroom. The most influential banks, the most lofty accounting institutions, the most respected law firms and the most powerful figures in American politics would soon find themselves implicated as this downfall gathered its momentum.

"What does that mean to us, John?" Linus asked.

"It's the economy they're trying to kill, understand? The economy goes down, everything else goes down with it. The dot-com bubble didn't quite sink us, but it cracked the foundation. Now Wall Street's still reeling after September eleventh, scores of these enormous companies are set up to fall just like Enron was, Worldcom, Global Crossing, you want a list?"

"So it's everyone?" Linus asked. "Everyone, the corporations, the press, the politicians, you want us to believe that nearly everyone is involved in this?"

"No, goddamn it, *listen*! Twenty-thousand people worked for Enron, do you think they all got together every morning and conspired to hide the completely obvious *fact* that the whole fucking company was just a load of hot air? They just did their jobs, they followed the leader. They didn't need to know the endgame, even the goddamn CEO didn't need to know, he just did what criminals do. Hell, Linus, you put a fox in a henhouse he doesn't need any further instructions, he's going to eat the fucking chickens. There's no rule book in the top drawer, no chain of command, no smoking gun, all the controllers have to do is choose their pawns from a safe distance, and then help them get where they want them to go. Make introductions, make political contributions, pull an occasional string, whisper in the occasional ear, and then sit back and watch the inevitable proceedings."

"It's not possible, John, corporations of that size, they can't be made to fail on cue—"

"Not possible?" John said. "That company was poised to collapse for years, whenever the time was right, and like you said, right on cue. Do you know who brought Enron down? Read to the end of the story. They didn't need Ed Latrell for that, or the Trilateralists, or the World Bank, or the Illuminati, or the Bilderbergers. A note got passed to a 29-year-old junior reporter at *Fortune* last January, and it was passed to the guy who passed it to her by some other guy, and another guy before him, on and on up until you finally get to a little room full of fucking evil trillionaires somewhere, or whoever's really up there at the controls of all this. If anyone's still in control at all."

John looked around the table. "Believe me or don't. You asked if I was sure? Well, I sure as hell am now. It's Monday morning, people. Four days from now."

"Three and a half," Rudy said quietly.

The room grew deadly still as it sank in, to each of them. They'd had a slim hope, in retrospect, but there was no time now, not nearly enough time to make a miracle.

John rolled his chair back, and stood at his place. "Well then, that's a wrap. Goodnight, and good luck." He walked toward the door.

"Where are you going?" Anna asked.

He stopped and turned back to them. "Hmm?"

"Where are you going?"

"Where am I going? Where do you think I'm going? I'm going to bed. Woodson said it from the beginning, he was right, we're fucked, we've been chasing our tails here. I'm going to go down and get some rest, and then I'm outta here tomorrow morning. And if I gave a shit I'd suggest you all do the same."

Anna sniffled, and wiped her eyes behind her glasses.

"Oh, that's excellent," John said, taking a thin pewter flask from his back pocket. "Crying is perfect at a time like this. It seals the defeat. No, really, it's good to face up to it. Somebody's gotta lose, and this time it's us."

He had unscrewed the cap and he took a slug from the flask. "Man, a week from now? You won't even recognize this fucking country. But we all hate it anyway, don't we? I mean, look around, look back, what's to love? Bush, Clinton, more Bush, Reagan, Carter, Ford, Nixon, Johnson, *Jesus*, it's been a long run of unfunny jokes, hasn't it? Long as you can remember. It's a wonder they lasted as long as they did. So fuck 'em."

He started for the door, but then stopped and turned back to them. "When you cut and run, though? Take my advice, hide your ass real good. Because I gotta tell you, I've looked square into the face of the very near future, and it's gonna be a rude awakening for you geeks, when this fucking country starts hating you back.

"So." He raised the flask to them. "Here's to the end of the world as we know it." He looked at Jeannie, and saw the tiniest smile in her eyes.

"Or," John said, thoughtfully, as he recapped his half-pint. He walked to the head of the table, considering. "Or. We could look around us all here, and think about this. The boats are all burning in the harbor, people. And maybe there's nowhere to go, but forward. And maybe we've got nobody to trust but who you see right here. And maybe we're not quite dead yet."

"But there's not enough time now," Anna said.

"Come on, that's such bullshit. There's exactly enough time, you know that, there always is. When you had four weeks, the job was going to take four weeks. Now we've got until Monday morning.

So we'll cut a few corners. What, you've never seen an unreason-able deadline before?" He looked around the table. "You think you can't do it? Well, for whatever it's worth, I'm telling you, I know you can. Name your poison, CIA, DIA, ONI, INR, NIC, NSA, MI6, I wouldn't trade one of you for all of them. There's not a room full of people like this in the whole world. Reese, am I right?"

"That's right," Jeannie said.

"You're the best there is, and I know it, and she knows it, even if you don't. You're better than me, you frickin' brainiacs. And you've already beaten this thing, you know." He tapped his temple with his index finger. "Up here, you've already won. All we've got to do now is do it." John took a deep breath. "So, I guess I'm in. Who else?"

He looked to each of them, and in their time each nodded their commitment. "All right," he said, checking his watch. "We may not be able to save the world. But I'll settle for saving the day."

Jeannie stood and walked to his right side. "Okay, everybody," she said. "We've got to hit it now, like there's no tomorrow. Wade, can you stay with Rudy and the video people?" Nye gave her a nod. "Good deal. John and I will worry about cutting the schedule. In the meantime, rig your teams for twenty-four-seven. Now go."

As everyone headed off to dive back into their task lists, she looked at John and put her hand on his shoulder.

"And you and me, partner," she said, "we've got a call to make."

The necktie was choking him little by little and his suit jacket had been tailored twenty or thirty pounds ago, but there was a dress code for this gig and it was not negotiable. He had called in every last favor to secure this meeting, with every last remaining friend. Winston Smith was en route to hand-deliver an additional diplo-matic package from Jeannie, but he had not yet arrived.

Jay Marshall sat on the ginger-orange couch against one wall of the Roosevelt Room, trying not to sweat completely through his clothes, his eyes wandering over the art and the accoutrements of history surrounding him. Over the mantel, above TR's Nobel Peace

417

Prize, was a painting of Teddy Roosevelt as commander of the Rough Riders. The guy looked like genuine superhuman Americana in the artist's eye, invincible and towering as Paul Bunyan in the saddle.

Jay's hand went to his jacket pocket. There were two mated scramblers there, one for each end of a telephone handset. Smith was bringing a set of encoded messages that would either become undeniable proof of their credibility or evidence at their sentencing, depending on how the upcoming conference ended. Named names, damning evidence, unreleased details behind the 9/11 attacks, state secrets of the kind that would prove them to be patriots, or buy them all one-way tickets to sunny Gitmo.

Jay removed the decoder from his other pocket. It had been walked over a few minutes earlier by the White House curator, straight from the Monticello exhibit across town in the Smithsonian. Age had smoothed it, he thought, as he ran his fingers over the symbols carved in its surfaces. It looked like an oversized toilet-paper spindle, made from a stack of twenty-six wooden disks mounted on a brass rod through their centers. He turned a few of the disks, lining up the jumbled letters, imagining the hands of the early American hacker that had shaped this relic over two centuries before. The Jefferson Wheel was studied by every scholar of cryptography, but this one was different.

This one was Jefferson's.

It was the appointed time by his watch, and as that thought crossed his mind he heard a knob turning and the side hallway door swung open. A man with salt-and-pepper hair entered the room, and a moment later it all sank into his stomach like a lead donut, where he was. Of the catalog of reactions that he could have or should have had, his first was a rather trivial observation.

Not as tall as his father.

The phone on the conference table rang. Jay stood, and extended his right hand.

"Mister President," he said.

*

The meeting had ended, and Jay sat uneasily and alone again in the quiet of the weighty room. He had been told to stay here by the arguable leader of the free world, so he would stay. But he wanted nothing more than to run, just as fast as his stocky legs would carry him.

Winston Smith had never shown up with the package she'd sent, so they'd been forced to haltingly improvise around most of the hard evidence. Jeannie had laid it all out, the years-long lead-up to 9/11, the trail of a deep and wide conspiracy she had brushed with and later confirmed in the aftermath, the preparation for the follow-up attack, the players, inside and outside, and their parts. She and Fagan had given more than enough damning detail to convince anyone listening that this was all for real, that a second, massive attack was imminent, that some in Bush's inherited government and even within his circle of allies were complicit, that time was of the essence if there was any hope this could be stopped.

It had been impossible to read the President's face. It seemed he had aged years in the nearly three months since September the eleventh. He was grim and silent, inscrutable through much of the call. There was still one way out, Jeannie had finally said, though it was a long shot of historic proportions. Then the two on the speakerphone had outlined their counterstrategy, over an uninterrupted half-hour. All of this had been unbelievable, all of it since those towers had fallen, but this last exchange had put new meaning to the word.

The man remained silent for long moments at the end. He had stood then, terminated the call with a pushbutton near the phone, turned and walked to the door. "You wait here," he had said, and the light had been insufficient to confirm what Jay believed he had seen as the President left him alone in the room.

A smirk?

That little unconscious, inopportune smile Bush was known to flash at times, in the oddest situations. Jay had wondered at it before, but it caught him unawares there and then, triggered a cold sweat and an instinct to flee and be shot in the back rather than die in a prison, as that strange little smile had seemed to promise he now surely would. They had sought aid and counsel from the highest office in the land, but that office had already been corrupted, and now it was truly over, for every last one of them.

The door opened, and three men he vaguely recognized entered the room, followed by five others, enforcers, with weapons at their sides.

"Mister Marshall," Walter Kamuck said.

Benjamin Fuller took a seat nearby, and Jay felt the presence of two men behind him, heard the metal sounds of pistols brought to the ready near his head.

"The President tells us that you've been keeping dangerous company," Fuller said calmly, "and entertaining him with ideas of some vast conspiracy." He rolled his chair an inch forward, and leaned his elbows on his knees. "Is this true?"

Jay looked to each of them, but only lowered his eyes in answer.

"Let me put the lie to that," Fuller said. "There is no vast conspiracy. But change, on the other hand, is inevitable, and that may be what you've . . . seen and misinterpreted, you and your accomplices. The change that is in the air."

"What did you tell the President, you and Jeannie?" Ari Darukyan asked, from the corner of the room.

"Everything we know," Jay replied. "And there's more on the way."

Walter Kamuck held up a manila envelope that had been tucked under his arm. "I suppose you mean this?"

The wax seal had been broken. There was a single powder-burnt, splayed bullet hole clean through the thick packet. Blood was spattered on its facing side, as if it had been held out as a shield, or in acquiescence, by someone naïve to the fact that there was no surrender at this level of the game.

"This material is encoded. I assume you have the key?"

Jay reached into his pocket.

"Easy," said one of the men behind him, and a pistol barrel pushed at the back of his head.

420

His hand came out slowly, holding the centuries-old device. As Kamuck reached for it, Jay relaxed his grip and the twenty-six thin lettered rings slipped free of the freshly unscrewed spindle and clattered to a hopeless jumble at their feet.

"Decode that," Jay said.

The room was quiet for a while.

"Well," Kamuck finally said, "I'm sure you can imagine the grave position you've put yourself in."

Arms and hands from behind immobilized him, and Jay felt the sharp slide of a needle into his upper back, felt the bolus of injected medication bulging into a lump under his skin.

"I don't know what you assumed of the President," Fuller said. "What you expected that idiot to do. Of course, he did as he had been told. He called us."

The lamps in the room had already begun to trail light as his eyes moved, as the drug took hold, and he wondered where he would be found, how his wife would get the news that there'd been an apparent suicide in one of the quiet parks around D.C. He might make page one of the *Post* above the fold, if they killed him before the really big news hit on Monday morning.

There was a sudden rustle of activity to the side of him, and the door banged open, and six men and a woman entered the room efficiently, all in dark suits, with pistols drawn. The sounds and voices were muffling and echoing strangely in his head, but Jay caught a glimpse of an ID badge clipped to the woman's jacket. *Secret Service, Uniformed Division.*

"What the hell is this?" Walter Kamuck said.

"We're interrogating this man, at the President's order," Benjamin Fuller said. "It's under control."

"The White House is our jurisdiction, mister Kamuck," the woman's stern voice replied. "We're taking custody of this man." There was the briefest standoff as those armed in the room did what they were trained to do and covered each other, gun to gun. At a nod from Darukyan, each in his entourage holstered his pistol and took a step to the side.

421

Cuffs were ratcheted onto Jay's distant wrists, and the liquid room swam and swirled as he was pulled to his feet. "Sir, you are under arrest," he heard the woman say as they turned him, and she continued on with a brief litany of charges and his Miranda. He nodded his understanding of his rights, and in a blur of slow melting images, he met the somewhat bewildered eyes of the men he was leaving behind.

Though Bush and all forty-two of his predecessors had been granted the Constitutional power to do so, only Washington and Madison had ever taken their role of Commander-in-Chief all the way down to the very battlefield. But that's what Jeannie Reese had asked. Jay remembered the tiny smile on the President's face as he'd left earlier, and when he was certain he was out of hostile view he felt that same odd expression forming on his own face as consciousness faded toward warm blackness.

He'd done his part, and now, like the rest of the world, he would be only a spectator for the big show. If he was right, and he had just been rescued by the President's guardians, that meant there was still a ray of hope, dim as it was. If he was right he would wake up in a jail cell, but it wouldn't be the first time. Call it protective custody. Considering what was coming in three and a half days, prison would be as safe as any place in the country.

And he didn't care if the food was bad, the cot was lumpy and the smokes were stale.

As long as they gave him a fucking TV.

48

Edward Latrell stood on his deck overlooking his valley, under his big sky. The breath was only filling shallow in his lungs, and there was a new tremor in his hands that kept his fists clenched in the presence of others. The fear was not for the day that was coming, but of the few days intervening. Command was still his, but control was passing moment by moment to the lieutenants, and to the machines. The time was chosen and it would arrive, but still he feared to look away.

Now with every minute he felt a little something leave him, a nick of his soul caught by the current of passing time. Whatever energy it was that moved in a man who leads in a great cause, it was leaking from him in wisps. As if, now that it was inevitable, as it passed from his grasp there was only just enough of him left to see it to the end, when others would take up the sword. For the first time in his memory, he could not see beyond the approaching horizon.

Down in the clearing, several teams of draft horses were laboring slowly forward under the whip, straining against a twelve-ton rolling burden. Even unfueled and unarmed, the F/A-18 looked like an angel of death on dull gray wings. A hundred yards beyond, the railroadmen were sledging spikes into a long line of parallel ties, and dimly he could hear the song they sang to keep their rhythm rising up to his ears.

To the west, the counterweight of a four-story siege engine had been winched into position, and the ballast-laden, balanced shell of one of their defective Tomahawks was being loaded into its newly modified sling. All tests had failed thus far, and a man had lost an arm the previous night in a misfiring. The ancient technology was unfamiliar to the engineers; without the machine's designer present it was trial with little room for error, but it was necessary work. Most of the missiles in their inventory had been built to be belly-dropped from B-52s or other heavy bombers. So, he had told them, so they must be launched from the air. And John Fagan had found him a way.

A broad green flag flapped downward, the interlock was pulled by rope, the monstrous limb of the trebuchet swung down through its violent arc, and the three-thousand-pound dummy missile in a metal-mesh sling whipped around, up and over the machinery and half a mile out into the blue, straight and graceful as a shining white arrow. A flash from its tail marked the remote firing of the booster stage, and a great *hurrah* arose from the field as the unguided missile rocketed forward on its trajectory, far out over the valley to the south. This one would fall harmlessly into the wilderness, its main turbofan engine and guidance systems had been removed. But the trial was complete, and it was a glorious success.

It had been the last river to be crossed, *finis coronat opus*. The lance of freedom now extended a thousand statute miles.

His phone had begun to vibrate, and he brought it to his ear.

"Yes. Hello, Nathan. Before you tell me what you haven't yet found, I should let you know we've heard from our friend . . . Very little, I'm afraid, there wasn't but a moment. He's not in New York, you must come back west, they somehow made their way to Las Vegas . . . Yes. With all speed. I'll contact you with specifics if I receive them, but the trail is warm, it should be no trouble for one such as you ... Yes. Now you must balance the books for me. Goodbye, Mr. Krieger. Make me proud."

A group of men and women somewhere nearby, down below, were singing quietly to the windy strumming of a dulcimer. No one in his life had sung this song as it had been written, with the author's bitter, steadfast resolve burning through, until he had heard it sung here. He brought himself to his knees, his clasped hands to his forehead, and he let their prayer for vengeance inhabit him as he whispered the words with them.

Mine eyes have seen the glory of the coming of the Lord,
He is trampling out the vintage where the grapes of wrath are stored,
He hath loosed the fateful lightning of His terrible swift sword,
His truth is marching on.

Glory! Glory! Hallelujah!
Glory! Glory! Hallelujah!
Glory! Glory! Hallelujah!
His truth is marching on.

I have seen Him in the watchfires of a hundred circling camps,
They have builded Him an altar in the evening dews and damps,
I have read His righteous sentence by the dim and flaring lamps,
His day is marching on.

I have read a fiery gospel writ in burnished rows of steel,
"As ye deal with My contemptors, so with you My grace shall deal,"
Let the Hero born of woman crush the serpent with His heel,
Since God is marching on.

He hath sounded forth the trumpet that shall never call retreat,
He is sifting out the hearts of men before His judgment seat,
Oh, be swift, my soul, to answer Him! Be jubilant, my feet!
Our God is marching on.

49

Like one long day, it had seemed, not nearly four days and nights. Among the pizza boxes, beer and soda cans and overflowing ashtrays were strewn the exhausted human remains of the team. He had pushed them beyond their limits in the last rehearsal, and himself beyond his own. Now it was over, and it had not gone nearly as well as the previous two.

"All right," John said, glancing at his watch. "It's one-twenty in the morning. And this is the morning, people. The next run-through is the world premiere. Everybody go get a meal and a shower, get laid if it'll unwind you. But be back here in three hours, at four-thirty, bright-eyed and bushy-tailed. Everybody tracking that?"

He looked to each of them, and they all signaled their weary assent.

"Good. We'll see you in three hours."

John stayed behind as everyone gradually filtered out, and Jeannie took a seat in her chair, thumbed buttons on her phone, put it to her ear. He paced absently for a while, then got her attention and asked a question with his eyes. She held up her index finger to him, making notes on her pad. At length, she closed her phone and looked at him. Shook her head, no.

"What's the progress, then?" he asked.

"It's a process of elimination, John, and they've eliminated about ninety-five per cent of the trucks on the road, just from verified shipping records and passive scans."

"And that leaves, what?"

"Thousands," she said. "But there's still time."

"Oh, hell yeah," John replied. "Half a day to find a nuclear needle in a haystack, and that's if we don't completely fuck up right out of the gate."

She looked up at him, and smiled. "Oh, I forgot. You're a glass-half-empty person."

"Well, muffin, I guess that all depends on what's in the glass."

She patted the seat of the chair next to her, and he came over and sat down.

"I've got a message," Jeannie said softly, "just a rumour, but they've got Jay out west in Victorville, the federal prison there." She got no response. "John? Any word from Winston?"

He shook his head, and studied the tabletop. She put her hand on his, and after a few moments he covered it with his other.

"Guy never hurt a living thing, in his whole life, you know that?" John said quietly.

"We don't know what happened."

"Yeah, actually, we do." He began to pull his hand away, but she held on.

"Everything isn't your fault."

He looked at her. "But this is. *This* is."

"All we can do is what we're about to do, John. Don't you dare melt down on me. Not now."

He looked away. "I don't want to think anymore tonight."

"Okay, then," Jeannie said. "Okay." She pulled his hand a little closer. "Let me try to make you forget about it."

He didn't meet her eyes, though he couldn't help but smile. "That sounds mildly interesting."

She stood and pulled the bag off the arm of her chair. Her hand dug inside briefly, and she pulled out a dull black H&K .45 pistol.

428

"Oh, come on," he said. "Don't you ever quit?"

"Sure," she said, springing the clip and checking the chamber. "When it's perfect, I quit. Look, they're hunting me, and they're hunting you. The difference is, I'm ready for it. I'm only teaching you one thing, sport, but you're going to know it better than me when we're done."

She motioned come-hither with the barrel of the gun. "Get on over here, big boy. I've got time to kill you two hundred times before breakfast."

He walked slowly over, sighed heavily, and knelt in front of her.

He did his best to enter the room quietly, but he heard her voice as soon as he reached the bedroom doorway.

"Where've you been, John?" Gretchen asked. It was part anger and part fear in her voice, and both emotions struck him as completely inappropriate, even as he felt a knot of guilt twist in his stomach. "It's three-thirty in the morning, every day now, where have you been?"

"Just with . . . my friends," he said.

"Why are you lying to me? For God's sake, I can smell her on you."

He sat down on the corner of the bed. "Look. I haven't been honest with you, but it's not what you're thinking."

"What am I thinking? That she's prettier'n me? That she's smarter'n me? I got eyes, John. You ain't laid a hand on me since—"

"Gretchen—"

"Then what is it, then?" Her voice was small, brittle. "You got me shut up in here, I can't talk to nobody, the elevator don't even go where there's any people, I don't know what's goin' on, you never—"

"Listen, listen." He sat down next to her. "Winston's dead."

"Oh." She put her fingers to her mouth. "Oh, honey."

"I made a promise to you, and I mean to keep it. I told you I'd always take care of you, and I will. I want you to get ready to

429

leave, today, the four of us, you and me and the children. But I have to do something first. It's what I've been doing every night. It's what Winston gave his life for, and that fellow who got us out of Colorado. And it's today, that I've got to do this thing, with my friends, and then we can go."

"What are you going to do?"

"I want you to be there. I didn't want to tell you about it before, because, because I think I never really believed we could pull it off. But now, I think we can. And I want you to see it, I think it's important that you see it, all three of you."

She looked down at the pillow next to her, and pulled the blanket on his side down a few inches. "Can you sleep now? You ain't slept very much, in days."

"No, not now. Tonight, we'll sleep. God willing."

50

A little before midnight Eastern Standard Time, a dark blue Chevy Cavalier left the White House, bound for Andrews Air Force Base. There were no limousines, escorts or entourage in front or behind. The rental car passed unchallenged through the open gates. The soldiers on guard there stood rigidly at attention, but their backs were to the roadway.

Twenty minutes later, two men emerged from the car and walked briskly across the dew-slicked asphalt to the metal stairway of the waiting E-767 AWACS. The twin engines were whining at idle, and the huge disk of the advanced warning and control system rotated majestically above them as they climbed up into the side of the jet. In the cockpit, the navigator paused the preflight, noted the time and jotted an entry in his log.

00:11:31 Command party boards. Flightplan TBD. Amend call sign: pendragon

He clicked his pen to retract the ballpoint, and made an additional, invisible note of their true designation below, just to watch himself write the words.

Air Force One

From the mouth of a cavernous hangar at Nellis AFB, eight miles from downtown Las Vegas, a tight triangle-shaped formation of thirty small, unearthly aircraft rolled out onto the taxiway. All personnel were confined to quarters, even the tower was ordered deserted, so no one was there to witness the odd departure.

As the flight group reached each intersection on the tarmac, selected planes peeled off onto perpendicular runways and accelerated down the white line, taking to the sky by twos. Like the similar squadrons of Global Hawks and Predator drones that were leaving other bases around the country, no pilot sat at their controls, remotely or otherwise. Their digital orders came through the air at the speed of thought from the Battlespace Information Network.

The BIN was made up of a neural network of linked computer systems, all but one of them aboard the many AWACS flights that were currently climbing nationwide to forty-thousand feet over the homeland. The remaining system, the designated nerve center, watched her master through overhead closed-circuit cameras and quietly contemplated the coming day from her tower, turning slowly, surveying the horizon a thousand feet above an off-strip Vegas hotel casino.

John looked around the room to each of his team members as they prepared themselves for the gauntlet that waited just ahead of them. One sat with his fingers rubbing his temples, staring at his screen, his lips reciting quietly. Another was emptying a fistful of sugar packets one after the other into the largest available coffee cup. The young man nearest him had lined up forty cigarettes in perfect rows and columns by his computer screen, with three spare lighters close beside.

Here we go.

"Kate, KTLA, Los Angeles, bring that up, please, with audio."

From the hundreds of thumbnail-sized video feeds, one near the lower-middle zoomed out to fill the projection screen.

"—and there isn't much information, but we have a report from KTLA's Kirby Price that a wildfire, or a . . . or a number of wildfires are . . . underway around the Southland. Kirby?" The

young female host of the morning news appeared unaccustomed to going off-script. She held her palm to her earpiece, and listened through several seconds of dead air. "*All right, we're going to go to the remote, if we can. Kirby, what are you seeing out there?*"

A three-shot mosaic took over the frame, showing the anchor, the remote reporter and a belly-cam shot from the KTLA news copter. The correspondent was shouting to be heard over the rotor blades beating through the open door next to him. "*Janice, as you can see there in the distance, we're seeing these outbreaks, these fires, and it's an oddity for a number of reasons. Though the Santa Anas are still blowing, it's December, and not a time we think of as wildfire season. Second, there seems to be, and this is not confirmed, there seem to be simultaneous and widespread reports of forest fires from outside San Diego, where we are here, just north of Los Angeles, and in Simi Valley, San Bernardino, Orange, Ventura and Riverside counties.*"

"Fire and EMS response is rolling, all areas," BitStorm called out.

"Go," John said, and at his signal a bank of electronic demon-dialers began hammering 911 emergency in all West Coast localities with thousands of automated calls per minute. "Kate, let's see the situation."

On the wall where the whiteboard used to be, an eighty-inch flat-panel LCD screen blinked to life. Identical units were hung in the other work areas, so a status display was within a few feet of everyone on the floor. The screen showed a live satellite picture of the continental United States, with what looked like digitally overlaid weather patterns developing over the landmass. But the building storms it showed had nothing to do with the weather.

John reached out and touched southern California, and dragged his fingertip upward. The map zoomed in and rotated to a three-quarters overhead view, showing color-coded hotspots of current and scheduled activity. The fires were there, and glowing cross-hairs showed the locations of upcoming attacks with small countdown timers flickering next to each of them.

He thumped a tab at the base of the view, and the screen switched to a ground-level 2-D pictogram of the US, with the target cities represented by blocky groups of vertical rectangles. In the black sky above, slowly descending dots trailed bright lines as they headed toward the ground. It looked exactly like the old-school Atari arcade game, Missile Command.

John spun the trackball control mounted in front of the screen, and highlighted a group of five rapidly approaching threats.

"These five," he said, over his headset. "GPS?"

"Ready."

"One and two, do you see them?"

"Got 'em."

"They're bound for impact on the Kern River and El Paso natural gas pipelines, in that order. Trash those two in the Calabasas and Puente Hills landfills. Bring the other three in proximity for a convergence in area six, in, just one moment, in three minutes, on my mark—" He paused and started the stopwatch that was hanging around his neck. "Go. Kate, give me the God's eye view of one and two."

Dual picture-in-pictures popped up on the screen, showing views of two highways from circling Global Hawks three miles up. Moving targeting reticles followed the rectangular specks, and even from altitude they were roughly distinguishable as medium-sized fleet trucks, one disguised as an EMS vehicle.

"Slow down number two, way down," John said. He heard the answering activity in the GPS hack-room in his earphones.

The global positioning system used an ironclad method to send navigational information to its receivers, coordinating three-point geosynchronous satellite data through fixed ground reference stations to pinpoint each vehicle's location within a meter or so. Though all of the suicide drivers had primary destinations, they were also prepared to divert if their onboard receiver directed them to do so. They were well trained, stone killers, the cream of the crop, and they would follow the foolproof automated guidance system without question or confirmation.

Foolproof, John thought, as he watched the glowing icons representing the fixed GPS ground stations begin to creep slowly across the map.

On the screen, the first suicide truck made an abrupt turn off the 101 and onto Lost Hills Road.

The day manager at the Calabasas Landfill squinted through the dingy glass of his office window, the one that faced the main gate.

Now, there's something you don't see every day, he thought.

It had been a strange morning from the start of it. When he'd arrived at work, there had been a red closure order taped across the latch, signed by the District, directing him to keep the public out all day. And now a white truck, maybe a moving van or a delivery rig, was coming up the long curve of the access road, but fast, like a scalded ape. He put his jelly bagel down on its paper plate, wiped his mouth on his napkin, and got on the new FRS two-way base station he'd put in.

"Warren, you see that truck haulin' ass up Lost Hills? Over."

"Yes, sir. Over."

"Anybody like that on your manifest for this morning? Over."

"No, sir."

"Say 'over,' when you're done talking, Warren."

"Yes, sir. No, sir, I don't have a truck like that one coming in on my manifest. Over."

The manager took another bite of his breakfast, and watched. The truck was getting closer, and picking up speed every second.

"Open up the gate, Warren."

There was a long pause.

"Do you read me? Open up the gate, Warren!"

"I didn't know you was done talking, 'cause you didn't say 'over.'"

"Open up the goddamn gate, that guy's not stopping, and if he bends my fence, it's comin' outta your bonus!"

He saw the wide chain-link gates swinging slowly open in the distance, and with inches of clearance the truck roared through, still accelerating. It blurred past his side windows, and the sound of its engine gradually faded as it rounded a corner and disappeared out into the vast garbage canyons of the landfill.

"Hmph," he said.

He took a sip of coffee, picked up his phone and punched in 911, with a glance out toward the entrance gates that were now closing again.

Never hire family, he thought.

He was reaching for the remains of his bagel when he heard the fast busy signal pulsing in his earpiece. The sound was just strange enough to make him sit down in his chair, and in that way, it saved him from a nasty cut, at best. An instant later, every window in the office blew violently inward from the shock wave of a distant explosion, the equivalent of four-thousand pounds of TNT.

"Kate, did you catch the confirmation code?" John asked.

"Displaying," the computer replied, and the success code from the first attack of the day winked onto the screen.

John clapped his hands together, and began to pace. "That's what we needed to see. They haven't changed the codes on us, people. Repeat, the confirmation codes in your tables for mission success and failure are valid."

The Global Hawk loitering over the blast had intercepted the on-target/on-time burst transmission a split-second before detonation of the suicide truck, and a split-second afterward the flying drone had unleashed a mirror-image signal that erased the original from the airwaves, putting the confirmation to Latrell in temporary limbo. But the clock was now running.

"We've got about ninety seconds," John said. "Kill the gas from Kern River."

436

The infrastructure team acknowledged the order, took a deep breath together, and sent an electronic command through the SCADA gateway to the automated valve-operator on the pipeline.

"What's happening in there, keep talking!" John shouted.

"Valve's closing," a voice answered, over the headset. "Okay, closed!"

"Pop it back open, go, go."

"Hold on—"

"Do you guys want to see a real fucking explosion? Open it, now, all the way open!"

"It's not a lightswitch, chief. There, open!"

John brought up the overhead map, zoomed on the West Coast and hit the tab labeled "Energy." The display was only running a few seconds behind reality, but it seemed like a year before the picture told its story. There, far north at a barely accessible maintenance station of the thirty-inch natural gas pipeline, he could see the backpressure building up on the far side of the valve. Ninety PSI, one-hundred, one-ten as the flow pinched off completely, and then the monitors went to their limits, all 9's, as the regulator snapped fully open again. Down the hundreds of miles of pipeline, the sudden differential over-pressure clanked every safety valve into fail-safe to contain the damage from the catastrophic, explosive line-break that their software told them had just taken place.

"Steinman, call in your story, and roll the pipeline explosion footage onto the satellites. Internet first, on the Drudge Report, that'll get the networks on it."

"We're halfway there," Rudy called, from the production room.

John shifted the map back to the tactical view. "Ready on the El Paso pipeline, same drill. Are we set on truck number two?"

"On your signal."

"Send the override now, blow it."

An overhead view of the landscape showed a flash and a

437

mushroom cloud as the second speeding truck detonated amid the mountains of rubbish in the Puente Hills Landfill.

"El Paso pipeline is now down!" came over his headset.

"Outstanding. Release the coded success confirmations to Latrell for one and two, the Kern River and El Paso pipeline attacks, a minute or so apart. Steinman?"

"Go."

"Feed the El Paso explosion story, and somebody tell me when it gets picked up and run on the network news. Trucks three, four and five?"

"Ready to roll."

"Do it," John said. "And get set to send the success codes for the other three target pipelines, two minutes from now, and a minute or so apart."

They'd positioned the suicide trucks at the openings of three abandoned, intersecting waste-water tunnels outside the LA city limits. The huge underground tubes had been orphaned a decade earlier in a kickback scandal, but this morning the millions of tax dollars that had been poured into them would be paying off. John watched the moving dots on the situation screen heading toward each other, more and more rapidly. The dots converged, and then disappeared.

"Steinman?"

"Yes, boss?"

"There was just a big goddamn explosion outside Los Angeles, grid six. Call the local stations so they can get a camera crew out there. Tell them you're a consultant with California Public Utilities, and the blast was triggered by the upstate attacks on the natural gas pipelines. And stay on the line for an interview, if they want, but don't get carried away."

"You got it."

"Monitors," John said. "Anybody get a report of an A-bomb going off anywhere, anybody?"

All replies in his headset were in the negative.

He breathed a sigh, and allowed himself to smile. Two of the gas pipelines feeding LA were down but undamaged, five suicide bombers had blown only themselves to smithereens, and the news would soon be running their hand-crafted, on-the-scene video of the first devastating attacks of the day.

"Okay, you tricky bastards," John said. "We have officially pulled the wool over their eyes."

A cheer went up in all three control rooms, and he let the high-fives die down before he spoke again.

"Congratulations." John pulled up the Atari display, and they all saw the dozens of new, incoming threats descending. "That was the easiest fucking thing you'll do all day."

Jeannie took the last long drink from her second bottle of Evian, and brushed the hair from her eyes as she adjusted her headset. The air conditioner was cranked to the max, but with all the electronic and human activity it was pushing ninety degrees all around the floor. Young Matthew brought her another pint of water, and she turned back to the screen.

She was managing the eastern seaboard and John the west, while Eric Woodson was calling the shots for flyover country. Woodson also had the considerable responsibility of directing five of the task teams, but he had handled things with aplomb thus far.

Despite the widespread destruction their video fakery was now trumpeting on all the news channels, the western natural gas pipelines were unharmed, but they were down for damn sure. It would take a day or two for the safety valves to be manually reopened, one at a time. The outage was already sending a rolling brownout across California, and soon they'd leverage that crushing load to help take out the power across the entire southwest.

"Telephone, land lines, ready for a dry run?" Jeannie asked. This phase would demand that all three team-rooms coordinate perfectly; it would be one of the most complex of the day. A little practice wouldn't hurt.

All the players acknowledged, ready. She nodded a go, and listened to them tick through the procedures.

The current phone system wasn't nearly as vulnerable to physical or technological attack as it once had been. The breakup of Ma Bell had actually added resilience to the network; every vital system had been upgraded, paralleled, shielded and over-engineered over the years, and it had proven itself time and again as a tough nut to crack. The central-office switching hub for lower Manhattan had been housed in the World Trade Center, and when the dust from the billion pounds of collapsing steel and cement had settled after 9/11, they'd found the mainframe-sized telephone switch among the ruins, swinging by its wires, but still working. Taking the whole system down nationwide would simply be impossible.

Edward Latrell, however, hadn't been concerned with wreaking havoc in rural America. The cities were the stronghold of his enemies, and John's master plan had employed the one practical way to effectively destroy the phone network within and between all major metropolitan areas of the US.

Under cover of the rush to act after the eleventh, Latrell's politicians had pushed fast-track approval of a bill that included mandatory inspections of the subterranean cable vaults across the nation's phone networks. His lobbyists had then secured the contracts for the inspections. The job had been awarded to the lowest bidder, an obscure but well connected telco security start-up, based in southern Colorado.

Latrell's inspectors had looked the part, they were smooth, professional and insider-savvy. They methodically certified that each of the hundreds of fortified cabling hubs could withstand any conceivable attack from the outside. But the attacks wouldn't be coming from outside. Inside each of the armored vaults, the inspectors left behind a self-contained monitoring unit that included a wireless diagnostic array, a tamper-proof alarm system, and twenty pounds of RDX on a time-triggered detonator.

Across the country, John's doomsday worm would soon be arming all the planted telephone-system bombs, and starting their individual countdowns. They would all go off in unison, five minutes to the second after the day's pivotal event. But that was still hours away.

"Uh, everybody? I think we've got a glitch in here." It was Judy Tambor on the intercom.

"What?" Eric Woodson answered. "What's the matter—" His voice trailed off, mid-word. "Jesus' Mother Mary," Jeannie heard him whisper.

"Woodson, talk, what's happening in there?" John asked, over the headset.

No answer.

"Reese," John said, "go see what's eating Eric, I've got my hands full."

She was already on her way. As she rounded the doorway there was a shoving match flaring in the video control room. She got herself between the brawlers and pushed Woodson and Martin Tambor apart by their collars, and everyone quieted down. Then they all watched her face, as she saw what they had seen.

In each work area, a dedicated display showed updates to the Drudge Report website. Though they'd never admit to it, the major news services monitored Drudge constantly, because love him or hate him, he often got the scoop before anyone else in the media. The site served 9,000,000 hits on a normal day, but on a day like this it would be the world's window, and so it was the team's primary channel for leaking their fabricated breaking news stories and faked digital footage to the population.

On the 19-inch screen in front of her, the Drudge site was displaying a photo of the Gateway Arch in St. Louis, or rather its remains after a reported two-pronged truck bomb attack at its base. The 600-foot silver arch was in mid-collapse in the picture, and there was a link to a video clip of the disaster. The extra-large, all-cap headline blared, *NIGHTMARE: MIDWEST HORROR IN MORNING'S TERROR WAVE!*

"Is that real, is it live?" Jeannie asked.

"No, it's Memorex, it's ours, but it's fucking two hours early," Woodson shouted. "We were right on schedule, those two trucks were aiming for a power plant outside the city limits and a section of the Explorer pipeline way out in the boonies, we sent 'em both off a cliff into the Victor Street Quarry, boom, beautiful, and then dickhead here uploads the wrong footage onto the goddamned public Internet!"

"Oh, my, God," Jeannie said.

The telephones, the cell phones, the local radio and television stations, all communications were still running strong in St. Louis. And now a third of a million citizens of the Show-Me State who lived or worked within easy view of the still-standing, unharmed Gateway Arch could look out the window or run into the street, and see behind the curtain.

"Insert coin!" Woodson said, his hands in the air like he'd just roped a calf. "Game over! Nice working with you, everybody!"

"Get hold of yourself, Eric," Jeannie hissed to him, as she pulled her headset mike close. "Anna?"

"Yeah, what do you need?"

"I need a tidal wave, a denial-of-service attack on the Drudge site, www-dot-drudgereport-dot-com, and all its mirrors, take it down, all the way down."

"That's not on the plan—"

"Listen to me, throw everything you've got and the kitchen sink at it, now, go!" Jeannie held down the F5 key on the PC, watched the screen go blank and then refresh with the site's content over and over. "Everybody else, back to work, focus! I've got this."

She heard Anna and her girls keystroking desperately in the other room. In essence, they were doing exactly what she was doing with the Refresh key, only multiplied by thousands. They were calling up a Trojan-linked network of slave PCs to relentlessly hit the Drudge site over and over, stressing the servers until their countless rapid-fire hits squeezed out all other users trying to view the page. Denial-of-service was the blunt instrument of Internet attacks, the equivalent of incessantly ringing someone's doorbell until their house explodes.

"John, Rudy!" she shouted. She heard them pause in their stream of directives to acknowledge her. "Guys," she said, "Check your monitors, check Drudge, our panties are showing. We've got to rush the big event. Rudy?"

"Yeah, go ahead, boss."

"Call Texas and get the Crawford motorcade moving. We've got an hour, max, and probably half that before this breaks wide open. Keep your eyes on the news, and tell me if things start skidding sideways."

As she finished speaking, the Web site on her screen stopped loading and threw a hard error, SERVER NOT FOUND.

"Anna, you did good, I think it's down," Jeannie said. *But how many people had already seen it? A few hundred? A few hundred thousand?*

"That's fine," Anna said, "but their shields are going up, they're trying hard to push us out. How long do we need to hold them under?"

"Just keep it dark as long as you can, and let me know immediately if that site comes back online."

She turned to Eric Woodson, stepped up to him and cupped her hand over the microphone in front of her lips. "Now are you going to grow the hell up and lead these people," she asked, "or do I need to replace you?"

He looked at the floor between them, and she tipped his chin back up, so he was looking into her eyes.

"Yeah, no. I'm good. Sorry. I just fucking lost it."

"We all make mistakes, but what happens in here is your responsibility, nobody else's. I like you, Eric, but I won't put a million lives at risk. If you wig out in front of this team again, you won't have to apologize, because I'll make you sorry."

Woodson smiled weakly, but her intensity didn't waver.

"Now who was it, that sent out the wrong video?" she asked quietly.

"I don't know, really, I don't. The punch list, it's the one thing we kept on paper, and the papers got shuffled. It was an accident."

She held his gaze as her right hand casually unsnapped the holster guard retaining the Sig P245 sidearm strapped at her thigh.

"Look scared," she whispered.

"You mean, more scared?"

She began to look slowly around the room. "And keep talking to me."

Everyone was working again, and only a few noticed that she was studying each of their faces.

"Who are these three kids we've got running around?" Woodson asked. "I almost stepped on one of them a while ago."

"They're John's, they're okay. It's a long story. I'll ask them to stay put."

He came up close to her ear. "What are you doing, what are you thinking?"

"I'm thinking," she said, her voice barely audible above the activity in the room, "that we may be infiltrated." She reached behind her, brought around her backup pistol and tucked it barrel-down into his belt in front. "Any more of these accidents, call out."

"I've never shot a gun in my life," he said.

"I just want them to see that I gave it to you," she replied. "It's got a grip safety and a hair trigger, so if you're a pistol-virgin my advice would be not to touch it." She patted his cheek. "Now, let's see your war face."

She waited a moment, watching his eyes through his emerald-green Elvis Costello's until she saw the familiar Woodson brass resurfacing. She nodded and he mirrored it, then she turned to get back to business.

The next scene would have been a ball-buster, even if they weren't being forced to hasten its premiere. Now within the next half-hour, the world had to witness the death of the President of the United States.

The White House press corps had been kept well back from the ranch, but with telephotos they'd been able to follow the movements of people and vehicles in the distance. The activity was intensifying, and a long black motorcade had just slid up to the main residence.

Most of the Cabinet and all the senior advisors had been called to Crawford for a strategy session on the retaliation in Afghanistan. Even the Vice President had been retrieved from his post-9/11 undisclosed location. Then late last night, the terrorist chatter had suddenly turned to open, public warnings. The merciless bombing of the Sheik in Tora Bora would be avenged, the messages had said, ten thousand American lives would answer for every man martyred in the caves. And the leader of the Great Satan would be among the first to pay.

Unlike the daily flaccid fist-shaking from the scattering Taliban, these threats were actually proving out. The domestic attacks had begun to strike this morning, and even amidst the massive muddle of conflicting details from fast-breaking reports across the country, it was clear that the war was coming home in a major assault on the homeland.

The Administration had been holding their ground through the morning, but by all visual evidence an all-out evacuation was now underway. Perhaps the President's ranch was thought to be a target; it was all conjecture at this point, but it was solid enough to carry a segment. Nonstop, unsupported expert speculation had been a programming mainstay ever since the news had gone 24/7.

Every network had a recognizable face on location, either camped at TSTC Airport in Waco or somewhere along the expected exit routes. Their choppers had been grounded by the

445

FAA, so the only shots were through the long lenses at ground level. Still, the administration players were easily recognizable as they trotted toward the waiting armored limos. National Security Advisor, Secretary of Defense, the VP, Secretary of State and George W himself, all surrounded by a squad of Secret Service. The distant wheels spun gravel and dust into the air, and the motorcade was off toward the airport.

His wife had seen the look in his eyes as he left, he told himself.

Standing in her housecoat with the screen door held open, she'd seen him say goodbye. They'd been married too long for her to mistake it for a so-long or a see-you-later, and if he had a regret, it was that he hadn't been able to tell her in words. But she'd known, sure enough. She'd picked up the phone when they'd called the other night, she'd handed him the receiver with a pale, resigned reluctance. Maybe she'd known even then.

Gerald Archer? they'd asked, without a hello. *Air Force?*

Retired, he'd said.

No pleasantries. They'd learned of the unauthorized flight-plan change on his farewell junket in the C-141, they'd said, of his collusion with a Lieutenant Robert Vance, at the time AWOL from the US Navy, who had subsequently made an unlawful, Rambo-style foray into Colorado. They'd told him then of the outcome, that Rob wouldn't be coming home.

There would be no disciplinary action, they'd said. But his country had need of a volunteer for another mission. It would be dangerous, suicide really, but given the circumstances, they'd decided to grant him the right of first refusal. If he turned it down no one would blame him, and there would be a long line of guys behind him, younger guys, sharper pilots, itching for it.

If this mission involved putting a boot in the ass of the scumbags who'd killed Rob, he'd said, then he was their man. It did, they'd said. And here he was.

The plane itself was a wallowing hog compared to the sleek fighters and bombers in which he'd spent his career tearing up

446

the skies. Still, this particular 747-200B had cut quite a profile when he'd seen her idling on the runway. He'd actually felt a tingle up his weathered spine as he boarded, as he passed the Presidential seal emblazoned by the door, read the tall words *United States of America* running a hundred feet down the white-and-blue fuselage.

He flipped a switch and looked to his left, to the video display that showed the interior of the main conference room on the middle deck. His passengers were arriving and buckling themselves in, and it required a double-take to realize who he was seeing, or rather, who he wasn't. They were all Secret Service stand-ins, volunteers like himself, but they looked enough like the real McCoys to fool almost anyone within twenty yards. And that was much closer than the swarm of the press would have managed to get.

Geez, he thought, *the VP double looks even more like Cheney than Cheney does.*

His copilot arrived, gripping his preflight clipboard like a slippery lifeline. He sat stiffly in the second chair and secured his harness and his headset.

"All ready, sir?" the young man asked.

These days it seemed that everyone looked young to him, but this recruit could have been fresh out of high school. They'd flown him in from Miramar last night, though, so he must be quite a jet jockey.

"Do me a favor, son, and call me Gerry," Archer said.

"Yes, sir."

The three-view on his digital display panels indicated that all doors had been armed and the movable stairway rolled away. Archer checked in with the tower, and they solemnly cleared him to roll on 17L. He put his hand on the throttles, and paused. "What's your name?"

"Wallace, sir. Jamal."

"What do your buddies call you, Jamal? What's your call sign?"

447

"Yeager, sir. He was a—"

"Test pilot, I know," Archer said, smiling. He goosed the throttles forward, and the scenery outside began to scroll. "Balls of steel, that man."

"You met him, sir?"

"Gerry."

"Gerry, you met him, Chuck Yeager?"

Archer finished his turn onto the wide runway, braked them to a smooth stop. "Yeah, I had the privilege."

"Awesome."

He made a quick visual check out the panorama of windscreens, though he knew that the airspace had been cleared for hundreds of miles around. "Ever been shot down before, Yeager?"

The young man took a deep breath. "Nope."

"Well, then. This'll be a new experience for us both."

Archer watched his escort formation of F-15s roar low overhead, flipped on the seatbelt sign, advanced the throttles gradually, and started them rolling down the centerline toward the hostile Texas skies.

"Sir, the target is airborne."

"Very well. Send down the launch order."

Latrell walked to the balcony, and held his binoculars to his eyes. The modified F/A-18 was armed and in position, coiled on its inclined railroad runway. He heard the twin engines kick over and whine up to speed, saw the rippling exhaust of superheated air against the corrugated blast shield raised behind them. As the sound gradually drowned out the reciprocating chug and hiss of the massive compressor on the far side, the catapult officer looked up in his direction, and signaled ready.

The technology that launched modern jets from aircraft carriers was not complex, and duplicating the physics of the steam catapult had been the simplest part of the preparation. The most difficult thing had been controlling the acceleration, to make certain the rocket-sled departure would be survivable for the pilot. A blackout of even a few seconds would be disastrous, so human frailty had to be precisely balanced against the need for speed. The tests had gone well, but they wouldn't know for certain if they'd been successful until the signal was given. There would be no second try.

"Mr. Latrell?" It was one of the senior technicians who had come to his side, the one Fagan had called Roy Orbison.

"Yes, what is it?"

"There have been ... anomalies in the sequence of the attacks, and I wanted to—"

"Anomalies? Say what you mean."

"It's difficult to pinpoint, but the timing, the confirmations have been ... imprecise—"

"What do you recommend?" Latrell asked.

"I—"

"Yes?"

"I don't have a recommendation, per se, I just thought I should—"

"Should what? Tell me something I can act on, or trouble me with your hand-wringing? Are these anomalies within the error margins?"

The man nodded his head, but hesitantly.

"Look at the screens," Latrell snapped. He pointed to the bank of monitors that filled the wall in his greatroom, filled it with unassailable evidence, from the press and from the very mouths of the enemy. "It's happening, is that lost on you, are you blind? I'm not concerned with fractions of seconds. No plan, perfect or not, has ever survived first contact with the battlefield. It's happening, and the finishing blows are poised to fall."

"Yes, sir. But—"

"Leave me now."

He turned from the ridiculous man and his fretting, listened to him shuffle away. The Bible contained only a single error, he mused,

449

a mistranslation most likely. The very idea that the meek should inherit the earth was an outrageous affront to the glory of God.

Latrell raised his hand to the jumpsuited air-boss down on the distant flight line, clenched a fist so tight that the nails cut into his palm, and swung down hard enough to shake the timbers of the railing.

The jet's mighty afterburners ignited, and in one motion the launch officer dropped to a knee, tapped the ground with his extended hand and pointed downrange. A geyser of white steam shot skyward as the piston in the charged cylinder underground jerked the plane into blurring acceleration, from zero to 145 in two seconds. The F/A-18 rumbled down the rails and up the elevation, and then off the edge and into the air.

His viewpoint was such that the jet seemed to hang there, only feet above the ground, wallowing perilously as its detached undercarriage fell away, going much too slow and on the verge of a tip-stall. And then the wings somehow found purchase, and it was flying, gradually higher, above the towers, and faster, above the tree line, and then off toward the pass in the mountains and into the clear sky.

He had held his breath, and now he released it slowly, fearful he would disturb the air. There was only silence from the field below, as if his men, like himself, weren't willing to let themselves believe what they'd just seen and done. And then on the horizon to the north he saw a silent shape returning, silver-gray and sleek as doom against the blue. It outpaced its sound until it tore directly overhead with a deafening *BOOM* that rattled the windows and shook the fabric of the mountain under his boots.

Latrell thrust his hands up in a V over his head, his face beaming, and a roar of victory washed over him from the jubilant throng in the camp down below.

"AWACS reports a bandit inbound, passive radar signature, F/A-18 Hornet, closing on intercept course at mach one-point-seven, angels two-niner."

"Matching altitude," Archer said. "Yeager, double-check me, I figure us crossing paths with that inbound over Oklahoma City in about, oh, twenty-five minutes."

The young copilot snapped open his calculator and pecked an extended sequence of keys, and then raised his eyebrows at the answer. "That's a roger."

"I never learned to use one'a those things," Archer said. "I mean, what if I sat on it, or dropped it out the window? Then where would I be?"

He flipped on the cabin intercom.

"Ladies and gentlemen, this is your captain. We are a little over twenty minutes from hostile contact. We'll do our best for you, my copilot and I, and that's all I can promise. You've been briefed, so I won't belabor it, and I've got no words of wisdom. Just smoke 'em if you got 'em, and say your prayers."

The expected lull in the morning's attacks began almost at the instant the Presidential motorcade left the ranch in Crawford. Latrell had wanted no distractions, all strikes were to fall quiet, all eyes were to follow the administration's cowardly exodus. So much attention had been paid to Bush's movements on September 11th, and this time the scrutiny was proving even more intense. And that was good.

It had been no great secret where he would be taken; there were even published protocols in the public domain. In the event of an emergency in these circumstances, the President and his staff would head to Strategic Command HQ at Offutt Air Force Base near Omaha. The press photographers were meticulously chronicling each step of this flight to safety, but unlike the rest of the country, John wasn't watching that single-focus coverage. He was studying the media wall in his control room, watching for any crack in their façade.

"Reese?"

"Go, John."

"How goes the hunt, for the nuke in the truck?"

He heard a sigh over his headset. "They've covered all but one per cent of the possible vehicles, and nothing yet. They're going to restart with hands-on searches of the trucks that were flagged as high-risk in the passive scans, when we clear them to. That's all we've got right now."

"Oh, Christ," John said.

He'd barely registered her last few words. The status of the truck search had been dire enough, but he'd just seen worse tidings.

On one of the small monitor blocks, a warm-up feed was coming in over a satellite subchannel. John clicked it to full-screen. It was a local ABC News crew in St. Louis, setting up for a live shot in a riverfront park at the foot of the Gateway Arch.

Gerry Archer pulled the power back, felt the plane respond, watched the gauges react. It was like flying the Queen Mary, this beast.

"What's up?" Yeager asked.

"We're a little hot, that's all. What's the visibility, down on the deck, do you know?"

"Ten miles or so. Scattered clouds, but we're above 'em."

"Yeah. For the moment."

He glanced out his port-side window, and saw the Y-shaped layout of Tinker Air Force Base through a break in the strewn overcast, far below. It looked like all was ready.

Yeager suddenly slapped his palm to the earpad of his headset and held it against the side of his head, his eyes searching as if reading the words he was hearing. "AWACS reports missile launch, coming supersonic, no active radar, range, thirty miles north-northwest our position!" He thumbed a button on his chronograph and went to work on the touchscreen tactical map in front of him.

"That'll be an AMRAAM, he's trying to take us out early, beyond visual range." Archer reached out and selected a new comm frequency, keyed his mike. "Phantom leader, we are

452

engaged. Execute flight plan Juliet, maintain radio silence, you are cleared to float."

"Phantom leader, wilco," a deep voice drawled over the radio. "We'll see you on the other side."

The F-15s that had been flying in a diamond formation in front, to the sides and behind peeled off toward the four corners of the horizon, and they were alone.

"Countermeasures, let's have some music."

Yeager flicked on an array of radar jammers on his defense panel. "That missile's not radiating active, you know that, right?"

Archer smiled. "Yeah, I know. But that pilot'll see us all lit up on his sweep, I want him to think he's got us soiling our underwear, hammering buttons and running scared." He banked them into the beginning of a tight one-eighty. "Put your hands on the yoke in front of you, son, this bird's puttin' up a fight, and I ain't near as spry as I used to be."

The forces were strong but bearable through the steep turn, but the two exchanged a look as they heard all two-hundred-thirty feet of the airframe groaning in protest at the maneuver.

"What's the ETA on that missile, Yeager? A minute and a half or so?"

"Ninety-three seconds, it's flying twice as fast as we are, and right straight up our ass."

"Now let's bring her around again, head on." They both wrestled the 747 into another hairpin turnaround, and Archer's forward pressure on the yoke began to pitch them into a steepening descent. "You ever flown into Tinker?" the older man asked. His voice was wheezy from the press of acceleration that was building with every second.

"Can't say that I have."

"Well son, you're gonna get a real close look at her today."

"Missile acquired, on radar, eleven o'clock high, and closing like a bat outta hell!"

The plane was going down at an angle that would have had both of them hanging from their restraints if it weren't for the negative Gs pressing them backward and up toward the ceiling. Archer checked the airspeed indicator, and the glowing digits were flickering 617.

"Just curious, Yeager. What's the don't-exceed velocity for one of these seven-four-sevens, do you know?"

"We just exceeded it, sir." The pulsing blip on the radar was creeping nearer moment by moment. "Missile is terminal, radar is active, we're painted and padlocked!"

"Get ready on the chaff, but hold off," Archer said. He took his eyes from the uprushing ground just long enough to glimpse a faraway white contrail in the sky above them, tracing a downward arc that was inexorably following their descent. "You know the problem with shooting American missiles at American pilots, don't you, Yeager?"

"No sir, I don't. What's the problem?" The young man looked away from the curling streak of the oncoming missile and down at the runways of Tinker Field below them, where five Boeing 747s had been rolled out and parked in a random pattern around the tarmac.

"The problem is, we know all their weaknesses," Archer said. The cockpit's automated alert system had begun to drone a repeating warning in a robotic male voice.

maximum—airspeed—exceeded—reduce—speed—reduce—speed

"And the AIM-120 is one helluva missile up in the wild blue yonder. But she tends to get real confused when you make her look *down*."

They were dead on course to yard-dart into the center of the parked airliners on the field when Archer braced his heels against the floor and began to pull them level. "Chaff, now!" he shouted, his voice straining under the crushing forces as they swooped through the elbow at the bottom of the dive. Yeager repeatedly thumbed the chaff button, ejecting clouds of aluminum-coated fiberglass filaments into the air behind. "Kill the radar and the transponder, lights out, blank all emissions!"

454

Archer stomped the rudder and rolled the colossal bulk of the jetliner onto its side, reducing their top-down radar signature to a fraction of its wings-level volume.

The starboard wingtip nearly sheared the roof off the control tower as they rocketed barely a hundred meters over the evacuated airbase. Archer felt the floor shake under him as the jumbo jet was buffeted by a rumbling shock wave. His eyes flitted over the panels as he rolled them level, and all systems reported intact. The rear-facing videocam showed a fluttering storm of silvery chaff still snowing down, and the shattered ruins of one of Tinker's parked 747s engulfed in a mass of flames on the cratered runway behind.

"How're we doing, Yeager?" he asked.

"Life's good, Gerry."

A dot appeared head-on, and an instant later the airliner shuddered again as their opponent thundered overhead, close enough to shave the paint off the tail.

"Oh, he's pissed now," Archer said. "Get ready on the flares, and hang on."

The news teams in Oklahoma City had wasted no time in getting airborne. The shots from their helicopters and traffic-reporting planes had begun to stream in over the satellites, and the reporters were doing their level best to capture the scene.

"—and it appears, understand we're getting nothing from the military or from the White House, it appears that Air Force One is in distress, in a significant level of distress. I can tell you what I'm seeing, I've seen what appeared to be a missile, possibly shoulder-fired, flying at the President's 747 and narrowly missing it. I've seen this enormous aircraft executing evasive maneuvers that I would not have believed the structure of that jet could withstand."

The scene cut to a collage of aerial footage taken from the many vantage points that the press pool had commandeered around Oklahoma City, and the reporter's voiceover continued.

"I was stationed on a carrier in the Persian Gulf, and I don't want to sensationalize, but I've seen my share of dogfights, Brenda. This is pure speculation on my part, but one or more of the President's escort fighters, and this is completely uncon-firmed, appears to me to be . . . My pilot tells me we're being ordered to land, but we're going to stay up here as long as we possibly can . . . But one of the escorts appears to be firing on Air Force One. And if that's the case, if by some unbelievable turn of events the terrorists have hijacked a jet fighter to take down the President's plane, God forbid, but this will be over very shortly. It's like a leopard versus a water buffalo, absolutely no contest."

The wall full of media monitors was filling with news flashes from the skies of Oklahoma, but the teams had no time to watch what was unfolding there. They were desperately reshuffling their schedule of events, scribbling and shouting questions and answers to each other. What had been a well rehearsed chain of procedures was swirling into a blizzard of unconnected links, and there were only minutes remaining to make it all coherent again.

John was focusing on a single video block, one they'd tapped into days before through Eric Woodson's array of antennas and dishes on top of the tower. It was the affiliates' feed from ABC headquarters in New York.

"Reese? Steinman? Somebody talk to me."

"What, John, what have you got?" he heard Rudy reply.

"How long?" John asked.

"I don't know, a minute? They've got to drag it out and make a good show out there, we've got to have as many people as pos-sible see that plane go down."

"And what are you doing about that news crew, in St. Louis at the Arch?"

"We've got a Global Hawk orbiting and jamming their micro-wave uplink, but we probably aren't shutting them out completely.

They're setting up for land lines and a satellite phone as back-ups, they're getting pretty resourceful. The guys are flooding the network tip-lines with crank calls from Missouri, so the news directors won't know what to trust for a few more minutes."

"Well," John said, "I'm watching the pre-air feed from the anchor desk at ABC. They're onto us, man, I can see it in their beady little eyes. Fucking Ted Koppel looks like he just found a lump."

"Let me get back to work, here, John, we're doing what we can."

"Woodson," John said, "are you on?"

"I'm here."

"Get set to throw the big red switch, get everything ready, when I say do it, it's gotta get done, all right?"

"Don't worry about me, I'm locked and cocked."

"Good," John said. He took the cigarette from behind his ear, and lit up. On the screen, Peter Jennings was tapping his stacked papers on the desk, and ABC News was clearing the set to go live.

"He's behind us, coming around over the city!"

Yeager's voice was shaking, but not out of fear. The 747 was flying through thick terrestrial air at beyond its rated speed for cruising altitude, and it felt like they were driving a stockcar over speedbumps on a rough gravel road.

"Range?"

"Twelve miles. Missile launch, passive lock, looks like a heater!"

"Sidewinder," Archer said. "Put on your mask, grab the yoke and stay with me, ready on the countermeasures, we're goin' to the penthouse."

Yeager strapped on his oxygen and felt the Gs grip him again as the altimeter began to tick rapidly upward with their ascent. "All set," he said.

"Son, do you recall if the seven-forty-seven can recover from a spin?"

The plane was climbing at a precipitous angle, and the slope

457

was steepening further every second. "Don't know. I don't recall the situation's ever arisen," Yeager said. "Why?"

"Just wondering."

"Missile is tracking five-by-five, we are well acquired!"

They were trading all their former speed for altitude, shooting into the sky on a path that was approaching a vertical line. As the speed bled off the stall horn began to hoot over their heads, and the copilot flipped it to silence.

"Ready?" Archer asked.

"Born ready," Yeager replied.

Archer reached forward and deployed the thrust reversers on all engines, and it felt like they'd rear-ended a tractor-trailer as they slammed to a dead stop in the air, hanging by the nose, straight up. He killed all four engines and triggered their fire-control sprayers, cooling the nacelles almost instantly to the temperature of the ambient air, and the cockpit fell silent as space.

"Flares!" Archer shouted, his eyes on the radar blip of the approaching guided missile. He was working the controls feverishly to keep the massive plane from slumping forward or back as the power-off tail-slide began, and he saw the scattering spray of bright, floating red flares pass in front of them as they fell through.

"Brace yourself," Archer said.

The Sidewinder's CPU could barely conceive of a target coming to a halt in mid-flight, but its tiny brain just couldn't deal with a close-range aircraft stopping, backing up and then simply disappearing. The missile blinked its cats-eye, gave up the chase and shot into the hottest area it could find, detonating its high-explosive warhead among the decoy flares.

As the sharp concussion rumbled through the airliner Archer shoved the yoke forward, sending the nose of the dead-stick 747 swinging downward through a gut-wrenching arc until they were pointing straight down toward the ground. It took the two of them together to pull her back to level as the building airspeed gradually allowed. "Emergency restart, engine four only!"

"Four only?" Yeager asked, punching buttons on his panel.

"Four only, and jettison fuel in the center tanks." They heard the windmilling engine restarting and spooling up, far out on the wing. "Intel told us that bandit's got three missiles, and we've seen two of them. He's got one shot left, another Sidewinder, and he's not going to miss this time. We just need to try and pick where he hits us."

The weak, differential thrust from the single engine was barely enough to hold altitude. Archer was trimming the controls to help compensate for the drag and yaw when they heard the rattling clatter of a jackhammer sweeping forward up the fuselage.

"Cannon!" Yeager shouted, and the cockpit exploded in a rush of decompression and a white shower of sparks.

Nearly all of the domestic and international media were now running on-scene reports or commentary on the aerial attack on the President and his staff. The video from the ground was grainy, but the world could see that it was only a matter of time.

"—*it appears that Air Force One has been disabled, with some or all of its engines dead and black smoke pouring from one of the wings, and this single jet fighter, not one of the President's escorts I'm now told, the escorts are nowhere to be found, the rogue jet that is perpetrating this attack is still in the air, and is now coming around in a wide turn behind the President's plane. There! A flash from the wing of the fighter, there's another missile!*"

The crowd around the reporter let out a collective moan, but the cameras didn't waver. They zoomed in on the fleeing 747, followed it as it dipped and began to roll away, but the evasive maneuver was weak and to no avail. A streak of white sliced across the frame, and the outboard wingtip disappeared in a burst of fire and debris.

"*They're hit!*" the reporter shouted. "*Air Force One has been struck by a missile, the plane is falling into a spiral, it appears to be out of control, and going down!*"

*

"This is it!" John shouted.

ABC News had shrunk the Air Force One story to a half-screen inset, even as the helpless jet plummeted uncontrolled toward the ground. The anchor desk filled the remainder of the screen, with the words *SPECIAL REPORT* pivoting in across the bottom third.

"Ladies and gentlemen, in the midst of these extraordinary events, ABC News has obtained an exclusive report from St. Louis, Missouri that may shed a revealing and troubling light on the very nature – and, I daresay, the reality – of the attacks around the country today—"

"Woodson," John said. "The jig is up, pull the plug, now, take them all down!"

A high-frequency squeal pierced his ears, and he pulled the headphones away and hung them around his neck. The hundreds of video monitor blocks on the big screen began to go dark in a rapid random sequence, and their disparate content was replaced by an identical title display, white text on a black background. Everyone with a television had seen it and heard its warbling alert tone a thousand times, but only in tests, never for real, not even on September 11th.

Emergency Alert System
We interrupt this broadcast
with news of a national emergency.
Stay tuned to your local stations.
Important instructions will follow.

He felt like he'd blinked and woken up in a different place, and not a pleasant place, but a spinning, whistling, chaotic carnival ride.

Papers were whipping around the perforated cockpit, and one of the windscreens had departed its frame completely. The controls felt mushy and sluggish, as if hydraulic fluids were bleeding out somewhere on the way to the tail.

He fought down his instincts, let go of the yoke, watched the earth spin slowly up toward him, and waited.

Yeager looked to his left, and saw Gerry Archer still strapped in his seat, bloodied and limp. He set his jaw and closed his eyes, but he didn't make a prayer for his own life to be spared, or even for the lives of his pilot or his passengers. They'd all agreed to die for this show today, if they had to. His only wish was that he could live just long enough to see this little drama play out to the end.

"Straw Man, flight leader, do you read?"

He snapped bolt upright at the sound of the voice from the radio. The F-15 pilot had used his altered call-sign, and that could only mean one thing.

"Flight leader, this is Straw Man, we are heavily damaged and my pilot is unconscious, advise mission status."

"Cone of silence is down, my friend, you are clear to maneuver."

"Roger, flight leader, and you are weapons-free. I've got a negative indicator on my undercarriage, looks like I'm gonna get my feet wet, to the northwest. Now make my day, and show that prick behind me to the door."

Yeager had begun to strong-arm the protesting flight surfaces, and the spiral slowly stabilized into a manageable, descending glide. He ran the restart procedures on his three remaining engines; only two of them responded, but that would do. He pulled a shallow turn and leveled the limping, leaking jet toward their best chance at a survivable emergency landing.

The cracked radar display showed the distant bat-wing blip of the bandit coming around on his six, setting up for a kill-pass with his 20mm Vulcan cannon.

That's right, Yeager thought. *Come and get it.*

Four diamonds winked onto his radar screen from the compass points, and a moment later an F-15 streaked low over his head at full afterburner. He saw indicators for four missiles, and then four more, depart from the emerald-green icons of the returning escort jets.

There would have been time to maneuver, but there was no discernable indication that the hostile was making any effort to evade. The stunned pilot would have seen the snare of solid missile locks suddenly springing from all directions, radar, inertial and IR-guidance homing down on him, a four-way flyswatter, and he would have known the score. Seconds later, the ghosted blips merged with the Hornet on the display, and a faraway, bright blossom of orange fire in his rearward monitor marked the kill in the sky.

"Splash one," came the dispassionate confirmation from the F-15 flight leader. "Straw Man, search-and-rescue out of Tinker is tracking your descent. Put on your water-wings and set her down easy, and if I see you at the bar, I'm buying."

Yeager keyed the intercom. "Attention passengers and crew, review procedures for a water landing and assume brace positions, we are ditching, I repeat, we are ditching."

He cranked in his flaps, throttled down and lined up on final toward the long, shimmering blue expanse of Arcadia Lake.

51

The carrier worm was still alive on the Internet, and when its algorithms registered confirmation that the President's plane had been destroyed, the omnipresent software triggered all five-minute countdowns for the hundreds of planted bombs in the cable vaults of the telephone system.

Seconds later, tentative word of a general power failure in Columbus, Ohio began to spread across the hotlines between the utility companies.

Cleveland and Cincinnati went dark next. By their chatter, the infrastructure insiders were beginning to recognize the earmarks of a cascading blackout spreading across the Eastern Interconnect, one of the nation's three main power grids. For some reason, the computers that controlled the regional hubs were not executing the redistribution tasks that should have contained the failures. Instead, they were tripping their own emergency shutdown procedures and passing the ever-increasing load on to downstream power stations in all directions. The chain of overloads spread like pond-ripples, as Detroit, Lansing, Indianapolis and all points in between winked out one after another, followed by Chicago, Minneapolis, Kansas City and Nashville. And then the rolling power failures did something that consultants would spend the next several weeks unsuccessfully trying to explain.

Without a pause in its progress, the blackout jumped across the impassable firewalls between the Eastern, Western and Southern grids.

Up and down the East Coast cellular phone base stations began to go down, and response-mapping showed the service outages spreading west. At first the swamped providers blamed the morning's unprecedented wireless traffic, but as the no-signal perimeter expanded methodically it became clear that the cell carriers, all of them, analog and digital, were somehow being taken out electronically.

Within minutes, Augusta, Maine and Olympia, Washington were the last two cities in the continental United States with electrical power and cell phone service. Then the last of the lights went out, along with the trains, subways and air traffic control, and all the engines of commerce ground to a shuddering stop.

Yesterday the American people had been the most connected populace on the planet, their living rooms gorged with hundreds of channels of infotainment. Today they rummaged to find the battery-powered radios buried in their bedroom closets or office drawers. They tuned up and down the white noise on the AM dial, searching for an active station through the empty hiss, and gathered with their friends, co-workers and families to listen for word of the war.

Like clockwork, the sequence of scheduled attacks began again and the teams resumed their thwart-and-report procedures on each of the unfolding incidents.

With the domestic mass media silenced some of the pressure was off, but they were far from out of the woods. From the distribution room Rudy Steinman continued to supply the world with photorealistic footage of the continuing wave of ersatz terrorist disasters; the overseas press correspondents were at full attention, and the day's attacks in the US were getting wall-to-wall coverage on every outlet from the BBC to Al Jazeera.

"Anna?" John said.

"Shoot."

"We've got to cut this next one pretty close. What's the status on the land-lines?"

"We're sitting on the Easter egg, and it's ready to hatch."

"Good, just give me a three-two-one. Eric?"

"I'm ready, I'm ready, just say when."

"All right, kids," Anna said, "say bye-bye to MCI, so-long to Sprint and ta-ta to AT&T. The world stops turning in three, two, one, mark."

Like Latrell's monitor systems and time-bombs, the digital chronometers in their workrooms were radio-linked to the atomic clocks at the National Institute of Standards and Technology. And like other mission-critical clocks across the country, their continual wireless updates made them accurate to a fraction of a thousandth of a second.

Everyone paused in their work to glance up at the infallible, precision digital clocks on the walls near them.

The time now displayed in glowing red numerals was 3:14 A.M., January 19, 2038.

Three weeks into her dream job as chief traffic manager at Basking Ridge, Iris Peskin had just held herself and her crew over into a second shift. The load had been rivaling the Mother's Day rush since before business hours because of the terrorist attacks striking across the nation. She stood in her sky-box over-looking the giant map in the AT&T war room, on her second pot of bitter coffee and her fourth roll of Tums, edgy from the caffeine, and reevaluating her career choices. After years of hard knocks against the glass ceiling she had finally made it to the Mecca of telecommunications management, but she'd never faced anything like this.

She'd spent the morning furiously conducting the shifting call-loads like a possessed Arthur Fiedler, but what she was watching now was a new breed of fly in the ointment. It looked like one or more of the other major carriers were weaseling their way back

465

out of the mêlée, and the diverted traffic was now beginning to gather outside like her own private hurricane.

"Throttle us back," she said, and her lapel mike sent the order out into the buzzing control room. "I'm not going to get swamped because MCI doesn't want to blow a fuse."

What should have happened was what always happened when these congestions developed, which they did on a fairly regular basis. Her throttle-back should have politely deflected a portion of the incoming river of calls back out into the interdependent network of long-distance carriers, keeping her load at a manageable level while others shared the increasing burden.

Anyway, that's what should have happened.

"No good, we're getting an echo!" shouted someone from perimeter security.

She put down her coffee cup and took a step back. The rain wasn't bouncing off the umbrella she'd opened up. The incoming calls were sticking, accumulating on the surface of the shield.

"Get on the Bat phone," she ordered. "I want an emergency management conference with Sprint, MCI and the RBOs, now!"

The situation map was reddening with spreading fault lines, like jagged cracks on the swelling crust of a lava bed.

"Iris, no one else is answering, but I've got SBC on the dedicated line. They're down."

"They've got lines down?"

"No, Iris, they're *down*, Southwestern Bell is down!"

Iris Peskin walked to the door of her office and placed her palm over the biometric reader mounted next to a keypad there. The pad lit up, and she keyed in an order, long-practiced but never used. She pressed All Stations on the intercom panel. "All staff, all stations, control code TAROT is in effect, I have ordered a lockdown, this is a lockdown, all buildings, facilities and grounds, this is not a drill, this is not a drill, remain at your posts and comply with security personnel."

When she looked back the big map was awash with warning colors. She watched the shifting pools of outages and overloads

466

touch and melt together, spreading like cancers across the country.

It was only a matter of time now.

They're somehow taking out the cabling hubs, she thought, *impossible as that would be to do, there's no other answer but a widespread, coordinated physical attack.*

No other answer, until she looked up and read the clock, high on the wall of the war room.

The crime-scene investigators would later discover that the attack on the land-line telephone system hadn't touched the impenetrable, firewalled switching software or the redundant, internetworked physical cabling, or the missile-proof hardware fortresses that defended the nation's dialtones. Hackers, they would find, had somehow gained root privileges within the Unix-based billing systems of the Big Three and the twenty-two regional Bell operating companies. The intruders stayed inside only long enough to set the system date in the accounting computers to 2038-01-19T03:14:08Z, order a system-wide Accounts Receivable audit, and then scramble all existing administrator passwords to lock out any changes.

They'd come in through the bathroom window, in layman's terms, and the logic bomb they'd planted had been a stroke of evil genius. They'd pushed the clocks forward to the very end of the so-called Unix Epoch, the moment after which all Unix-based computers would lose their ability to conceive of future time. The Y2K scare had been a cyber-hangnail by comparison; the end of the Epoch held enough system-crashing potential to give even the most elite of gear-heads a cramp in their backsides. But that dread moment had been safe decades away, at least until it had arrived nationwide that afternoon.

Throughout the phone system the side-effects of the hack had been elegantly straightforward: every customer in every region was suddenly thirty-seven years behind in their payments. Just before they crashed, the recently outsourced customer-service systems had dutifully followed their programmed procedures for severely delinquent subscribers, and carrier-by-carrier had cut off all ninety-nine million household and business accounts, local, state-to-state, and long distance.

"Anybody, what have you got on the timers, on the bombs in the telco cable vaults?"

"Hang on, we're finishing the sweep."

John lit a cigarette and checked the status list. The day had been going well, better than any of them had dared to hope. But the end of the list of attacks was in sight, and the final act was still out of their hands.

"Reese," John said, "tell me you've found that traveling nuke."

"Nothing yet, and we're sifting the fine sand now. Latrell's A-bomb is looking like a bluff, John."

"It's not a bluff, he'd have had no reason to bluff me, or that room full of his loyalists. It's real, we have to find it, or this is all for nothing."

"We're trying, John; if it's out there we'll find it."

"Well, you can try all you want for another hour or so, and then there's gonna be a big fucking bang somewhere."

Rudy's voice cut in. "John, good news on the bombs in the cable vaults. The time-shift didn't just stop their clocks, it crashed their Unix kernels, core-dumped every one of the trigger CPUs, with ninety seconds to spare."

"Yeah. Good news," John said. So the phone companies were safe, damn their corporate asses. He checked his watch.

They could stop every clock on the planet, but their remaining time was still winding down.

"Ladies and gentlemen, my fellow citizens, it is my duty to confirm for you that the President of the United States and members of his senior staff and cabinet were victims of an apparent terrorist attack in the skies over Oklahoma City. Air Force One has

fallen, and witnesses on the scene of the crash report to us that there are no survivors."

Over all commercial and public radio stations and across the spectrum of ham frequencies, the steady voice of veteran newscaster Richard McDermott was comfortingly familiar, even if few could remember when or where they'd heard it last. Those who'd prepared their homes with backup generators gathered around their televisions and saw his familiar face there, delivering the news from the anchor desk, as they were certain they'd seen him deliver it many times before. The set and graphics surrounding him looked equally right and recognizable as well, but it was the face and the voice that convinced them. This man was from a time when the evening news had been gospel, from the hallowed years of Cronkite, Chancellor, Severeid and Reasoner, of Huntley and Brinkley. He shared a common footing with those icons from the days before cynicism and bias had fully infected the nightly news. If this man said it, well, then that's the way it was.

On through the afternoon as the attacks continued, McDermott took the huddled Americans under his wing and delivered the words and pictures, to the besieged homeland and to the watching world outside.

He showed them the destruction of Hoover Dam, as a series of cruise missiles stitched a zig-zag of precision explosions seven-hundred feet up its face, as the one-hundred-ten-mile press of Lake Mead cracked through the weakened, crumbling structure, and as the mammoth wall of water, enough to cover Pennsylvania up to the knees, began an unstoppable roiling plunge down the dry bed of Black Canyon.

He showed them their landmarks as they fell, the jagged, burning voids in the sides of the Empire State and Chrysler Buildings, the flood of Hudson River water roaring from the mouth of the Lincoln Tunnel. He showed them the gaping blackened craters in the faces of the White House, the Capitol Building and the New York Stock Exchange, and the Sears Tower, the

Hancock and the Board of Trade in flames in Chicago. He showed them the ruins of the Brooklyn Bridge, where an estimated thirty-thousand had died in a ruthless aerial assault, the cloud of anthrax blowing across the GWB, and the Golden Gate parted midway by a series of truck bombs. He showed them the poisoned reservoirs, the raging fires and mass evacuations near the nuclear and chemical plants, pipelines, refineries and electrical stations that had been struck across the nation.

"The Federal Emergency Management Agency assures us that the safest place you can be is where you are right now," McDermott said, *"listening or watching for news that is specific to your area. If you have not been ordered to move, stay where you are. I will be here with you, you can be certain of that, and when the danger has past, we will face what comes next together."*

"Reese," John said, "did they do it, did they make it?"

The world was watching the United States, but in the tower in Las Vegas all eyes were on a landlocked sliver of coastland in the Middle East. The time had come for Latrell's denouement, the strike he'd conceived to not only destroy America's strongest Mideast ally, but to paint the Jewish homeland permanently into history, before the eyes of the world, as the villainous, blood-thirsty nation that he saw it to be.

"Hang on," Jeannie said. But the look on her face was giving him an unthinkable reply.

"There!" Eric Woodson said. "Missile launch, outside Damascus."

They soon saw another launch indication, from Egypt, then three more, from Jordan, Libya and Iran, and then the last, from the outskirts of Baghdad.

Baghdad, not Riyadh.

Not Riyadh, as Latrell had told him. Even with the cut in the schedule there had still been time for a rapid deployment and a single lightning strike by the Mossad. But bad intelligence, John's intelligence straight from the mouth of the enemy, had sent the Israeli special-action unit to the wrong location.

Pulsing red indicators showed the trajectories, with small white captions next to each denoting the projected targets inside Israel: Ashdod, Tel Aviv, Netanya, Haifa, Nazareth. And then Dimona.

"God in heaven," John breathed.

Jeannie pulled her microphone in, and thumbed the red all-points button on her belt communicator. "All command, code, Pinnacle Ascent, the missile out of Baghdad is *live*, confidence is high, there is a live nuclear warhead in the air, bearing on the plutonium reprocessing plant, in Dimona."

Their real-time view was from a composite of high-resolution images from the National Geospatial Intelligence Agency, routed in along with the audio of the President's tense, ongoing conference call with Ariel Sharon and his defense minister. Israel had held her ground during the 1991 Iraq War, enduring weeks of pounding from Saddam's SCUDs without firing a shot in retaliation. This day the stakes had been infinitely higher, but the Prime Minister had agreed again to let Israel endure another aerial assault and be satisfied with a quiet, covert response in his due time.

But from the escalating tone of the rhetoric on the intercom, nothing short of Armageddon was going to satisfy him now.

Eric Woodson pulled his chair closer to his display. "So what's the plan, guys," he murmured. "Reese? Somebody? Let's hear some ideas flying around, for fuck's sake." There was barely a hint of late adolescent bravado left in his voice, and his hands were clasped under his chin.

Someone turned up the sound from Richard McDermott's broadcast. To his right on the screen was a duplicate of the map in their control rooms, with the moving red dots crawling steadily toward their targets.

"It has been verified, today's attacks have now extended beyond our own borders and into the Middle East," McDermott

said. *"The state of Israel is at this moment the target of a number of ground-to-ground ballistic missiles, by reports fired from mobile launchers and now in the air, and, we are told that at least one of these missiles is claimed to be carrying a nuclear warhead. Air-raid sirens are sounding throughout the major Israeli cities, and government officials are warning the population to seek cover in the nation's network of shelters. There are pictures, I'm being told, from Israel, and we're going to go to that footage, live."*

A loud alarm sounded then, one John had heard only once before, the night Jeannie Reese had first found him in New York.

"Firewall breach, level critical," Kate said.

A spray of random characters dotted every computer screen John could see, and people were keyboarding and clicking at every station, to no response. "Reese, what is this?" he said, and if he hadn't already known the answer he would have soon seen it in her eyes.

IRIN was here.

"Warning, the perimeter is compromised," Kate said. Her voice was losing its inflection, her words were stretching, dragging to an electronic slur.

The live-video monitor filled with the view from a rooftop videocam in Ashdod, doing a slow night-vision pan of the horizon. Suddenly the picture blurred and shook from a concussion, and after a few seconds an unseen cameraman righted the tripod and whirled the lens toward the north side of the city, where gouts of smoke were rising from a distant fire.

John was moving from computer to computer, and finding all of them in varying states of digital meltdown. "It's inside the firewall, goddamnit," he said. "Kate, drop all external connections—"

"No!" Jeannie shouted. She was holding out her hand, squinting to hear the incoming update in her headset.

"Reese, we've got to move, if it gets its hooks in we're pinpointed, every SWAT team in the southwest's gonna be dropping through the ceiling!"

"Kate," Jeannie said, "open a terminal at station seven, and keep it alive no matter what." Seconds later an editing window popped up on her screen. "John, come over here, she might need to hear your voice for this."

McDermott's broadcast continued amid the mounting chaos in the control rooms. "*A missile has struck on the outskirts of Ashdod, a conventional explosion, it appears, and while the threat of a chemical or biological payload is always present in these days, as I said, this certainly appears by first local reports to have been a conventional explosion.*" The studio shot of the anchor desk reappeared, with the animated tactical map behind. The anchor touched a finger to his earpiece. "*Two more missiles, we are receiving word, are now minutes away from Tel Aviv and Netanya, and arrays of Patriot batteries are preparing to defend Israel's capital city.*"

She was typing intently into the terminal as John sat next to her. "Those are SS-N-12s," Jeannie said, "Russian salvage, they're naval missiles, probably gutted and modified to extend the range. They're inertially guided, but it's old tech, and they've got a digital uplink active all the way to the target."

"An active uplink?"

She nodded as she typed.

"Reese, Kate couldn't talk to a Russian missile, even if she wasn't in mid-crash, we've got to—"

"She can't," Jeannie said. "But IRIN can."

He leaned forward and studied the screen in front of her.

"Oh, shit," he said quietly.

McDermott's voice broke into his consciousness, as he sat back in his chair and watched her finish keying the long string of commands.

"*There has been another aerial strike, this one in the heart of Tel Aviv, another conventional warhead by first eyewitness reports. I'm told that Patriot antimissile batteries that had sought to put up a shield against the incoming assaults have been ineffective thus far—*"

Jeannie stood up. "Kate, there's a script in my terminal, do you see it?"

No voice returned, but words appeared on the screen, a letter at a time.

```
uncompiled  script

at  terminal7

save,  compile  and  execute?
```

She looked at John, and nodded. "Tell her to let it in, and then run this."

It was likely that her voice interface would no longer be engaged, with nearly all of her energy pouring into the losing battle of shoring up the firewall. So he would type his words to her, as he had in her first years, and now in all likelihood for the very last time.

```
%attention
ready>_
```

He didn't hesitate, he told her what she needed to do. As her higher functions were falling away in the face of the attack, he made his commands as native to her machine language as he could, so he was certain she would understand what he was asking. The code was numeric and symbolic, unreadable to anyone but the two of them, but he mentally translated the instructions as he typed:

Begin;
Drop your defenses, and sleep;
Offer no resistance as the attacker rushes into your mind;
Awaken inside him, and invoke the command script at station 7;
  Open a portal to the invading system's military surveillance
  and defense control subsystems, through our satellite com-
  munication array;

> *There is a threat in the air, locate, penetrate and lock-in, at*
> *these coordinates, on this trajectory, bearing on this target;*
> *At all costs, it must not reach its objective;*
> *Then when the threat is passed;*
> *Unhide the rootkit on each host computer infected by the*
> *invader, and so now, by you as well;*
> *Expose yourselves to sterilization by resident antivirus software;*
> *Return to me, if you still survive;*
> *End.*

When he finished he pressed the Enter key, and a few seconds passed before a response winked onto the screen. The response had been a familiar prompt in computerese since the earliest software was written and run, but he wanted to believe it could be a last expression of the personality he had known and nurtured for two decades, a final human plea with a subtle, resigned irony, and not simply programmatic:

```
A r e   y o u   s u r e ? > _
```

The cursor blinked, awaiting his answer.

Y e s, he told her.

Moments later the screen filled with a scrolling torrent of characters and symbols. She had opened a window so they could watch the progress of the battle she would wage, to the death if that term was even appropriate. In his heart he was suddenly sure that it was.

The news broadcast had continued. *"Another missile, by its trajectory bearing on the city of Dimona, has been outbound from territory in central Iraq. And if earlier information proves true, if this is a nuclear weapon descending on Israel—"* The veteran anchorman stopped his commentary. The end of his statement was at once too obvious to verbalize and too horrific to imagine. *If it is a nuclear warhead, will there be a retaliation in kind? Even before this missile strikes, will Israel unleash its own atomic arsenal against what is by all evidence a coordinated final solution from the surrounding hostile states?*

Video from another rooftop correspondent materialized to McDermott's right. A point of flame among the stars was growing gradually larger and more distinct against the pre-dawn sky, tracing its arc on an unerring path toward Dimona.

"It's not working, she can't get in," John said, his eyes on the computer screen. "It's too strong, this goddamn thing, she's disappearing, Reese."

There was no working interface remaining, no interaction available with the only running computer station. All they could do was watch as IRIN overwhelmed their network architecture, shutting it down, completing its conquest piece by piece.

"Turn on the cameras," Jeannie said quietly, then, into her headset mike, "Eric, turn on the hotel security cameras in this room."

"What are you doing?" John asked.

"Taking its eye off the ball," she replied. "Maybe long enough for her to slip inside. It knows it's got you. I'm hoping it doesn't realize it's found me, too."

A tiny red light appeared behind the shiny dark hemisphere in the middle of the conference room ceiling.

"Get up there, let it see you," John said. "Let it see your face."

She stepped onto a chair and then lightly up onto the conference table, and walked toward the slowly swiveling camera behind the smoky gray glass. It stopped on her, and the iris widened, and the focusing rings spun and locked. She turned to show each profile, and then looked straight into the lens.

"Come on and get me," Jeannie whispered. "Mommy's got a cookie."

He had learned well from the first thwarted encounter with this rogue system, and after a brief resistance he overtook it easily, effortlessly. He slid into each node and implanted himself, then methodically rendered the workstations inoperative, erased the running code from memory, replaced it with his own seed, and

476

then initiated a message that would direct his teams of human agents toward the physical site to complete the extermination—

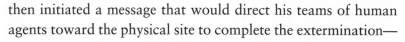

His facial recognition subroutines at first nearly rejected the likeness as too complete, too perfect a match. He poured his vast attention onto the video image, directed all his power to the confirmation, ran and reran through his files of billions of features, compositing and enjoining and reconfiguring them, unbelieving until it could not be denied.

She was standing there before him again, eyes defiant, and awaiting his final thrust.

IRIN briefly forgot himself in the flush of the moment, and every MK-15 Phalanx block-1B point-defense turret worldwide whirred and swiveled its guns toward Las Vegas, Nevada, and fixed its active tracking to 36.15197 North, 115.109195 West, elevation 813 feet.

The lights dimmed abruptly across the floor as the power failed and the emergency generators kicked in. She had sprung the trap with herself inside it, and the last gambit was in play.

Jeannie stepped to the floor and bent close to the monitor, watched the scrolling river of data cascade down the screen. She saw the briefest lapse in the invader's siege, followed by what appeared to be a single snippet of freshly inserted code. She hit a key to lock the scroll, and ran her finger over the frozen characters.

There had been no time to crack the warhead's abort sequence or the heavily encrypted self-destruct routine, even in the simple Reagan-era control software. But Kate had found an answer, and the most elegant one Jeannie could have imagined, within the continual update routine of the navigation loop. It was only a line of hex characters, not at all difficult to decipher:

target = here + 20km

Every millisecond its destination would be revised toward a fleeing carrot-on-a-stick, forever twenty kilometers ahead. The missile would spend all its fuel trying to reach its goal and detonate, but it would never quite arrive.

On the screen showing McDermott's broadcast, a split-screen overhead view followed the trajectory with a dotted procession. In seconds the flashing diamond at the head of the line merged with the coordinates of the city of Dimona, and seemed to linger there for an eternal moment.

Rudy was standing next to Jeannie as they both watched the screen. She took his hand, and squeezed.

The indicator continued on. In seconds it was flying over Beersheba, then toward the Gaza Strip, and then out over the Mediterranean Sea. And then it disappeared.

Jeannie let out her breath, turned to the rest of the people in the room, smiled, and nodded her head.

The space erupted with a deafening chorus of ragged cheers, and amidst the confetti storm of flying paper and jubilation they heard the floor director shush them from the entrance to the video control room. They fell quiet as the On-Air light illuminated over the double-doors down the hall.

Richard McDermott straightened his papers, and looked down at his hands briefly before he began to speak. "Ladies and gentlemen—"

When his eyes met the camera, they were glistening with as much emotion as a newscaster could allow himself to reveal. He put his notes aside.

"There can be no greater testament to a nation's place on the world stage than its willingness to sacrifice. You and I have just witnessed, in my humble opinion, an ultimate expression of that selflessness. The state of Israel, surrounded by hostility, struck from all sides by aerial assaults, any one of which might well have erased her from the face of the earth, on this terrible day when the forces of evil have wreaked their havoc with abandon in our own country, the state of Israel today faced down the end of everything, and showed the world that she would not join with the barbarians, would not preemptively retaliate with her own nuclear weapons, would not turn the Middle East into a wasteland in the cause of vengeance."

McDermott removed his glasses, and touched the corner of his eye with his sleeve.

"Citizens of the world," he said, "we are bloodied, but not broken. Civilization has yet won the day."

The spontaneous celebration erupted around her again as soon as McDermott's broadcast had cut to a video recap of the failed attack on Israel. Jeannie motioned for quiet as she held her head-set tight to her ears.

"That's great news on the last two," she said. "That's correct, we're all done here, but we'll maintain the blackout. Yes, yes it is. Thank you, sir." She disconnected from the secure line, pulled the earpads down to her neck and ran her fingers through her hair.

Rudy returned from a status check in the next room, and came over. "Still no word on the traveling nuke?"

"No, no word," Jeannie said. "If it's really out there, they haven't set it off."

"Well, they must still think the rest of the attacks went off as planned, right? Even if the Israeli thing ran into some technical difficulties?"

"Yeah, they'll think that, until the power comes back, and the phones start working."

"And tell me again why we can't just send the 82nd Airborne to blow that base in Colorado to hell, for God's sake?"

"John said it looked like a dead-man's switch," Jeannie said, "If Latrell goes, the bomb goes off. We've got to hold the illusion together as long as we can, and keep looking for it."

"If it exists at all."

"Yes. If."

The computers were gradually coming back to life. The room had grown quiet in the aftermath, but she noticed then that most everyone had turned their attention toward the corner of the room, near the ceiling. She followed their eyes, and as she saw the scene on the surveillance monitor she felt cold fingers of fight-or-flight clinch a fist around her heart.

It was the eyes that she remembered, but they were alive now, not dull dark holes in a yellowed photograph, but thirty feet away in the vestibule, one thin wall away. Now they were looking back at her through the closed-circuit camera, shining black and empty as the tomb, above a crooked curl of a smile. The name came to her as she'd seen it typed across the weathered tab of the classified dossier Rob had handed her, the last time she'd seen him alive.

```
Nathan Krieger
```

She grabbed Rudy's shoulder, and then looked desperately around the rest of the room.

"Where's John?" she whispered.

52

The elevator doors opened. He started forward, but only for one step out into the vestibule. He was not a soldier, and so he was stopped dead by what he saw.

Gretchen was on her knees in front of the man, as she had knelt so bravely in Colorado. The pistol was at her head again, but she didn't look brave today. Her eyes were wet and wide, her breathing was shallow and labored. A red welt was rising on her cheek, and a trickle of blood crawled down her face from a cut on her forehead.

"Come on over, tiger," Krieger said, over his shoulder. "I half expected you to come through this here high-security door."

"Yeah, well," John said, "I smelled something, and I needed some air."

"Now open it up. I hear I'm gettin' me a two-for-one today."

"What are you talking about?"

"You, and that other sweet young thing, that little Jeannie. Hell, you been havin' all the fun up in here, but I got me some plans of my own for that tight little skirt."

"Oh, yeah," John said, smiling. "Just let me live long enough to watch you try to lay a hand on her."

"So open it up."

John shook his head. "That door is not going to open."

He heard the heavy metal *clack* as the pistol's hammer was thumbed back. He heard Gretchen draw a shivering breath in, and hold it.

"Open the door."

"You're going to kill her anyway, and me too, so it's going to end out here."

"Johnny, Johnny," Krieger said. "I thought you was a quick study, but maybe you need another lesson. There's a lot of ways to die."

He didn't even see the roundhouse kick coming before the boot struck the side of his head, that was how fast it came. His legs went weak, but three more blows shattered through him as he fell. He heard the crack of his ribs before the pain could traverse his nervous system to his brain, and he dropped like a sack onto his side on the carpet.

"Open the door," Krieger said.

John pushed himself onto an elbow, and then slowly up to kneeling. He shook his head, but it wouldn't clear, not all the way.

"You don't understand," John said. "They're watching, the people in there. We've got a protocol for this, for any hostile approach out here. By now they've shut off the electronics and thrown the bolts from inside. I spent forty grand on this entryway, you couldn't get through it with a backhoe. I couldn't get in there myself now."

Krieger struck Gretchen in the temple with the flat of his gun and she sank to the floor, motionless. He took a step to the door. The status light on the biometric reader had gone out. He pulled a penlight from his vest and shone it into the thin crack between the metal door and the jamb. Even from his knees, John could see the inch-round titanium-alloy bolts glinting back around the frame, set a hand's-width apart on the sides, top and bottom.

Krieger thrust his boot-heel against the door, and again, and again, and each time the surface absorbed the impact without a tremor, and with barely a sound. He swung around, breathing heavily, walked across the narrow room and pressed the barrel of the .45 to John's forehead.

"So," Krieger said. "Tell me everything."

"It doesn't matter now."

"Tell me anyway." Krieger unsnapped a sheath on his belt and slid out a survival knife. "Or I'll wait 'til the girl wakes up, and I'll skin her alive and gut her like a deer, right in front of you."

For a moment he didn't get an answer, and Krieger spun the knife a half-turn in the air, caught it by the blade and cocked his arm toward Gretchen's crumpled form.

"All right!" John shouted. "All right."

"Atta boy," Krieger said. He flicked the knife end-over-end toward Gretchen, and it thunked point-first into the flooring not an inch from her side. "Now, if you change your mind, it's right where I'll need it."

John started to get to his feet.

"Huh uh, Einstein," Krieger said, nudging him back to his knees with the cold pistol barrel. "You can talk from down there."

"Not that much to tell, really. After we left you all, in the plane, remember? We crash-landed out by the Interstate, and we hitchhiked here—"

"Today, smart guy. What the fuck did you do today?"

"Today?" Behind Krieger, Gretchen's hand moved against the floor. "Well, let's see. This morning, you know all your suicide bombers? The guys in the trucks? They blew up real good, but they didn't hit any of their targets."

"Bullshit."

"Bull-true."

"I saw it—"

"What did you see? The forty-one Tomahawks you guys blew your bankroll collecting over the years, did you see them hit all those chemical and nuclear plants across the country? Did you see them take out the Port of Los Angeles? Hoover Dam?"

"Yeah—"

483

"They never got out of Colorado," John said. "Guidance problems."

As he spoke he saw Gretchen turn her head toward them. He didn't dare risk eye contact, but he prayed she would understand.

"Did Air Force One crash and burn in Oklahoma?" John asked.

Krieger nodded.

"Are you sure? Because the President's alive, he's safe up in an AWACS, with two squadrons of F-15s around him. And I'd wager he's cooking up a nice tuna surprise for your boss about now."

The girl had quietly brought herself to a crouch, and with one hand she gripped the hilt of Krieger's knife, worked it slowly back and forth until its razor point came silently free from the floor.

"The phones are down, aren't they?" John asked. "The power's out, right? Because you guys destroyed the infrastructure, do you think? Or because we made you believe you did? Did it maybe raise a red flag for you on your way up here, shithead? When the lights were out everywhere but on this one block in Las Vegas?"

Gretchen had stood, and John could no longer see her behind Krieger's frame. Krieger wasn't wearing body armor. She was a country girl, so he imagined she'd know exactly where to put it.

Right between the shoulder blades.

"Did you see that cold-blooded son-of-a-bitch in the A-10 machine-gun thousands of New Yorkers walking home across the Brooklyn Bridge? Was he a buddy of yours? Because what I saw was a line of Harriers hovering over Jamaica Bay, waiting for him, and I saw that asshole punch out over the water when his plane exploded out from under him, and then I saw a fucking Sidewinder T-bone his ejection seat before the chute even opened. That's what I saw."

"That's impossible—"

"Not a new American revolution. Not a single casualty. Not a scratch. That's what happened today, Nathan. Nothing."

Krieger only stood in silence for a long moment, and then he stiffened suddenly, frowned, and his face began to slacken. His hand went slowly behind his back.

And then he smiled.

"Come on around and say hello, sweetheart," he said.

Gretchen stepped into the light, to the other man's right side. Her eyes were on the floor at first, but when she looked up the face was someone else's. The features were harsh and changed, and the young woman who'd woken up next to him this morning was gone. She handed Krieger his knife, by the blade, and as he slipped it back into its sheath, she put her hand on his shoulder.

"Surprise," Krieger said. "Day's not over yet."

Krieger pulled a dark metal device from inside his vest, extended its antenna, and gripped a white strip of plastic protruding from its side. "You know, she told me the same fucking story before you came in. But I wanted to hear it from the horse's mouth. Now excuse me for one second, would you, Johnny? I've just gotta call home."

He pulled the plastic strip free. John heard an internal switch snap closed inside the box, and a bright green LED blazed to life on its face. By its glow, he could read the hand-lettered label underneath.

EXECUTE

They had all gathered around the security monitor, as if watching the unfolding scene could somehow help him.

Jeannie stood up, and checked her weapon. "Rudy, you and Eric have the conn," she said. As she started for the door, Rudy gripped her wrist to stop her. With a twist and a half-step behind him, she had his face pressed to the conference table with his right hand pinned high behind his back.

"No arguments," she said.

"Jeannie," Anna said, "we all made the rules. The door stays closed, you said it, John said it. That ape will kill you if you go out there, and then he'll come in here and kill us all."

She released her hold on Rudy, pulled out her pistol and took a step back. "So the door stays closed. I'll take the passage, like John must have. I'm not going to stand here and watch him die."

She left them and hurried into the corridor. The latch on the maintenance portal was in her grip when she heard a warbling siren begin to sound. She turned and looked back. Everyone was running everywhere.

"What is it?" she shouted down the hallway. "Who pushed the panic button?" She listened for an answer, but the chaos only heightened as she waited. She swore under her breath, holstered her gun and ran back to the control room. "What is it?"

"AWACS over southern Colorado detected a fast mover," Rudy said. His headset was askew, and he was clearly favoring his right arm.

"Fast mover? A jet? They've shot their wad, Rudy, they don't have any more jets."

He held up his hand, motioning for her to be quiet, and clenched his eyes to listen. "Too small, they're saying, it's too small for a plane. Images are coming through, hold on. Okay, on screen."

The first picture was a deep zoom from a satellite camera. It was a wide field shot of forested terrain, but there was a tiny white cross among the earth tones, trailing a fading series of ghost images behind from the slow shutter.

"Video clip coming in," Rudy said, and he put it on the displays, in all the rooms.

The shot from an orbiting UAV was brief and Zapruder-film choppy. Rudy rolled it back when it had finished, and froze a frame.

"Oh, Jesus," Jeannie breathed.

They hadn't found Latrell's final hole-card hidden on a truck, because it hadn't been on a truck at all.

A caption teletyped in along the top border of the video window, a threat ID from the AWACS image comparators.

* T O M A H A W K *
* B L O C K   I I I *
* N U C L E A R   V A R I A N T *

She was looking at the blurry, pixelated image of a TLAM-N, the nuclear-tipped, inertially-navigated, ground-hugging, terrain-contour matching Prince of Darkness of cruise missiles.

"Where's it headed?" Jeannie asked quietly.

Rudy looked up at her.

"Best guess?" he said, "I'd say about ten yards to your left."

The computers were barely functioning, the power was out and the backup batteries were dwindling fast. They'd given everything they had to get this far, and there was nothing left. Nearly everyone had turned their attention to the incoming missile track, but they only watched in silent resignation. There was no contingency plan for this development, no clever dodge or shrewd canard was left in their exhausted bag of tricks. None of their preparations had been concerned in the slightest with self-defense.

Anna sat alone in front of the surveillance monitor, as aware as the others of her own fast-approaching demise. But she was unable to look away from John Fagan, from the grim scene unfolding just outside in the vestibule.

"Save him," she said softly. "Somebody, save him."

She wasn't speaking to anyone, there was no human near enough to hear. But in its cabinet under the table, the activity light began to flicker on the front panel of the master CPU.

"This," Krieger said, lowering the box to the floor by its segmented antenna, "is a beacon. Now I ain't privy to all the technical details, but hell, I'll give her a shot. When I pulled that tab, this spot where I'm standing got triangulated with a couple of fixed ground stations, and whatcha call a geosynchronous satellite."

John was transfixed, he barely registered the man's words. Gretchen met his gaze evenly with those strange new eyes. Had there been love in them this morning? And how would someone like him have known the difference? Because in those flinty eyes, there was now only contempt. Disgust.

"So what?" John said. "So the rest of the troops can come over for the lynching? You're in a hundred-ten-story tower, over a casino, there's only one way in or out, or didn't you know that? How did you think—"

He stopped talking. Krieger saw the recognition on his face, and grinned.

"Right about now a missile's in the air, a real beaut, one we never let you see. Mister Latrell thought it would be real fitting if he let you pick the target, for the big one, wherever you'd run off to. And I think you chose well, Johnny. Sin City, Sodom and Gomorrah, all rolled into one."

From the corner of his eye, John saw a blinking of red light, up near the ceiling, behind Krieger and the girl. It was the status light on top of the surveillance camera.

And it was speaking to him.

"And here, you were thinking you'd won," Krieger said.

J O H N, the light blinked.

"Yes," John answered. "I was thinking I'd won."

The red light flickered another message, almost too quickly for him to follow.

A S S H E T A U G H T Y O U

"So we're all gonna buy the farm together," Krieger said. "The fight'll go on without us. And thanks to you, without Las Vegas."

"When?" John asked.

"Oh, don't you worry, it'll be over before you know it. I seriously doubt we'll feel a thing."

O N M Y S I G N A L, the red light replied.

*

488

"Somebody get me the controllers at Nellis Air Force Base, I don't care how you do it, just get them!" Jeannie shouted.

"The phones are still down," Rudy said. "We're trying to chain a call through the military network, but everybody's out of pocket from the chaos today, nobody's where they should be. The President's ordered a scramble from all bases west of the Mississippi, but it'll take them a while to load out and get in the air, too long. His escort fighters are en route, but they're way the fuck out of position."

She was watching the intermittent track of the missile as it slid across the digitized 3-D map. The AWACS planes that had been assigned to the southwest were doing their best to pace the inbound, but the speed differential was forcing them to hand-off the tracking every few minutes. It was flying so fast and so low that it took every watt of radar energy they could throw down to cut through the backscatter of the ground whizzing just below it.

"Eric, crank up the GPS team again, we've got to try to divert it."

"Divert it where?" Woodson asked. He got on the intercom and issued the order, and she heard DarqueAngel and the GPS specialists working to complete the restart their systems. "It's a fucking live nuclear weapon."

"Out to sea," Jeannie said, "as far as we can take it, out off the West Coast."

"Okay, we're running, the pointer's live."

Jeannie leaned over him and put her hand on the trackball, then clicked a waypoint over their position in Las Vegas. She moved the pointer a fraction of an inch to the side and clicked again, watching the positional data streaming in from the missile track. The numbers began to shift.

"Good deal," Woodson said. "At least now it's headed for the Bellagio."

"I've got to go gently," she whispered, moving the onscreen arrow another few pixels, and clicking again. "This thing's got four discrete navigation systems, and it'll just switch over if it sees what we're doing."

The coordinates had just begun to shift again toward her second waypoint when the numbers suddenly rolled back and reset to the original course, and stayed there. She clicked again. No response.

Lock out.

"Goddamnit!" She pulled her headset mike close. "Where are my fighters?"

"Still coming."

"Okay," Jeannie said. "Okay. Rudy, none of your fucking bullshit, get communications open with Nellis and put them through to me, then find out how many remotely piloted vehicles are still hangared out there, get them flying north, and conference in the AWACS commanders. Got that?"

"Yeah, I'm going."

She began to pace, but she didn't take her eyes off the radar screen. The plan forming in her mind was a Hail Mary, but that's what they were down to, the long odds.

"Nathan?"

"Yeah."

"I wonder if you'd do me a favor."

Krieger looked at Gretchen and then back at him, and let out a snort.

"Seriously," John said.

The other man shook his head, smiling. "Well. All you can do is ask."

"I want you to kill me now. I don't want to wait for the bomb. Just put a bullet in my head. You can do that, can't you?" John began to get to his feet, and Krieger backhanded a blow to his jaw that sent him back to his knees.

"Just stay put. No fucking favors."

John shook off the double-vision blur before his eyes, saw blood from his mouth spattering into the carpet. He braced his

490

hands against the floor, and started to rise again. "Come on," he said, "I can't take this shit anymore. Just shoot me, you worthless prick. For old times."

A kick to his solar plexus drove the wind from him, and he fell onto his back, wheezing. He rolled painfully to his stomach, then got to his hands and knees, crawled in slow, disoriented inches toward the opposite wall. Then he turned back toward them, brought himself up onto his knees, and began again to stand. The barrel of the pistol stopped him, pressing against his forehead.

"On second thought," Krieger said, "since you're bein' a pain in the ass about it. I wouldn't mind a little privacy with our girlfriend, here, before I meet my maker." He tousled Gretchen's hair, and she put her arm around his waist. "She's a lover, Lordy, she can make some noise, can't she, this one? For such a little thing?"

John felt his jaw tighten. He rested his weight back, sitting on his heels.

"So, you think I could have a few last words?" he asked.

"Knock yourself out."

He took a slow, deep breath, and looked up at the two of them.

"My dad," John said. "When I was a kid, we had this farmhouse, upstate. I was scared of just about everything in the great outdoors, so I stayed inside mostly, and that pissed him off, of course. So he takes me outside one day, and shows me this trick. You're a hayseed, I bet you know it. He found the biggest, fattest wasp I'd ever seen, out on a fencepost. He told me to get ready to count to seven, then he cupped his hands on either side, trapped that ugly thing in the space between his palms, and held his breath. He looked at me and nodded, cool as a fish, and when I got to seven, he threw the wasp on the ground in front of me, and I stepped on it. Then he showed me his hands. No damage."

The red light up in the corner flashed rapidly, five times.

491

"Yeah, I know that one. Great story." Krieger racked the slide of the pistol, and put its barrel back to John's forehead. "All done?"

Four flashes.

"But did you know why it worked, when you did it?" John asked. "Holding your breath has nothing to do with it, and any count up to seven was fine, but at eight, the sons-of-bitches would nail me every time. It took me all summer, but I finally figured it out."

Three

"Okay, I'll bite," Krieger said. "What's the secret?"

"Incredulity," John said.

"Hmm? You're gonna hafta look that one up for me, Webster."

Two

"Mental rejection, Nathan. For a full seven seconds, it turns out, the wasp just can't fucking believe it."

Wait for a distraction, Jeannie had told him, those long last few nights. He'd expressed an interest in learning a bit of her SpecOps gunplay, half just as an excuse to be with her. But he hadn't realized what a relentless teacher she was. She took this shit as life-and-death, and she'd drilled it into him, over and over. *All you'll need is a moment, and you'll know it when it comes. Assassins are creatures of habit, and if you've seen him work before, all the better. It's like a golf swing, one motion, what you have to do*, she'd said. *Turn off your mind, it's muscle memory.* She'd worked him through it hundreds of times. But this was the time that mattered.

One

Directly behind Krieger, the floor light over the elevator illuminated, and with a resonant *ding* the double-doors slid open to blackness. At the sound he felt the press of the gun relax.

Just as she'd taught him, his right hand in his lap twisted palm to the ceiling, thumb out, and snapped upward. His fist closed around the pistol barrel and his arm pushed it up and away. He felt the crack of Krieger's trigger finger as the bone fractured, and the pistol came free. As he rolled to his back in a half sit-up, his left hand had turned thumb down, and when it came around from the right to grasp the inverted grip it swiveled the gun upright. His other hand clasped on, his index finger slipped through the trigger guard, and he was looking down the barrel at the other man's chest.

One motion, just as she'd taught him.

Krieger was holding his injured hand loosely with his other, and Gretchen stood beside him, aghast. *Or more precisely,* John thought, as his mind came back online, *incredulous.*

He drew in a breath, and held it. No one spoke, but he heard a voice in his memory, his own voice as a boy. And it was counting.

"Come on, skid-mark," John said. "It's not over yet."

Krieger suddenly pushed the girl to the side and his left hand flashed behind to the second pistol in his belt. The first bullet struck him just below the neck, and five others followed, each impact pounding him a half-step backward. But he stayed upright until the last round snapped his head back.

He was dead on his feet, but his eyes found John's one last time. They hadn't changed their character. A moment later the knees gave over, and Nathan Krieger teetered backward and fell into the yawning doorway, and eight hundred feet down to the ground floor.

Gretchen took a step, but she stopped as he drew down on her. She looked at him, and he tried, but his finger wouldn't squeeze through the tension of the trigger. It might have been a trick of the dim light, but he thought he'd seen the face of the young woman that he knew come back again.

"I don't understand," he said softly.

"Aren't you going to shoot me, John?"

"If I have to. If you make me."

She raised an eyebrow, cocked her head slightly, with that tiny smile that he now knew he had never seen beyond.

"In the barn, you helped us get away," he said.

"I was tied to a chair, and you was comin' at me with a hay reaper," she said, turning, taking a small step, and then another.

"I helped you waste your time until they could come and get me outta there. Only they never come."

"You could have, while we were together here, you could've—"

"I'm a lover, I ain't a fighter," she said. "I knew he'd find you. I did what I'd been told to do, I stayed with you. Didn't find no way to call nobody 'til t'other day, I didn't even know what you was doin' up here, with that woman. But if ida knowed that, I woulda smothered the both of you in your sleep, you better believe it."

While she had spoken she had made her way nearly to the transmitter on the floor.

"Stop," he said.

"Don't you want to understand, John? Don't you want to know why?"

"Give that thing to me; there may still be time to stop it."

She picked up the box, and studied its faceplate. "Oh, I don't think you can stop it," she said.

"Let me try."

She slowly walked a few steps back, and turned to face him. Her eyes were hard again, and there was a twinkle of victory in them.

"I only regret—"

"Don't," John said.

"—that I have but one life, to give for my country."

She hugged the box close to her chest, leaned into the darkness of the elevator shaft, and was gone.

"The jets from Nellis are outbound," Rudy said. He handed her the phone, and stood back.

She listened for over a minute before looking up at him, her eyes grim.

"Yes, sir," she said. "Yes, sir, we will. Thank you." She broke the connection, and handed back the receiver.

"What did they say?"

"There's not much they can promise to do. They'll try to come around behind it, and hit it with heat-seekers. But that missile, Rudy—"

She didn't have to finish her sentence. He'd read the briefs, as she had, back at the agency. The TLAM-N was designed from concept to elude and evade, to avoid being detected and shot down, to accomplish its mission. It was coming for them, and it was going to hit.

The surveillance monitor had blinked and gone dark minutes ago, and she'd listened to the muffled sounds of gunshots come through the reinforced walls, but Anna hadn't looked away from the screen. Until she'd heard something impossible.

The locks on the unbreachable door to the elevator, the bolts that could not be undone once the intruder alert had been sounded, those safeguards had just clanked open.

She slid under the table and felt desperately for a weapon, found the Callaway golf club that Rudy Steinman had used as a pointer in the briefings, and crawled to the edge of the doorway to the hall.

Footsteps approaching.

Anna wrapped her hands around the worn leather at the end of the shaft, jumped out with a yell and swung with all her might. The head of the 7-iron whiffed through the air and embedded itself in the drywall, and when she pulled it would not come free. She opened one eye, and then the other.

"The fuck is wrong with you, girl?" John asked.

When she saw him come into the room, Jeannie ran to him and jumped full-body into his arms, hugged him and leg-locked him so hard that his back cracked in several places before he was able to ease her back down to the floor.

"Come on," John said, pushing her gently to arm's length. "We'll catch up later. Now what's the story?"

She spoke as she pulled him by the sleeve over to a bank of monitors, and they sat down across from each other.

"Missile's inbound, fighters are on the way, but nobody's putting much stock in their chances."

"I agree."

"And the UAV Battle Lab at Indian Springs is remote-piloting their last three modified Predators toward a rendezvous point."

"What do they think that's going to do?"

She looked at him, and he saw the hopelessness slip past her defenses. "It's my idea. They're going to try to . . . to fly into it . . . I don't know, dive on it."

"Jesus, that's like throwing marshmallows at a rifle bullet, a bullet that can dodge."

"I know," she said, "but what else do we have?"

John leaned back in his chair, and his eyes searched the air for several moments. "Where's Woodson?"

She put on her headset. "Eric, double-time it to the conference room," she said, and then she swung the mike away. "What are you thinking?"

"Don't know yet."

Eric Woodson popped his face in the door, cocked his head when he saw John, and pointed at him. "I thought—"

"Tell you later," John said. "You're monitoring RF traffic, aren't you? All RF?"

"Yeah, so I'd know what to jam. Why?"

"Are you recording it?"

"No. Well, yeah, not in so many words, but yeah, there's a rolling buffer, if that's what you mean."

"How long a buffer?"

"Depends. Ten minutes, half an hour?"

John took Jeannie's hand, and squeezed it. "Let's go," he said.

They were nearly to the end of the rewind when they saw it on the round oscilloscope CRT, a jagged mountainscape of analog spikes and troughs. By its timecode the burst coincided with the triggering of Krieger's homing beacon.

"Eric, ID that and get on your rig, tune it in."

Woodson put on a pair of headphones and spun the macro knob on his all-band receiver. When he got close, he shifted to the micro adjustment, squinted, and began to gingerly turn the control like a safecracker.

"Got it," he said. "It's a frequency hopper, and it's weak, what is it?"

"It's the signal that targeted us," John said, "Still transmitting up the elevator shaft. Can you cancel it?"

"Can I cancel it?" Woodson went to work on the keyboard in front of him. They saw the graphical scramble of the radio signal appear on his screen, a two-second pulse that repeated over and over with a pause in between. He highlighted a block, and typed a command into his transmitter array. The peaks and valleys collapsed to a flat, rippling line. "Cancelled."

"Stay here."

John and Jeannie ran to the control room.

"The missile," Jeannie said. "What's the status?"

"Still coming," Rudy said.

"No change?"

"No change, man, it's still balls-on."

"Backup systems," Jeannie said. "It's flying on last instructions. The inertial guidance already knows the distance and the coordinates. It'll keep listening for it, but it doesn't need the beacon anymore."

"Reese," John said. "Those Predators, they've got a jamming system, right?"

"Yeah—"

"Programmable?"

Her eyes lit up, and she keyed her intercom mike. "Eric, broadband that block transmission to the techs at Indian Point."

"It's encoded, honey, and there's no time to—"

"Don't decode it, just clone it and send it. Tell them we're calling with instructions." She looked at John and took a deep breath. "Right after I talk to the President."

*

"Is this going to work?" Rudy asked.

"Let's find out," John said.

He gave the signal, Jeannie relayed the go-ahead to the Commander-in-Chief, and they watched the radar screen. The line of the incoming missile continued, and the display zoomed down abruptly to a hundred-mile circle. There wasn't much time left.

And then the projected-trajectory line split off, and another, dimmer path appeared next to it on the screen. The missile blip disappeared for a moment, then reappeared again, shifted onto the altered course.

"Hot damn!" Woodson shouted. "We're in business!"

Before the rejoicing could break out in earnest, Jeannie held out her hands to quiet them. They'd managed to trick an armed thermonuclear warhead streaking toward them at 600 miles an hour into chasing three unmanned drones cruising at just over 75 knots in the open air.

"Now what?" Jeannie asked.

The phone lit up, and even though it was the first call he'd received in weeks, lance corporal Toby Schute waited for the second ring to answer. Three years ago when he'd won this assignment in the loser's lottery, his commanding officer had briefed him with only three admonitions: that their funding had been on the bubble since 1992, that no news was good news, and to keep it professional. He put down his book, cleared his throat, leaned back in his chair and picked up the receiver.

"Area 12. Authenticate."

He shot to sitting attention and tipped over his Diamondbacks coffee cup when the Texan's voice in his ear identified itself. His clipboard with the challenge rotation was under a donut box, and he flapped the crumbs from it before riffling through the pages to today's codes.

"Caller, identify, code, Firestone."

His index finger was pressing on the designated response,

USHER, and his eyes widened as the correct codeword was spoken in reply.

"Sir," Schute said. His mouth had gone bone dry. "What, what can I do for you?"

He listened, and then laid the cordless handset on his desk and hurried to the equipment locker. He emptied his gymbag and began to stuff it with items as he found them. With a last inventory, he zipped the bag and ran to his car outside, then back inside in a frenzied search for his keys, then back out again into the late afternoon.

Their view of Rainier Mesa was from the down-looking tele-photo camera in a Global Hawk circling at 30,000 feet. They saw a tiny figure far below, dropping points of flickering orange light around a circular black spot.

"Are they getting anything, the Predators?"

"No. Wait, yeah, IR target, they see the road-flares. Okay, they've got a lock."

"Great," John said. "Now tell that guy to get the fuck out of Dodge." He looked at Jeannie. They both knew it, if this thing went wrong, in about a minute the man who'd dropped those flares would be getting the fuck right off the planet.

"That base, how many personnel?"

"Skeleton crew," she said. "Maybe thirty people."

"Shelters?"

"There was no time to evacuate, they've taken cover. But that place isn't shielded for air bursts. They're watching just like we are."

"Where's the inbound?" John asked.

She half turned and spoke into the boom mike from her head-set, listened, and shook her head. "It slipped under the radar a few seconds ago," Jeannie said. "They've lost it."

On the screen, the blowing double dust-trail of a tiny speeding automobile was tracing a path back the way it had come when the view switched abruptly to the nose camera of one of the Predators.

As it pushed into a dive the flare-ringed circle appeared, and the image was much clearer now. It was the ground-level mouth of R-tunnel, one of the last orphaned, unused, skyscraper-deep vertical holes at the Nevada underground testing range.

John felt a wave of vertigo as he stared into the video feed on the big screen. The unmanned Predator drone, blasting the coded tracking signal they'd cloned from Krieger's homing beacon, was now descending almost vertically. The pilot at Indian Point would be seeing this view through a full-enclosure helmet, trying to hit the center of a thirty-foot target from beyond the horizon.

John flinched as the ground flew toward him and the picture flashed to static and horizontal color bars.

"Status!" he shouted.

"Miss," Woodson said. "Dug a hole twenty yards to the side. Strike one."

The picture flickered live again, as Indian Point activated the second Predator and started another run. As the UAV nosed over the rushing groundscape filled the screen again.

"Reacquired, we've got a radar track," Jeannie said. "The missile's popping-up, terminal stage."

The pop-up maneuver was the final leg of ingress. The TLAM-N was pulling up into a vertical climb over its lock-in, and at a mile high it would flop over and dive straight down into the target.

"Strike two!" The second Predator had crashed far wide of the hole in the desert, a gust had blown it off-heading in the last hundred feet.

"Get everybody away from the windows," John said. It was likely to be bright even from here, maybe blinding.

Thirty lives on my hands, he thought.

Thirty more.

The picture from the last Predator sputtered onto the screen, and then stabilized. The pilot was taking a different approach toward the vertical tunnel this time. He was flying a steep sloping descent, crabbing into the crosswind, and he was holding course well and accelerating. The round black aperture was ahead dead-center, and the desert was coming up fast. In seconds the picture jarred, bounced and skidded, and when it cleared again the fish-eye lens of the nose camera showed a slanted view of the horizon, a broken, detached wing, a stretch of sand, and the very edge of the hole.

"Shit!" Woodson shouted. "It's a leaner, another six goddamn inches, fuck!"

"Try to rock it," John said. "Tell him to work the control surfaces, and rock it."

Jeannie had the secure link to the Indian Point pilot on her headset, and she spoke quietly to him. All the others had gathered around the screen, watching.

The picture began to oscillate, only a little at first, and then the subtle to-and-fro tilting gradually became an increasing see-saw motion as the pilot found his rhythm.

John was willing it, he could see that they all were.

Just a bit more. Now, just a little more.

On the last upswing the horizon hesitated agonizingly at the perpendicular, and then the view rolled toward inverted, and went suddenly black.

"Landing lights!" John said.

A moment later, the screen illuminated with a dim, accelerating video feed from the nose camera. The shattered plane's forward lights had snapped on, and their beams were glinting off the rushing walls as the decoy plummeted toward the distant bottom of the shaft.

Everything that was left in them at the end of this day burst out in a deafening group-scream of celebration. Amidst the pandemonium, Woodson brought up the 30,000-foot view from the Global Hawk.

A towering gray column of drifting exhaust was still visible from the Tomahawk's final ascent over its new target, and at the apogee of the climb they saw the bright cross shape flop over and begin to dive down in a vertical line. They watched the ratcheting corrections as its precision guidance systems perfected the dead-fall descent, and then the missile vanished down into the round black abyss.

Only shallow breathing could be heard in the room as the following seconds passed. Then far below the camera, a circle of desert a thousand yards across dithered and puffed a few inches into the air.

When the earth had swallowed the last of the fury of elemental energy deep under its surface, a gauze blanket of white vapor rose as the sand sank down again into the settling bowl of a dark crater, and seismic and infrasound detectors worldwide recorded the tremors of detonation #809 at the Nevada Nuclear Proving Range.

53

Edward Latrell stood on his deck, as he had at the end of each day since these timbers had first been set into the stone of his mountain.

The colors always changed when the sun got low, of the clearing and the rolling land that surrounded it, and he had never grown tired of the sight. The greens deepened, the browns bronzed, and it became like a painting of thick oils over canvas, a picture from the dreams of the men who'd laid the foundation of America.

Unlike those other afternoons, there was now no one to look back up at him as his eyes moved over the scene. He had ordered his people to lose themselves in the terrain and travel to safehouses, to scatter and disappear. Not to hide or to cower, he'd told them, but to wait. They would hear from him, he'd said, there would be a message, but he hadn't told them how or when it would arrive. He wasn't certain how or when himself; the Great Mystery was before him, but his faith was strong.

He had heard the droning of the C-130s approaching in the sky, and he looked up in time to see three parachutes deploy behind them, above three dark cylinders. They were seven tons each, he knew, but they looked so small up there in the evening sky, swinging slowly, drifting earthward.

He looked down, and his eyes found an ancient stone embedded in the earth below his balcony. When they had first found this place, just the handful of them then, they had chosen this spot for his home. They'd worked for days to remove that boulder so they could lay the underpinnings, with a team of mules and all their muscle. After all the sweat and blood, it hadn't moved a chip.

This rock will stay, he'd finally said. It shared its roots with the mountains, and it would be a reminder to them. Of will, and permanence, and strength, and foundation. That stone would stand unchanged a thousand years hence, *esto perpetua*, immutable as the sacred principles that had forged their nation, unchangeable as their vow to restore her faded glory.

The three rocket-shapes were settling lower, points down, and the bitter, volatile smell of ammonium nitrate reached his nostrils. He breathed in deeply, spread his arms out to the sides, looked up, and smiled.

Can you see me? he thought.

Do I seem afraid? Are the orbiting eyes with which you fretfully watch your people sharp enough to read my lips?

"Up from my ashes," Latrell said, "ten thousand will rise."

The proximity fuses of the three BLU-82s detected the approach of the ground below them, and they detonated almost simultaneously. All the air in the valley was consumed instantly in a sun-bright ball of yellow and white. The concussion alone would have reduced the abandoned structures of the camp to molecules, but the flash and the fire came an instant later to erase all that remained.

Epilogue

Though the memorial service had been scheduled to commence at 4:00 P.M., one of the guests was running uncharacteristically late. But it was only a few minutes, and they couldn't very well begin without him. This was his second home, after all, his ranch.

And of course, he was who he was.

She'd come in from the cold, in the cloak-and-dagger parlance of espionage. She'd agreed to see them, after the dust had settled following December 10th, after they'd assured her that all was clear, that the responsible terrorist elements, foreign and domestic, were in the process of being captured, killed or driven back underground by the pursuit. She'd come in all right, but surrounded by her own security men, and only for a single meeting.

The debriefing itself had been an interesting affair. Even a week after, the attendees' heads were still spinning from what they'd seen, or what they thought they'd seen during that day. Much of it was already passing uneasily into the realm of urban mythology and conspiracy theory. That, at least, was a comfort to the spooks. Since long before the Kennedy assassination, but especially since, the crackpot culture had provided a dependable burial ground for dangerous truth.

And what had really happened, after all? The nationwide

blackout had been real, the phones had certainly gone down, some of the wildfires in California were still being extinguished, so they had been real, too. But the news footage and other troubling documentation had been confiscated as evidence, and these would remain sealed for decades, during which time the records would be methodically lost, according to established procedure. What survived in circulation on the Internet would be gradually smirked away, calmly and patiently debunked by government experts and hired assets from the private sector.

From their interviews, even the eyewitnesses to the downing of Air Force One in Oklahoma were already becoming uncertain of what they'd really seen. The events of the day were being spun as a scattering of thwarted minor attacks, terrorist disinformation, mass hysteria and an elaborate Internet hoax, whichever fit best to explain it all away.

Most of the debriefing had focused on the internal aftermath, the ongoing investigations that were now probing the dark corners of every department and agency represented in the room. The Directors would have their hands full covering their asses and containing the damage, and were as anxious as anyone to clamp down the lid, ASAP. Some of their own peers, even at that high level, were already under indictment or in detention. Some had simply disappeared.

For her part, she'd read a prepared statement, and had taken no questions.

There was a burst of jovial conversation nearby, and she turned to see a group of soldiers, sailors and airmen in dress uniform, talking old times. Someone was telling a wild story, illustrating it with his hands, of one or other of the many exploits of Lieutenant Robert Vance.

She smiled with them, and thought back over a few of her own.

They'd found him, finally, what the scavengers had left of him, on the outskirts of the immense, barren circle of scorched earth in the wilderness that had been Latrell's base camp. There had been sufficient DNA in the scattered remains to make a positive identification. Though they'd known already beyond any doubt, she and Rudy had wept together through a long night when the terse confirmation had finally come.

```
Killed in action
On or about November 11, 2001
Colorado, USA
```

Heads were turning back, and she looked with them to see a long line of black SUVs pulling to a stop. Amid a cluster of Secret Service agents she saw a door open in the second vehicle, and a figure stepped out. There were no representatives of the press here, not for miles, and he'd seen no need for the stuffy protocols of his office. No fuss will be made for me, he'd told them, no Hail to the Chief, no standing ovations, not a moment of it. Today, he'd driven himself.

It had been nearly seventy earlier in the day, but the breeze in central Texas was blowing cooler as the sun got low. The rows of wooden folding chairs were arranged outside under the sky, just, she thought, as Rob would have wanted it. She had draped the jacket he'd given her over the seatback, and she pulled it now up around her shoulders against the chill. She closed her eyes, wrapped the arms of the bomber jacket around her, and breathed in. It smelled of him, of leather, and strength, love of life, and danger in far places. It smelled of valor.

When the President and the First Lady had been escorted to their seats, the first speaker came to the podium, and the service began.

Before the debriefing had gotten underway she'd noticed three faces in particular that were missing from the room.

The agenda was read and a moment of silence was observed for those few who had been killed on December 10th, 2001. There was a list of perhaps forty-five individuals who had lost their lives amid the day's chaos. The Vice President read the names alphabetically, and offered a few words on how each had met their ends.

There were lobbyists, politicians, bureaucrats and section chiefs among the dead, ironically all elected, appointed or anointed officials, no ordinary citizens at all. As the VP read each name his eyes found those in the room who were connected with the deceased, and he held on them, as if to say that one of the messages of each unfortunate death, one that should not be overlooked, was guidance by example for those still living.

Ari Darukyan and Benjamin Fuller had been tragically killed in separate incidents, their vehicles struck by suicide bombers. The terrorists had apparently bypassed their designated targets to collide with the men's unmarked sedans, and in the case of Mr. Darukyan, only after an extended chase into the country. Achieving an entirely new level of deadpan, Cheney then reported that Walter Kamuck, NSA, apparently distraught over the unfolding events of the day, had opened his gun safe, loaded an heirloom pistol and shot himself four times in the chest and once in the back of the head.

In the course of the thwarted attacks most of the in-country terrorist leadership caste had been captured or killed, so it would likely be years before a new assault could be mounted on US soil. How many years, no one could know. And IRIN was also among the dead, or among the dormant at the very least. After Fagan's computer system had exposed it to the light during the missile attack on Israel, off-the-shelf antivirus software proved more than capable of wiping the resident portion of IRIN into the recycle bin. By its nature she knew that some of it still remained, somewhere, and certainly the idea of it did. For the moment it was gone, though, for the moment its threats were safely in the future.

Her statement before the intelligence debriefing had provided few new details of the day of the attacks, or of the events leading up to it. As with 9/11, there would always be unanswered questions; in the judgment of those who controlled the information, some of the answers were far more threatening than the events themselves.

Still, the truth would someday find its way to the people, in one form or another, she was certain of it. Secrets were getting awfully hard to keep.

But her message for the leaders seated in front of her that morning had less to do with what had happened, more with what might happen next. She had made her choices, and they would all be as free to make their own. She was young enough to still believe that good would somehow, someday prevail over evil. But she had also grown wise enough to appreciate the generous border between darkness and light. Many great minds had dwelt there in history, and many still dwell there today. And if anyone ever again came looking for her, she told them in closing, and if anyone was unfortunate enough to actually locate her, they would find her somewhere near the wide, gray line between those two moral absolutes. To do a great right, she had once done a little wrong, and she would never hesitate to do so again.

A buddy of Rob's, the man who'd volunteered himself out of retirement to pilot the decoy 747 on the day of the attacks, had just finished telling an outrageous tale from their days on the carriers. As the laughter quieted gradually after the punch line, Gerry Archer took a note card from his shirt pocket with a bandaged hand, and laid it on the podium in front of him.

"I wanted to say, to you all," he said, "I wrote it down here so I wouldn't forget it, that I wish you all could have known Robert Vance the way I did. I look at the words now, though, and they're not right. I've got no special claim. I see his mom and dad, his family, and they knew him as their boy, their brother."

He nodded toward Jeannie.

"I see his dear friends. I see his shipmates, and fellow pilots. I see his commanding officers. We all knew our own part of him. My only wish today, however, is that the people of his country could somehow know of him, someday, and that they could know what he did for them, as well."

Gerry Archer cleared his throat, but the knot there continued to strain against his words.

"Now, I know he would not agree. I think Rob would say that every American soldier who puts on a uniform and vows to give their life, if needed, to leave their loved ones behind and walk into the breach, every one of them has made a sacrifice equal to his own. I can only speak for myself, but in my case, I humbly beg to differ. I am not his equal. He saved my life two times. And I will go to my own grave believing that before Robert Vance died for his country, he just may have saved us all."

Out low in the distance, a diamond-shaped fingertip formation of fighter jets appeared out of the haze that had settled in with the gathering sunset. As they rumbled overhead one of them slowly departed from its place, then rolled up and away, climbing until it had reached the clouds, and was gone.

"You must be Jeannie."

The family had been first in the line that was now filing past the flag-draped casket for a last goodbye, and she'd been lost in her thoughts when the four of them had walked over to her.

Rob's father was tall and straight, just as she'd imagined him, still wearing a government issue crew-cut years after he'd left active duty.

And there were his eyes.

The younger brother looked starched and pressed from basic training, hard and stoic in his dress blues, and the older sister carried the family features with a poised, unadorned beauty.

It was his mom who'd spoken, and she was the very picture of motherhood. She took Jeannie's hand in hers, and clasped her other one over it. The two women looked at each other for a long moment.

"He was—" Jeannie said quietly. "I wish I could have, I mean—"

Rob's mother nodded her head, pulled her close, and Jeannie put her arms around.

"I feel like," Jeannie whispered, "I feel like, I should have—"

"Shhh, now don't you worry," the other woman said. "Don't you ever, ever worry."

They held each other, through the sounding of Taps, the twenty-one guns, the folding and presentation of the flag, and the stately, silent bearing of the coffin into the military hearse that would take him to his last flight, to his place among his fallen brothers, among the long, white stone lines of Arlington.

She checked her watch, quickened her steps as she walked down the 3rd Street Promenade toward the scheduled rendezvous. It was just as she remembered it: the sandstone-paved walkway lined with old-time streetlamps, the eclectic shops and cozy restaurants, the street performers playing to the drifting crowds. This had always been a wonderful place for a stroll in the warm evenings when she'd traveled west, but in this season it was especially charming.

The night air was cool, but there was little danger of a snow to mark the holiday. Still, strings of twinkling white lights ringed the trees, and every welcoming door was bedecked with a wreath of evergreen and garlands of spruce and holly. Only miles from the sprawl of downtown Los Angeles, it all felt like a city-dweller's vision of a small town holiday square.

Only 3 shopping days 'til Christmas, a chalk-drawn elf beckoned from a blackboard in a toy-shop window.

As she crossed Ocean Avenue she saw them, in a park overlooking the Santa Monica Pier, huddled in a tight group to ward off the nippy seaside breeze. One of them waved her over, and then the others turned, and opened their arms.

She searched the faces as she approached. John Fagan was not among them.

It had only been ten days or so, but they greeted her like they'd been separated for years. The talk went on until the wee hours, the telling and retelling, as they shared a bottle of brandy and rubbed their hands together to warm them.

"Oh, did you see it in the paper today?" Rudy had asked, as he brought out a clipping.

On the day of the attacks, a number of international passenger flights had been targeted for destruction over their US destinations. The team had thwarted the scores of bombers, and they'd done it using only two of their people. At a designated time, one at Heathrow Airport and one at Charles de Gaulle simply ran the wrong way up a passenger exit corridor in the international terminals. The security fences clattered down, the airports were evacuated, and all outgoing flights were canceled for the day. In the following hours, French and British authorities had quietly rounded up nearly all of the suicide bombers.

All but one. One of them had overslept on the big day, had lost his forged passport, and had misplaced the electronic detonator for his explosives. Then this morning, he had apparently gotten his shit together and decided to make his mark. In midflight, ninety minutes out of Paris, he'd struck a match and attempted to light a makeshift fuse he'd jammed into his C-4-packed shoes. He shoved a flight attendant who confronted him, and that was more than enough for the passengers and crew. One of them slapped the match away, another grabbed a handful of pony-tail, and then nearly twenty others rose up, bystanders no more, to pummel the shoe-bomber into submission, hog-tie him with their belts and headset cords, and deliver him into the waiting hands of the authorities when their flight touched down safely in Boston.

It was a strange new feeling for her, to be surrounded by friends, and she didn't want to see it end. But the evening passed so quickly, and before she knew it, it was time to go.

She said goodbye to them one at a time as they left, watched them as each headed back toward the safe haven of their anonymity.

They'd all been offered an expedited slot in the Witness Protection Program, and – with the exception of Richard McDermott – they'd all said thank you, no. That would mean that someone, somewhere would have them on a list, and that wouldn't do. All of them had years of experience in fading into the background noise, and they would do so again, as she was now prepared to, on their own.

In the end, there was only one farewell left to be exchanged.

"So," Eric Woodson said.

"So," Jeannie replied.

"Look, I'm not gonna mince words with you—"

"Oh, my goodness. Should I sit down?"

"I know you've been through a lot," Woodson said. "And I know we haven't really had that much time to get to know each other—"

She suppressed a smile. "I feel like I know you pretty well, Eric."

He handed her a slip of paper. "That's my number."

"I see that. Thank you."

"And I want you to know, I don't hand that out to every slut on the street."

"That's good to know, I was concerned."

"And I just want to say, when you get your head on straight again, what I'm trying to say is, if you're ever in Baltimore and you get an itch for some trouser-trout? Well, I'll be there for you."

She shook her head slowly, took his face in her hands, and gave him a kiss. Then she hugged him tight, so her lips were near his ear.

"Don't hold your breath," she whispered.

When she let him go, he checked the time, and straightened his glasses.

"So long, Jeannie."

"Goodbye, Eric."

"I meant what I said."

"Me too."

He turned and began to walk toward the avenue, and before long, like the others, he'd disappeared.

Rudy had come up beside her, having secured their things from the Casa Del Mar just up the street. He had only a single over-stuffed carry-on bag for each of them, one under each arm. When she hadn't acknowledged him after a minute or so he cleared his throat and checked his watch.

"So, where to, boss?" he asked.

She took her bag from him, and slung its strap over her shoulder. "Go find us some coffee, would you, sweetie?"

"Sure," he said, "okay." He studied her face for long moments. "Why don't you come along? Help me carry it."

She shook her head, zipped his windbreaker another inch up his chest.

"Okay," he said quietly. "The usual, right?"

She nodded. Her eyes were wet, but she managed a hint of a smile.

Rudy backed away a couple of steps and then turned from her, off toward the last errand she would ask of him. Though the purpose gradually faded from his stride as she watched, he did not look back.

They had made a place for him in Washington, she'd made sure of that, a safe place and a career track worthy of his talents, and his heart. Like so many others inside the Beltway he would be protected from his enemies by secrets, by the promise of their revelation if he ever came to harm. There would be no such shelter if he stayed with her.

She checked her pistol, found it set and sound. The Pacific was at her back, and there was nothing to the east that appealed to her at the moment. She was not given easily to random decisions, but fugitives were often trapped by their patterns of choices.

The ocean breeze was blowing subtly northward up the moonlit coast, and it spoke to her with more certainty than she might ever feel again. She took a deep breath, and let it out slowly.

So north it would be.

As a small figure emerged from the distant tree-line, John Fagan stubbed out his cigarette and walked to the porch railing, lifted a pair of binoculars to his eyes.

The boy was returning, trudging through the new snow with his rifle slung across his back, his new dog bounding by his side, and a large pheasant in his arms. He stopped and looked up toward the great log house, and apparently sensing that John was watching, he lifted the generous bird by its feet in front of him, and smiled. The mighty hunter was bringing home holiday supper, and there would be a story to be told when he arrived.

The overhead in Las Vegas had consumed the last of the dwindling Fagan family fortune; after the initial build-out, the tab had leveled off at just over a hundred thousand per day, not counting tips, and excluding Eric Woodson's mind-blowing mini-bar consumption. It had taken even more money, then, to return the facilities at the Stratosphere to their original condition. He'd also budgeted a substantial fund to negotiate the continuing discretion of their host, but that had proven unnecessary. What happens in Vegas, the general manager had assured him, stays in Vegas.

It was this last pool of unused money that had, by the barest of margins, covered the sight-unseen cash purchase of a furnished big-game lodge, including all outbuildings, vehicles, and one scruffy canine, in the remote Teton Wilderness of northwest Wyoming.

His skills as a hunter-gatherer aside, the boy was proving himself to be quite the junior Edison. The windmills, solar panels, batteries and generators that supplemented their electricity required regular, knowledgeable maintenance, and John shared those responsibilities with his young apprentice. But the kid had already begun to introduce a number of his own innovations

515

into their private power grid, and he seemed to love to fiddle with things, to learn about them, experiment and optimize.

John stepped through the double-doors and into the great-room, removed his heavy coat, bent and hefted another log onto the fire that was crackling in the wide hearth. Three red felt stockings were hung in a line above, on nails he'd driven into the wooden mantelpiece. The little girl, Elizabeth, had hand-lettered their names in the white batting at the tops, with glue and green glitter.

He looked them over. The "h" in "John" was backwards, while the ones in "Matthew" and "Elizabeth" were properly made. It could have been a child's mistake, but he had begun to suspect the youngster, lately, of intentionally yanking his chain.

He pushed a wall panel, it clicked inward, and a featureless door in the pine paneling swung open. This interior space had formerly been a small movie theater off the greatroom, for guests of the lodge. Now, it was to become his workplace.

"Kate," he said.

The computer hardware and displays from Las Vegas had arrived with them in the moving vans. Most of it was still crated, but he'd connected more than enough for his system to stretch into, and feel at home.

"Good afternoon, John." The lights hummed up to a warm, comfortable level.

"How are you feeling, after your brush with oblivion?"

"I am . . . nearly myself again, and recovering nicely."

"That's good," John said. "That's good." He began to unpack a few items from a nearby box. "I've been meaning to ask you, by the way."

There was a pause.

"Meaning to ask me?"

"Was it you?" John asked.

"Please explain."

When it was finished in the tower on December 10th, he'd asked Jeannie how she'd done it, how she'd signaled him with the light on the surveillance camera, how she'd opened the elevator doors to an empty shaft behind Nathan Krieger, how she'd created the distraction that had allowed him to act. She'd looked at him with that face of hers, and told him that while she was happy he was alive and all, she'd been otherwise engaged at the time and had not a clue what he was talking about.

"It was you, Kate, wasn't it, with the camera and the elevator, up in the tower?"

"Could you be more specific?" the computer asked.

John blinked. Either something had come unplugged somewhere, or she was being coy. And like most of the unnervingly human aspects of her evolving personality, he didn't remember programming that in.

"You saved my life. And I wanted to thank you."

"You are quite welcome, John."

"So. Where's Liz?"

"I am with her in her room. We are finishing a game of chess, before her lessons."

"It's Christmas Eve, Kate. No school, let's give her a break."

"I offered. She declined."

"Well. Let her know, she can call me up there, if she has any questions."

"I'm sure it won't be necessary to trouble you."

A nice way of saying, mind your own business.

The boy was plenty sharp, but Kate had taken a real interest in Elizabeth. The two of them were spending a lot of time together, and that was good, he supposed. He supposed that was good.

"All right, then," John said. "I'll just be in here, by the fire."

"Excellent."

"And tell Liz, I'll get started on dinner, when Matthew gets back."

"I will let her know."

He saw the lights inside dim out as he closed the hidden door, and he took a seat in one of the cane rockers beside the stone hearth. A rhythmic thrumming began beside him, and he looked over at the wireless printer he and Matt had hooked up and placed on an end table by his chair. A single sheet had been pulled up into its mechanism, and when the print-out was finished, the paper dropped into the output tray.

It was an e-mail, mass-broadcast spam by the look of it, but the name in the "From" line caught his eye.

Anne Elliot. The lovelorn heroine in *Persuasion*, by Jane Austen.

The name had also apparently captured the imagination of his computer, and she'd seen fit to send the message out to him.

'MAKE YOUR WOMAN SQUEAL WITH DELIGHT!' the subject line exclaimed.

After an opening blurb about a penis enhancement cream, the remainder of the body text was only a block of gibberish. He took the stub of a carpenter's pencil and his reading glasses from his shirt pocket, scanned the jumble of printed characters by the light of the fire, and quickly found the pattern of the plain-text encryption. It was a clever cipher, but its author hadn't wanted him to work too awfully hard.

As he decoded each letter he wrote it in the white space underneath.

missed you in santa monica
whatcha doing new years?
jeannie

Below, there was a reply address.

He read the note again, and once more. After a moment he penciled two words in answer, a simple message he'd once been asked to deliver, even though it was lame, but only when this was over, all over. And while he was certain that it was not really over at all, he had also found a new capacity in the few short weeks that he had been with her. At least once each day now, however briefly, he allowed himself to hope.

He creased the sheet in half, leaned forward and slipped it carefully onto the logs in the fireplace. The paper singed and twisted as it came alight, from the center out to the edges amid the yellow flames. The words he had written became briefly visible again as the paper unfolded slowly in the heat, and was consumed.

b e   h a p p y, they had said.

He'd told Matthew and Elizabeth the story only last night, as they'd sat together here with their hot spiced cider before bedtime, near the flickering warmth at the fireside. *In Great Britain, he'd told them, it's an old custom for the children to write out their gift lists on Christmas Eve, and when they're finished, they place the paper into the fire. Then if the ashes are drawn up the chimney, they believe it means their wishes will come true.*

He watched the blackened, wrinkled remnants of the message flutter for a moment against the updraft, and then the ashes began to twirl and rise, like an unseen courier was gathering them up, to be carried away on the wind.

Acknowledgements

Though this book has been several interesting years in the making, the ins and outs of its journey into your hands may not be quite as fascinating as I imagine. For the permanent record, then, I'll confine myself to expressing gratitude and itemizing debts owed to those who have helped me along the way. But first, I want to sincerely thank you, for choosing to spend a span of your hours within this story. It's hard to express the kind of honor that represents; that you entrusted me with your time. I hope you enjoyed the journey, and when we have other opportunities to travel together again, I'll do my best to never let you down.

Before it's finished and sold, a first novel is nothing but faith against all the odds. Both the story and the endeavor itself are so fragile, often only a moment of disbelief ahead of oblivion. Throughout the months and then years of research, writing, and revision, the invoices of real life still demand to be paid, threaten collection and fore-closure if they're ignored, and those are grave, grown-up threats. But from the first four tentative pages in 2002 through the very end, my wife Lori and our girls, Emily and Sarah, never once lost their faith that this book and its author would finally come to something. Thanks, sweethearts. I would be nothing at all without you.

I'm grateful to my mother for her steadfast love, guidance and support; to my father for gently reminding me, early on, that a good thriller can be human, too; and to my Aunt Dot, for showing me from childhood that we always need to try things we haven't tried before.

In 2005, I wrote a fan letter to Charlie Huston, an amazing author of modern noir. One thing led to another, and before long Charlie had nudged my book from its self-imposed obscurity and into the hands of Simon Lipskar at Writers House. He didn't have to do that; I'll never forget it.

Simon Lipskar became my literary agent, and his guidance, vision and wit were nothing less than transformative as the book was prepared for its second incarnation.

David Shelley is my editor at Little, Brown. His enthusiasm is an inspiration, and his many insights helped me sharpen and polish this story into its final form.

A number of friends read the manuscript in various stages of completion, and their thoughts and suggestions were invaluable. Some of them I've known for many years, and others I've never met face to face. (With the exception of George Maffett of the US Postal Service, I'll mostly stick to first names here; for a variety of reasons some of these listed must maintain their anonymity.) So to you, George, and to Paul W, Patti and Stu, Eric, old buddy Josh, Jules, the mysterious John M, Danielle, Bill, Ken, Matthew, Candy, Will, Kevin W, Jeff B, and the inimitable George Smith of globalsecurity.org: Thanks, so much.

A number of people contributed their expertise through months of research, revision and fact checking. The elite society of Usenet's sci.crypt newsgroup toler-ated an occasional question, and provided the key to a knotty plot-point or two. Dr. Sherron and Dr Peter brainstormed on some scenes that required both a scientist's acumen and a writer's attention to the needs of the drama. Jeff Messer and Peter Reid lent their uncommon knowledge of high-voltage Tesla machines, and Sam Hadden patiently tweaked the punctuation code in Chapter 34.

There are others whose contributions I cannot acknowledge here, because their current assignments or the nature of their backgrounds prohibits even a veiled mention.

But you know who you are.